BLACKWELL'S HOMECOMING

BLACKWELL'S HOMECOMING

by

V.E. Ulett

www.OldSaltPress.com

Published by Old Salt Press
Old Salt Press, LLC is based in Jersey City, New Jersey with an affiliate in New Zealand

978-0-9882360-7-3
National Library of New Zealand Cataloguing-in-Publication Data

Ulett, V. E., 1962-
Blackwell's homecoming / V.E. Ulett.
(Blackwell's adventures ; volume III)
ISBN 978-0-9882360-7-3 (pbk.)—ISBN 978-0-9922636-2-1 (PDF)
I. Title. II. Series: Ulett, V. E., 1962- Blackwell's adventures ; v. 3.
813.6—dc 23

Cover design by Broos Campbell
The Heroism of a Maori woman by Angus McBride, and Polynesian clubs and insignia of rank, from 'The History of Mankind', Vol. 1, by Prof. Friedrich Ratzel reproduced by arrangement with Bridgeman Art Library.
Interior design elements by Sabrina Frontiero

Publisher's Note:
This is a work of historical fiction. Certain characters and their actions may have been inspired by historical individuals and events. The characters in the novel, however, represent the work of the author's imagination. Any resemblance to actual persons, living or dead, is entirely coincidental.

CHAPTER ONE

The cob given Captain Blackwell by the Nelson Arms was a used up, scarred, pot-bellied disgrace of a beast. Captain Blackwell wondered, as the horse plodded head down toward his home at Merton, whether the insolent wags at the inn meant to suit beast to man. He was still merely a post-captain at his advanced age. Vice-Admiral Lord Horatio Nelson, for whom everything in those parts was named, had been made post at twenty, and vice-admiral at forty-three. Like the pitiful animal, Captain Blackwell was knocked about and had seen his share of active service.

Yet he did not feel quite ready for the knacker's yard. Captain Blackwell had retained a finer figure later into life than many of his fellows, thanks to an experience in the islands of the Pacific that had changed his diet and activities drastically for a time. He'd also come away from the Great South Seas tattooed across his buttocks and loins, making him a curiosity in the Royal Navy, and earning Captain Blackwell the nickname of Black Savage. He knew about it, of course, though none were bold enough to call him so to his face. And as his son was also in the Service, they distinguished them by Black Savage the Elder and the Younger.

Needless to say Captain Blackwell was proudest of this son who had just passed for lieutenant, he'd left Aloka celebrating in London. Captain Blackwell had been summoned home to attend his daughter's first London season. "Do come, if you can, just for the first balls and routs. If we go in with a show of force to begin, and give them to understand she isn't an unprotected girl no one cares for, why, then if you must leave again I am sure we will manage tolerably," his wife Mercedes had written. The Black Savage was commanded to appear to affright the beaux. Captain Blackwell was perfectly willing to comply, aside from the fact that he could refuse Mercedes nothing.

The dejected cob had brought him in its shuffling pace at last to Merton. He approached the house over a bridge spanning the Wandle river. When Mercedes had let the house of Emma Hamilton on their return from the Pacific, a great attraction, alongside its proximity to London, was a netting Lord Nelson had constructed where the house fronted the river to prevent his daughter Horatia from tumbling in. Captain Blackwell's children had been small then, and not yet grown into the ciphers they'd now become to him.

Captain Blackwell had hoped, as always, to meet Mercedes first when he came into the house from the stable yard. He walked through the kitchen, grunting a greeting to the one-eyed, former Navy cook already about his business at the early hour, imagining the joy on her face when he would appear. It was always the same, a constant delight to Captain Blackwell. But it was his eldest son he met in the passageway, who'd appeared from his first floor rooms in breeches and stockings, with his stock hanging untied about his neck.

"Edward, there you are, son. How do you do?"

"F-F-Father." Edward stuttered, and turned his intense blue gaze to the wall.

"No one was in the mews, son, and the Nelson's nag wants attention. Scare up McMurtry or Mr. Martinez, won't you?"

Edward turned abruptly from Captain Blackwell and retreated into his rooms.

Captain Blackwell hardly had time to feel confounded, to hear in imagination those ugly phrases "idiot" and "half-wit", for Mercedes called out to him.

"Jim! Jim!"

She did not launch herself from midway downstairs into his arms as she'd done on previous occasions, but Mercedes was yet light on her feet and she ran down quickly to greet him.

Captain Blackwell was not disappointed in that tender look he'd been thinking of, nor in the feel of her in his arms, nor in the delightful sensations she caused him.

"Tio Severino is out riding with Emma. They shall return soon and he will see to the Nelson's horse."

"Ah, good. In that case..." Captain Blackwell nodded to his son. Edward lingered just inside the doorway, swaying back and forth. "Your mother and I have a few things to discuss upstairs."

He put his arm round Mercedes' waist, steering her along, and did not notice the glance Edward and Mercedes exchanged.

Once inside her bedchamber they did not make it to the bed, he had her up against the bedpost where he lifted her skirts.

"What the deuce is this?"

"Bloomers, Jim," she said, "its cold in this country you've brought me to."

"I should think you'd be warm enough with all these petticoats you have on."

"You can take them off me."

Blackwell would have liked to take them off her with his teeth, but he wasn't as young and supple as he used to be. She was generous in their intimate relations. He liked those positions best that gave him a full view of her, and what he was doing to her. Sometimes she would cover her face with her hands, when pleasure overcame her. But aside from that Mercedes never tried to hide or withhold her body from him. On this occasion she did move his hands from her breasts to lower down, which turned out well for both of them.

"Can we get in bed now?"

"Certainly, sweetheart."

They took off the rest of their clothing and lay down in Mercedes' bed together. Something about their encounter troubled him, and he suddenly said, "Have you not lost a deal of flesh, Mercedes?"

"Most men complain of their women growing old and fat."

"Oh, I ain't complaining, it is only—"

"I may be somewhat reduced, but I would not say a great deal of flesh. And I daresay I shall be better now you are here to relieve my cares. I hope you have not had the devil's own time getting away?"

"It helps when the commanding officer is one's father-in-law. Admiral Gambier was only too willing to put a jobbing captain in my place. No, sweetheart, do not be concerned. He seemed sincere in his well-wishes, even good natured, no easy feat on blockade duty. Now tell me of these cares I am to relieve you of."

Mercedes turned with a sigh under his encircling arm, so that her back was to him. "No more than the usual domestic dust ups, but I am so glad you are home."

She was probably the only one in his household who was glad of his return.

"You worry over your children, no doubt."

Mercedes did not answer and in a moment Blackwell realized she was asleep. He hoped he had not tired her unduly with his attentions, it was only nine o'clock in the morning. Perhaps she had not been sleeping well, in her preoccupation over Emma coming out and Edward's...well. And then she truly frightened him, for Mercedes was suddenly covered in a sheen of sweat. Had it happened earlier during their intimacy it would not have shocked him so. She was lying there asleep, dashing the moisture from her face in unconscious movements with the sides of her hands.

"Mercy, sweetheart," Blackwell said, leaning over her.

"Leave me alone, can't you? For once."

Blackwell lay back, shocked.

"Hell and death," Emma Blackwell said, returning from her morning ride and finding she had to stable her hunter with the horse from the Nelson Arms.

"Easy, girl," was Severino Martinez's only comment as he moved off to attend to the horses.

Mr. Martinez was a family retainer, in the way Captain Blackwell's old steward McMurtry now was. One of Mr. Martinez's duties was to act as groom and attend Emma on her solitary rides. Mr. Martinez had a fierce appearance still, but such an old man could not be supposed to have protected her from much of anything. Fortunately there was little to fear in the surrounding countryside, and the other servants—chiefly disabled seamen—were disgraceful horsemen. Besides, Emma had a fondness for Mr. Martinez, as her mother's family friend, a man of few words and no nonsense whatever.

She walked into the house and sought Edward in his rooms.

"What are you about at this hour with your stock all ahoo?" Emma asked. Edward was hunched at this desk reading Herschel's 'Astronomical Observations relating to the Construction of the Heavens'. "Has not Mama been down?"

"He's home."

"I was afraid of that, when I saw that sorry cob from the Nelson Arms. They will give him the most disreputable beasts. And he will not utter a word, but oh how he roars at home."

Emma had come round Edward's desk and was tying his stock for him. Her father's presence in the house always made her feel small, just a girl and of little consequence, the least of God's creatures. How many times had Captain Blackwell greeted her, "How do you do, Emma?" after a considerable absence, and not even waited to hear her answer.

"I don't know why she endures him," Emma said, an oft repeated lament. "She is lovely and dashing enough still to have her choice of smart London men. Instead she's shackled to that...sailorman."

"Don't make her choose between you," Edward said. "She is surpassing fond of him. No one knows why."

Edward went back to studying the drawings of nebulae that accompanied Herschel's paper, preferring the mystery of the cosmos to the more earthly and mundane.

In an upstairs bedroom on Greene Street Aloka Blackwell had unveiled the mystery of what lay beneath the fine evening gown of a Frenchwoman he'd met in Ranelagh Gardens. Aloka gazed upon very white skin and a quantity of red hair, as he held the woman's legs against his chest. He had a Polynesian's aversion to body hair and he could wish the woman would not throw her arms over her head in that ecstatic way, exposing great muffs of it in her armpits. Aloka watched the woman intently, until the trembling of her thighs and the clenching of her body spoke to him, and he let out a great war whoop.

He was just recovering and beginning to consider how to extricate himself, when there was a slamming of doors downstairs.

“My husband!” the woman cried.

Even at nineteen Aloka was not foolish enough to waste time protesting she had said she was a widow woman. He snatched up his clothes and dressed double quick. In spite of the second floor bedchamber—a height as nothing to a seaman—he would have been out the window and safe away had not the woman grabbed at his ankle for some unaccountable reason as he sprang from the sill. It overset him. He fell headlong, twisted, and landed on his back, the wind quite knocked out of him. Aloka rolled over, pressed against the side of the house, just as the man and woman set up a great screeching over his head.

He’d left behind his midshipman’s top hat, and he was so knocked up at first he was obliged to crawl away. Aloka considered, as he recovered and was able to walk upright once more like a man, the loss of the scraper was not grave. He had his commission in his pocket, and would have to come down upon his father for a lieutenant’s rig in any case. Aloka directed his thoughts and steps toward Merton.

CHAPTER TWO

The Blackwells were an awkward foursome at supper, with many more such meals in their immediate future. Mercedes had never been a chatty woman, but her company was the most welcome to Captain Blackwell. The secret desire of his heart was to have her back aboard with him. Just her, as it had been in the days before their children arrived. They were to launch Emma into society and if a decent man could be found for her, Captain Blackwell did hope and trust to realize his wish. In the not very distant future he would reach flag rank, and no one could dictate to an admiral in the matter of carrying a wife. Once he would have defied the Admiralty over that particular, but then Emma had come along. A man-of-war was no place to raise a lady, no one could argue with that. Emma had come between them in a way the Admiralty never could have done.

"Those were the best fried potatoes I ever had, Mercedes, I thank you," Captain Blackwell said. She always prepared one or two of his favorite dishes herself when he was home.

"I'm glad you liked them."

Mercedes rose from her chair, preparing to leave Captain Blackwell to his port. Everyone else stood too. Edward never stayed with Captain Blackwell after supper unless Aloka was at home.

"Emma, I'd like a word, if you please," Captain Blackwell said.

Emma took a seat again at table, folded her hands and looked down at them in her lap. She was not merely pretty. Emma was beautiful, and she had a mature womanly shape, more buxom and much taller than her Mama.

"I'm concerned for your mother. How has she been of late?"

"What do you mean?"

"Does she eat enough? She seems thinner to me, and weary. How is she of an evening? Does she sit up with you and Edward or retire early?"

"She's just as she's ever been. She reads a great deal of an evening, and we talk, she and I and Edward. Sometimes Edward reads from his articles, and tries to explain the heavens to Mama and me."

"Well, I'm glad of it. I must rely upon you, Emma, to send to me if she were unwell. Edward is no use in such matters."

A contemptuous look crossed Emma's face. "He is of much more use than you suppose, Father. He hardly stutters except when you are by. And if Mama is thin and weary, perhaps it is because you importune her so."

Captain Blackwell was not quite sure he heard her aright, for he could hardly believe she could be such a bold faced chit, suggesting what he thought she was suggesting. They stared at one another with unconcealed displeasure. Captain Blackwell was on the point of telling Emma she hadn't noticed her mother's health because she was a froward ill-natured brat, when there came a knock at the dining parlour door.

A tall man in the King's coat walked in, followed by Aloka with a wide grin upon his face.

"Father, I do beg your pardon for bursting in upon you. May I present Captain Lord Cochrane. Sir, m'father Captain James Blackwell."

The gentlemen exchanged bows and handshakes, and Captain Blackwell turned to present Emma. Her aspect had changed entirely; from the disagreeable child to a woman that was stunning, and meant to be. Captain Blackwell had seen such a look on Mercedes' face, and he glanced quickly between Lord Cochrane and Emma.

"Your lordship, may I present my daughter, Emma Blackwell."

Lord Cochrane moved nimbly round Captain Blackwell and took Emma's hand, expressing himself delighted to make her acquaintance in the most gentlemanly, modest manner. Mercedes and Edward came back into the dining parlour, having heard the commotion, and a new round of introductions took place.

Mercedes came over to stand at Captain Blackwell's elbow, from where she whispered in his ear.

"Ah, yes. McMurty! McMurtry, where is the villain? There you are. Glasses and a bottle of ..."

"The Lafite with the long cork, if you please," Mercedes interjected.

When the wine glasses were brought in and filled Captain Blackwell said, "Ladies and gentlemen, raise your glasses, if you please. I give you Lieutenant Blackwell!"

"Lieutenant Blackwell!" the rest cried.

Round the table, at that moment, there were truly happy faces.

In a short time, after Mercedes had given the newcomers supper and only the ladies had this time withdrawn from the dining parlour, the glow of pride and happiness in his son's step had vanished. Captain Blackwell felt instead a greater mix of uncertainty and dread than he'd experienced in many a long day in the professional line. Aloka was all fierce and eager attention, as Lord Cochrane unfolded the Admiralty's intention to allow him to direct a fire ship attack against the French in the Basque Roads.

His lordship, in his soft Scottish voice, explained how he'd protested his appointment was inappropriate, without the commander in chief's knowledge, and over the heads of many more senior captains. The First Lord of the Admiralty would not hear it, calling him back the day following his refusal, and representing to him the exigency for the nation. Captain Blackwell thought Lord Cochrane put too fine a point upon that last.

"Their lordships seem to acknowledge all the enemy's vessels may be driven upon the Isle of Oleron by sending fire vessels to the eastwards of the Isle d'Aix. You've served some time in the Channel Fleet, under Admiral Gambier, sir," his lordship said to Captain Blackwell. "How do you think this plan shall fall upon him?"

"Not the least well, to be truthful."

"Not the least well, what an understatement," Captain Blackwell told Mercedes as they prepared for bed. "He has a perfect horror of this explosion and fireship type of warfare. I don't know but what I am of one mind with Gambier this time. I hope that don't make me timid and old maidish."

"Why do you say so? Not the old maid part, the being of one mind."

"I don't like the enterprise above half, what I know of it. You should have seen Aloka's face. He is with child to have a part in the mission."

"Remember what it is to be young. He has not yet established himself and is eager to do so. It's an anxious time for all of them."

"I hope I don't grow such a gray beard as that, only I could wish my son were less willing to do his duty. Explosion vessels are outside the rules of warfare, do you see? Any man captured from one can be hanged, no exchange for the officers, no prison for the men. Not even the galley."

"Oh!" Mercedes gasped. "Oh, James."

"I'm sorry to distress you. I'm overset myself. Aloka is sure to find his wish gratified, I believe he hopes to be given command of one of the fireships. That's only a fond dream. Lord Cochrane is a sensible man and would not move a junior officer up so rapidly. Still, having been a mid in *Imperieuse* all this while, and now as her third officer, he's sure to be given a berth of some kind."

"Will you be leaving too?"

Mercedes' voice was constrained. She lay curled on her side, her shoulders slightly hunched, with one arm protecting her painful left breast.

"Not before I see you and Emma settled in London. Then all will depend on the Admiralty." Captain Blackwell was silent a moment. "Has Emma made Lord Cochrane's acquaintance before?"

"No, this is our first meeting. Just as you."

Lord Cochrane actually lay in the next room. They'd given him Captain Blackwell's bedchamber with its grand bedstead from Polynesia and the dressing room connected to it. Mercedes and Captain Blackwell were sharing her bedchamber, with a screen set up for the close stool and wash handstand. Captain Blackwell had been all for evicting Edward from his rooms, except Mercedes would not have it.

"It is only that they both looked...conscious somehow."

Mercedes imagined the meeting, and unlike Captain Blackwell, she pictured Aloka very much present in the room. She could not contain a great sigh. She'd meant to tell him right away about her troubles, the worst one a hard little lump in her breast. She was afraid, fear almost overwhelmed her at times, and she wanted his strength. Mercedes could not share this with her children, did not wish to burden their already somewhat fraught lives. But she'd hesitated, out of vanity mostly, for Mercedes still wanted Captain Blackwell to think her strong and brave. She'd waited and now he had worries of more moment, and he would be going away again soon.

"Mercy, sweetheart," he said gently. He was like a great pillow she was relaxing into. "You would tell me was I to...to, well, importune you."

"Importune me? Darling, you know I love you. You and your big cock."

To one degree or another, sex was on all their minds. Aloka's back still ached from the fall out the Frenchwoman's window. Underneath his fine linen shirt he had a livid bruise covering one side of his back from the band of his breeches to his shoulder. He shifted his shoulders uncomfortably. Normally, Aloka, Emma, and Edward, were much gayer when they were together, the talk lively and natural. They were lounging about in the small upstairs parlour of the house on Curzon Street in London, waiting for their parents to conclude their conference downstairs with Lord Cochrane. His lordship had come to beg permission to call upon Miss Emma.

"Now Emma is to be launched upon the *ton*," Edward turned to Aloka, "and has her first serious admirer, you should share the advise Father gave you when you first—"

"Ed! That ain't fit for ladies." Aloka blushed beneath this dark skin tone, remembering Captain Blackwell's few words of wisdom. 'Ladies first, son, always. See to her pleasure, and she will welcome you. There is never a reason to force a woman, or be unkind.'

"If she isn't fit to hear it, I don't know who is. Seems she is to be paired off first of all of us."

Edward was the only one at ease after that remark.

"Suppose they are disposing of your hand at this moment?" Edward said. "Then you shall be married to the Royal Navy, just like Mama!"

"Should you like that, indeed, Emma?" Aloka cried.

"Hell and—"

"It is a good thing his lordship don't hear such talk or he might reconsider his attachment," Captain Blackwell said, walking in with Mercedes.

Emma flashed Captain Blackwell an injured look. "If his lordship is anything like the rest of you, no manner of oaths and vulgarity shall shock him."

"T-t-tell, F-f-father, did you give the chit away?" Edward said.

"There is no giving anyone away, you should both be ashamed." This came out as 'a-chamed', in Mercedes' slight accent. "Lord Cochrane merely asked if he might call upon Emma. Very agreeable and gentlemanly he was too."

"He may be an e-e-earl one day, Emma. You should like being a countess."

"We told him," Mercedes came and took Emma's hand, "we had to consult you first. To discover your inclination."

"*You* told him, Mama, I'm sure." Emma glanced at her father.

Captain Blackwell and Aloka were standing shoulder to shoulder, nearly identical perplexed looks upon their faces.

"Well, what is your inclination? That's what we'd a-a-all like to know."

"I haven't even come out yet, nor seen a scrap of London or society. Am I to be made to decide immediately if I will have a man twice my age just because he expresses a passing fancy?"

"No, no, of course not." Captain Blackwell shook his head, frowning. "He's merely asked to call, not to take you to wife. But it would be impolite not to give him an answer as soon as may be, after how handsomely he expressed himself."

"Yes, I'm sure his feelings are important to you, Papa," Emma said. She rounded on Mercedes. "What do you think, Mama?"

"I think these Navy men are not to be trifled with, nor any of the male persuasion."

All the Blackwell men now had the good grace to look somewhat conscious.

Few fathers were left in attendance in the ballroom, most of the gentlemen having retreated to the card rooms. Edward was among those at the whist tables, and he was the only male attendant with Mercedes and Emma this evening. First Lord Cochrane and Aloka had departed to rejoin *Imperieuse*; then, with the London season only a fortnight old, Mercedes had to bid farewell to Captain Blackwell. She thought of his dear battle scarred face and said a silent prayer for his safety, and Aloka's.

The ballroom was insufferable. Mercedes was mashed up with other mamas on dusty sofas lining the walls, and there were so many dancers her toes were nearly trodden upon as the couples went up the dance. After weeks of festivities Mercedes did not know if she could bear another ball, rout, levee, soiree, or excursion to Ranelagh Gardens, the opera or theatre. Mercedes certainly felt as if she couldn't tolerate the tight bodice of her ball gown much longer.

The throbbing in her breast was very bad, and the heat and airlessness of the room oppressed her. Emma was brought back to Mercedes by Lord someone or another. Her radiant daughter employed her fan for several seconds, and was led away into the next set by a different gallant. When she'd gone a groan escaped Mercedes.

A tall gaunt gentleman in the black evening dress of an earlier era, sitting on the other end of the sofa, must have heard her for his head swiveled in her direction. He regarded Mercedes with pale, expressionless eyes.

"Sure, beauty can be a curse," he said. "And she is a diamond of the first water."

"How kind in you, sir. Well may I groan when I think how young girls are brought out these days."

"So it is, too, a pernicious round. May I make myself known to you, madam? My name is William Russ. Allow me to present my wife, Christine."

Mercedes shook hands and they were just discovering a connection, for Doctor Russ was a physician in the Navy, when they were interrupted by the appearance of the couple's own daughter. She was an exuberant, talkative, handsome and showily dressed young woman. Mercedes guessed she must be of an age with Emma. One instantly wondered how such a lively creature could have sprung from Dr. and Mrs. Russ, equally unfashionable, unimposing, and shabby. But surely the same was thought of her and Captain Blackwell when seen in company with their offspring. None but Aloka took after them in point of looks. Aloka resembled Captain Blackwell, they were the same height though Aloka was heavier of build, and few knew he was not Mercedes' son.

She rose when the Russ family moved away, and curtsied to them. Doctor Russ took her hand, and Mercedes felt a card pressed into her palm.

"Forgive the freedom with which I address you, Mrs. Blackwell," he said. "I know pain when I see it. You must go home and remove that gown, and you will be much easier. Do not delay, I beg."

The passing of the card and the doctor's speech were done with a discretion and an effortlessness that drew no attention in the crowded room. A protest was on Mercedes' lips, when she was suddenly flushed and sweating.

Mercedes mumbled, "Yes, sir, thank you, sir," before sitting down hard on the sofa. She nearly collapsed, and a sudden panic seized her that she should not be able to hide her condition much longer. When she'd taken leave of Captain Blackwell, she had cringed, *cringed*, in his strong embrace.

The pain in her breast had actually ebbed with the fright the doctor had given her. She took deep breaths to calm herself. Slipping the card he'd pressed on her into her bag, and tilting it to read, Mercedes received another jolt. She'd expected to see 'William Russ, Physician', or something very like. No name appeared on the card, only 'Physician of the Fleet' and the insignia of the Royal Navy. Could the man in the worn and shiny black suit be the Physician of the Fleet? She'd nearly fainted in front of him.

Mercedes was sufficiently disturbed, vague hopes from the encounter with the doctor mixed with other sensations, that she made Emma sit down beside her when next she returned.

"Listen, my dear, I must go home. I do not feel at all well."

"Oh, no, Mama! They have not even danced the Roger Decoverley, and I've promised it to Lord Marlborough."

"Lord M., is it? And Lord Coch—"

"Do not say it, Mama. You know I do not care for him, and see him only because he is in the precious Service." Emma had the good sense to pitch her voice low as she spoke. "May I not stay? Edward is here. You go and take the carriage. Edward and I shall come home in a cab."

Mercedes bowed her head. She longed to remove her gown, she felt if she were forced to stay in the ballroom much longer she must shrink into a corner and rip her bodice down the front. At the same time she knew it was unwise, most unwise, to leave a girl of Emma's vivacity and beauty unattended. Yet she believed her daughter a sensible being, and another wave of pain and sweating decided her.

She stood up. "Let's go speak to Edward."

Lord Castlereagh was so disturbed by the sight of Edward Blackwell's sister standing at his elbow, he could hardly complete the hand of whist with any credit. Leaving aside Emma Blackwell was a damned fine looking girl, flashing green eyes, graceful womanly curves, at the end of the hand Lord Castlereagh would lose his partner when Mr. Blackwell must escort his sister back to the ballroom. His lordship was extremely unwilling this should happen, with Edward Blackwell for partner he was for once trouncing the insufferable Mr. Canning. The young man sat there mum, his Apollo's head cocked slightly to the side, playing brilliantly.

"Stay, Mr. Blackwell, won't you?" Lord Castlereagh said, rising when Edward did and moving to his side of the table. "Should you not like to finish out the round? I do not wish to keep you from your duty, but I am sure your sister is a good girl. One who no more needs a minder than a nursemaid."

Lord Castlereagh ended by speaking directly to Emma, as Edward turned his head and gaze to the side. The tall handsome girl gave him a frank considering look, but even she could not help but be swayed by what was obviously the Secretary of State's preference.

She turned to her brother. "Should you prefer to remain in the card room, I shall do very well in the ballroom until you are quite ready to leave."

Lord Castlereagh had counted upon Emma Blackwell being too spirited a girl to cry out, "But Mama said!" He carried the day.

Mr. Blackwell walked his sister back to the ballroom, and then returned and took his seat at the card table. When they all rose from it some time later not one of them gave a thought to the dancers in the adjoining room, they each ordered a carriage or hackney cab and pursued their way homewards.

Emma was collapsing with fatigue, her feet ached from the heeled satin pumps she wore, and she guessed it must be four o'clock in the morning. She was more than willing to retire, but when she looked into the card room she gave a little gasp. The card tables had already been taken away, and there were only servants remaining, carrying out chairs and glasses. She hurried, her heart thumping a little, and took a place in the line of people waiting for their carriages. It was always she who ordered the hackney or their carriage to be brought round, that was not a problem, but Emma missed Edward standing near her. She felt she must be conspicuous, an unescorted female, especially after the attention paid her earlier.

When her turn came at the head of the line, Emma spoke up. "A hackney coach to Curzon Street, if you please."

"Oh, no, Miss! Not for you." A man in pigtail and seaman's garb was suddenly at her elbow. "His lordship, Captain Lord Cochrane sends his carriage."

Emma recognized the coat of arms on the carriage, and with a murmured, "How kind", she allowed herself to be handed in by the rough seaman. The man shut the door of the carriage and jumped up on the box alongside the driver. Emma sank back into the padded seat with a sigh, put off her shoes and promptly fell asleep.

She awoke when the carriage lurched to a halt. The door was opened by the same seaman, the steps let down, and Emma was out of the carriage and upon the pavement before she looked about her.

"This is not Curzon Street. Why have you brought me to Harley Street? This is Lord Cochrane's house, surely—"

"Pipe down, Missy."

Another man had appeared at Emma's side, together the two seamen hustled her up the house steps and into the foyer.

"How dare you." Emma shook them off. The men let go of her as soon as the house door was closed, the second man melting away into the interior of the place. "His lordship could not have ordered this, he is not even here in London. Do you know who I am?"

"Oh, aye, Missy. But I ain't shy of no Black Savage, not John Bargeman."

"How do you feel about the Younger? What do you think Mr. Blackwell will say when he hears of this caper? Lieutenant Blackwell is a great favorite of Lord Cochrane."

This seemed to give John Bargeman pause, a considering look came over his butcher-like countenance. Then he brightened. "Ain't I heard his Lordship say, "If her parents do not favor my suit, I declare I shall steal her away. An elopement to Scotland, just the thing a spirited young lass loves.' Well, you see, I'm just helping his lordship's plan along like. Keeping you away from them other leaping lords in the meantime, besides."

Emma noticed sand bags stacked in the foyer, against the walls facing the street. She'd thought matters would be straightened out in a moment once inside the house, and she would be on her way home. Her heart misgave her looking into the credulous yet menacing face of John Bargeman. Emma recalled her father speaking of 'awkward sods' who sometimes attached themselves to commanders, following them unwanted from ship to ship, often violent men of great strength but addled wits.

She made a dash for the front door. John Bargeman caught her in a painful and too intimate grip.

"Don't make me have to give you a little correction, eh, Missy? Bruises will heal by the time his lordship returns, and he may even thank me for bringing you up."

He hauled her up the stairs and into a grand bedchamber. Emma went quiet. She looked about for a weapon and tried to keep from sobbing aloud. They marched through the large bedchamber and its adjoining dressing room, to a smaller bedchamber beyond. John Bargeman shoved her in, clapped the door to, and Emma heard a key turned in the lock.

The room was cold and dark, the light of day not yet reaching the miniature west facing window. Emma immediately went to this sole view upon the world and looked out, at the blank façade of the next town house. A wrought iron grating surrounded the whole of the outside of her window.

Such was the cheerless apartment meant for Lord Cochrane's lady, with the only entrance and exit through the master's chamber? Emma began to sob, but it was the last she thought of Lord Cochrane for some time. She longed for home, her own bed, and most of all for her mother. Why hadn't she gone home with Mama when she said she was unwell, instead of staying on at the ball like a goddamn fool? From thoughts of Mercedes, which made the tears fall fast, Emma passed on to other members of her family. She curled up on the bed under the coverlet with her ball gown still on, imagining Aloka coming to release her from this prison, and at last fell asleep.

CHAPTER THREE

Aloka was in the great cabin of the flagship *Caledonia*, thunderstruck, as were his father and Lord Cochrane. Admiral Eliab Harvey had just stormed in. "'I do not care if I am passed by, and Lord Cochrane or any other junior officer appointed in preference, I will strike my flag, and resign my commission!"

Alerted by the hallooing Admiral Gambier and his secretary rushed in, and hurried Eliab Harvey into the admiral's apartments. Lord Cochrane, Aloka, and Captain Blackwell were left in the captain's cabin, where they'd been awaiting Admiral Gambier's pleasure. They could not so much hear the words as feel the concussion of Eliab Harvey's booming voice. He was occasionally silenced when they imagined Gambier must be trying to interject a pacific note. Admiral Harvey was not having it, and he burst out again through the adjoining door, red in the face.

"I understand you are Captain Lord Cochrane, sir," he said, advancing straight at his lordship. "I mean no personal offense to you, sir. Captain Blackwell, young Sa...Mr. Blackwell." Admiral Harvey bowed to them. He heard Admiral Gambier and his secretary advancing and fury rose to his countenance. He spat out, "I never saw a man so unfit for the command of a fleet as Lord Gambier", and stomped out of the cabin.

The secretary came out to them, and they walked into Admiral Gambier's apartments where the Admiral was working to subdue his anger and indignation. Admiral Harvey's attack seemed to have aroused no sensibility in him to the hostility in the fleet, or of the ill will he'd created by not allowing one of his own officers to move forward and lead the fireship attack. Gambier focused instead on criticizing the Admiralty's plan, calling it "A horrible mode of warfare, and the attempt hazardous if not desperate". Then he desired Lord Cochrane to lay the details before him.

Lord Cochrane proceeded with the logistics of the attack. Four explosion vessels and twenty-one fireships, some brought out from England and some to be prepared from captured enemy craft and transports on hand in the fleet, all to be sent against the French anchored near the Ile de Aix.

"To cause confusion and consternation among the Enemy," Lord Cochrane said. "And to open the way for His Majesty's line of battle ships to burn, capture, or run the enemy's ships on shore."

"The Master of the Fleet says there is insufficient depth in the Aix Roads for a line of battle ship. To say nothing of the battery on the Ile de Aix."

"The threat of the battery on the Ile de Aix, Sir, with respect, has been overstated. I reconnoitered in *Imperieuse*, the battery is in a ruinous state. I saw it from my own maintop, the inner fortification is completely destroyed. We counted thirteen mounted guns and several mortars."

Admiral Gambier studied the list of the explosion vessels and fireships and the officers selected to command them with a pursed countenance. Nothing concerning the attack could fall well upon him, since the whole had been planned without his knowledge. All of the seamen chosen to take part in the fireship attack would be volunteers, of course. After raising more cautions and objections, which Lord Cochrane patiently put down, Admiral Gambier turned to Captain Blackwell.

"I do not like the assignment of a lieutenant to command the only heavy fireship we have, the 44-gun *Mediator*. Woolich does very well in your *Valiant*, for the moment. Will you take *Mediator*, since you are yet to return to your command?"

Aloka was already assigned to *Mediator* as her second in command, and he could not help looking sharply at his father. Captain Blackwell's expression was stony, unreadable. Aloka knew his father's distaste for the proposed action, one he shared with most men of his age and service history.

"It will be an honor, sir," Captain Blackwell said.

A bristling resentment rose up in Aloka toward Admiral Gambier at that moment.

The first in line of the explosion vessels, the one Aloka had wished to be assigned to—aboard were Captain Lord Cochrane and his lordship's brother Basil and Lieutenant Bissell—had blown up with a brilliant flash that revealed the enemy fleet lying at anchor south of the Ile de Aix. The explosions of the next vessels and fireships in line illuminated the confusion among the enemy, anchored close together in two rows of line of battle ships. It was a perfect night for such an attack, one that even a timid commander in chief could not refuse to sanction; very dark, a strong onshore breeze, and the tide flowing toward the French fleet. Two lighted British sloops marked the limits of the channel up which the fireships and explosion vessels raced.

Aloka was on the quarterdeck of *Mediator*, the large fireship meant to break the boom the French had constructed in front of their anchored fleet. Lord Cochrane had discovered this barrier when they'd reconnoitered in *Imperieuse*. The boom was a formidable affair of spars, yards, beams and tubs weighted with stones and securely moored by heavy anchors and cables. Aloka admired Lord Cochrane for his care in planning the entire enterprise, it spoke of a commander concerned for the preservation of life: British life in any case. Congreve's rockets mounted in the tops and rigging of the fireships, which were taking fire and darting through the air directionless, were not one of his lordship's more brilliant strokes.

Aboard *Mediator* Captain Blackwell was forward conning the ship, his long-time coxswain and follower, Narhilla at the wheel. A gunner, Mr. Seggess, Aloka, and Mr. Midshipman Monroe made up the remainder of the crew.

Towing behind *Mediator* was a four-oared gig, bumping over floating debris and waves caused by the vessels already exploded. Captain Blackwell had the difficult task of judging their distance from the boom and the enemy fleet, and ordering when to light the fuses. Beneath their feet, on the lower deck, were long wooden troughs laid fore and aft. Crossed over these athwart ships were more troughs, filled with tarred canvas, oakum, and gunpowder. They'd even doused the whole with turpentine taken from enemy merchants. Below and amidships were large casks packed with gunpowder, standing on end and lashed together with cables, surrounded by grenades and several hundred shells. *Mediator* was a sailing bomb.

"Light the port fires!" Captain Blackwell called.

Aloka, Mr. Seggess and Mr. Monroe immediately went to work firing the fuses. Captain Blackwell and Narhilla were securing the wheel with lines to keep her on her course. Straight before them was the enemy fleet, several French line of battle ships were falling on board one another in their haste to move away from the burning vessels. Aloka's heart leapt to see the enemy's force so close.

"Mr. Seggess, Mr. Monroe, Narhilla, into the boat," Aloka ordered.

He waited with a pounding pulse until the men were looking up at him from the gig. Aloka turned and shouted, in defiance of his fear, "Straight at 'em, Father!"

An explosion amidships and a consuming roar. Captain Blackwell was flung into the air and over the side. Next moment Aloka was in the water. The strong wind had halved the time of the fifteen minute fuses. *Mediator* held her course, blowing up as she went. Ragged wood, barrel staves, shredded canvas were in the water with Aloka. The severed head of Mr. Seggess floated near him just under the surface, impaled on a pike like whack of planking jutting out from the port cover of a gun. He dove underwater, swimming, swimming up channel against the tide.

Shouts when he surfaced. "Mr. Blackwell! Mr. Blackwell!"

Aloka stroked over to the gig, grasped both gunnels of the craft, and heaved himself inboard.

"Where's the Captain?"

"Missing, sir. Captain and Mr. Seggess are missing."

"Mr. Seggess is dead. Pull down channel."

"Oh no, sir. We must make for the frigates." Mr. Monroe looked imploring. "We shall be fortunate to reach them with this tide race. We must start now."

"Bugger that!" Aloka threw himself back over the gig's gunwale.

"Oh, Christ!" Mr. Monroe cried. "Oh, the Savage!"

Narhilla had already shipped his oars and was following Aloka. Aloka swam off in a diagonal to the channel, the tide pushing him and the following gig closer and closer to the enemy. There was no more boom, *Mediator's* weight, the explosions, and wind and tide had combined to break it. The water thickened dangerously with casks, spars, planking, canvas. Aloka surfaced underneath dangling legs in the water. He grabbed the back of the man's sodden blue jacket and pulled him face up. "Father! Hang on, do you hear?"

Swimming backward, clutching Captain Blackwell round the chest with one arm, Aloka met the gig. He heaved and Narhilla hauled, and they brought Captain Blackwell into the boat.

"Face down, over the thwart!" Aloka ordered.

They pounded upon Captain Blackwell's back. He coughed and belched out a quantity of water and moaned. On his right side Captain Blackwell's clothing was completely burned away, and the skin of his exposed arm, shoulder, and neck looked as though it had been flayed.

"Good Lord," Mr. Monroe breathed.

"Help me move him into the stern—"

Captain Blackwell pushed himself upright with his good arm, and croaked out, "Tiller."

They understood him, and handed Captain Blackwell aft where he took hold of the tiller with his good arm.

"First trick. Ship your oars."

Aloka and Narhilla pulled the entire way back to the British frigates. Mr Monroe remained in the stern, bailing and trying to keep Captain Blackwell upright, in the end taking the tiller. Aloka needed all his considerable strength, pulling against the headwind and tide. Constantly before him was the sight of his father struggling, so wounded, to keep control of the tiller, to sit upright. Captain Blackwell must be brought to one of the frigates, to medical attention. Aloka gritted his teeth and pulled, wishing to make the gig cleave the water like a native canoe, pushing down his own terror as they navigated between fireships aflame before and behind them, with fiery rockets shrieking overhead.

The first frigate they encountered Aloka shouted to Mr. Monroe to come alongside. Captain Blackwell was slumped insensible in the stern. It was their own ship *Imperieuse*, and her people immediately brought them aboard.

Mercedes awoke so much refreshed and eased that she was almost ashamed of her desperation in leaving the ballroom the evening before. She'd slept well into the morning, and once dressed she found Edward installed in the downstairs library behind a desk piled with books and papers.

"I am sorry to have dashed off last night," she said, as she tied Edward's stock for him. "Is Emma yet abed?"

Edward shot up from his chair, yanking the cloth from Mercedes' fingers. He looked at her in horror, and then bolted from the room.

He ran up the stairs, Mercedes following behind, and flung open the door of Emma's bedchamber. They both walked in to an unoccupied room, the bed still made up.

"I am so sorry, Mother," Edward stammered. "I came away, I forgot—"

"Do you mean to say you left without Emma? She has not been home all night?" Mercedes' voice rose high and shrill toward the last.

Edward's frightened expression told her all, and for once she could not contain herself. Mercedes grasped him by the lapels of his coat and shook him. "How could you? How could you leave your sister alone? Where is she? *Oh, Dios mio.*"

Mercedes sank into a chair and stared at Emma's empty bed. A parent's worst fear. London was such a big, sprawling, wicked city. It could swallow the child she loved and had raised so tenderly, because she had been so weak as to leave her alone in it. Mercedes did not notice when Edward left the doorway of Emma's room, and Mr. Martinez appeared in his place.

"*Hija,*" Severino Martinez said, approaching her chair. "Shall you send for the Captain?"

Captain Blackwell had always trusted her with the care of their children, saving Aloka, of course, who'd gone to sea when still a boy. The ache in her heart was matched by the throbbing pain in her breast, making her gasp. "No, with all the will in the world a message could not reach him for weeks. And for him to return? No, I will not sit with arms crossed. But how to find where she's gone!" Mercedes and Severino Martinez stared at one another. Mercedes' mother, Arabella de Aragon, had run away from the life her family had planned for her, and pursued her own wild, reckless course. "I cannot send to the Marlboroughs to inquire if they might have seen my daughter. Such a thing could ruin her."

"Will you hear my advice?"

"I should like it of all things, Tio. I feel unequal to this, to tell truth."

"Hold on, girl. Do not despair. You must take one of the Captain's men into your confidence. That McMurty is a sly, insinuating fellow, and loyal to Captain Blackwell and this family. There is nothing servants do not see. Send him to make the round of the footmen and coachmen from last night. We pick up traces of her, then we make another plan."

Mercedes had been on the receiving end her whole life of Mr. Martinez's ability to retrieve errant females.

"Do you think he can be discreet? It is of the first importance it not be known I have lost Captain Blackwell's daughter."

"Calm yourself, girl," Mr. Martinez reached out and took Mercedes' hand. "McMurtry loves Emma too."

"Oh, Tio." Mercedes sobbed. "Let it be so. *Que Dios nos ayuda.*"

Severino Martinez patted her hand kindly. He turned and jerked his head at Edward, who came and took his place.

"Asses' milk?"

"Aye, Missus, ten gallon of it, delivered to the servant's entrance and taken in by that cully John Bargeman. Certain unsophisticated coves believe as how elegant females must always bathe in asses' milk. Then Severino and me, we lay hands on one Spotted Dick, an awkward sod as was bringing provisions to the house." McMurtry paused and rubbed bruised knuckles. "We persuaded him to let us in on the caper, like. We're near certain sure without actually clapping eyes on her he has our Miss Emma. He ain't right in his top hamper, John Bargeman, do you see?"

Mercedes put her face into her hands and Severino Martinez shook his head, casting McMurtry a withering look.

McMurtry hastened on. "That's not as whose to say he'd harm our Miss. John Bargeman may be a half wit but he fair worships Captain Lord Cochrane, and —"

"Thank you, McMurtry, I am infinitely obliged to you. I'll pass the word when we're...when we —"

"Right, Missus. Choose your weapon and wait for the word." McMurtry knuckled his forehead and walked out of the parlour.

"Spotted Dick says the house is buttoned up like a fortress, ready for a siege," Mr. Martinez said. "Sand bags on the first floor. I don't know how many men we'd need to break in."

"We cannot recruit a file of men and cannonade Lord Cochrane's house. It must be done quietly. If only we could surprise him, gain admittance to the house."

"I can get us in," Edward said. The timber of his voice changed. "Open this door, John Bargeman, goddamn your eyes," Edward said in a perfect imitation of Aloka's accents. Then in Lord Cochrane's aristocratic Scots, "Do you no ken the Master? Open this door."

"That caps it," Mercedes said. "Tonight late we shall go in. After he has had a chance to drink his grog."

"You cannot mean to go yourself?"

"I do too, Tio. Edward and you and I and McMurtry. We must arrange what to do with the man, we cannot have him spreading this tale about London."

"*Estas loca, hija.* But don't trouble yourself for John Bargeman. McMurtry and his cousin Clark fixed up a berth for that one. We need at least two more for the subduing part."

"I think what he's saying, Mama, is that it cannot be done by two old men, a half-wit, and a sick woman."

"So long as they do not see Emma," she said, "you may bring the fleet."

When Severino Martinez had gone out to arrange matters with the seamen, Mercedes said, "I suppose I am fooling no one, then?"

Edward had put off the morning callers, mostly gentlemen Emma had danced with, saying 'Mrs. and Miss Blackwell are indisposed'. There had been one very interesting interview Edward did not tell Mercedes of because it did not bear upon Emma, who was the whole object of her attention and concern.

"I beg you will see a physician, Mama."

"As soon as Emma is back. How I hope..." Mercedes bowed her head, trying to master her fears. "Come, Edward. *A la espada.*"

Both her children knew how to handle a sword. Mercedes had considered fencing lessons as essential a part of their education as dancing. She returned after changing her outfit to spar with Edward, unaware her face was set in a grimace of pain.

Mercedes was dressed in volunteer's attire, a relic from a previous day. She was made to stand in the back, behind McMurtry and Mr. Martinez. Edward was at their head, pounding upon the front door of Lord Cochrane's Harley Street townhouse.

At last they heard, called through the door in a strong seaman's voice, "Go away. His lordship ain't t'home."

"His lordship bloody well is to home. Open this door, John Bargeman!"

Scrabbling was heard the other side of the door and it was flung open. Edward immediately stepped inside, grasped John Bargeman by the front of his coat, and gave him such a crack to the head—with his own head—they both staggered backward like struck billiard balls. McMurtry and Mr. Martinez rushed in, caught John Bargeman beneath his arms and dragged him backwards toward the servants' regions. McMurtry dealt him a few more sharp raps with a cudgel on the way.

Mercedes closed the street door, and began shouting for Emma. McMurtry had by this time let his cousin Clark and his mate in through the kitchen entrance. Between them they had John Bargeman well in hand.

Edward tried to raise his voice to call for Emma, but mainly he staggered in a circle holding his head. Mercedes ran up the stairs, calling frantically, and at last when she stopped to take breath, she heard an answering, “Mamaaaaa!”

She tore through a bedchamber and dressing room, and found a little locked room beyond. Mercedes turned the key and Emma burst out upon her. Clutched in one hand was a great heavy silver candlestick, and she still wore her ball gown. It was by now quite frowsy and disarrayed, giving her a lunatic appearance, and she swayed on her high heeled pumps. They fell into an embrace and a babble of exclamations and questions that went unanswered. Within moments Mercedes declared, “*Vamos, vamos!*”

They ran downstairs, Mercedes crying out, “Don’t sit down, Edward!” He was weaving toward collapse upon one of the steps.

Edward jerked round toward them. “Oh, Emma! Oh so sorry!”

“Never you mind it, dear, dear Edward,” Emma cried, grabbing his wounded head and smacking him a kiss.

“Lord, you smell like —”

“Sour milk. Because why? Because that goddamn—oh, Mama!”

Mercedes was pale of face, sweating, doubled over and gasping. She unbuckled the sword belt she wore and thrust it at Emma. Emma snatched up the weapon, buckled it round her own waist, and grasped Mercedes by one arm.

“Edward, take her other arm.” Emma said in the gentlest tone, “What now, Mama?”

“A carriage, up the street. Harley and G-g-greene Street.”

Out Lord Cochrane’s front door they fled. Emma resembled more a pirate wench than a young lady of quality, Edward was dripping blood, with Mercedes in young gentleman’s garb supported between them.

Imperieuse’s surgeon Mr. McNeath had done what he could for Captain Blackwell. The truth was the most learned of the medicos probably could not help him; he needed to grow new skin. In the meantime he was a swollen, suppurating, blood colored mess. He spent the majority of the time lying on his good side in a cot in the sick berth, willing the canvas sides not to touch and stick to the rawest patches. Between the carefully divided doses of laudanum Mr. McNeath allowed him, Captain Blackwell was managing the pain.

Aloka came to him in the evening. Lanterns were lit in the sick berth, so Captain Blackwell knew it was night, but the evening of which day he could not tell. It was unclear to him how much time had passed since the night of the fireship attack.

"You would not credit it, Father, the timidity, the shameful cowardice." Aloka spoke to him low and in Hawaiian, because of the delicacy of the subject. "His lordship signaling all morning. 'Half the fleet can destroy the enemy. Seven on shore.' And then, 'Eleven on shore.' The Admiral would not budge. The fireship attack drove eleven ships of the line aground. Only two were afloat, with the rest falling aboard one another, and still he will not order in the fleet. When the captain saw the enemy beginning to heave off with the tide, what does he do?" Aloka's eyes glowed with the recollection of that day's action. "He allows her to drift down stern foremost and we played our guns upon one of their big ships, the *Calcutta*. All the while his lordship is signaling the admiral, hallooing for assistance. Two of our line of battle ships did come down, and five frigates. Your *Valiant*, sir, came on like a good 'un."

"Poor Woolich will earn no favor by it." Captain Blackwell shifted carefully in his cot.

"What ails the man? Is he old, addled in his wits, or merely craven? Now I see what Admiral Harvey was on about, never was a man so unfit to command a fleet."

"Hold hard, son. Help me up, if you please."

"Do not tell me you will defend the man? After he threw you into this action." With a large man's gentleness Aloka assisted Captain Blackwell from the cot, and to a seat on a stool.

Their conversation continued in Hawaiian, the sick berth patients who were not so bad off exchanging winks and nods. Captain Blackwell rather cherished the Hawaiian language he'd acquired at such cost. It linked Aloka to his forebears, a line of chiefs. Captain Blackwell would not otherwise have been able in a crowded man-of-war to speak so intimately with his son.

"It is the most irksome thing, I am not comfortable in any position. No, I won't defend him. There is no love lost between us, believe me. But, listen to me now, son." Captain Blackwell gave

Aloka a serious considering look, and changed tack. "You would not do anything to injure Mercedes, I suppose, nor cause her discomfort of any kind?"

Aloka was silenced, taken aback. Captain Blackwell glanced down at himself. He was horrible to look on, bare to the waist, wearing only a pair of cotton trousers, his wounds smeared with goose grease.

"What the dear soul will think of me now, I cannot say."

"She will love you as heartily as ever, Father. You know that, more so even."

Tears were in Aloka's eyes. He always said his earliest memories were of being aboard Captain Blackwell's ship coming away from the Sandwich Islands. He'd contracted a series of agues, and was so gravely ill they almost despaired of him. Whenever he'd surfaced from delirium there had been Mercedes sitting beside him, willing him to live. He'd recovered and grown remarkably hearty, experiencing barely a sick day since. She'd always cared for Aloka, shielding him, even within his own family, from the taint of being a bastard.

"I should never wish to cause her the least discomfort," Aloka said. "Or a moment's anxiety. But what can she have to do with that —"

"This is not my tale to tell, I hope you will bear that in mind. That timid old man is Mercedes' natural parent. Hard to credit, ain't it? But it is so. Never was a braver, truer hearted creature than Mercedes, and that she should have sprung from such a canting, hypocritical, shrewish man..."

Captain Blackwell shook his head. He and Aloka stared at one another, considering the accidents of progeny.

"He never owned her," Captain Blackwell went on, "he is not man enough for that. But if there is crying out about timidity and cowardice, it might yet wound her. I beg your pardon for speaking so free, but your captain is just such a man to raise the hue and cry. Not but what he does not have cause. In your case son, being so closely related as it were, best be silent."

A tremendous roar and a concussion, and the ship gave a great lee lurch, throwing Captain Blackwell and Aloka from their stools. Captain Blackwell screamed when he hit the deck, loud and full-throated.

"Let's get you into the cot, Sir." Aloka's voice shook. He glanced anxiously round at the dumbfounded sick berth patients.

"That would have been a ship exploding." Captain Blackwell groaned. "Thank you, son. You may be needed on deck. Tell Mr. McNeath I would like my draught now."

It was a ship that blew up, the 50-gun *Calcutta*. Almost as soon as *Imperieuse* had begun to play her guns on *Calcutta* earlier, the French commander led her abandonment, climbing out the stern windows. The British had set *Calcutta* afire, and the flames at last reaching the magazine caused her explosion. With a bitter feeling at his heart Aloka watched her burn.

Captain Blackwell's remark that Captain Lord Cochrane was the sort to raise a hue and cry had not fallen well on him, it had at first rankled. Aloka had slept little in the last forty-eight hours and lived hard. The horror and fear of those hours was still with him. He and Mr Monroe had been sprayed by viscera when a cannon shot took out the whole of a seaman's bowel, standing before them on *Imperieuse's* forecastle. As the long night wore on, and repairs to *Imperieuse* went forward, Aloka became convinced his lordship would continue engaging any French ships within reach in the morning. It had been a mistake to bring Captain Blackwell aboard Captain Lord Cochrane's command, to be tossed around in a ship in action.

Imperieuse was once again preparing for action next day. Repairs from the previous day were still going forward, enemy shot holes in the ship's sides and deck plugged, the foremast had been shot through, the standing and running rigging was much cut up. For a time *Imperieuse* had exchanged fire with *Calcutta* and two French 74-gun ships as they lay aground. About midday three brig sloops arrived from the fleet and anchored near *Imperieuse*. A boat from one brought a letter for Captain Lord Cochrane.

'My Dear Lord,

You have done your part so admirably that I will not suffer you to tarnish it by attempting impossibilities, which I think, as well as those captains who have come from you, any further effort to destroy those ships would be. You must, therefore, join as soon as you can, with bombs, etc., as I wish for some information, which you allude to, before I close my despatches.

Yours, my dear Lord, most sincerely,

Gambier'

Then there followed this extraordinary addendum:

'PS — I have ordered three brigs and two rocket vessels to join you, with which, and the bomb, you may make an attempt on the ship that is aground in the Palles, or towards the Ile de Madame, but I do not think you will succeed; and I am anxious that you should come to me, as I wish to send you to England as soon as possible. You must, therefore, come as soon as the tide turns.'

Lord Cochrane naturally chose to regard only the portion allowing a further attack on the French, and ignore the recall order. *Imperieuse's* officers and crew continued with their repairs and preparations. Yet it became obvious to all that the French, by this time, could not be effectively engaged. Four of the French warships had managed to heave themselves off and were proceeding up the river Charente. Ships' boats and fisherman were taking stores out of the wrecked French vessels. Those French ships still aground were unloading their guns into local vessels lying alongside, in order to heave off with the next tide.

Aloka imagined Lord Cochrane's fury, when a little more expedition would have annihilated the French fleet. Napoleon could not have come back from such a blow this war. With the tide turning, Aloka requested to speak to the captain.

He was immediately admitted to Captain Lord Cochrane in the great cabin. His lordship was in a vexed humor, pacing up and down.

After saluting Aloka said stiffly, "Sir, with respect, I'd like to request Captain Blackwell be sent aboard the ship to England that will carry the dispatches. You are aware he is gravely injured, and I am sure he will recover best at home with his wife to attend him."

Lord Cochrane looked rather startled. "Certainly he must do better with that incomparable woman by his side."

Aloka's face took on a hard, reserved expression. Was Lord Cochrane speaking of Miss, not Mrs. Blackwell?

"I shall do everything I can to oblige you and Captain Blackwell," Lord Cochrane said.

"Thank you, sir. Your servant." Aloka bowed. He was convinced Lord Cochrane was considering his consequence with Emma more than Captain Blackwell's well being.

"What has Admiral Gambier against Captain Blackwell? Threw him into the worst of it headlong. Come in." Lord Cochrane called in response to a knock at the cabin door.

A post-captain was ushered in by *Imperieuse's* premier, and a letter handed to Lord Cochrane. He glanced at the brief note, and as it concerned his officers, Lord Cochrane read it aloud.

'My Dear Lord—It is necessary I should have some communication with you before I close my despatches to the Admiralty. I have, therefore, ordered Captain Wolfe to relieve you in the services you are engaged in. I wish you to join me as soon as possible so that you may convey Sir Harry Neale and those despatches to England.

Yours, etc. Gambier'

CHAPTER FOUR

Imperieuse weighed anchor and sailed out of Aix Roads to rejoin the fleet. The tenor of the meeting between the fiery Scottish commander and his evangelical admiral could be guessed from the furious set of Lord Cochrane's face on his return to *Imperieuse.* While they awaited Sir Harry Neale, Admiral Gambier's flag captain, to come aboard, store ships and a boat from *Valiant* came alongside.

Mr. Midshipman Monroe sought Captain Blackwell out in the sick berth. "A letter from home, sir, I believe."

"Must obliged, Mr. Monroe, that is welcome of all things."

Mr. Monroe bowed and left Captain Blackwell to his letter.

'Curzon Street, London

Dear Papa,

You said I must send for you if Mama were ill, and I find myself distressed to have to obey your command. Do come, Papa, as soon as ever you can. She is unwell and she suffers, but she will take no measures without you are here to give your consent to the treatment proposed to her. Her physician is most urgent with her to proceed, but she is intractable in her position. I am sorry if I astonish you, we have all been dreadfully frightened for her. There is another Circumstance that may have given Mama such anxiety as to have measurably contributed to her current reduced state. I cannot tell you of it in the present, though no one is more sensible of where the blame lies for this Circumstance than me. I shall give you a full accounting when you are home, and that you should be so at the earliest are the wishes of,

Your ever dutiful,

Emma'

Captain Blackwell was still holding his letter when Aloka looked in on him later.

"What is it, Father? You've gone all white beneath your red and blue."

Captain Blackwell handed Aloka the letter, and gave him a bare few seconds to read before he blurted, "Hell and death, son, I could not bear it if ...". Captain Blackwell swallowed hard. "It must be very bad indeed for Emma to write such a letter, and sign herself 'ever dutiful'."

Aloka was silent. He gazed at the letter and rubbed his thumb over Emma's signature. His jaw clenched and his face became grave.

"There's not a moment to lose, Sir."

On *Imperieuse's* arrival in Portsmouth, Captain Blackwell was offered a seat in Lord Cochrane's carriage. His lordship was posting immediately to London and the Admiralty. He accepted and was graciously set down before his doorstep in Curzon Street.

"No, I will not get down, sir, I thank you," Lord Cochrane said. "I will save that felicity for another time. Your family will be anxious to receive you."

A pretty speech, Captain Blackwell thought, as he adjusted his clothing before going in. Bad weather in the Bay of Biscay had delayed them, and given Captain Blackwell time to heal. He looked somewhat less like a creature of the knacker's yard. He wore a shirt draped over one shoulder with the badly burned arm in a sling against his body. No waistcoat, with the King's coat over all, one good arm in and the other pinned up as for a one-armed man.

"There you are, sir, God preserve us!" McMurtry said, letting him in the front door.

"How do you do McMurtry? Take this coat, won't you."

"Any dunnage, sir?"

"In the port—". Captain Blackwell broke off, seeing Emma poke her head out the library door and then come running toward him. "This side, sweetheart." Captain Blackwell gestured, holding out his left arm to her.

She pressed herself to his breast, underneath his encircling arm, as he'd never remembered her doing before. Then Emma looked at him, really looked, and the more familiar, slightly disapproving expression returned to her eyes.

"What has happened to you, Papa?"

"He's been blown up. Ain't it obvious?" Edward followed Emma from the library.

"Oh, my God, Aloka!"

"No, girl. He's fine. Hale and hearty and with *Imperieuse*. She is paying off in Portsmouth. He will be here soon. How do you do, son?"

"Better than you do, Sir. And better than dear Mama."

"Go up to her right away, Papa. She will probably be awake. Her physician left a letter against your return."

"Your letter frightened me very much, Emma."

"I'm sorry for it, and for your wounds."

"Aloka, Mr. Monroe, and Narhilla, all suffered minor burns. My gunner Mr. Segesse was killed."

Emma and Edward murmured their sympathy.

"You do not ask after Lord Cochrane?"

"I do not, and I shall tell you why but not just now. You must prefer to see Mama."

"I do. I do, indeed." He leaned down and kissed Emma's cheek and clutched Edward's shoulder as he passed him.

He was made anxious by their behavior. Emma had never encouraged him to go to Mercedes, she'd always behaved more as though she resented his taking her mother's time and attention. Captain Blackwell crept up to her room. He expected to find her writing letters at her little desk, sewing, or reading. Instead she was asleep, albeit in her morning dress, looking small and fragile beneath the counterpane. Captain Blackwell sat down in a chair at her bedside, tears starting in his eyes.

She was pale and, at intervals, would come out in a sweat, yet Mercedes slept heavily. Captain Blackwell thought it might be the effects of laudanum and this brought fresh tears to his eyes, that she should suffer so much as to need it. She didn't wake while he sat there blubbering, nor when he recovered and walked about her room. In a little glass dish on her vanity, he found a letter addressed to 'Captain James Blackwell, R.N.' and a calling card with naval insignia and bearing in script Physician of the Fleet.

The calling card gave him pause as he sat down to read his letter, it had no name upon it.

'Dear Sir,

Forgive the liberty with which I address you, having never made your acquaintance. I desire you will wait upon me at 22 St. James Street near the Greene Park. I had the pleasure of meeting Mrs. and Miss Blackwell at a ball our daughters attended, and subsequently Mr. Edward Blackwell when he and his sister called upon me. A discussion of Mrs. Blackwell's condition and prognosis is of the first importance, for she will not be moved until she has consulted 'her partner in all'. I use her words, sir, and I know you will understand the importance of there being not a moment to lose.

Your humble, obedient, etc.
W. Russ'

"The Physician of the Fleet," Captain Blackwell said aloud.

There was no time to wonder at Mercedes having met such a man. He wiped the tears from his face and went over to her. Captain Blackwell longed to embrace her, to kiss her pale cheek, but he did not wish to wake her and destroy what little peace and ease she was finding. In the barest whisper he told her he would return directly.

Captain Blackwell ran downstairs with the doctor's letter in his hand, his own injuries of little importance, calling to McMurtry for his jacket.

Captain Blackwell followed a tall, superbly dressed young woman down the hall to the doctor's study inside the house on St. James's Place. The young woman had a graceful carriage, striding along with her head high, a delicate beauty in the curve of her neck.

She rapped twice upon the study door and opened it.

"Here is a wretched man to see you, Father dear."

Doctor Russ glanced up. "Here is a wretched captain, you meant to say, Daughter dear."

Captain Blackwell assumed he'd been presented, for Doctor Russ and his daughter were speaking Irish, he bowed and said, "Captain James Blackwell, sir, at your service."

"How do you do, sir? You are come at last. Thank you, Brigit, dear."

Both men bowed to her, and Brigit withdrew with a look Captain Blackwell could not interpret, but which he'd seen often on certain young faces at home.

"I hope I did not frighten her, with my appearance," Captain Blackwell said. "But I was obliged to come by your letter, sir, and from my own fears for my...for Mercedes. I collect you have waited upon her in a profession capacity, sir?"

"I have, indeed. Mr. and Miss Blackwell called upon me, they discovered a card I gave Mrs. Blackwell at the Marlborough's affair. When your wife became very ill, knowing no other physician in London, they sought me out."

"I should beg pardon for their intruding upon you, but I cannot, if it brought her the best care to be found in this city."

Captain Blackwell immediately felt he'd spoken indiscreetly. Doctor Russ regarded him through colored spectacles. He was shabbily dressed, even grubby, which offended Captain Blackwell's particular seaman's sense of cleanliness and order. Doctor Russ, though, was a great man, a renowned physician. A man who had only succeeded to be Physician of the Channel Fleet after much active sea-going duty as a ship's surgeon. Doctor Russ had served at Trafalgar. Loving Mercedes as he did, Captain Blackwell had to bear in mind Doctor Russ's great condescension in attending a woman.

"You do me great honor, sir. The case is this, Mrs. Blackwell has a mass in her left breast. Over time it has grown larger and harder, and is causing her greater and greater suffering. It is almost certainly cancer, sir, I am sorry for it. Now I shall speak yet more to the point. The only remedy is the knife, let there be no delay. It may already be too late."

Captain Blackwell was stunned. Though he might blubber sitting alone by his wife's bedside he could not do so here, with Doctor Russ observing him through slitted eyes from across his desk. It was difficult to make out any expression on the doctor's face, but Captain Blackwell fancied even without the colored glasses there would be only cold dispassion. Perhaps that was what was most requisite in a physician. He had a brief and mortifying vision of this ill-kempt man touching Mercedes' tender breast. He had to close his eyes and banish the thought from his mind.

"What do you mean by too late, Doctor?"

"Even if the peccant part is removed, the cancer may have spread beyond the breast to other parts of her body—"

Captain Blackwell's grunt of dismay stopped the doctor's speech. They gazed at one another, and for the first time he thought he saw a glint of compassion in the doctor's expression. Then again, it might have been approval that he had at last understood the seriousness of Mercedes' condition.

"I must still urge surgery, sir. She is a most extraordinary woman."

That simple statement almost undid him. Tears rose to Captain Blackwell's eyes, he agreed wholeheartedly. He wanted her by his side always. Always.

"She shall have the surgery." He bowed his head a moment, quickly adding, "Is it what she wants? You have discussed it?"

Doctor Russ smiled for the first time, a fleeting, weak affair that passed over his features and vanished like a ghost.

"I did indeed. Mrs. Blackwell said, and I hope I commit no breach by repeating, that she wanted to live, even if she had to endure an operation, for she must help the Captain with his children."

"She is a very fond mother, to be sure." Captain Blackwell shook his head. "Though they are all oldsters now."

There was a pause, during which Doctor Russ looked as though his mind were far away from St. James's Place. Captain Blackwell prepared to take his leave.

"I have found myself in the position of being inside your family circle, Captain Blackwell, if you will allow, during my attendance upon Mrs. Blackwell. She is a fond mother, and her children are necessarily concerned with her well being, so I have had much conversation with both Mr. and Miss Blackwell. I must congratulate you, sir, on your son's success, in his particular sphere."

Captain Blackwell thought of Aloka, burns on arms and shoulders, hands flayed of skin from the pull the night of the attack, days and nights of hard labor, loss of life and bloodshed, for a sort of half-victory. He had a hard time imagining what success Doctor Russ referred to. Unless he meant to be ironical, in which case Captain Blackwell must bid him a good day. The doctor pushed a paper across his desk toward him.

'Discourses on the Construction of the Heavens' by Edward James Blackwell.

"A great accomplishment, to be published in the Royal Society's *Philosophical Transactions*. Little do I know of mathematics, but I have a particular friend who assures me Mr. Blackwell's philosophy is quite sound. And he not yet a university student."

Captain Blackwell was astounded. He'd known Edward to be forever reading and studying astronomical papers and articles, but he'd certainly not been aware of the depth of his scholarship. To be published by the Royal Society! The last tutor Edward had was a Jesuit brother Mercedes had discovered. Public school had not answered. There had been many thrashings in Edward's defense when Aloka was at school with him. And Edward generally outstripped the local masters in point of intellectual acuity.

"I have not yet had the pleasure of reading it, sir. I...I take it, it is a discussion of Mr. Herschel's findings?"

"Just so," the doctor said. "Sidereal time, an infinite space, perhaps many universes not unlike our own. Astonishing."

"I quite agree. I must take my leave, sir. I've taken enough of your time."

"I will have a look at your injuries before you go. Take off your shirt, Captain Blackwell, if you please."

Captain Blackwell wanted nothing more than to fly home to Mercedes, to take that dear, treasured woman in his arms. He'd been astonished, frightened, humbled by what he'd learned in Doctor Russ's study and he wanted to be alone, and with the woman he loved to absorb it all. Trained to obedience, however, he patiently stripped off his shirt.

"Don't get up, sweetheart," Blackwell cried.

He strode into her room and knelt beside her chair. This time he found her altering one of his shirts, so the shirt opened with buttons up the front. He wrapped his left arm round her waist and they leaned their heads together. At first he could barely speak.

"James, darling. You've been wounded again. Take off your shirt, and let me see. Tell me, I need to hear it from you. Aloka is unharmed?"

"Outside of a few scrapes, he's prime. He fished his old governor out of the drink, he won't tell you that. Pulled me out before I could drown or die of—"

"Oh, Jim!"

"I beg your pardon, sweetheart, it wasn't so bad as all that, and I shall do just as you say in a moment. But first..." his voice faltered, "first, I want to hear about this trouble, the thing that is troubling you. I wish...I wish you had told me, as soon as ever you felt unwell."

"I wish I had too!" she cried. "Then you might not have gone off to be so terribly injured."

"Mercy, sweetheart." He embraced her again. "You must think of yourself from time to time. Now, you must show me, and tell me what is to be done."

Mercedes nodded and rose, going into the dressing room that joined their bedchambers. A few minutes later she emerged, having removed her gown and stockings and underclothes, and wearing instead a dressing gown. She sat up in her bed with the bolsters at her back and held out her hand to Blackwell.

When he was seated on the edge of the bed facing her, Mercedes dropped the gown from her shoulders. She grasped his good left hand and put his fingers beneath her left breast.

"It was a little hard pea, now it is a large angry lump. And it is from there all the trouble and pain arises."

Blackwell felt oddly shy of touching her, though he'd done so eagerly for what seemed like the entirety of his life, or at least the part that mattered. He did not wish to cause her pain, and he touched the foreign hard lump he could feel beneath her soft skin gingerly.

"It is what my mother died from," she said suddenly, with a little sob.

He had his arm around her again, and he wanted to free his other arm so he could hold her properly.

"Help me with this blasted shirt, my love."

"At least your handsome face wasn't burned," she said, carefully lifting the shirt over his head. He'd taken off his jacket immediately upon entering the room, the heavy fabric chaffed his wounded skin.

"Only you would say such a thing. Come here, if you aren't afraid of me."

She instantly settled against his good left side.

"This isn't California, and you've managed to secure to yourself the finest physician in London. You shall not share your mother's fate, you mustn't think of it."

"Doctor Russ has been a great comfort. I don't know what we would have done around here without him these last days, bringing us all up with a dozen neat turns."

"He is a peculiar, reptilian sort of a cove though, ain't he?"

"How unkind! He is an eminently learned, practical, straightforward man of science. He has become a great friend to Edward."

"Ah, yes. It was humbling to learn of Edward's paper from a stranger. Published by the Royal Society!"

"I am sorry for it. Emma and I knew he was writing, but you know Edward, he has his own reasons and keeps his own council."

"The problem is I don't know him. I should like to do better."

"I love you so."

They kissed, and held one another carefully.

"So you must have this surgery," Blackwell said. It was half a question.

"Yes. The Doctor has been most urgent with me to proceed, but I could not do it without you were here. Not because I could not decide, I know I must submit if... I know I must have the surgery. But I couldn't do such a thing before you knew, we are supposed to be one flesh, this is your body too."

"Mercedes." He gave her a gentle shake. "You had better say, we are partners in all. I will not bring you up for your scruples, they do you too much honor. But now I am home, and if you must have this surgery, I shall be here to care for you."

She sat up suddenly. "What did the Doctor give you for the burns?"

"Why, a tin of cream and a packet of leaves of some South American plant to be made into a fortifying tea. Mercedes, I beg you will not—"

She was already up, searching in his jacket pockets. "I told you, such a resourceful man. I love Doctor Russ, I knew he would prescribe. I'll put this on for you."

Mercedes returned to the bed and as she gently salved his wounds, she told Blackwell the arrangements she'd made with the Physician of the Fleet.

Emma heard Captain Blackwell leave his bedchamber and walk downstairs. The old people may have been abed this long time, but she had not been, instead she'd anxiously waited about in her nightdress, dressing gown, and slippers. She followed her father downstairs and surprised him where he was deeply engrossed in the pantry.

He actually cried out when she walked up to him, looking about somewhat desperately. He had on only cotton drawstring trousers, no shirt nor shoes of any kind, in spite of the chill in the house.

"Never mind it, Papa," Emma said. "I shall run up for a dressing gown if you wish. If you will light the stove, I shall make you eggs and sausage."

"It is only I can barely stand to wear clothes these days." He blushed. "Might there be such a thing as an apron?"

Emma turned up one belonging to the cook Dickens. Captain Blackwell seemed as immune to the brutish, ludicrous appearance he presented as he was to the cold. After tying on the apron he went to work with a flint and steel.

"Is it to be surgery, then, Papa?"

"It is. She has it all planned with Doctor Russ. We are none of us allowed to be here to support her."

"What?"

"Your Mama will have it all her own way. Just as she would not be moved until I came home, now she tells me I am not wanted and must go away for the duration of the surgery itself. She will not even have the servants in the house, so don't begin to cry out."

"But...no one at all to support her, to hold her hand? What are we supposed to do?"

"She told me exactly. I am to take you and Edward to Windsor, to view Herschel's great telescope. She says he's been invited to do so this age."

"We are to have an outing while she suffers this operation, not even Tio Severino in the house?"

Captain Blackwell merely shook his head. For a time Emma fried eggs, onions and sausages in silence. She went into the pantry and found two small loaves of bread. She filled the rolls and put the sandwiches before Captain Blackwell.

"Thank you kindly, Emma. Won't you join me?"

"No, Papa, I had my supper. Unlike you."

Captain Blackwell fell to his midnight repast. Halfway through the first sandwich, he said, "We must allow her to arrange matters as she sees fit, of course, we haven't any other goddamn choice. But I shall be back here the moment, the moment it is over. You have something to tell me I believe. About the circumstance that caused your Mama such anxiety. I hate a mystery, girl."

From Mr. Martinez 'girl' was acceptable, but not from her father. She hated it from him, and she was surprised by what felt like a sudden attack, though this very explanation was the reason she'd followed Captain Blackwell downstairs. Emma knew she wasn't as important as her brothers, she was just a girl, but she did not like to lose any part of the small esteem her father bore her.

Emma lifted her chin and told Captain Blackwell of the Marlborough's ball and what took place in Lord Cochrane's townhouse afterward. Her mother had advised her to give her account officer-like, adhering to the events and exactly the words spoken. She said nothing of her fear and panic, much less of the fantasy of rescue that had sustained her in captivity. Captain Blackwell abandoned his last half-sandwich, his jaw clenching.

"If any violence was done you, Emma—"

"It wasn't. I will not pretend I don't take your meaning, Father. I was most sincerely frightened, and threatened, and thrown about a little. But I was not violated, or anything unthinkable of that kind."

"I shall make him marry you, after what you've been through, if it is what you—"

"I most decidedly do not wish it." Emma sucked in a breath. She should have known the whole affair would come down with him to a reason to fob her off. "The very last thing I want is a hue and cry. Mama agrees. She sent Tio and McMurtry back to Lord Cochrane's house to scrub the place of my presence. I might never have been there."

"McMurtry and his cousin Bosun Clark took care of John Bargeman, Sir," Edward said, walking into the kitchen.

"There you are, son. Sit down. Should you like this? I've lost my appetite."

Edward reached across to Captain Blackwell's plate and stuffed the remainder of the sandwich in his mouth in one go. Captain Blackwell looked at Edward rather ruefully, but he was not to be distracted, and he turned back to Emma.

"I wish I'd been here to knock a few heads together, and for your dear Mama. She must have been beside herself, the time you were missing. Has the whole experience decided you against Lord Cochrane?"

"I never was for Lord Cochrane, Papa, nor anything near."

"You are so taken against him, I half suspicion there is another man in the case."

Captain Blackwell started back in his chair when Emma leapt to her feet.

"What if there is? I can never be with him!"

She ran from the kitchen.

"Hell and death, son, is she in love with a Frenchman? One of those wretched émigrés?"

Edward could have said it was much worse than that, but he was still chewing. His father was tolerably transparent, he was obviously making a mental note to ask Mercedes what was afoot.

"May I congratulate you on your paper? Doctor Russ showed it me earlier. Why did you never remark on your writing?"

"Thank you, F-f-father." Edward made a little bow from the waist in his chair. "It's a rather pitiful thing to call oneself a writer, don't you think? I believe as Doctor Johnson did, only a blockhead ever wrote except for money."

"But there is no money in the case, it only pays in honor to be published in the *Philosophical Transactions.* A very great honor, nevertheless, and a very great accomplishment."

"Do not give me too much credit. I am the man that l-l-lost Emma. She will not have told you that, sir."

Indeed she had not, and Captain Blackwell looked quite confounded.

CHAPTER FIVE

Doctor Russ called upon the Blackwells with a crate of bandages, linen, and towels, and he brought with him Doctor Lally, a French physician. He was actually an army surgeon, taking refuge like many of his countrymen in England. Doctor Russ, without colored spectacles today, looked pointedly at Captain Blackwell as he explained how Doctor Lally had performed the surgery Mercedes was to undergo while he had not.

"Do you know Madame D'Arblay, ma'am?" Doctor Russ turned to Mercedes. "Née Francis Burney."

"Oh, the author of *Evelina* and *Cecilia*!"

Doctor Russ bowed. "She is the sister of Admiral James Burney, sir," he said to Captain Blackwell. "Doctor Lally performed this surgery for Madame D'Arblay. She is recovered, and living here in London for the present. I trust there will be no objection to Doctor Lally's attending at your surgery, ma'am?"

Mercedes glanced at Captain Blackwell, they instinctively reached for one another, and both meekly murmured there should be no objection. The doctors left them alone after that, going off to see to their theatre of operation in the library.

Doctor Russ walked in on Mercedes while she was alone in the small parlour later that day. He slipped into the room so silently Mercedes started when she looked up from the shirt she was working and saw the doctor standing there.

"The day and time is fixed, ma'am. Mr. Blackwell has had a reply from the Herschels. Tomorrow at noon Doctor Lally and I will attend you."

"Sit down, Doctor Russ, if you please."

"I know you must feel a great disturbance of spirit. I want to speak to you of the actual operation. Tell me, did you cry out, did you scream when your children were born?"

Mercedes blanched a little before his stare, before that question.

"My children were born aboard ship, Doctor. Men-of-war. No sir, I did not cry out."

"You must have no such scruple tomorrow, ma'am. I must absolutely charge you to scream, to do otherwise would be detrimental to your constitution. You must expect to suffer, I do not want to deceive you — you will suffer — you will suffer very much."

"I know, Doctor, you have already warned me. It is the reason I insisted dear James and the children go away. Even the servants." Mercedes added in a small voice, "Even Tio Severino."

"I shall be with you, Mrs. Black—"

"Call me Mercedes, please sir, we are about to be very intimate."

Doctor Russ flushed beneath his swarthy skin tone. "I will be with you, Mercedes. You must tell yourself you shall endure it and you will recover from it. Our minds have a power far greater than our feeble shells."

"My mind is all confusion at the moment, and my feeble shell fairly quakes."

"No, ma'am, no. You are made of tougher stuff. I should know, I too was bred of it." This last Doctor Russ said to her in Spanish, surprising her.

Tears came into Mercedes' eyes with memories of her mother, and the wasting away and suffering at the end of Arabella de Aragon's life. Surgery would be a terrible blow, but she meant to live. Mercedes rose and fetched several folded sheets from a small desk in the corner, and gave them into Doctor Russ's hand.

"Here is the document I prepared after your kind suggestion, may you put it into the hand of the Notary, if you please, sir. And these are letters, for James and the children, in case...I understand it is the custom, before going into action."

Doctor Russ gave Mercedes a long appreciative look. He took her Will and letters, and put them in his pocket without a word, and in a short while the doctor took his leave.

It was not a restful night for any of them. Captain Blackwell stayed in Mercedes' bedchamber at her request. He could really only lie on his left side comfortably, and Mercedes on her right. They were a pair. Even her left arm ached, one more part of the general malaise. She would have liked Captain Blackwell to love her, but with all the will in the world, neither could manage it.

Morning came too soon, and with it the difficult task of taking leave of them. Captain Blackwell embraced her and whispered, "I love you with all my heart and soul. Don't...don't leave me." She and Emma could do nought but cry and cling to one another. Edward was last to embrace her. "We need you, Mama. Be strong. Survive."

Mercedes sat still, stunned, and stupid after they departed for Windsor. She'd meant to use the time before the doctors arrived to write James and each of them little billets, to add to the letters she'd enclosed with her Will. But for a time she could not move, and she was grateful to have written her letters when her mind was more composed. She had a terror of the operation, but forced herself to rise after a time and walk about the empty house.

She ended in the library, where she stood in fascinated horror before the sea chests over which the doctors had layered several old sheets. Both being military men they were accustomed to operating on such a surface and had chosen to stay with what they knew. Leathern straps with buckles were fixed to the trunk that would in a short while restrain her. A quantity of linen, compresses, and bandages was neatly arranged on a table. Mercedes felt if they did not come soon she would climb out a window, in her dressing gown as she was, and run away.

The doctors called her from the library, pounding on the street door. She was obliged to answer herself, clad as she was. Mercedes was infinitely glad Doctor Russ had thought to engage a nurse, a big competent looking woman he presented as Mrs. Mulvaney. She wanted a woman to support her, to hold her hand, and arrange and cover her when she could not do it herself. There was no lack of women friends she could have called upon, but she could not bring herself to expose any of them. And Emma, the woman she most wanted in such a crisis, least of all.

"Thank you, Doctor."

Mercedes gave Doctor Russ the empty glass, that had contained a wine cordial laced with laudanum.

"Come, Ma'am."

Doctor Russ led her to the operating table. Mercedes was trembling, even before she was told to remove her dressing gown. She lay down upon the hard surface, naked except for a pair of bloomers such as the Captain once teased her about. Doctor Russ buckled the leather straps over her thighs and midsection. He gave her a look of great compassion before he laid a large cambric handkerchief over her face.

Mercedes did not know if they were aware she could see through the fabric. Both doctors immediately came close and bent over her, but they did not speak. Instead an unspoken communication took place. Doctor Russ lifted her left breast and made a motion underneath it in the area where the lump was most felt. Doctor Lally shook his head, and made a circle with his finger.

"Mrs. Mulvaney, hold this breast, if you please. Jesus, Joseph, and Mary!" he cried.

The nurse had turned and fled from the library.

"Mrs. Blackwell, I beg your pardon. I was assured she was a reliable person," Doctor Russ said.

"I will hold the breast for you, Doctor. It is just here," Mercedes touched her breast and indicated the part underneath, "from where the pain starts, and from there reaches into every other part."

The doctors heard her very gravely, but then Doctor Russ took her gently by the shoulders and arranged her again as before. He laid the veil over her face, and turned to Doctor Lally. The French physician inscribed a circle, and then an X through the circle with his finger. Doctor Russ nodded, and took a scalpel into his hand.

Mercedes shut her eyes as the doctor bent over her. She screamed, a prolonged shriek that lasted as long as the first incision.

The pitch of her screams rose when he withdrew his cold instrument and the air met the fresh wound. A million raw nerve endings felt on fire. The scalpel bit in again on the other side of the breast. Doctor Russ paused; Mercedes thought the surgery might be at an end and she opened her eyes. No. The surgeon was taking hold again, slicing all the way round the breast. She screamed, panted, and writhed on the table. It either must be over soon or she would die there.

She opened her eyes and watched the doctors' pantomime. Doctor Russ motioned Doctor Lally forward. He came and craned over her trembling body, pursed his lips, and pointed to an area where he perceived yet some offending tissue. Doctor Russ's scalpel came down again, Mercedes felt it scrape against her breastbone. She fainted, and when she became conscious once more the handkerchief had slid off. Doctor Russ bent over her, his face blood splattered, and underneath the gore a grieved, almost horrified expression.

"How I pity you, Doctor."

No one answered his knock and finding the door unbolted, Aloka walked in to the house on Curzon Street. He stopped dead in the vestibule as a scream jolted him, sending a cold spike of fear through him. He'd heard the cries of wounded men before. This was much worse, the shriek of a woman under torture. He was paralyzed where he stood.

When the agonized animal shrieking stopped, Aloka forced his steps forward, his heart thudding. He stood in the open doorway of the library, gazing at two old men bending over Mercedes. They were bandaging her, carefully and methodically layering bandages and lint, and wrapping the whole tight round her. Mercedes had fainted and the doctors were lifting her gently as they worked.

"I am glad she is insensible, the poor dear creature. How we are to move her to bed upstairs, I cannot tell."

"Shall we send for the Captain's servants? That ill-looking steward told me they would be just down the way at the Pig and Oaks."

"I have a notion the Captain would not like it above half, and they are nearly as old as we, colleague."

"I shall carry her." Aloka advanced into the room, his heart still pounding. "Aloka Blackwell, gentlemen, at your service."

Doctor Russ turned to him and actually smiled. He was a gruesome sight, with blood on his face, apron, and sleeves.

"Mr. Blackwell, you are come at the opportune moment, sir. Lieutenant Blackwell, is it not? I am William Russ, and may I present Doctor Lally." The doctor meanwhile gazed long and keenly at Aloka, particularly at his face. "We shall be ready for you in a moment, sir, we must just complete the dressing."

The two doctors went back to work, titivating the bandages to a degree Aloka found old womanish and over fussy. He wanted to step over and cover Mercedes, he knew it would be what she would want. At last he was called forward.

"May we wipe this blood from her other side, Sirs? And where is her nightdress?"

Aloka found Mercedes' dressing gown over a chair while the two doctors sponged her right breast. He spread the gown over her front and was directed to lift her from her right side. The doctors had bound Mercedes' arm against her left side so as not to disturb the wound. She felt insubstantial in Aloka's arms, like a child. He carried her upstairs, Doctor Russ plodding at his side with his chin upon his breast.

"I'm so sorry you should have returned at such a time," Mercedes said, jostled awake.

Aloka felt his throat constrict with emotion. "Hush, dear Ma'am. You must do no more now than recover."

"God bless you for what you did for your father. Has he been sent for?"

"I shall do, just as soon as your doctor gives me leave. And you know I should not dare come home without the Governor, you would not have me."

"Nonsense. You are always welcome here, come what may."

He set her gently down on her bed, backing away with tears in his eyes. Doctor Russ moved in immediately and arranged Mercedes, offering her a draught he had prepared and just at hand. The doctor spent some time sitting beside Mercedes, taking her pulse, checking her pupils, and speaking softly to her. Aloka waited near the door, his legs apart and his hands clasped behind his back.

Doctor Russ stood up. "You may send for Captain Blackwell, sir, if you please."

"You will stay with her?"

"Of course I shall, sir," Doctor Russ answered sharply. "Do you think I should leave my patient during this critical time?"

Aloka saluted before he could stop himself, received his father's direction of the doctor, and went out without another word to arrange a messenger to Windsor. On his way home he called at the Pig and Oaks to collect McMurtry and Mr. Martinez. When he returned to Mercedes' bedchamber at last, Aloka found both Mercedes and the doctor asleep. Doctor Russ was slumped in an armchair at her bedside. Aloka woke the doctor.

"Sir, why do not you lie down? I understand you are to remain overnight, in Edward's chambers. I shall sit with her and call you if she wakes, or at any other indication you care to name."

Doctor Russ led Aloka to just outside Mercedes' doorway and gave him a list of changes in her he was to watch for, and specifically when he should be summoned.

Aloka listened attentively. "May I beg, sir, that room downstairs be cleared before m'father and Miss Blackwell return. And forgive me, sir, but if you could change your shirt and wash your face I am sure you shall spare them a...Well, you shall spare them."

"We must have a private word, sir, sometime in future."

The doctor bowed and went away. Aloka had expected a sharp retort, learned men do not like to be told their business. Doctor Russ's remark was inscrutable, and Aloka wondered if the doctor, old as he was, meant to call him out.

That absurd notion was given no further thought as he sat down beside Mercedes' bed. She slept on, whimpering or moaning now and again, and Aloka thought it must be a drugged sleep. He pondered why the doctor had not given her such a dose beforehand to lessen her suffering. Aloka stared at the little, unassuming woman in the bed, so very much a part of each and every one of them.

Some while later McMurtry opened the door a crack. “Mr. Al, sir, a word if you please.”

Aloka met McMurtry in the hall, softly closing Mercedes’ door behind him.

“It’s a caller, sir, as won’t go away. Captain Lord Cochrane. I told him the family wasn’t to home, but he insists he will wait Captain Blackwell’s return. A matter of the first importance.”

“Hell and death.” Aloka gazed down the hallway as though he might see Lord Cochrane appear. “I shall speak to his lordship. Pass the word for Mr. Martinez to sit with the Missus.”

“Which Severino is abed, sir. He’s what you might call paralytic. This here was too much for him, it being the second time round like.”

“Very well, wake Doctor Russ.”

“Oh, no, sir. Not me, that wicked man will rip me a new—”

“Wake Doctor Russ, McMurtry, that’s an order. I shall await the doctor before I see Lord Cochrane.”

McMurtry slumped away, setting his own evil countenance to the task of jerking the doctor from his slumbers.

After he’d yielded his chair to Doctor Russ, drooping with fatigue but clad in a clean shirt, Aloka went down to wait on Lord Cochrane.

He found him in the vestibule, pacing. No one had offered that Lord Cochrane should come farther into the house.

“Lord Cochrane, sir, how do you do? I regret to say you have called at a most inopportune time—”

“It cannot be helped. I must speak to Captain Blackwell and Miss Emma on a matter of the first importance.”

Aloka was astonished to hear Emma named, and he stared at Lord Cochrane. He’d frankly never seen him in such a state; no, not during the hottest part of a battle. His lordship had lost his usual calm reserve.

“Captain Blackwell and Miss Blackwell are not at home, sir. Nor could you see them to-day if they were.”

“What the deuce mean you by that, sir?” Lord Cochrane cried.

“I beg you will lower your voice, sir. Mrs. Blackwell is unwell upstairs.”

"I don't believe it, that is merely a rumor put about—"

The street door opened and Emma walked in. They were all three struck dumb a moment. Aloka thunderstruck by Lord Cochrane's words and behavior, Emma with a look of horror on seeing the two of them standing there together, and Lord Cochrane with choler and surprise.

Lord Cochrane recovered first. "Emma, I must have a word with you."

Emma evaded him, moving quickly to stand near Aloka.

"Sir, I don't remember giving permission for use of my Christian name."

That brought Lord Cochrane up, and he spluttered, "Where is Captain Blackwell?"

Captain Blackwell had been outside paying the hired coach. He walked in with such a look of anxiety and concern, anyone who knew him would not have crossed his hawse. He and Lord Cochrane were not so well acquainted.

"Not now!" Captain Blackwell anticipated Lord Cochrane, and held up a hand.

"She's upstairs, Father," Aloka said.

Affronted, Lord Cochrane moved as though he would block Captain Blackwell's path to the stairs. Aloka checked him. He did not put his hands on his lordship, but he threw him a good body block all the same. Captain Blackwell reached out in passing, and he and Aloka gripped forearms in the native manner. Low, in Hawaiian, Captain Blackwell said, "See to your sister."

He ran up the stairs, two at a time, for all his injuries and age.

Apparently even aristocrats can sense when they are about to get punched in the face. Lord Cochrane held his peace until Captain Blackwell was out of sight.

"I don't know what can excuse Captain Blackwell's behavior. If he will not see me, I really must insist on a private word with you, Emma. I came here today on a matter of honor."

"No one gives a damn for your honor, sir!"

Aloka stepped in front of Emma at this juncture, and she even took his hand.

"I came here for you!" Lord Cochrane declared. "To offer for you, and save your reputation after what was done in my name and without my knowledge. But I find honor is thrown away here, where the entire family are nothing but Sava—"

"Enough of that infernal noise, sir! There is a sick woman upstairs."

Doctor Russ hadn't spoken loudly, but his sudden presence, his quelling looks, instantly subdued them all. Aloka might have done some punching of his own if the old doctor hadn't intervened, and that would not have served any of them.

"Doctor Russ, I beg your pardon, I—"

"Your lordship." Doctor Russ acknowledged Lord Cochrane with a brief bow. "Miss Blackwell, if you will come with me, I will acquaint you with your mother's present condition."

Emma took the arm Doctor Russ offered and he led her away. For a few seconds Aloka and Lord Cochrane considered one another, emotions running high, with the uppermost, for Aloka at least, a sincere desire to knock the other's head in.

"I thought Mrs. Blackwell being ill was a story put about to explain Emma's absence from society, and to recall Captain Blackwell as soon as possible. But if the Physician of the Fleet—"

"No ruse here, sir. No joke."

Lord Cochrane had the good grace to look ashamed. Aloka seized the moment and moved to open the street door.

"My reasons for calling have not changed. I really must have a word with Captain Blackwell and Em—ah, Miss Blackwell, under calmer circumstances. If I were to call again..."

"She might be out of danger in a fortnight. Or perhaps you'd like to ask the Physician of the Fleet?"

Lord Cochrane gave Aloka a sour look, jammed his hat on his head and took his leave without so much as a 'good day'. Aloka would have liked to give the street door a resounding slam behind him, but he was conscious of Mercedes' fragile state, as she lay abed upstairs. Aloka closed the door. In the short time he'd been home he'd witnessed a terrible thing done to the dearest woman in the world, and managed to insult and offend his former captain and the Physician of the Fleet.

He went immediately and found the old gentleman with Emma. She was trying to be brave, listening to the doctor with her hands clasped in her lap. But when Aloka appeared in the doorway, she turned on him such a gaze as quite melted his heart. Doctor Russ, too, must have seen that look. He rose and bowed, wished them good evening, and walked into Edward's bedchamber adjoining the library, and shut the door.

Aloka opened his arms and Emma flew into them. He held her for a long time while she sobbed on his chest. Aloka even dared to stroke her hair: precious moments for him.

The first thing she said was, "You saw her. How is she really? Poor, poor Mama!"

Aloka chose his words with care. "She knew me, and she knew where she was. We spoke about her getting better. While I watched beside her, she slept soundly. You shall go to her yourself, unless the Doctor forbids it. But first...Emma, I must ask what Lord Cochrane could have meant by all that."

Emma wiped the tears from her face with her fingers. A proper gentleman would have produced a handkerchief, but Aloka hadn't got one. He waited while she composed herself, and then recited a most astonishing tale. Her account of being in the power of a man like John Bargeman made him grit his teeth. Aloka could see she'd spoken of all this before. She ended by saying Captain Blackwell knew the whole.

"I am sorry, Aloka. I know you value Captain Lord Cochrane, and now your chances for another commission under him are quite dashed."

"You are to set the notion of my being injured aside, I assure you there is nothing in it. More importantly...would you have him had he come when your Mama was not so ill?"

Emma looked away. "There is no point in such a question. He will not return after the way I spoke to him."

"You much mistake men, and particularly a man like his lordship. They value a prize the more when it's difficult to obtain. Oh, Emma, don't—" Tears had come into her eyes at his boorish remark. "Forgive me. Between this and your Mama, you have been through a great ordeal. It is only my anxiety that...that you not accept him, made me say such a deuced awkward thing."

"Never," she said. "I never shall."

He was clasping both her hands in his, and they sat pressed together on the sofa.

"He is not the man for you." Aloka looked down at her lovely, upturned face. "Promise me..."

Then he did what he'd been yearning to do for ages. Aloka plunged ahead and took advantage of her vulnerable state over her mother and the wretched business with Lord Cochrane, and he kissed her. It was very far from a brotherly kiss. She moved right against his chest, almost into his lap, kissing him back. The surprise and delight of it nearly overwhelmed him. Since he'd started it, he also ended it, pulling away from her.

Aloka could not look on her with anything other than affection; shame was the last thing on his mind. "Promise me, dear Emma," he touched her face, "no one but me." He was not sure how he'd grown so bold.

If she had rejected him, Aloka would have had to walk off and shoot himself. Instead Emma gave him a beautiful smile, a tender look, and fell on his breast. What she said exactly he could not hear, her words were muffled against his chest. For several glowing moments he was happy, just in the knowledge she would not be another's, and they held one another in silent contentment. Aloka had a capacity for living in the moment; a trait bred into sailors, that helped him greatly as a sea-officer; but Emma, being younger, and much more English, did not.

"Shall we ever be together?" she said.

"We must not think of that now."

"Oh! You are right. How could I be so evil? Oh Lord! Edward!"

"Yes, where is the fellow? I should think he would be here."

"The Herschels begged him to stay, to view the heavens at night through the great forty foot telescope. He really could not refuse, besides wishing to do so, and Papa would not stay. We were to send to tell him how Mama does. Now all this time has passed, and what shall he think has happened to her?"

"You are not to worry. Ed shall have his head so far up the great telescope and the cosmos, he will not be aware any time has passed. I will go out this minute and send a messenger. Or ought I go myself?"

"Oh, no, stay. I...I need you here. I'll just dash off a note to Edward." She ran to a writing table, and moments later put her folded letter into Aloka's hand. "I'll go up to Mama now. McMurtry will see a bedchamber is made ready for you, and I'll speak to Cook about supper for you and Papa and Doctor Russ."

"Bless you, Emma."

He kissed the hands clutching her letter. They stared at one another. Aloka wished for another kiss and embrace, and he thought he read the same desire in her eyes, but he hoped they were neither one of them fools. He smiled and bowed and ran out the front door.

Mercedes woke in the dark. Her entire left side, her arm, breast, chest and torso felt paralyzed, the whole on that side of her body was a great throbbing mass. She was thirsty, her mouth and throat dry, and her bladder full. Mercedes turned her head and there was Blackwell, asleep in a chair at her bedside. A small table held glasses full of various liquids that she could not reach on her own.

"James. James, darling."

Her voice came out a croak, quite destroyed from all the screaming. She shivered with the recollection, swallowed, and mustered her strength.

"Captain on deck!"

He came awake with a start and was instantly beside her.

"Water, if you please."

He selected a glass from the bedside table and put a pipette the doctor had left into it, and held her and it so she could drink.

"Thank you, darling. I need to use the p-o-t."

"Oh." Blackwell looked confounded. "I can't carry you, one armed as I am. I'll go fetch Aloka, or Edward if he's returned."

"No, no, I can walk. The Doctor said I should try." It was a lie, but Mercedes did not want Aloka or Edward to have to help her. Bad enough Blackwell should have to do so.

He put back the bedclothes and she swung her legs out of bed slowly. Blackwell helped her sit up, she felt a wave of nausea that frightened her very much, and then clinging to his shoulder and arm she was on her feet. They teetered into the dressing room.

Passing her full length mirror Mercedes had to look away from the sight of the two of them, once so young and dashing.

Blackwell eased her down on the close stool. He knelt on one knee beside her and turned away his head. Mercedes still clung to his arm, and she rested her head against his shoulder. Her urination felt hot and sick, just like the rest of her.

After one of the most intimate moments of their married life, Blackwell helped her back into bed. He pursed his lips slightly pulling the bedclothes over the mountain of bandaging on her left breast, struggling to maintain a neutral expression. Mercedes began to cry.

"Is the pain too bad, sweetheart? Doctor Russ has left a dose of laudanum should you want it."

"I'm mutilated, Jim. I thought they would cut into the breast, take out the offending part. They took the whole! The whole!"

Now he looked at her speechless and appalled. What had she expected? She took a gasping breath.

"What are the other draughts?"

Blackwell swallowed hard and turned to the little table. "There is barley water, a broth if you are hungry. It has gone quite cold, but I'll warm it if you wish. Water, and the small glass has the laudanum."

"My stomach is a bit uneasy. I'll have the barley water, if you please."

She did not want Blackwell to be uncomfortable in the chair by her bedside all night, and she knew he would not leave her. He was sitting upon the bed facing her now, and Mercedes did not care to be looked at so much at this juncture.

"I'm cold, James. Won't you get in bed with me?"

"I don't want to disturb you, sweetheart. I'll fetch another blanket."

"No, I can't stand anything else on top of me. Please."

He leaned forward and put his hand on her cheek, kissing the other side of her face. Then he stood up and took off his breeches and shirt. His skin was healing, he would be well quite soon. Blackwell eased in beside her. She sighed with satisfaction at the feel of his shoulder and chest against her right side. They might both sleep now.

He had snuffed out the candle before getting in bed, and his voice came out of the dark. "All those tender names you always call me—darling, dear—they apply more to you. You are the center of my life Mercedes, all I care about is that you are here with me. There would be no love, no tenderness for me without you, no home to come to, no country worth fighting for. You have given me all, all."

"Oh Jim! But now? Now I don't know when I will be able to be a proper wife to you again."

"You have only had the surgery this self same day. You must give yourself time to heal."

"Perhaps I should say if I will be able to be a proper wife to you. If you need to be with other women, I will try not to be hurt by it."

"Sweetheart! What would you have done if I'd come home missing a leg, or an arm, or an eye?" She was silent beside him. "Eh? I shall tell you, you would have nursed me and loved me until I was better. Why would you think I should do anything less for you?"

"Some men resent their wives for illness. And one of this kind, such a mutil—"

"Those men would be what you might call scrubs. Listen now, sweetheart, I'm going to be a bit severe upon you. I do not want to hear any more talk of mutilation. You did what you had to do to save your life, and now your only duty is to get better. When you are well and strong, I guarantee you will feel differently about fobbing me off on other women."

"Oh, James! Oh, Jim!" She turned her face into his shoulder and wept.

Mercedes had asked for the dose of laudanum, and now she slept profoundly beside him. Blackwell hoped her mind was somewhat eased. During their conversation, one of Doctor Russ's little lectures had been in his mind. The doctor had said that for men the sexual act was all instinct and reaction to a woman's sweet form. For a woman, on the other hand, much went on in her mind. How she felt about herself and all the circumstances surrounding coitus; it seemed a man might be the least part of it. Blackwell lay in the dark fervently wishing—he could not pray, having once been quite nearly a pagan—the doctors had removed the entirety of the cancer, and she might not have suffered the operation only to die that most lingering and painful of deaths.

Such a fate could not befall her. He kissed Mercedes' hair, her head was resting against his shoulder. He still cherished his dream of taking her back aboard with him, when he should have her to himself again.

Aloka, Captain Blackwell, and Doctor Russ were the only ones in attendance at breakfast next morning, and a steady gunroom reserve presided. None of the three were apt to share their dreams and wishes. Edward had come home in the early hours, and finding the Doctor, who suffered bouts of sleeplessness, awake and in the library, he had received an account of Mercedes' condition. Their talk had turned to Doctor Herschel, whom Edward described as equally kind and learned, and the wonders Edward had seen through the great telescope. As the conversation had lasted until dawn, Edward was now abed. Emma was upstairs helping Mercedes wash and prepare for the doctor's attendance.

"May they not disarrange the dressings in their zeal," the Doctor said, a look of disapprobation on his face.

"I should not interfere with the ladies in that regard, Doctor. I take it as quite a good sign that she should care about her appearance."

Captain Blackwell nodded to his table companions, and nearly smiled. McMurtry walked into the room and presented a calling card to Captain Blackwell on a silver tray. Captain Blackwell took the card with a wry look for McMurtry, and his show of gentility before the Physician of the Fleet.

"Hell and death, its Admiral Gambier. Is he waiting below?"

"He is, sir, though I did say as the family wasn't to home. No one seems to mind it these days."

"That'll do, McMurtry. Excuse me, gentlemen. I suppose I must see the Admiral." Captain Blackwell rose and tossed his napkin upon his chair, exchanging a conscious look with Aloka. "Doctor Russ, do go in to her whenever you are quite ready, do not wait on me. I must also beg an interview with you later, sir, about your and Doctor Lally's attendance on Mrs. Blackwell."

He bowed and closed the parlour door on his way out, leaving Aloka and Doctor Russ quite alone. Aloka supposed the time might have come for the doctor's few private words.

"Has your mother always been fastidious, so?"

Certainly not the words Aloka had expected to hear.

"Edward and Emma's mother, sir, not my own. Though she has always been as kind to me as if I were her own son."

Why he had told the sharp eyed doctor such a thing Aloka did not know, unless it was out of a desire people should begin to understand he and Emma were only half-brother and sister.

"I should like to have that private word I mentioned yesterday, sir, if it is not inconvenient."

Punctilious old gentleman. Aloka bowed from the waist in his chair.

"You are probably unaware, sir, given your involvement in the recent action, and your family circumstances, that the King and Queen of Hawaii are paying a state visit in England. Both you and Captain Blackwell speak the language, I am told, and it would be disingenuous to suppose anyone connected with the Service was not aware why you are called the Black Savages." Aloka smiled at the doctor, he liked a man who would call him that to his face. "In short I have been commissioned by Sir Joseph Banks, with whom their Majesties are currently residing, to present you to the Royal couple. I know this is not the time for social calls, but I was to extend the invitation for sometime in future. Sir Joseph strongly wishes to present one of their own, turned English gentleman, if you will, sir."

Aloka was taken aback, and he perceived Doctor Russ was not quite comfortable with this commission from Sir Joseph.

"I would be most honored to wait upon the King and Queen, sir. Please give Sir Joseph my best respects and gratitude. If the invitation might include my family, when Mrs. Blackwell is recovered, m'father has a closer association to that nation than I. Edward still knows the language, and I'm sure it would be a great comfort to the Queen and her ladies to have the acquaintance of Mrs. and Miss Blackwell."

"I am sure you are in the right of it, sir." Doctor Russ rose and bowed. "I shall convey your acceptance, and your suggestion, to Sir Joseph. I must go in to Mrs. Blackwell."

Doctor Russ was relieved Aloka Blackwell had not taken offense, he'd expressed his apprehension beforehand to Sir Joseph. "He is a sea-officer, not a social experiment or a creature for display." Sir Joseph had pooh-poohed his fine scruples, and the young gentleman, too, seemed to make nothing of them. He had not expected to meet with such a family, and certainly not at a London ball.

From the time Doctor Russ had made Mercedes' acquaintance, he'd felt an uncommon interest in the Blackwells. She had immediately brought to his mind his own mother and his aunts in Spain. Small, unremarkable women except for their backbones of tempered steel. He went to an upstairs cabinet where the bandages, linen, and compresses were stored to collect material to change Mercedes' dressings.

He hoped she was strong enough to recover from the trauma of the surgery, and that, with the blessing, all her cancer was removed. Doctor Russ much doubted he would perform another such operation. It had taken a great deal out of him, he still felt unnerved by the experience. If he was only to do one breast surgery, he was happy it should have been for such a woman as Mercedes.

He had been curious to meet the man she called lord and master. Doctor Russ had found Captain Blackwell to be the best kind of sea-officer; circumspect, disciplined, with a weather beaten, open and kindly face. No doubt brave as a lion, and his tender regard for his lady did him a great deal of credit.

In Edward Blackwell Doctor Russ had found quite simply the most interesting mind outside his official capacities he'd ever encountered; it was the reason he'd promoted the young man with the Herschels and the Royal Society. Now he had made the acquaintance of the last of Captain Blackwell's offspring, and found the native son to be a man very much like the father; physically as well as in manner. Doctor Russ was fairly certain he'd been witness yesterday to a scene in the library no one was meant to see. He thought of his own spirited and lovely daughter, and of the delicacy of the female reputation.

Captain Blackwell imagined Admiral Gambier might have heard of Mercedes' illness, perhaps from Lord Cochrane, and come to inquire after her. He felt a pang for not having dealt with Lord Cochrane himself, and he had not yet spoken to either Emma or Aloka about the outcome of that meeting. He was aware he was not doing his duty as he went in to meet Admiral Gambier, a man who was no stranger to avoiding the obligations of fatherhood.

Admiral Gambier disabused him almost immediately about the reason for his call. After inquiring into the state of Captain Blackwell's wounds, he brought up Lord Cochrane.

"I tell you this in perfect confidence, Captain Blackwell, because of our long association. Government is contemplating a vote of thanks to me for the success of the late action, but Lord Cochrane has informed the First Lord if the matter was raised he felt it would be his duty as a Member of Parliament to oppose it. Can you credit the flippant and pert behavior? His duty! After I wrote some very handsome things of him in my official report to the Admiralty. Very handsome, I do assure you. Lord Cochrane has made such a noise that I may be obliged to demand a court martial, and I've come round to discover if you will stand by me in the matter of the recall orders."

Captain Blackwell gazed at the self-centered brute, amazed that his lovely Mercedes could have sprung of such a parent.

"Sir, I may have been aboard Lord Cochrane's command, but after the night of April 11, I assure you I hardly knew day from night. I was never on the quarterdeck except in a stretcher, so I was not privy to orders received by *Imperieuse's* officers from the flag and when they received them. You shall have to rely on the logs of the ships involved, like all Naval officers in a court martial."

Captain Blackwell and Admiral Gambier regarded one another with dislike on both sides. It always had been so.

"It would be understandable if you felt I have not been sufficiently grateful for your taking a problem off my hands, all those years ago. We might discuss remedying that situation."

"You had better stop there, sir," Captain Blackwell said, real anger in his voice. "I considered no one's convenience but my own in my choice of Mercedes for wife. Nor have I had one day's, no not one moment's regret of my choice."

"Well, no, I wasn't suggesting—"

Captain Blackwell stood up. "What I must suggest, sir, is that you call again another time. If there is anything further to be discussed on this subject. Had you inquired after Mercedes' health I should have told you, she is not at all well. I am past due to sit with her and to consult her doctor."

Much like Lord Cochrane the day before, Admiral Gambier did appear shamefaced, priding himself as he did on being a Christian. As Captain Blackwell hustled him to the door, the Admiral rushed out many wishes for Mercedes' speedy recovery of health. Captain Blackwell hardly attended, he shut the street door upon him, and turned immediately to go upstairs. Anyone calling upon them now must expect to meet with scant welcome.

CHAPTER SIX

Blackwell did not like the pale look of her, the dark shadows under Mercedes' eyes, her lips and fingernails were bluish colored; but Mercedes rose every day and dressed. She tired easily, and Blackwell had begun to think of taking her away into a warmer climate. He could not see her enduring another English winter.

They did not make calls or go out though they did receive callers, one had just left them. Blackwell would have liked to take her back to Merton, to the quiet countryside, but for reasons he did not fully grasp Mercedes wished to continue in London. It might have been to remain near her doctor. Emma's London season had been effectively curtailed. She didn't seem to regret the balls and routs, and appeared content for Aloka to escort her to London attractions by day and to remain at home in the evenings. In the six weeks since Mercedes' surgery Lord Cochrane had not called upon them again, Admiral Gambier's court martial was going forward, and they'd just received news from Missy Bourne. Missy had taken her leave moments before.

"He beat her, you know. That is why she left him." Mercedes said of Missy, the wife of Blackwell's naval companion Captain Enoch Bourne.

Blackwell made a face. "I did not know."

"She has a good heart, and she's brave. She offered to be with me during the operation."

“Enoch told me once the old Lord, his governor, used Lady Oxford cruelly. I suppose it is hard for us not to be our father’s sons.”

Mercedes smiled at him quite kindly, a sight that always lifted his heart.

“I cannot regret her news, either,” Blackwell said. “Lord Cochrane is not the sort of man I should wish for Emma.”

Missy Bourne had told them it was generally known to the *ton* that Lord Cochrane had fixed his interest upon a seventeen year old little nobody, and eloped with her to Scotland. Mercedes gave Blackwell a serious considering look, her hands had left the garment she was working on.

“I believe he has a jealous evil temper,” Blackwell explained, “the sort who will hold a grudge. He and Emma could not have started fairly after what happened. And then this court martial promises to be a deuced awkward affair.”

Many of the officers concerned, particularly those who might side with Lord Cochrane, had been offered foreign commissions. Blackwell had been offered a commodore’s pennant on the North American station, Aloka had received three offers of ships. Why Aloka had turned them all down, Blackwell could not comprehend.

“What kind of man should you like then for Emma?” Mercedes asked.

She leaned forward, the camisole like lacy affair of Emma’s design with one of the breast cups filled with cotton batting forgotten in her lap. Her eagerness to hear him made Blackwell ashamed he’d given so little thought to a mate for Emma.

He answered in a bluff tone. “I should like to see her with an honest, straightforward fellow, who would treat her kindly, and protect her, I suppose. Someone near her own age, for she seemed to object very much to Lord Cochrane on account of his advanced years.”

She looked beautiful to him, quite nearly her old self, when she smiled as she did now.

“A difference in age has not worked out so badly for us,” Mercedes said. “Though I never thought I should be the one failing first.”

“There is no failing in the case, sweetheart. None at all.”

"I've given the matter of a match for Emma a great deal of thought. One of the worst things about my condition is that she should have missed the London season."

"She don't seem to mind it overmuch. At least not since Aloka's been home."

Mercedes gave him a sharp look, and it came into his mind to ask her what Emma could have meant when she cried out she could never be with her choice of sweetheart.

"I should want just the same as you for Emma," she said. "A man who will treat her kindly. Were she to be as fortunate as I in the way of a husband and a lover, it would be all I could wish for her. Nothing else would matter. It is of the first importance the man one fixes upon should have a good heart and be decently behaved. Only look at poor Missy."

Mercedes was looking at him fondly, and he felt the kindness and compliment in her words. But he had no time to respond, nor to recall his question, for Doctor Russ was announced and walked in.

Doctor Russ surmised he'd interrupted a tender scene, and he was not yet so gelded by age that he didn't feel a twinge of jealousy. Few men deserve their women, and for Doctor Russ at least, fewer still could merit such a woman as Mercedes Blackwell. She was his ideal, and had he been a score years younger and a bachelor he would have taken her from Captain Blackwell, great warrior though he might be.

"Forgive the intrusion, and this not my usual day," he said.

"Not at all, Don Guillermo, do sit down."

She could not consent to call him William as he'd ask her to do. Still, the more formal address from her lips warmed his heart. He'd long ago determined to do what he could for her and hers.

"Distressing news, I regret to say. King Liholiho has contracted the measles, along with his Queen. The King does not appear in imminent danger, but his lady is very ill indeed. Sir Joseph has sent you this, sir," he handed Captain Blackwell a letter, "to which King Liholiho has appended his note."

Captain Blackwell excused himself and moved away to the chimney piece to read his letter. Doctor Russ took Mercedes' pulse and subjected her to the usual questions.

"We are summoned, Mercedes, by Mr. Canning and by the King, Liholiho that is. But I much doubt you should go."

"Oh, I shall go, I have had the measles." Mercedes even rose from the sofa. "I should have called on Queen Kamāmalu before this, I'm very much ashamed not to have done so."

She wobbled slightly on her feet, and Captain Blackwell instantly had her under the elbows. His expression was a plea to the doctor, but Doctor Russ looked away as he'd often seen junior officers do to avoid their captain's gaze.

"Just let me fetch a pelisse, and my cloak," Mercedes said.

She was going out of the room, Captain Blackwell uttering objections, when Miss Blackwell and Lieutenant Blackwell walked in. Their faces were shining, full of youth and high spirits, and Doctor Russ wondered at the blockhead that could miss the affectionate glances between them.

"Mama! What are you about?"

The explanation was given, and Doctor Russ had to wait through a round of crying out and protests. Mr. Blackwell, of course, instantly resolved to accompany them. He had already met the Royal couple, had even attended them in the King's box—King George's, that is—at Covent Garden Theatre. Miss Blackwell was dispatched for her mother's wraps, and Mercedes made to sit down. In another half glass they did manage to quit the house on Curzon Street, Mercedes well supported between Captain Blackwell and her daughter.

On arrival at the Osborne's Hotel, Emma was surprised to be shown directly into the Queen's bedchamber. A great company was crammed into the apartment. The King and Queen's entire suite were present, and a number of official and professional looking men whom Doctor Russ immediately joined. The King lay in bed holding his poor ailing Queen.

Captain Blackwell left Mercedes' side with a little warning glance at Emma, which she neither appreciated nor needed to do her duty. Her father and Aloka advanced and prostrated themselves on hands and knees before the Royal couple, according to the custom of the Hawaiian Islands. Led by Foreign Office Secretary Mr. Canning all the Englishmen present shifted uncomfortably, and seemed momentarily unable to decide where to direct their gazes.

Mercedes, holding Emma by the arm, moved to the Hawaiian ladies, sitting on mats on the Queen's side of the bed. They seated themselves in back of these women, and Mercedes murmured, "Wahine Mercedes Blackwell, wife of Captain James Blackwell, and my daughter Emma."

The woman appearing to occupy primary place among them inclined her head. "Li'liah, wife of Boki, minister to King Liholiho."

More introductions were made in low voices. Then, on her mother's expressing distress on the Queen's condition, Li'liah cried, "Oh, the poor sweet Queen! And she the sacred wife, and sister of Liholiho."

Emma's head came up and she gazed intently at the Royal couple. While he spoke with her father, the King yet encircled his Queen in his arms. His affection, anxiety and concern for her were etched on his features. Emma's heart was pounding. She could no longer concentrate enough to understand the Hawaiian language spoken around her.

"I shall lose my voice," the King said to Captain Blackwell. "I shall lose my voice, and so I make my wishes known while I am yet able to speak. We have ever valued our friendship with King George and the British people. My mother and my father's wife Ka'ahumanu, who rule in my absence, remember *Ali'i* Blackwell with esteem. Mr. Canning is aware it is my desire you should be the first British consul-general appointed to the Kingdom of Hawai'i."

"You do me great honor, Your Majesty." Captain Blackwell bowed, surprised and taken aback. "But I am no diplomat, just a sailor in the King's Service."

"You speak our language, you lived among the people. Who better? I have expressed my wish to Mr. Canning, and I shall do so to King George when we meet. I cannot say if your government will consent. All kings fear a divided loyalty."

How well Captain Blackwell remembered that feeling of being caught between two worlds. He made all proper acknowledgements for the King's great condescension. King Liholiho addressed a few considerate remarks to Aloka, and then the Queen stirred on his breast. He inclined his head to Kamāmalu, her breath so short and labored only he heard her, afterward asking everyone to leave them.

In the press in the adjoining sitting room Emma found herself standing next to Doctor Russ. Captain Blackwell had placed a chair for Mercedes near the Queen's ladies and the four medical men in attendance. When there came a lull in the doctors' conversation about inflammation of the lungs, a constitution unaccustomed to a cold climate, the dangers of falling damps, Emma meant to interrogate Doctor Russ. Edward had said of him, "He is a very learned man, a polyglot. Has sailed the world in the capacity of physician and natural philosopher. What you might call an infinitely knowing cove."

Emma seized her chance when Doctor Russ turned toward her. "One of the Queen's lady's, Madame Li'liah, told Mama the King and Queen are related. Can this really be, Doctor?"

Doctor Russ gave her that cold dead fish-eye stare of his, but answered in a neutral tone. "Half-brother and sister, born of the same father and his various wives. Kamāmalu was Kamehameha the Great's favorite daughter, and so he married her to his heir."

Emma swallowed. "How...different their customs are to those of Europe."

"And to think Lord Byron was run out of England for his *tendre* for his half-sister." Doctor Russ gazed at her shrewdly. "The Polynesians consider a marriage between brother and sister, especially of the noble class, a union beloved of the gods."

Emma strove not to appear too much agog. Captain Blackwell detached himself from the circle around Mr. Canning and knelt before the Queen's ladies. They held a grave conference. Emma could not attend to what was said, and then her father rose and it appeared they were to take their leave. Farewells were exchanged. Aloka, deep in conversation with King Liholiho's men, particularly with his admiral, Kapihe, was requested to remain to finish their discussion.

Aloka walked out of the hotel and waited with them while a carriage was summoned. Of course there was no chance for a private word, and Emma should not have felt dissatisfied. She'd spent the best part of that day with Aloka. He'd taken her to see the pictures at the British Institution. And promised to escort her to those sights one could not see unless under the protection of a man: Vauxhall and Ranelagh Gardens.

Emma was obliged to maintain a composed silence, but she wished for nothing more than to blurt out the question uppermost in her mind. Did both Aloka and her father know of this custom of marriage between siblings? Her father was too much taken up in Mercedes' comfort and well being to notice her agitation. And, if she did not imagine it, Aloka was avoiding her gaze.

Two days later Queen Kamāmalu died after exposure to measles, followed by an inflammation of the lungs. Measles was a disease for which the Hawaiians had no resistance. Her brother and husband held her to the last, as she took her final labored breaths. Liholiho could not at first consent to her being taken from him. He held her until he felt her spirit must have gone over the rainbow, and then he relented.

Following this the king agreed to everything proposed by the British in accordance with their customs concerning the dead, after the Queen's body had been first arranged by Li'liah in the Hawaiian manner. Unclothed to the waist, with ankles and feet bare, her hair dressed and adorned with flowers. King Liholiho's firmness of decision at first encouraged his doctors to believe in his swift recovery from the measles. But from the day of the Queen's death his spirits failed. His cough became much worse, and Liholiho even declared he could not long survive.

Captain Blackwell was sent for. Liholiho had not yet had his presentation to King George, and no official appointment had been made of a British consul to Hawaii. But King Liholiho felt King George would not ignore the wishes of a fellow sovereign. It did not occur to Liholiho to consider Captain Blackwell's feelings. The king knew only his desire to do right for his island nation. He also wished to have an Englishman who understood Hawaiian like a native by him, while he made his last will known to his own subjects and those of King George.

"I am dying," Liholiho said to the little assemblage comprised, besides his countrymen, of Captain Blackwell and Mr. Canning, and four medical doctors. "I am dying, and I will follow the English manner of making a Will. Kuanoa has written it for me, and Boki, Kuanoa, and Mr. Canning shall witness it. I am following Kamāmalu in placing my feet on the rainbow. I leave my property here in England to Boki, for use by you *ali'i* that you may live and return to our homeland. I desire my body and that of my Queen be conveyed to our native Islands. This is the Will of King Kamehameha II."

King Liholiho was lifted up and he, who wrote the best hand among them, was too weak to do more than make a mark on the paper to signify his signature. After he'd done this, Li'liah was instantly at his side, easing him back on his pillows with great kindness and tenderness. The witnesses and most of the men left the bedchamber. Captain Blackwell was asked to remain.

"I entrust to you, Captain James Blackwell, presents to the *ali'i* that I desire be made in my name. These shall be delivered to you, to be conveyed on the vessel that will take my body home. Here are written instructions, of the most confidential nature. To be given to the Regents who rule in my stead, my mother and Ka'ahumanu."

Captain Blackwell took the envelope with a bow. "I am honored, Your Majesty, and if I am not selected for the commission, I shall put this into the hands of Britain's appointed consul with every caution as to confidentiality."

The King gave him a concentrated, though fevered stare. "I should be happier if you said you would take it to Hawai'i in any case, like a proper king's *kanaka*."

Captain Blackwell stood mum, his hands behind his back. He was the older man. Liholiho was but eight and twenty, and he was not this King's man to command.

"Very well, Captain James Blackwell, I entrust my letter to you. May you return to my Islands, and may you prosper there. You and your children. But hear this and beware. The descendants of the Papua Guinea men, your Ata Gege, are not to be trusted."

For some time Captain Blackwell sat with King Liholiho after this, with his face turned toward him and his eyes fixed on him, as was the custom of the Polynesians before Royalty. When he was replaced by Boki in this vigil, Captain Blackwell went away with mixed feelings. He resented Liholiho's reference to Ata Gege, for Aloka was his direct descendent. And he doubted he had the headpiece for a diplomatic role. He might forget he was not aboard ship, and start flinging out orders and curses. Yet he had wanted to take Mercedes away to a warmer climate, her comfort and convenience were ever present to his mind, and he needed the means to provide for her. His sympathy for King Liholiho in his grief was sincere. Had it been Mercedes who had died, he might be the one following her out of heartache and loss.

'Bulletin — The King of the Sandwich Islands departed this life at four o'clock this morning. His doctors state that his anxiety and depression of mind after the death of his queen seven days prior aggravated his disease, which, but for this cause, might have terminated prosperously. The alarming symptoms of his disorder rapidly increased within the last few days, and King Kamehameha II at length sunk under it without much apparent suffering.'

Doctor Russ was with them early the day the Blackwells were invited to view the Royal couple. Afterword some of the party, the men primarily, would accompany the caskets to the church of St. Martin's in the Fields. In the vault under this church the British government had decided to deposit the bodies, until such time as Kamehameha II's wishes could be complied with.

"What I should like to know," Doctor Russ called to Mercedes, putting on her clothes after his examination in the dressing room, "is how you feel about this appointment. Should you welcome it, do you wish to remove to the other side of the world, my dear?"

"I cannot help but feel it would be good for James and the children. It will be much easier for James to find another woman there, if the cancer should come back—"

"God between us and evil," Doctor Russ said.

"Amen, sir. But you know what I mean, not that he could not find a woman in England. It is just they view relations much differently in the South Seas, in a way that I know will bring him comfort. And as for the children..."

She walked out of the dressing room and saw the exasperated expression on the Doctor's face.

"I beg your pardon, Don Guillermo, you asked me how I would welcome the appointment. I will encourage him to accept it, because I'm quite serious about his happiness. I do not care to see it destroyed. I want to see my children settled and contented too, and those islands, that culture, may be the best chance they have."

"For two of them, I quite agree."

She leaned forward and took Doctor Russ's hand. "The only hesitation I have, this is hard to admit even to a medical man because it springs of vanity. The Hawaiians go about without much clothes at any time, and they bathe often and in communal pools."

Tears stood in her eyes. They seemed to put Doctor Russ quite out of countenance.

"You have a beautiful body despite the children and the surgery, it is a simple matter to cover the wound. And as for bathing, you shall just have to find a private pool. Or you might forego it, a lack of washing is not insalubrious, I find."

"I'm afraid I could never do that, Doctor."

Mercedes smiled, she could almost have laughed but for a wish not to offend, and she wiped the tears from her eyes. She was grateful to be alive. Today they were burying a twenty-two year old woman and a twenty-eight year old man.

The bodies of the King and Queen of the Sandwich Islands had been prepared by their countrymen, and then properly encased and sealed by the English into an inner coffin. The coffins were then fitted in large caskets, and it was these that were on formal display on a raised wood platform in a large apartment of the Osbourne hotel.

The two Royal caskets were draped in crimson velvet ornamented in intricate patterns of embroidered gold thread.

"It would be a pleasure to die in England," said the King's treasurer, Kuanoa, "to have one's body so honored."

The Englishmen in their black clothes formed a ring around the periphery of the room, on the three sides facing the caskets. Before them, on fine woven mats, sat the King and Queen's followers. The wood platform on which the caskets rested was completely obscured by capes and mantles covered over in yellow, red, and black feathers.

"The yellow are from the Nectarina Niger or *Uho* in the native," Edward told Doctor Russ. "The black is the Drepanis Vestiarius, and the red is Nectarina Coccinea. I made drawings of them, part of my juvenilia, if you will, sir. They are at Merton."

"I am with child to see them," Doctor Russ said. "How fascinating to view the gorgeous plumage of those birds in life."

"My brother is with child to discover who will command the ship that will carry the Sandwich Islanders home. Can't comprehend why. What do you say to it, Doctor?"

Doctor Russ's cold stare was elicited, but as Edward's gaze was turned away it did not profit him.

"Lord Byron is suggested."

"The Right Honorable Baron George Anson Byron Byron," Edward said. "Otherwise known as Foul Weather Jack."

"You are acquainted, sir?"

"Not at all."

Doctor Russ could still be surprised in conversation with Edward, who never forgot a thing once he'd read or observed it.

"If his lordship declines, Captain Verson is spoken of."

"Ah? Perhaps for his experience with m'father on the survey mission gone wrong. Captain Verson knew us as nippers, Aloka and I. I daresay no appointment could better suit Aloka."

Captain Verson received a letter shortly after his appointment to *H.M.S. Blonde*, 46-guns, from Lieutenant Aloka Blackwell requesting an interview. Aloka arrived promptly on the day named for the meeting in rural Chelsea, on the outskirts of London. Captain Verson shared a house there with his long time companion and particular friend, Mr. Juan Luis Montelongo.

Mr. Montelongo ushered Aloka into a parlour, where Captain Verson was waiting and rose to shake his hand.

"Mr. Blackwell tells me Miss Mercedes has been most unwell," Mr. Montelongo said, after the initial handshakes and greetings. "I was just about to inquire if she is well enough to receive visitors?"

“I should think so, sir, she receives one or two friends at home. She suffered from a cancer, and was obliged to endure a surgery.”

Captain Verson and Mr. Montelongo both looked deeply concerned, and said so.

“They are much taken up at the moment with this diplomatic appointment proposed to my father.”

“I cannot image a man better suited to the post,” Captain Verson said.

“You are very kind, sir. Those were apparently King Kamehameha’s feelings as well. It is on a related matter that I intrude upon you today, Captain Verson. I understand you are to command the *Blonde*, the vessel that is to return the Sandwich Island chiefs to their home.”

Captain Verson, from his seat in an arm chair, bowed his assent. He was thinking how like Captain Blackwell’s son was to him.

“I’d like to volunteer for the mission, sir. I served under Captain Lord Cochrane in *Imperieuse* the last four years, and I was with her during the action in the Aix Roads.”

“We’re very much aware of the battle in the Aix Roads, Mr. Blackwell. Mr. Montelongo was Master of *Indefatigable* in Rear-Admiral Stopford’s squadron. He will be *Blonde’s* sailing master. Government is decommissioning at an appalling rate, so I must ask why you wish to join as volunteer, sir, and not seek an officer’s commission to the ship?”

Aloka shifted his shoulders and stared down at the threadbare rug.

“May I offer you a glass of wine, sir?” Mr. Montelongo said. “Perhaps hock or cider?”

“Cider would be most welcome, thank you, sir.”

With his refreshment in hand, Aloka took a deep breath. “I wish to volunteer, not be appointed, because there are a few irregularities...that is to say, this will be a one way voyage for me, sirs. I will most likely not be returning to England. And I will have a young lady under my protection, if you will accept her as a passenger, Captain Verson.”

Captain Verson and Mr. Montelongo exchanged an unconcealed, startled look. Apparently there were more similarities between father and son than mere physical resemblance.

"What young lady, Mr. Blackwell?"

"Miss Emma Blackwell."

"Your sister?"

"My half-sister, sir."

"But will not she travel with Captain and Mrs. Blackwell in the *Blonde* anyway, if they are to take up residence in Hawaii?"

"My father intends to accept the appointment, with the condition government share in the expense of a ship for his use in the Islands. He will make the voyage to Hawaii in that vessel. I know it is irregular, sir, but I have particular reason for wishing Miss Emma to travel aboard the *Blonde*, under my protection."

Captain Verson could not at first conceive what those reasons might be, until he chanced to look at Mr. Montelongo. The eager attentive way he leaned forward caused Captain Verson to think of all the younger man meant to him. The situation revealed itself at a stroke.

Captain Verson rose and strode over to the window, where there was a view of his neighbor's kitchen garden and orchard. He did not need to ask Aloka to return until he should decide. He was a post-captain used to making critical decisions on the instant, without recourse to anyone else's opinion. Captain Blackwell and his lady had always treated him and his with great consideration and esteem, never any judgement in the case, and Captain Verson was perfectly willing to return their kindness. He considered Aloka Blackwell, nervously awaiting his reply, so like the man who had mentored him in the Service. Then too there was self-interest. If Lieutenant Blackwell left the ship, Captain Verson could move up his own son, also commissioned on the *Blonde's* cruise. Young Jack Verson had lost much active service time as a prisoner of the French, having just been exchanged.

"I will take you aboard as second lieutenant, volunteer, provided their lordships at the Admiralty do not object, Mr. Blackwell. As to Miss Blackwell, if she is a member of King Kamehameha's suite, I have nothing to say to it. I will be berthing in the gunroom for the voyage to the Islands, giving the captain's quarters entirely over to the King's people. We shall endeavor to accommodate Miss Emma as genteelly as is possible in a frigate, and if you have no objection, the crew shall be given to understand she is your cousin."

Aloka had leaped up and was wringing his hand. "None at all, sir. Thank you, sir."

"I will send word as soon as I have confirmation from the Admiralty. You will wish to speak to Captain Blackwell without loss of a moment."

Aloka sobered. "Yes, sir. I will speak to him."

Out of mercy Captain Verson turned the conversation to more general topics, and Mr. Montelongo put into Aloka's hand a letter for Mercedes.

After Aloka had taken his leave, Captain Verson sat down again in the shabby parlour. "I should not like to be present when that news is communicated. The poor fellow is likely to be blown up worse than he was in the Aix Roads."

"Black savages ain't in it," Mr. Montelongo said.

The house on Curzon Street was all ahoo. The Blackwells were packing in preparation to remove to Merton, and then to Portsmouth to take ship for the Sandwich Islands. Captain Blackwell disliked the domestic hurry and bustle, and was concerned the move be beneficial to Mercedes' health rather than cause a depression and strain upon her spirits.

Captain Blackwell was alone in the small parlour that adjoined the upstairs bedchambers, having encouraged Mercedes to retire early, when Aloka walked in.

"Can I have a word, sir?"

Aloka waited for his nod before taking a seat.

"I constantly have a feeling of having forgot something," Captain Blackwell said. "It must be old age. I worry like an old woman whether we are to be too much cheek by jowl, in *Albion*."

Albion was the ship Captain Blackwell had purchased with the subsidy of the British government, a neat schooner of the type called a Baltimore clipper. The captain's private quarters might not be quite large enough for four people, especially given the temperaments of Edward and Emma.

"I wished to discuss something with you that bears upon that, Father. I've arranged for Emma to travel in the *Blonde*."

Captain Blackwell gave Aloka a quizzical look.

"As part of the King's suite, and under my protection."

He frowned. "I don't know what you can mean by either of those things, son. She is the daughter of a British subject, how can she be part of Kamehameha's suite. What's this about then, and under your protection?"

"I intend to marry her, Father, when we reach the Sandwich Islands. Emma has accepted me."

Captain Blackwell's eyes narrowed, a pain starting up in his chest. He could hardly credit what he'd heard.

"You intend, you've arranged. You presume an enormous lot. We don't do what you are proposing in England. How could you think I should sanction such a thing? And how do you think that woman who loved you as a mother shall feel about this?"

The pitch of Captain Blackwell's voice had risen with his indignation.

"Nothing to say? I'll tell you then. She shall feel betrayed, having raised and loved a half savage creature all these years only to have him steal away her dearest child. Mercedes dotes upon that girl. She is to marry an English lord."

"No, sir, that she is not. And I have stolen nothing. We are in love, sir, the long and the short of it. Many girls Emma's age are already married."

They were both on their feet now, toe to toe, speaking in loud quarterdeck voices.

"Not to their brothers!"

"I know a place where such a thing is countenanced, even approved. Emma is nearly of age, and may soon do as she pleases."

"You had better leave now."

Aloka turned abruptly and marched over to the parlour door, Captain Blackwell close behind him. Out in the passage they met Mercedes and Emma. Mercedes was in her dressing gown, both were wide-eyed and shocked. Aloka shook his head, casting a sad and rueful glance at Emma, and hastened down the stairs and out the front door.

"Papa! How could you—"

"Go to bed."

He turned on Mercedes.

"Will you order me to bed, too?"

In reply he gave a disgusted snort and slammed into his own bedchamber.

Mercedes went over and put her arms around Emma.

"Oh, Mama! What if he never comes back?"

"Nonsense, you know how fond your father is of him. Which probably hurts him the more, he feels betrayed."

"Betrayed? This is not about him! We did not fall in love expressly to vex him."

"Hush, Emma. Let me speak to him. You shall sail in *Blonde* with Aloka, bear that in mind will you? You are almost eighteen."

Mercedes was able to leave Emma more composed with that thought. She recommended Emma go down and see if Edward had come back from the Royal Society meeting. Mercedes then crept into her bedroom and through the interconnecting dressing room. She stood in Blackwell's doorway.

He lay in the dark on top of his bed, with his breeches and shirt still on, one arm behind his head, gazing abstractedly before him.

"May I come in?"

He rose rather wearily and came over to her. "Of course, sweetheart. Come. Forgive me for speaking chuff just now."

Mercedes went and lay with him on the bed.

"Tell me what happened with Aloka?"

After a short pause, he said, "I hardly know how to say it, I am so astonished, and unhappy." He related his conversation with Aloka. "I beg you will not be too much wounded by this, nor let it overset you—"

"I know, James. I'm sorry. I know they are in love, your son and my daughter."

"How in the hell!" He turned to her, rising up off his pillows. But the sight of her arrested him, and he fell back again. "I suppose I must accustom myself to be the last in this family to know anything."

"Forgive me, it is not the sort of thing that is easy to speak of. I had hoped Emma's affection might change when she had her season and made the acquaintance of any number of gentlemen. It is partly down to me that did not happen, and it seems the attachment grows stronger. Once they learned the Royal couple were brother and sister, there was no stopping them."

"I should like to stop them, indeed, and I deeply regret foisting my bastard on you all those years ago. Only to bring you this scandal and disgrace."

She moved immediately closer to him and laid her hand on his arm.

"Don't say that, Jim, there's no disgrace, you cannot mean it. And as to scandal, we are leaving the country. They fell in love. It isn't suitable or convenient, but—"

"Do not tell me you condone this relationship?"

"I don't think it matters what I condone. You may remember, when we fell in love it wasn't convenient for either of us. And you did not at first wish to marry me."

"Because I was a goddamn fool, but you bore with me. Even though you could have had my brother, handsomer, richer, and certainly smarter than a mere sailorman."

"Darling." She was lying on his chest now, hugging him with one arm. "The point is we really can't help who we fall in love with. Aloka didn't do this to hurt, or vex, or betray you, any more than he has led Emma astray. You know her, I don't believe she can be led. He has arranged everything like a man, and declared his intentions to you."

Blackwell ran his hand up from her waist, Mercedes was glad she still had on the little top under her dressing gown. If she could have made love to him, she would have given him the kind of comfort and release for his emotions he most needed now. But he had not seen her naked since the surgery, and Mercedes could not bring herself to initiate intimacy.

"You believe the attachment to be more than a thing of the moment?" he said.

"Oh, much more."

"And to think I was afraid she'd fallen in love with a Frenchman." Blackwell sighed. "Aloka could have left me to drown in the Boyart Channel. It might have suited his convenience to have the roaring old man out of the way."

"Except he didn't because he loves you, and because he's a decent and good hearted man."

Captain Blackwell lay still for a long time, Mercedes having fallen asleep on his breast. A great part of his anger and indignation had sprung from how he thought Mercedes would feel, and his wish that nothing interfere with her delicate health and recovery. But her kindness and the extent of her love knew no limit, felt no pride. She was willing to endure a long voyage to live in one of the remotest parts of the world, because it would be best for the rest of them. He kissed the top of her head.

His feelings about retirement from the Navy and the cause of it, his children, were complicated. Aloka had always been his favorite, there was no point not calling a spade a spade. Edward was peculiar, and not particularly attached to any one of them. And Emma, well, Emma was a female. A female who never seemed to have liked, approved, or had any use for him.

Captain Blackwell remembered coming home on leave when they were small. The boys would play peek-a-boo with baby Emma. Dandle her on their knees where she could not see her father, then turn her suddenly to face him. She would invariably cry out, tears streaming down cherub cheeks, with a look of pain and grief in her eyes. They would roar with laughter, until Mercedes or Aloka himself put a stop to the capers.

He'd always had a particular bond with his native son, from the time they'd made a canoe voyage together from the island of Kauai where Aloka was born. He'd survived that journey at a tender age, a strong, agile, good-natured, obedient little boy. Aloka had grown into the sort of man, Captain Blackwell realized with a little jolt, he'd described to Mercedes as one he should like to see Emma married to. The thought gave him considerable pause, and a creeping feeling of shame. Did he actually feel gratitude toward Aloka, who was proposing to relieve him of a troublesome girl and allow him at last to have Mercedes to himself?

Maybe he was just as low a creature as Admiral Gambier. Captain Blackwell's words to his son rang in his mind: a half-savage creature. Aloka had come away as a little boy and been raised in England, he did not remember having lived in those islands. Captain Blackwell did, and recalling his time there, he knew he was the one deserving the name of half-savage. His breast was in a turmoil and he eased out from under Mercedes, unfortunately waking her.

"Do not stir, sweetheart. I can't sleep. I'm going to find Aloka. I threw him out of the house earlier, and now I am heartily sorry for it."

Mercedes took off her gown and underclothing, while he turned away to oblige her, and slipped beneath the bedclothes. "I love you so."

He leaned over and cupped her face in his hands, and kissed her. She looked so fragile, her dark eyes large in a pale face. He felt a tenderness for her that bordered on adoration. Whatever this woman wanted or needed for her peace and comfort, he would give her, the rest of the world be damned. She'd followed him to the far side of the world once, and the miracle was she was willing to do it again.

Captain Blackwell dressed and went downstairs. A light was on in the library and the door stood open. He stuck his head in the room.

"You are up late."

"I was reading the mathematical paper presented by Admiral Audrey this evening," Edward said. "A particular friend of Doctor Russ. He made me known to the Admiral."

"I am glad to hear it. Did you speak to Emma?"

"Oh...yes."

"I was wondering if you might know where young fellows retreat to when they are thrown out of the house?"

"Where would a young spark go to get away from an irrational, bawling parent? Shall I go with you?"

"I wish you would."

Aloka did not gamble. His pay was too hard earned and there was no money to spare in his father's household. But in his distracted state he'd wandered off to the Coco Palms, a gaming hell frequented by the Bucks and Beau of London. He did not drink either, outside of wine and small beer taken with meals, and the grog that was practically part of his duty when aboard ship. Yet early in the morning hours, with the place in full cry round him, Aloka was most decidedly drunk.

His great vice heretofore had been women. Aloka loved their soft bodies underneath his, pressed on top of him, their sweet cries, and most of all the feeling of being fully alive when he was with them. Since he and Emma had declared their attachment Aloka had refrained from womanizing. All he could think of was her lovely face and perfect body. He'd seen what venereal disease looked like up close, and he had a perfect horror and dread of bringing illness to that dear, lovely creature.

He placed his chit on a number and then watched his money swept away off it. Turning to call for another bottle, Aloka found Edward at his elbow.

"Ed, old fellow! What do you here?"

"You shall lose your money," Edward said. "The odds of winning in this game are three thousand four hundred and thirteen point six-seven, six-seven to infinity to one."

"Stubble it, can't you?" said a beau in a high starched collar.

Aloka ignored the rude remark. "If you aren't here for the play, why've you come, brother?"

"Father's in the next room. Wants a word with you."

"Place your bets, gentlemen," the house declared.

"In or out, cully?" The starched beau next to him was become bold.

"Out," Aloka said, removing his chits to his pocket.

He was turning to follow Edward when the beau said, quite loudly to the table in general, "Good! We need no Blackamoors here, and may you take that addled counting idiot with you!"

Aloka tapped the man on the shoulder and when he turned, planted him such a facer the beau fell back upon the faro table. There was a resounding crash, and cards, chits, and sterling flew in all directions.

The other gamblers at the table, companions of the starched beau, took exception to Aloka's behavior and a general brawl broke out. Edward retreated to stand against the wall, turning his face away to mark his indifference. The set-to was doomed to be short-lived, none of the Londoners being fighting men. Aloka, in his present emotional and inebriated state, was in a fair way to thrashing them single-handed, when the thugs employed by the establishment and Captain Blackwell bore down upon them.

Captain Blackwell showed a certain diplomatic flair, his brother Francis might have been proud, in dealing with the people of the gaming house. He made them aware that their patrons had attacked a King's officer, and hinted at his own importance and influence in such a way that the Coco Palms desisted in their cries for reparation. They jumped instead on the beau and his companions, whom their thugs had been sitting on just in case.

Relying on his air of command and authority to carry the day, Captain Blackwell had managed to extricate them without giving their names. He hurried them outside and into a hackney cab.

Aloka slumped in his corner of the coach, reeking of spirits, his clothes disarranged. On the morrow he would look like bruised fruit. Quite the picture of a gentleman and eligible suitor he must present to Edward and Captain Blackwell.

"Thank you, Father," he did manage to say.

Captain Blackwell leaned forward and gripped Aloka's knee. "There would be no living with the ladies, son, was you to stay away. I, for one, value my lady's peace and comfort. I suggest you begin to do the same."

His father sat back and exchanged a bow, initiated by Edward.

Both Aloka and Captain Blackwell maintained a severe reserve. They knew how to behave in the face of men with whom they'd quarreled, but still must live by. Yet when Aloka met with Captain Blackwell's cool and stern demeanor, he wondered if he'd imagined the kind words and touch in the coach returning from the Coco Palms. He valued his father's confidence and trust, and apart from the wine and the bruises, Aloka was low in his spirits. Under other circumstances he might have been all gaiety, with his future opening before him.

Another cause for discontent was, they'd had to explain the circumstances of his late debauch to the ladies. Captain Blackwell refused to be thought to have thrashed his own son; "For that's what they will believe, when they see your phiz." Next day Aloka was to leave and join the *Blonde*. Captain Blackwell would make one of the party, along with the natives going to Woolwich. Perhaps it was none too soon for him to take his departure.

The looming voyage had already sent Mercedes and Emma into a sort of shopping frenzy. Sea chests had been purchased, and filled with clothing for different climes, woolens, linen, scents, soaps, and other necessaries. The fact that Emma should as well have a trousseau, and the emotion surrounding that subject, had pushed Mercedes toward a relapse. At least today she kept her bed, a thing Aloka had never known her do except immediately after the surgery.

He was surprised when Mr. Martinez came to him. "Will you join them in Miss Mercedes' bedchamber, sir? They are all up there."

"She is not..."

"Oh, no. It is your father insisting she must rest."

Mr. Martinez had meant it when he said they were all there. His father and Mercedes, Emma and Edward. Even McMurtry hovering just inside the open doorway, where Mr. Martinez joined him. Captain Blackwell was on one side of the bed, Emma and Edward on the other, so Aloka took up a station at the foot. Mercedes gave Aloka a kind smile, and Captain Blackwell cleared his throat.

"Boki and the King's people have sent to invite Emma to travel with them to Portsmouth, that she may be immediately one of their number."

Captain Blackwell had not spoken directly to him, but the others in the room must already know. Aloka was silent, his hands clasped behind his back.

"I want to refuse their kind invitation," Emma said. "I wish to travel with Mama as far as Portsmouth, since we are to be separated for the rest of the voyage. Do you think I will give offense?"

She glanced first quickly and furtively at Aloka, and then rather shamefacedly at Captain Blackwell. This time it was Captain Blackwell who refused to speak.

"I cannot imagine there should be the least objection or offense taken," Aloka said. "They make the offer out of the generosity of their natures, and shall perfectly understand your reason for declining."

How happy and relieved Emma looked then.

"That's settled then, I shall make your excuses to Boki," Captain Blackwell said. "Edward, since we are sorting out berths, you said you had something to bring up."

"Why, yes, sir. Only that I will not be joining you in the Islands."

There was such an outcry and uproar that Aloka was sure this was the first anyone had heard of Edward's intentions. Edward slipped around Emma by the bedside, and took Mercedes' hand.

"Oh, Edward!"

"Forgive me, Mama. I'll accompany you back to Merton, but when you leave for Portsmouth, I am returning to London."

"But Edward, you could botanize. Even transport a telescope in pieces and set up your own observatory."

"That is a charming picture, and I may do one day." He looked around at them all, for once making eye contact with his odd blue gaze. "But there is no Royal Society there, no University. I shall start Cambridge in the new term—"

"Congratulations, Ed," Aloka cried. "Well done."

His father seconded the sentiment, as did everyone in the room.

Edward acknowledged their compliments with a bow. "What don't strike me so agreeable, is being mewed up for months with the four of you. I much doubt even those islands shall be big enough to contain you, much less two tiny ships."

Another hullabaloo broke out, but Edward overrode them.

"Mama, you are to consider. Someone must maintain a home here, in case any of you need to come back."

It was hard to argue with Edward's logic. But Mercedes would worry over how he was to get along alone, Captain Blackwell harangue him for upsetting his Mama, and Emma and Aloka lament they must do without their best friend since childhood. Finally it was settled that Mr. Martinez would remain with Edward; he felt himself too old for the adventure; and Mercedes was infinitely relieved. Edward would have Mr. Martinez's practical head and capabilities to rely on. McMurtry, on the other hand, must go. "Who else can look after the Captain and our Missus?"

Doctor Russ walked in. "Jesus, Joseph, and Mary! Everyone here, and not a soul below to answer my call! Pounding at the door this quarter hour and more, and you yourself, my dear, lying abed!"

CHAPTER SEVEN

The same family group was gathered, saying their goodbyes before the portico of Merton, with the carriage waiting to take Mercedes, Captain Blackwell, and Emma, on to Portsmouth. Mercedes and Mr. Martinez could not pretend there was much chance they should see one another again this lifetime. Many tears were shed and promises made in Spanish. It was difficult taking leave of Doctor Russ, too, who had saved Mercedes' life and worked ever since to make all easy for her. He had secured a fine surgeon to attend them aboard *Albion*, a Swede by the name of Anders Sparrman, also sending aboard a fully stocked medicine chest and a prodigious store of laudanum. Mercedes knew he'd done this in case her cancer came back, and she blessed him for it. By far the hardest farewell was with Edward.

Mercedes and Emma took turns embracing him and crying on his breast, and Edward bore it all with a good grace. They had been close companions, the three of them, sharing many a fireside discussion of the universe and their place in it.

"Take care of Tio and the Doctor, Edward," Mercedes whispered. "They grow old. Find someone to love, my darling, woman or man."

"I love you, Mama," Edward said, careless of his tears. "You have always understood."

Parting from him was very hard. Mercedes remembered the baby, the dear little boy. Edward was not only the man before her; now grown tall and exceedingly handsome, with his brilliant and odd ways; he would continue to change and she would not be there to see it. Captain Blackwell at last steered them toward the coach. They climbed up and were away, with not a dry eye among them, saving the driver. No one, not McMurtry up on the box, nor Captain Blackwell riding inside the carriage, was ashamed of their tears.

On the day Mercedes, Emma, and Captain Blackwell were to go aboard ship, in another carriage riding toward Portsmouth Hard, Emma asked Captain Blackwell, “Do you have any advice for me, Papa?”

Captain Blackwell looked surprised, and then his face took on a serious considering expression.

“Don’t interfere with Aloka’s duty, unless you want to disgrace him and me both.”

Mercedes half gasped, and put her hand to her mouth. Captain Blackwell glanced at her.

“Come what may, Emma, you shall always have my love and protection, and a home where ever your mother and I may be.”

There were smiles then and tender words, and Captain Blackwell was all complaisance handing them out of the carriage.

“Boat ahoy! What boat is that?” A marine officer hailed, as they approached the *Blonde* in their crowded boat.

“*Albion!*” roared Narhilla, Captain Blackwell’s follower and longtime coxswain.

The shrill call of the bosun’s pipe rang out.

“Hell and death,” Captain Blackwell muttered, immediately rising to his feet and springing for the ladder.

On the quarterdeck they met him with salutes, the official clash and stamp of the Marines, and broad grins from the officers. Sensible of the honor they did him, in his civilian suit of clothes, Captain Blackwell raised his hat to them. He could not help turning anxiously to look over the side as Mercedes came up.

There had been a time when she’d climbed a ship’s side with relative ease and agility, but now she rose shakily to her feet.

“Guide me, if you please, Narhilla. Otherwise the Captain shall make me use the bosun’s chair, and be hoisted aboard like cattle.”

Narhilla snorted. This was his last voyage with them. He would return in the *Blonde*, having a large wife and six children in England, for whose maintenance Captain Blackwell had advanced three years' pay.

"No, Missus, we cannot have that."

He held her in a steady grip, and practically lifted her onto the first rung as the boat heaved up on the swell. Other hands were extended to bring her in, and almost without effort on her part, she was standing beside Captain Blackwell. No one dared give Emma quite so much assistance, but she received just as much attention, and more interested stares, when she came aboard *Blonde*.

Captain Verson stepped forward, after dismissing the assemblage on the quarterdeck, extending his hand to Captain Blackwell.

"Captain Blackwell sir, Ma'am, Miss Blackwell, welcome aboard *Blonde*. Boki and all the King's people are just come this morning, and are settling in. May I show you your quarters, Miss Blackwell?"

Emma took the arm Captain Verson kindly offered. As the only single female in the Hawaiian king's party, Emma had been given the coach to herself. She was still obliged to share the quarter-gallery, the captain's private toilet, with four other women and six men.

Captain Blackwell stepped in to the space normally used as the captain's dining parlour, glanced round at the narrow fixed berth, Emma's sea chest already brought in, and tried the latches of the door leading into the captain's quarters and the one giving onto the passage near the quarterdeck companion ladder.

"I will go pay my respects to Boki and the others. Ma'am, meet me on the quarterdeck when you are ready." Captain Blackwell bowed to Mercedes and Emma. He gave Emma a smacking kiss upon the cheek by way of private farewell, and turned to Captain Verson.

"Jack," he said in a low voice, as they left the coach, "I should thank you to put locks upon those doors."

Mercedes and Emma had their own private and rather painful goodbye, Emma clinging to her.

"Don't leave me, Mama," she murmured.

Mercedes' heart ached, in the way a mother's does when she knows she can no longer protect her child. The coach was meager quarters compared to what Emma was used, and for the first time she must make her own way among people she did not know.

"Find occupation. You have many books, and you can sew, and learn from Li'liah and the other ladies the ways of the Hawaiians. Practice their language. I used to volunteer in the sick berth, but I don't know if Mr. McNeath shall allow that here."

"I don't know I have the stomach for that, Mama. Seriously."

"Just keep busy, and let it be of your own devising. Need I speak of Aloka's duty?"

"I wish you would not. His sacred duty!"

"Allowances must be made for the Service, my love. It has fed and sheltered us all these many years. Come, we must greet Li'liah."

"Oh, not yet. Just a few more minutes."

They could only linger together a short while longer. Mercedes was aware Captain Blackwell waited for her. They knocked and walked into the cabin where Li'liah, two other ladies and two men, Boki and Kuanoa, met them. The Hawaiians were eager to show Emma all the conveniences of the quarters, and while this was happening Mercedes said, "Excuse me just a moment. I shall return directly."

Mercedes hurried into the passage outside the captain's cabin, and along the gun deck. She did not mean to go far, in her quest for a midshipman.

A young man in uniform rattled down the after hatchway companion ladder.

"Oh, Jack! Mr. Verson, how glad I am to see you."

"Miss Mercedes!" Jack exclaimed, as he'd done when he was a boy of five.

Mercedes had been his school mistress, and taught him his letters. He was now a lanky young man, whose face had a hollow appearance from the depredations of his time as a prisoner.

Mercedes gave him joy of his release, and Jack said, "It is an honor to have both Mr. and Miss Blackwell with us this cruise, Ma'am."

"You are very kind. Do you know if it is Mr. Blackwell's watch at the moment?" Mercedes looked abashed asking the question, she knew a thing or two about Naval etiquette.

"No, Ma'am, it is not. May I be of service to you?"

"I would be obliged if you would ask Mr. Blackwell to join me in the captain's cabin, if he is at leisure." Mercedes looked at Jack Verson, and then she suddenly embraced him. "Bless you, dear Jack."

The two captains were anxious to set sail on the evening's tide, the wind being fair to carry them out of Portsmouth. They had discussed the wind and tide, the state of the ships and their crews, and neither being particularly talkative, Captains Blackwell and Verson had long since exhausted their store of conversation. Yet they stood together on the weather side of the quarterdeck, the domain of senior officers only, in a companionable silence.

Captain Blackwell lost his cheerful look when Mercedes and Emma at last appeared on deck, followed closely by Aloka, who gave Emma his arm as soon as they'd gained the deck. A stern expression came over his features, and remained in place during the leave taking. All of the ship's officers appeared on deck, and they exchanged bows and handshakes, and, in the case of Mercedes and Mr. Montelongo, kisses upon both cheeks. The two women clung to one another. Whatever Mercedes said to Aloka in parting brought tears into his eyes.

The first into his boat saving his coxswain, Captain Blackwell had the satisfaction of guiding Mercedes himself, and settling her safely beside him in the stern. He glanced over at her during the pull to *Albion*. The sea was choppy and the breeze had turned fresh.

"Come, sweetheart," he said, putting his arm round her waist and pulling her against his side, "no tears, now. You shall see her again directly."

He sincerely hoped not too soon, however. If the wind dropped, who knew but that they might be stuck in Portsmouth harbor some days. An idea repugnant to his feelings; Captain Blackwell longed to be under way and at sea. He looked forward to the comfort of naval routine and an ordered way of life, enlivened by the much cherished woman beside him. He wanted an end, or at least a respite, from the complications of shore life.

Emma had imagined a certain closeness to Aloka, walks together upon the deck under a blue and sun filled sky, surrounded by a placid ocean, intimacy and private moments of conversation. Instead there were continual squalls of rain, and a choppy and cross-grained sea that kept the officers constantly at their duty, and the passengers confined to their quarters. Except for a brief stop in Madeira, when the Hawaiians went ashore to recruit themselves, conditions were singularly disagreeable.

She was seasick, along with some of the Hawaiian contingent, and many of the landsmen in *Blonde's* crew. During these episodes the last thing Emma wanted was to be seen by Aloka. Even in the worst weather he came to the cabin daily to enquire after her. What Emma longed for when she was low and vulgar with nausea was her mother's cool hand on her brow, her loving and practical presence. She sincerely hoped Mercedes was being looked after, and not too cruelly flung about. Kuanoa, the King's treasurer, and Kapihe, his admiral, were seafaring men, both had made voyages to China. They went about unaffected by the sea's motion. Li'liah and the native ladies, and the *Blonde's* surgeon Mr. McNeath, late of *Imperieuse*, attended to Emma.

The passage from England to Brazil seemed to Emma an interminable misery, but to Captain Blackwell and Aloka, and the rest of the professional seamen it was nothing more than a bit of squally weather and lively seas. And then they were gliding into the harbor of Rio de Janeiro in splendid weather.

Emma was recovered and up on deck. Aloka approached her, as they passed through the harbor's narrow entrance, and she felt her heart throbbing like the vibrant prospect before her.

"I am sorry you have been so unwell, Emma," he said, with a considering gaze. "You are very much paler, but no less beautiful."

Such words could not be unwelcome at any time, much less when Emma thought she was not in her best looks.

"I shall hope to be a better sailor directly. What a glorious place you've brought me to."

The *Blonde* slipped past the great rocks on either side of the narrow harbor mouth and opened the view of the bay and anchorage, with steep and forested mountains rising up round it.

"I've brought you to? That would be me, Captain Verson, his officers, and two-hundred ninety men." Aloka grinned and took her hand.

They gazed at the neighborhood of Botofogo away to larboard, and on the opposite shore, amid groves of citrus trees was the village of Pray a Grande. Aloka told her of these places, for he'd been here before, while holding her hand in a firm and caressing grip.

"Captain Verson shall come to anchor just opposite the city. That is the church of Nossa Senhora de Gloria standing on its own upon the hill. Rio de Janeiro has a fine aqueduct and a number of churches and convents. I shall take you on shore, to see the sights, with your Mama if she pleases. There is *Albion*, already snug in her berth."

The swift sailing schooner had preceded them. Captain Blackwell had her swinging to her cables. She was naturally easier to bring to anchor than a 46-gun ship of war. The first lieutenant called all hands to moor ship, and Aloka moved away with a final warm squeeze of Emma's hand.

Aloka did squire Emma and Mercedes to those sacred places. The last shore party they, and others from *Albion* and *Blonde* were attending was a great entertainment given by King João of Brazil's purveyor, Don Eduardo de Paiva. This suave, cunning, and enterprising gentleman courted the company of Kuanoa during the *Blonde's* stay in Rio, with an eye to current and future profit. The highlight of the evening was to be a phantasmagoria Don Eduardo was presenting to the Hawaiians.

Don Eduardo and Kuanoa stood together to the side of the long gallery where the phantasmagoria was to be presented, watching a contingent of local officials and their wives file in from the supper parlour. They were followed by the Hawaiians and the British visitors. Captain Blackwell was there, with Mercedes on his arm,

Mr. Montelongo representing *Blonde*, and Aloka and Emma. They took their seats in rows of chairs.

"A fine and elegant creature, Miss Blackwell, no?" Don Eduardo said. "She would be worth a ship's load of sandalwood in China, perhaps two."

"I should like to marry with her," Kuanoa said.

"Is she not promised to the young sprig sitting beside her, all eagerness and attention?" Don Eduardo gave his companion a penetrating sideways glance.

"Maybe."

Kuanoa shrugged, a gesture among the Hawaiians expressive of many things.

"My friend," Don Eduardo said, "perhaps we can be of use to one another."

Don Eduardo's principle pursuit in life was being of use, the preferred partner in trade and nefarious doings, while above all serving his own interests.

The Hawaiians having all sat down, on chairs or on mats as best suited, Don Eduardo and Kuanoa found two chairs. At a signal from Don Eduardo the spectacle began. The Tower of London, London Bridge, and the Thames were first pictured. The variety of craft and commerce upon the river loomed up, the great buildings with steps leading directly down to the Thames, and next the crowded London streets. Excited exclamations rose from the Hawaiians as they recalled seeing these sights for themselves. Next came the Tuilleries in France, and the canals of Amsterdam. They were viewing the Danube when Boki suddenly jumped up and faced the assemblage. The projected image wavered over Boki's body, and he raised his arms over his head.

"Stop, I beg you."

"What is it, Mr. Boki?" Don Eduardo was on his feet, waving his hand so that the candle in the projection lantern was blown out. A little groan went up from the gathered company as the image disappeared from the wall.

"I beg you will save some of the pictures for my countrymen in O'ahu. The *Ali'i* of all the kingdom will wish to see them, and we must not use them all."

Don Eduardo pursed his lips; altruism, self-sacrifice, these were sentiments almost unknown to him. He looked attentively at the expectant faces of the Hawaiians, his esteemed guests, and calculated their worth.

"Mr. Boki, your laudable request shall be honored." Don Eduardo bowed to Boki, and then turned to the company in general. "Ladies and gentlemen, thank you for your kind attendance this evening."

There were murmurs of disappointment, even disapproval from the locals in the room. Many felt Don Eduardo ought to have made the nature of the phantasmagoria known to the island savages so the entertainment could continue. Don Eduardo was indifferent to the opinion of these guests. Before the Hawaiians, and Captain Blackwell and his party, Don Eduardo asked to speak to Kuanoa, the King's man of business, about the remaining projections.

The two men retired into an adjoining room, and the majority of the company left to await their carriages. Captain Blackwell and Mercedes, along with most of the Hawaiians, said their goodbyes and departed. A short while later Aloka and Emma, and Mr. Montelongo, chatting companionably, were moving toward the door. Emerging from the room where he'd met with Don Eduardo, Kuanoa rushed after them.

"Your father?"

"He took his leave. He has returned to his ship."

"He means to keep the entire amount," Kuanoa said, his voice ringing with distress. "The whole of the three thousand dollars I gave for our provisions. Don Eduardo says between what has already gone aboard *Blonde*, our expenses ashore, and these pictures Boki will have, there is nothing due in return."

"I shall send for my father," Aloka said.

"No." Kuanoa reached out and grasped Aloka by the forearm. "There is no time for that. You must help me. Don Eduardo will listen to you, you are an officer in King George's service."

Aloka hesitated, glancing at Emma and Mr. Montelongo. They had both assumed neutral, non-committal expressions. He returned the pressure of Kuanoa's clasp.

"Emma, you will not mind if Mr. Montelongo sees you back to the ship? I shall follow directly. I must support Kuanoa and the King's people against this sort of ill-usage."

Aloka could not quite comprehend why Don Eduardo de Paiva was in such a furious temper. He had very meekly asked for an accounting of the items that had been purchased by Kuanoa on behalf of the King's suite.

"You will have a list, will you? Why then, greens, fruit of a dozen sorts, onions, sweetmeats. Fresh meat, poultry and pork are very dear. And then there is the water and wine."

"The King's people do not take wine, sir. The wine and water would have been for the ship's account."

Don Eduardo's face went livid. "How dare you suggest any irregularity of that sort! And then there is the matter of the phantasmagoria. The magic lantern and the pictures upon glass!"

"I did not mean to suggest any irregularity, as you call it, sir." Aloka took a step toward Don Eduardo. "But three thousand dollars is a grand sum for the King's people to have spent in a single port."

Now it was Don Eduardo who leaned in close to Aloka. "I am not obliged to give an accounting to a junior officer. To an insolent puppy who need not concern himself in what is not his business, business he could not comprehend if it was."

Aloka's head jerked as though he'd received a blow. His expression grew cold and he stood upright, preparing to make his bow. "I shall make Captain Blackwell acquainted with your proceedings, sir. Good—"

At the same time Aloka bent forward at the waist, he was shoved violently from behind. He fell into Don Eduardo, head butting the older man to the floor. Don Eduardo instantly began to abuse him in much stronger terms than puppy. 'Black bastard' was a particular favorite, until he switched from English to Portuguese. Aloka heard him shout "*Guarda!*"

His hand sought the sword at his side, as he disentangled himself from Don Eduardo on the floor. A trio of soldiers rushed into the room. One dealt Aloka a tremendous blow to the back of the head as he tried to rise.

Men were moving in the shadows between the commercial buildings. Emma and Mr. Montelongo were nearing the quay, in an area of warehouses and storerooms quite deserted at this hour.

"Mr. Montelongo, there are men up there before us."

"There are several more behind. Your Mama taught you to use the sword? You must take my dirk. I wish I had another blade to give you."

Mr. Montelongo handed Emma his steel dirk. It was not finely edged, meant as it was for disciplinary purposes.

"Listen now, Miss Emma. I shall set up a great cry for our men, and with the blessing they shall hear, the night being so still. We will meet the attack like the Romans, back to back. And whatever happens, Miss Emma, do not let them separate us."

Emma barely had time to gather her skirts, and roll material up under the waistband of her gown to give her feet freer play. She adjusted her weapon in a good grip, and the attackers rushed them: three from behind, and two in front.

"Blondes!" Mr. Montelongo shouted. "Blondes, to me!"

Mr. Montelongo yanked Emma down, and a stout wooden cudgel whistled over their heads. Straightening and lunging, Mr. Montelongo paid the man with a sword thrust through his guts. A hand reached out and scrabbled at Emma's upper arm. She brought the hilt of the dirk down hard into that grasping arm. There was a cry, she stabbed out toward it. The weapon met resistance, she yanked it back and struck at another man fronting her. Emma shouted along with Mr. Montelongo, shrieking the name of their ship into the still night.

They fought close to one another, trying to keep in step. Emma was the taller and larger of the two, but once or twice she reached out and grasped Mr. Montelongo's jacket or his arm. The ruffians had fallen back after the initial attack. They had no edged weapons, but menaced with wooden cudgels and clubs. Three unwounded men faced them, schooled to respect for Mr. Montelongo's sword. These men bunched together and circled them, edging round toward Emma. Mr. Montelongo turned with them, as though in a dance, placing himself and his steel between Emma and the attackers.

"Blondes! Blondes!"

They heard the sound of running feet pounding toward them.

"Thank God! The lobsters," Emma cried.

Musket shots, and their attackers turned from them and ran like hares down the street. Four of the youngest, fleetest seamen sped past Emma and Mr. Montelongo in pursuit.

"Cease fire, goddamn it!" Mr. Montelongo called. The Marines, enthused, continued discharging their weapons. "You shall hit one of ours."

Mr. Montelongo called back the pursuing seamen. They dragged between them the two wounded ruffians.

"What to do with these sorry fuckers, sir?"

"Mind your language, Bates, there's a lady present."

Mr. Montelongo ordered the midshipman, Mr. Whittemore, the son of the man who'd once been Captain Blackwell's premier, to proceed to the boat with Miss Blackwell, four of the Marines, and all but two of the seamen. Emma departed with a reluctant glance at Mr. Montelongo but, schooled in the ways of the Navy, she knew an order when she heard it.

The remaining Marines Mr. Montelongo directed to face the street and watch for any approach, while he and the two sturdy seamen hauled the wounded men against the side of a store house. Only one man was capable of responding to Mr. Montelongo's questions. He was wounded in hand, shoulder, and thigh, and his refrain was "*No Ingles, no Ingles.*"

"Should we carry him to the ship," Bates asked, "give him a couple good knocks, to loosen his tongue like, sir?"

"We're going to leave these men here. Captain Verson does not want scum near his ship. Their mates may come back for them, if they will." Mr. Montelongo knelt down so he was face to face with the ruffian. Forcefully and directly into the man's face, Mr. Montelongo said in Spanish, "Tell whoever sent you the Royal Navy doesn't give up our own at the first salvo. If we find out who is behind this, they will be made to smell hell."

The last remark gave Mr. Montelongo great satisfaction. He'd once heard Captain Blackwell use it before an action. Many years had passed since then, when Mr. Montelongo was the midshipman interloper from Spain Captain Blackwell had taken into his ship out of pity. He had admired the English mariners greatly then, and his feelings had not changed a great deal since. His party returned quickly to the quay and the *Blonde's* boat.

Mr. Whittemore yielded his seat next to Emma in the stern and moved forward to the bow. He greeted Kuanoa, who had slipped into the boat and was taking a place near him.

"Should you like to be rowed to *Albion*, Miss Emma?" Mr. Montelongo asked gently, as they neared the two ships. "To pass the night with your parents?"

Emma had been trembling, sitting beside him.

"No, thank you, sir. Much as I should love to fly to Mama, Aloka will expect to find me aboard the *Blonde*. You will send a boat back to await him?"

"That must be for Captain Verson to command, ma'am. I cannot help but think Mr. Blackwell should have been with us. You were very brave, you have your mother's quickness and spirit."

"You are kind, sir, and I daresay more heft behind my blows than dear Mama. It was your skill and courage truly carried the day." There was a hitch in Emma's voice, and very low in Spanish she said, "I am so afraid for him, Juan Luis, I can hardly bear it."

Blackwell lay stretched out in his cot aboard *Albion*, one arm propped behind his head, thinking over the evening's entertainment. The lady of the governor of Rio de Janeiro, reckoned to be one of the handsomest women in Brazil, had been present. But Blackwell did not think she compared to Mercedes. She hadn't Mercedes' charm, gentleness of manner, nor her quick intelligence. Blackwell did not consider how much Emma threw all comers into the shade; he simply could not think of her as a sexual being. There were more subjects on which Blackwell's mind refused to turn. Edward's oddness and his affinity for the company of women, along with his inability to form a fonder connection with one—in spite of his Adonis looks. Then there was Captain Verson and Mr. Montelongo's on-shore relationship, living together in the house in Chelsea these many years. One train of thought, however, never failed to captivate him. He tried to ignore his painful hard erection.

His door opened and Mercedes slipped inside the cabin. Blackwell was immediately up and at her side, in spite of his nakedness.

"Are you unwell, sweetheart?"

"Not in the least. May I join you?"

"I wish you would."

She pointedly looked at the bed instead of at him. Blackwell was sure he was a ludicrous sight, with his scars and his burns and his native tattoos, his cock like a pikestaff. Mercedes shed her dressing gown, naked underneath except for the little camisole top that covered her wound. Blackwell's heart began to thud as she climbed into the berth before him, exposing her lovely round bottom to his view.

He immediately settled beside her and took her in his arms. "Should you like me just to hold you?" She'd come to him for comfort before, not yet strong enough for anything more vigorous.

"Then what would you do with this?" She touched him intimately, causing Blackwell to suck in a breath.

"You know I cannot help it. I've been thinking of you and...just you let me worry about it anyway, Miss, and don't provoke me."

"Darling," she propped herself on his chest, considering him with a gaze of love, "I wouldn't tease you. I love you too much, and I feel quite well. I would have come to you sooner but for the weather being so rough in the crossing, and how busy you've been in port."

She followed this by kissing him. A good long kiss that began gentle and ended with Blackwell trying to tuck her beneath his body.

"Like this, Jim," she whispered, turning her back to him and pulling him against her.

Blackwell thought he knew why she wanted that position. He leaned over her, and moving her hair aside he kissed the back of her neck and her shoulders.

"I don't want to make you uncomfortable, sweetheart, and I won't touch you there or even look at you if you don't like it. But, would you take this off for me?" Blackwell touched her upper garment. "I want to feel only your skin against mine."

Mercedes hesitated a moment, and then she sat up and unclasped her top and put it to one side in the berth. She lay down again with one arm clamped over the wounded spot where her left breast had been.

Blackwell kissed her from shoulder blade to the small of her back. He put his hand over her buttock, a gentle squeeze, then plunged it between her thighs to caress her intimately. A groan escaped him when his fingers met warm, wet flesh.

"I've been thinking of you, too."

"I thought only men were that way."

She smiled and gave a little chuckle, looking back at him. "Put your legs outside of mine."

Blackwell made a queer face at this instruction. He was perfectly willing to do whatever she wanted, but he did not know how she came by such notions. In the next moment, all thought of the why and wherefore disappeared from Blackwell's mind. Mercedes put her hand underneath her body and guided him, and when he slipped inside her, it felt like being wrapped in the finest, tightest, wet, warm silk. He nearly lost his head, it had been so long since he'd lain with her. He waited with great concentration and self control until Mercedes cried out and gripped the bolster beneath her cheek.

His first concern after his own release was to remove his weight from her.

"This side, if you please, darling."

Mercedes shifted and he squeezed between the bulkhead and her body. She immediately lay half over him, her damaged side pressed against his body and the mattress.

"How did you know it would be like that, my darling?"

"Eh?" Blackwell couldn't think what she meant.

"You said I must wait and see how I felt about fobbing you off on other women. I think I should call them out if they tried to take your attentions from me."

She kissed his chest affectionately and Blackwell felt his heart glow.

"I only hoped. Hoped and trusted what had been so good between us would not be at an end." He gave her a squeeze, and then with trepidation and in a low tone he said, “Mercedes, had you better not...you know. I’m sorry I did not pull out, I was too excited.”

“No. No need to now. All of that is over for me. The cancer and the surgery seemed to have hastened what might not have happened to me for years You are living with an old, damaged woman. I can have no more children.”

Blackwell’s feelings at this news were quite, quite mixed. “Are you sure, sweetheart? It would be a disaster was you to become with child.”

She began to cry and Blackwell cursed himself for a fool. Of course what was a relief to him, was a sad loss to Mercedes’ tender heart.

“Forgive me,” she said. “Blubbering is part and parcel of growing old, I fear. I should be less sad if I had more hopes of a grandchild, but between Edward, and Emma and Aloka...”

She broke off, sobbing. Blackwell cast about for a means of consoling her, and making amends for his stupid blunders.

“You shall always be younger than me, Mercy, sweetheart. And never, never damaged in my eyes, I do not like to hear you talk so. I love you just as you are, and I’m grateful. Grateful for every day you’re with me, and willing to come into my arms.”

This made her cry harder for a time, but he was happy to hear her say at last, playfully, “Did you like what we did? Did it feel good?”

“Yes.” He actually blushed in the gloomy cabin. “But...”

“But?”

“It made me feel like a fat arse, if you want the truth. You are so little and tender, I felt like I was too much all over you. Besides,” he ended in a low abashed tone, “I like the feel of your legs around me.”

She stroked his face and kissed him, and murmured that he was no kind of fat arse, and she would not hear such talk. It gave Blackwell a feeling of having come home again. He was a little surprised when she went to sleep in his arms. Usually, Mercedes left him to sleep in her own cot undisturbed. His attentions might have caused such fatigue, but Blackwell thought more could be put down to the emotion she must have experienced in working herself up to come to him. She rolled upon her back, completely relaxed, her vulnerable position confirming him in his suspicion.

Blackwell raised himself to look at her now exposed chest, which he had not seen properly before. His eyes were perfectly adjusted to the gloom of the cabin. The healed, scarred area where her left breast had been was not so ugly, to his mind, as the corrugated flesh of his torso and right arm where the burns had healed. He'd noticed for some time past, that when he was on top of her his paunch hung down upon her. None of these things, not his scars or his native tattoos, not his bulk or his bastard son, seemed to weigh with her. Her love had remained unchanged since their earliest days together.

Blackwell knew that the illness, the surgery, and its aftermath she'd just told him of, struck at the essence of her womanhood. He pulled up the bedclothes and gently covered her, kissing the top of her head after lying back down, grateful she'd had the courage to return to his bed. He began to devise ways to make her comfortable with him again, to regain that perfect unconstraint he valued so highly.

Aloka awoke in a dank, gloomy, fetid atmosphere. There was a tremendous throbbing in his head, and a stench worse than bilge. He let his eyes adjust to the gloom, keeping his head quite still because moving it caused sharp pain, and he felt around him. His fingers met slimy straw, he rested on a heap of it. Aloka ceased to stir up the straw, for it caused the smells to waft up and assault him. He raised his arm and carefully probed an egg-sized knot on the back of his skull. A low moan escaped him, and then he gave a violent and painful start at the slamming of an iron gate.

He pushed himself to a sitting position against the nearest stone wall, to face the guard if one was coming. Aloka collected he was imprisoned, remembering the sequence of events that put him there in bits and pieces. His naval coat, sword and belt with its clasp knife, and his silver buckled shoes were gone. After sitting propped against the damp stone wall for a time, Aloka's thirst became overpowering. His tongue felt fat and sticky in his mouth.

The only light in the cell came from somewhere down the corridor, and by its feeble gleam Aloka made out a bucket on the opposite wall. He rose to a standing position by small degrees, and with one shoulder propped against the cell wall he began to make his way to the bucket. He lurched along, his head pounding, and his vision so blurred at times it frightened him. Half way there he had to rest, panting slightly, his parched tongue almost hanging from his mouth. When he was nearing the bucket, heeled boots were heard ringing on the stone floor, and Aloka thought they approached his cell.

At last he stood over the bucket, but looking down Aloka gave an agonized grunt, for it was a slops bucket. He leaned farther over and added his own contribution, vomiting into it. A guard halted outside his cell. Aloka turned his whole body to face the man.

"*Agua.*" He'd learned some Spanish words from Mercedes.

The man laughed just as screaming started up in another quarter of the prison. Aloka remembered Mercedes' screams. A man under torture this time.

"*Punição,*" the guard said matter-of-factly, and moved on.

Captain Blackwell was on his quarterdeck in the cool of the early morning, breathing in the fresh sea-scented air, feeling remarkably relaxed and well. A low mist hung over the water that would dissipate by noon. He began to plan the day ahead, they were to move both ships to St. Catherine's to complete their water and wood. The sound of oars reached *Albion's* quarterdeck before the *Blonde's* gig emerged from the mist.

"Boat ahoy! What boat is that?" called Mr. Stapleton, master's mate.

Captain Blackwell could make out a three-cornered, gold laced hat, and a lady's bonnet in the stern of the boat. He hardly required the answering "*Blonde*!" from the boat's coxswain to recognize Captain Verson. He smiled, thinking how pleased Mercedes would be to see Emma again so soon. He felt certain Emma was the lady in the boat.

Albion had no young gentleman for Captain Blackwell to send scurrying below to warn Mercedes of their visitors. She also lacked sideboys, but *Albion's* bosun stepped up and piped Captain Verson aboard. The minute Captain Verson took off his hat to acknowledge their salutes, and Captain Blackwell had a good look at both their faces, he knew this would not be a visit to bring Mercedes pleasure.

Immediately after greeting Captain Verson, he stepped up to Emma. "How did you come by that bruise?" His heart felt cold and heavy as he took in the angry blotch on Emma's lovely face.

Captain Blackwell forestalled Emma's response. "We had best go below, if you please."

Given the grim looks on their faces, Captain Blackwell dreaded to hear her answer, most especially before his men. He feared it must have something to do with Aloka. He hoped they would not find Mercedes still abed. Though she looked somewhat flustered, she was there in the cabin in a morning dress with her hair pinned up.

"Mama, you look remarkably rosy this morning." Emma walked in and kissed her mother as usual.

"Perhaps because your father and Doctor Sparrman keep me wrapped in cotton most of the time." Mercedes cast a concerned look over Emma's shoulder at Captain Blackwell. "I wish I could say the same for you. You look as though you haven't slept. And what is this great mark on your face, the whole side of your face is bruised."

"She was just about to explain that," Captain Blackwell said.

They all took seats, and Captain Verson reported the previous night's attack on Mr. Montelongo and Emma.

Mercedes gasped. "Juan Luis?"

"Knocked about, ma'am, but otherwise well enough," Captain Verson said. "I shall tell him of your concern, and I thank you. The reason for our visit, other than that Miss Emma might have the comfort of seeing you, is Mr. Blackwell never returned to the ship."

"Oh, Papa!" Emma cried. "Do you not think the two events related? What might have happened to him?"

He exchanged a glance with Captain Verson. Normally, a missing lieutenant in port would not be cause for any great alarm. They would simply flush out the brothels and drinking dens until the man turned up.

Captain Blackwell cleared his throat. "I shall call upon the British consul and make inquiries, if Captain Verson thinks it proper."

"Exactly my thought, sir."

He took his ladies aside for a private word before departing with Captain Verson.

"I never thought it appropriate your mother should have taught you the sword, until now. I'm very glad, very grateful, you were able to defend yourself, and stand your ground with Mr. Montel—"

"Until the blessed lobsters came!"

"Just so. You will be so good as to stay with your mama until I return. And you are not to worry. Do you hear me now? There are a dozen reasons a young man might be detained in port."

Captain Blackwell pursed his lips and glanced down after uttering that last. Perhaps he'd said too much. Most of those reasons, especially in the case of his son, would have to do with women.

Captain Blackwell became much less sanguine when no one else thought a woman was involved in the case. In company with the British consul, Sir Walter Hornsby, Captain Blackwell had spent hours at the governor's mansion, while the governor sent his aides round to look into Mr. Blackwell's disappearance. The whole occupied such a long space of time that Captain Verson was obliged to excuse himself, to return to his ship and his duties.

In the afternoon Captain Blackwell and Sir Walter were at last summoned to the governor's office. The governor gestured to a perspiring young man.

"Ensign Balbao is returned from Don Eduardo de Paiva, King João's treasurer. Don Eduardo says yesterday evening Mr. Aloka Blackwell insulted and abused him, and as he was in fear of further violence from the young man, he was obliged to have him taken up."

There was a brief silence as he and Sir Walter absorbed this news. Captain Blackwell had already observed Sir Walter was a retiring, quiet sort of man, so he spoke up. "I should like to see him in the fortress of Santa Cruz, sir, and I would be obliged to you for leave to do so. If there were any insult offered, I am sure an apology to Don Eduardo can be arranged."

The governor's face reddened as the ensign, still standing, spoke up.

"Mr. Blackwell was not taken to *fortaleza* de Santa Cruz, Captain. He is in the gaol at Botofogo."

Heat rose up Captain Blackwell's body, he felt as if it would explode out the top of his head. "Goddamn, hell, and death, sir! You do not mean to tell me my son, a King's officer, sir, is in gaol with common criminals and runaway slaves?"

"Captain Blackwell, sir,..." Sir Walter squeaked.

"I demand he be moved at once, sir. At once to the military prison! That is the honor due his rank and service as a British Naval officer. I shall certainly write to my government. I am sure there are one or two Brazilian gentlemen in London who could be welcomed at the Tower."

Shocked exclamations followed his declaration, the moral force of which was strengthened when Captain Verson was announced and walked in. He brought with him Lieutenant Blackwell's naval coat, sword and belt, and shoes, which had been sent to the *Blonde* anonymously by one of the boats bringing stores to the ship.

"It was all I could do to persuade them to move Aloka to the military fortress," Captain Blackwell explained to Mercedes and Emma. "Captain Verson very handsomely said if he is not liberated in three days time, when the *Blonde* returns from St. Catherine's, the consequences would be most unpleasant."

Captain Blackwell met the distressed, and rather blank stares, of Mercedes and Emma.

"He cannot say fairer than that," Captain Blackwell said. "Nor in conscience can he fire upon the shore, yet threats are often effective."

"I knew there was no woman keeping him ashore." Emma glanced pointedly at Captain Blackwell. "But I cannot credit he insulted and abused Don Eduardo de Paiva. Kuanoa was upset when Mr. Montelongo and I left, but Aloka was perfectly calm and composed."

"Kuanoa, do you say?" Captain Blackwell replied sharply.

He drew out all the details, listening carefully to Emma's narration of their parting with Aloka the evening before. His heart ached for what might have happened to the girl, and what could be happening to his son. He certainly thought the two events related, as Emma had suggested earlier, but he did not like to say so.

"When did you come by that great bruise on your face?" he asked at last.

"To tell truth, I think Mr. Montelongo elbowed me in the head. We were fighting so close together." Emma looked from his face to Mercedes, tears springing into her eyes. "May I worry for him now, Papa?"

Early in the morning the guard entered Aloka's cell and pulled him to his feet. He barked something at him, while pinning him to the wall with a meaty fist on his shoulder. The guard gestured toward the open cell door with his head, and dropped his hand.

"I can walk." Aloka's voice came out a croak, he was so parched.

He staggered just in front of the guard, his heart pounding, for they were moving in the direction from which the screams always came. Down a corridor, Aloka's stockinged feet slipping on the moist stones, up a pair of stairs, and into a courtyard. Aloka's heart lifted with the sight of the new day. At the same time he tried not to look too closely at his immediate surroundings. They passed whipping posts and wheels stained dark with blood, as they made their way through the prison yard.

The guard halted at the great wood and iron door, undid the antique lock, and waved Aloka through. Aloka stumbled forward, and the guard helped him along with a boot to his backside. He sprawled face forward in the dirt of a cart track.

Several pair of hands lifted him up, dusted him to some degree, and Aloka found three Portuguese soldiers looking at him not unkindly. They made wry faces at the smell of him, took him by the arms, and bundled him into a cart pulled by an ancient mule. The soldiers climbed in with him and signaled to the equally ancient mule driver.

Aloka swayed upon his bench.

"*Agua, señores. Favor.*"

One of the soldiers handed Aloka his water flask, and when the others saw his greed and his joy, they immediately offered their own. After this reviving draught, the sweetest he'd ever had, and the civility with which it had been given, Aloka felt his heart soar.

He poured a small amount of the water remaining into his cupped hand and rubbed it over his face, but he dared not touch the lump on his skull matted with hair and blood.

The cart brought them to a small jetty, and the soldiers assisted him from the cart into a six-oared boat. Aloka was out in the clear day, his heart beating with excitement, and once more upon the water, after a confinement in gloom, darkness, and fear. He relished the clean smell of the air, slipped off his slimy stockings and dropped them over the side. He began to look about him like one of the living again. The oars were manned by diminutive men with ropey muscled arms, who were pulling for the fortress on the outcropping of rock they'd seen when coming into Rio de Janeiro.

He had uncommonly good eyesight and was able to just make out *Albion* in her berth opposite Pray de Grande, but *Blonde* was nowhere nearby. Aloka thought briefly about escape. He could slip over the side of the boat, he was not shackled, swim a few hundred yards under water and come up at some distance. In peak shape he could have swum the entire distance to *Albion*, it not being so very great. But his head was tender, he was shaky on his pins after having eaten nothing for two days, and if he had not had the precious water to drink he believed he might soon have expired. Aloka remained seated, and followed the soldiers meekly when the boat ground upon the stony beach and they led him into the fort.

The governor's boat was sent for Captain Blackwell in the middle of the morning watch. He'd been up early, after a night during which none of them rested, and was meeting with Captain Bowles. Captain Bowles had been a lieutenant under Captain Blackwell on his previous South Seas voyage. He was now a fleshy, red faced, fair haired, and close to middle aged post-captain. On the beach for six years in England, Captain Bowles had been eager and pleased to accept the berth of first officer aboard the *Albion* yacht.

"Warp her out to a position here," Captain Blackwell said, pointing to a hand drawn map of the bay and its approaches, "and then dispatch Narhilla in the gig with the men as we discussed."

"I should very much like to lead them, sir."

"Thank you, Captain Bowles, I am obliged to you. But I must have you aboard *Albion*, for the sake of the ship and my ladies."

Captain Blackwell hoped this planning would not be necessary, and there was to be a diplomatic resolution. Aloka would offer Don Eduardo de Paiva his apologies, and be released into Captain Blackwell's custody. Yet if there were difficulties, he still intended returning to *Albion* in company with his son.

The governor's boat received Captain Blackwell, not in naval uniform, or to any piping ceremony at the side. He wore a black frock coat, a sword dangling at his hip, and carried a package under his arm like any civilian gentleman. Mercedes and Emma were upon the deck waving their handkerchiefs as the boat bore him away. More concern and worry were evident on his lady's face than Captain Blackwell ever cared to see there.

At the entrance to the fort of Santa Cruz, Captain Blackwell made himself known and was almost instantly attended by a captain of artillery. The officer greeted him cordially in Portuguese, casting an appraising eye up and down Captain Blackwell's person, and led him to the officers' mess. Aloka sat at one of the long mess tables with his head bent over a bowl, a heel of bread clutched in one hand, asleep.

Captain Blackwell moved over to him, a great lump rising in his throat, and squeezed his shoulder. "Son."

Aloka straightened with a start, looked at him closely, and threw himself upon his breast. Aloka clutched him for such a length of time, Captain Blackwell was obliged to say, his voice heavy with emotion, "Lord, son. You smell like a privy."

The young man stepped away, sniffled, and wiped the tears from his face. "That's because I've been in one. I never dreamed humans could treat each other so."

"Do the Dons speak English?" Captain Blackwell asked in a low voice.

"The fat fellow on your right, and the mustachioed, feminine looking one near the end of the table," Aloka replied in Hawaiian.

"Sit down, son," Captain Blackwell continued in the same language, causing some of the officers dining near them to stare. "Finish your soup. You were about to plant your head in it when I came up."

"I don't think I shall take anymore, my stomach feels queer. But I will make the motions while we talk."

Captain Blackwell inclined his head. "They say you insulted and abused the King's treasurer. Is that true?"

"The insults and abuse were flowing pretty fast and heavy both ways, sir, as I recall. But I cannot think how it all started, except if it were when I stumbled, or however it happened, and knocked the man down."

"Where was Kuanoa in all this?"

"Kuanoa? Last I remember he was just at hand. I was taking a cold but civil leave of Don Eduardo, and then we were upon the floor grappling, and when I tried to rise someone dealt me a most prodigious thump to the back of my head."

"Are you wounded, son?" Captain Blackwell cried. "I thought you were merely covered in smuts."

"It ain't so bad now, Father, pray do not raise the hue and cry. I don't want to be prodded by one of their doctors, I can wait for Mr. McNeath. If I am to be released, that is?"

The mix of youthful bravado, eagerness, and hope in Aloka's voice struck at Captain Blackwell's heart.

"You should be, but an apology may be necessary. Can you manage that?"

"That and more to gain my freedom, to be back aboard ship, to see my darling...". Aloka trailed off with a sudden, conscious look.

"I am rejoiced to hear it. Though whether an apology is owing I much doubt. You should never have been in that gaol, you should have been here in military detainment and treated with the proper respect and civility due an officer. Whose spite put you in that place, I cannot say."

Captain Blackwell's voice had become severe, and Aloka shuddered.

"I wish I could forget it," Aloka said.

They were silent for a time, seated side by side. The officers had finished their dinner and gone away. As they were quite alone, Aloka leaned against his father's shoulder.

"Speaking of things better forgotten," Captain Blackwell said, with a little clearing of his throat. "I have the sad duty to tell you, Emma and Mr. Montelongo were attacked the evening you were taken—"

"Oh, my God!" Aloka tried to leap up, hit his legs on the edge of the table, and landed again on his rump.

"Easy, son. They held off the attackers, five thugs with clubs and cudgels, bawling all the while for the Blondes, who came up like good 'un's and set the ruffians to their heels."

"I should have been there!"

"Yes, you should have. It was a grievous mistake to leave Emma. The attacks were coordinated, do you see? They meant to separate you, and steal her. Had we lost her, it would have been a blow Mercedes could not recover from, to say nothing of the dear girl. Even if we'd gotten her back, how long do you think it would take a woman to recover from being in the hands of such rough men? Her experience in Lord Cochrane's house would be nothing to it."

Aloka looked too miserable to speak. He hung his head, his expression pained and remorseful.

"The *Blonde* has gone to St. Catherine's to complete her water," Captain Blackwell said. "Emma is aboard *Albion* with her mama. I'm sure Captain Verson and Mr. Montelongo would have taken great care of her, but her mother and I did not think it proper, since she was under your protection."

"I shall do better, Father. She shall be my priority in everything. Unless...unless you see fit to keep her with you aboard *Albion*?"

"No," Captain Blackwell answered at once. Mercedes would not like to be intimate with him with her daughter in such close proximity. He felt guilty this was his reason, and he said in a different tone, "Everyone deserves another chance. I don't know if I ever told you that Mercedes was taken from me once. Because of my bad judgement and another man's greed and ill-will. I was given a second chance, through fortunate circumstance and her own strong will to survive. I should not like to see you suffer through the same regret and guilt. It might have poisoned the rest of my days had things not turned out as they did. A woman like Emma is a treasure, son. Don't think other men will not try to take her from you."

Captain Blackwell was conscious of having delivered a long and perhaps unwanted lecture, but Aloka sat up straight and looked him in the eye.

"I want to get back aboard, sir, back to all my duties," he said. "I can fight if I have to."

Captain Blackwell helped Aloka to his feet, gave him his arm to lean on. "Have you given your parole?"

"None has been asked of me, sir."

In a few words Captain Blackwell told Aloka about the disposition of *Albion*, and how his gig's crew would be with them shortly.

"We shall wait, however, and give the governor a good while to do the right thing."

They walked slowly to the main gate of the fortress, no one paying them the least heed, and halted where two sentries stood either side of the arched entrance. Captain Blackwell took Aloka to a bench and sat him down.

"I'll go see whether Narhilla is come with the gig. I shall return directly."

Aloka nodded, and when Captain Blackwell looked back over his shoulder, he had slid down to lie upon the bench.

Captain Blackwell found Narhilla round one side of the fortress. He was alone, the gig had not been allowed to land at the dock belonging to the fortress. He had brought the boat in to a civilian landing place pointed out by a helpful old muleteer.

"What orders, sir? How fairs young Mr. Blackwell?"

"Poorly, I'm afraid." Captain Blackwell put a shoulder belt with a pistol Narhilla handed him over his head, and replaced his coat on top of it. "For the moment we wait. Leave two men in the gig and spread the others out within shouting distance. Then return to the fort entrance and await my signal."

"Aye, aye, sir."

Captain Blackwell found the captain of artillery with Aloka when he returned. The captain had one booted foot on the bench near Aloka's head, and was bending over him. Captain Blackwell quickened his pace.

"Captain Bernal?" he said.

"Ah, Captain Blackwell. A letter has been sent you from the governor."

He hastened to prop Aloka in a sitting position, noting how his eyes seemed to swim in his head at the change in posture. Captain Blackwell took his letter with a bow and a word of gratitude, and excused himself to read it.

"You know the letter's content?" Captain Blackwell asked, returning to them with the brief note in his hand.

"Oh, yes, sir, its intent, more or less." Captain Bernal smiled. "Mr. Blackwell is quite free to go."

"Exactly so." Captain Blackwell read from the letter. "'Don Eduardo de Paiva having been persuaded that Mr. Blackwell acted only out of the impetuous temperament of youth.'" He gave both Aloka and the captain of artillery a severe look. "We shall take our leave, Captain."

Aloka stood on his own and made Captain Bernal a shaky bow. "Thank you for your hospitality, and the very good dinner, Captain Bernal."

Narhilla had appeared at the open fortress gate.

"May my coxswain pass in?" Captain Blackwell asked, nodding at Aloka, who he had taken under one arm.

"Of course, Captain." Captain Bernal signaled to the two sentries. "Tell me, sir, do sailors always go about so draped in weapons?"

Narhilla hurried up to take Aloka's other arm, a pistol and tomahawk in belts across his chest, and a cutlass at his waist.

"I don't know about sailors, sir," Captain Blackwell said coldly. "Seamen do. When ordered to do so. Good day to you, Captain Bernal."

Aloka stumbled so in bare feet on the sharp rocks of the beach, that Captain Blackwell and Narhilla almost carried him to the boat, collecting the boat's crew as they went.

Before getting in, Aloka asked, "Can we stop short of *Albion*, sir? I'd like to wash, I do not like to offend the ladies."

"Of course we can, son," Captain Blackwell said. "Mercedes has sent some of my clothes for you in this package."

"I hope that means I have not entirely lost her good opinion." Aloka pulled his shirt over his head, dropped his breeches, and left both on the beach before climbing into the gig.

Captain Blackwell accompanied Aloka into the water, when he ordered the boat to halt, in case he should need propping up. Aloka moved better in the water though than he had on land, always having been something of a porpoise. Together they swam a ways apart from the boat.

"There they go, the Black Savages," said Barnes, at stroke oar.

All but the oldster, Narhilla, were disappointed at not being allowed to give the Portuguese soldiers a good thumping.

"Shut it, do you hear? And keep it shut," Narhilla said, but without enthusiasm. He understood the men's disappointment, even if he did not share it.

Blackwell watched Aloka bathing. He submerged carefully and repeatedly, combing his long hair underwater with his fingers. From a boy, both in his native land and in the Navy, he'd been raised to cleanliness. Seeing how diligently Aloka scrubbed himself with his hands, Blackwell could imagine what he'd suffered. When Aloka was done and resting in the water, Blackwell stroked over to him.

"You must think me uncommon nice to be so overset by a two-days' confinement," Aloka said, "when you endured years of captivity. On several occasions."

"No one ever put me in a sunless hole. The French, and then Ata Gege, treated me with decency. Your people did far more than that, taking me to their hearts the way they did."

Blackwell paused, panted, treading water. Aloka stirred the water far less than he did and still kept upright, hardly moving his upper body.

"The Hawaiians are a generous and good hearted people for the most part," Blackwell said, when breath returned. "But they have the same failings as other men. Greed, lust, envy, and violence."

CHAPTER EIGHT

If Aloka had any doubts about how Mercedes, or anyone else aboard *Albion* would receive him, they were dispelled almost from his first moment aboard. He was whisked below to the captain's cabin by Doctor Sparrman, leaving his father on deck with Captain Bowles. In the cabin they met the ladies, and he and Emma immediately fell into each other's arms.

Neither could speak a word, and they only gradually became aware Mercedes and Dr. Sparrman were standing by trying hard not to gape at them. Aloka at last stepped back and extended his hand to Mercedes.

"Forgive me, dear ma'am, for not taking better care of Emma. You begged me when we parted on *Blonde*, to remember how you used to hold me on your lap, and be kind to your daughter."

Aloka began to cry. In fact they all did, saving Dr. Sparrman, who looked on them askance.

"I shall do better, ma'am."

"I hope and trust you will, dear. We are rejoiced to have you back, so glad. Now, you must allow Dr. Sparrman to examine you."

Mercedes led Emma away to the captain's sleeping quarters, after giving orders to McMurtry to bring a tankard of water and start a broth preparing for Mr. Blackwell. Aloka was taken into Doctor Sparrman's hands, who palpated, prodded, completely undressed and examined him, for the Swede was a thorough man of his profession.

"Does your vision trouble you, Mr. Blackwell?"

Doctor Sparrman was mercilessly handling the now marble-sized knot on the back of Aloka's head.

"The day after they pulled my cork, my vision was bad at times. My head hurt something tremendous, and I was nauseous on moving about. That has passed off, thank God, though my head does still hurt if I turn it certain ways."

"The worst danger from a blow to the head comes in the hours immediately following, and you have come through that. Under ugly circumstances, I collect, sir. I am sorry for what you have been through, I've seen the places they keep slaves prisoner at the Cape."

Aloka bowed, he could not at first trust himself to speak. "I wish there were something to be done for those poor souls. Perfectly inhuman treatment, because their skins are dark like mine."

"Slavery gives rise to excesses, wantonness, and cruelty." The doctor seemed absent for a moment, a pained and almost savage expression on his face. He shook himself and gave Aloka a kind but thin smile. "The head injury bears watching, Mr. Blackwell. And a reduced duty, if there is to be any duty—"

"Oh there shall be, Doctor, if I have my way. I have one or two I must return to without loss of a moment."

"You may put on your clothes, Mr. Blackwell. For the next twenty-four hours you are to rest. And I do not like that rash upon your torso, sir."

"Why, Doctor, the place was full of vermin, you know. These are nothing more than insect bites."

Two weeks later the bites had not disappeared and Aloka was inclined to believe good Doctor Sparrman in the right; it was a rash. Still he did not think it of sufficient importance to call upon the *Blonde's* surgeon, Mr. NcNeath. He could certainly not spare the time now, with Emma waiting for him to escort her on deck. The ship was becalmed, but they would eventually pass through the variables and then there would be the heavy work of sailing round the Horn. Aloka wanted to make the best of this time with Emma before duty consumed him. He finished dressing, pulling his shirt out a bit from his breeches so the cloth would chafe less.

The officers had been allowed to dispense with waistcoats, and many wore straw hats in place of their Naval scrappers.

Aloka ran up the after companion ladder to the upper deck, feeling giddy and with a racing heart. There had been signs in their relations of late that Emma would soon grant him the ultimate favor a woman could bestow, and invite him to her bedchamber. In this Aloka had refused to make the first move, she being so young and innocent, but he knew the Hawaiian ladies had been working upon her. Since his imprisonment in Brazil they'd been particularly strident in urging Emma to seize life and all it had to offer.

Such advice could not displease him. He fairly leapt up on deck, and was staggered by the brilliance of the day. Really, it was shockingly bright. Aloka put his head down, hurried the few steps to the door of the coach that gave onto the upper deck, and knocked on Emma's door.

"Who's there?" Her sweet voice answered at once.

He was glad she continued to follow this protocol, impressed upon her while they were yet aboard *Albion*.

"Mr. Blackwell, at your service."

She immediately emerged from her apartment, looking lovely as a spring day—an English spring day, he couldn't compare her to the airless stillness they were experiencing at present—and wearing a demure little bonnet to shield her face from the glare. Aloka clapped his own hat on his head with a happy smile, and gave Emma his arm.

They made a circuit together of the deck, walking down the starboard gangway to the forecastle, and then back along the larboard side. Forward of the break of the quarterdeck was the area where the men and the watch on deck gathered, so Aloka did not stop or linger, but moved steadily along. The seamen knuckled their foreheads, and the other officers greeted them. All eyes, he was aware, were on his companion.

The only time they halted was when Kimo approached them, one of Admiral Kapihe's servants. The boy had adopted Aloka, acting as his servant as well aboard ship, while intimating it was the old admiral's wish.

"The Admiral sends to invite you and Wahine Blackwell to join him under the *tapa*."

Captain Verson had caused an awning to be rigged on the lee side of the quarterdeck, for the comfort and convenience of the King's suite. It was to the shade of this sail-cloth covering they were invited. Aloka and Emma directed slow steps to the quarterdeck.

Several of the Hawaiians were playing a game very much like English draughts, with fourteen rows of black and white pebbles laid out and undisturbed by the ship's gentle, rocking motion. The *Blonde's* head was gradually drifting through all points of the compass. The Hawaiians had brought their soft, woven mats up on deck, and many lay reclined full length upon these, watching the ship's business, or with eyes closed and half-smiles on their broad faces.

Kapihe was one of the lollers about, but one eye popped open at their approach. He welcomed Aloka and Emma with uncommon zeal and invited them to a seat upon his mat, which, however, he knew they must refuse. Aloka because he was a ship's officer and could not sit upon the quarterdeck, and Emma because she was his companion. She often sat upon these same mats in the cabin, in company with Li'liah and the ladies.

"I had a dream about how you should be tattooed," Kapihe said, smiling on the pair of them.

"Did you, sir? I am obliged to you for the condescension. May I know in what the design consists?"

Aloka's formal way of speaking Hawaiian always pleased Kapihe. The old man launched into a description of the complicated symbols for waves and sea that he envisioned, acting out some of these with the motions of a *hula* or dance.

Emma and Aloka listened with great attention and respect, grave looks upon their faces, except during the *hula* parts when they had to smile.

"I do not propose the designs be on your backside and loins."

Aloka glanced quickly at Emma, he was unsure how much Hawaiian she understood. She stood with her gaze cast down and a slight flush on her face. He could make nothing of that, however, for it was a warm day.

"No, that is a thing the present generation cannot like," Kapihe said, "as being of their grandfather's day. I propose you put the tattoos here and here."

The old man grasped Aloka's upper arms and beamed into his face.

"Could be, he's afraid of the pain, Kapihe," Kuanoa said, flexing his own biceps and chest muscles.

This made Kuanoa's tattoos stand out, the name of the great king Kamehameha I, and the date of his death. Aloka suddenly became aware he was exposing Emma to bare chested men and loose talk.

He tried to keep guilt from his face as he stepped back a pace, and gripped Kapihe by the forearms. "Thank you for relating your dream, sir, I shall consider of it deeply and we may discuss it again. There are many days between now and when we shall reach the Islands, so I trust I will have sufficient time to work up courage for the event."

Aloka stared pointedly at Kuanoa as he uttered this last. Kapihe's face broke into a wide grin, and he clapped both Aloka and Kuanoa on the shoulders. After taking leave of the Hawaiians, Aloka drew Emma's hand back on to his arm. He escorted her to the taffrail, where Aloka thought they could not be heard by the King's people.

Emma was relieved to be away from them; she liked all the Hawaiians except for one. She could not like Kuanoa, nor the way he stared at her, suspecting from her father's questioning he'd had to do with Aloka's imprisonment. She turned to Aloka, they were somewhat alone at last, the officers on the quarterdeck having moved considerately away.

"My Hawaiian is grown quite good, you know, spending so much time with Li'liah and the ladies."

She gave him an arch look, and it had the intended effect. Aloka smiled, then laughed, and she watched the tension go out of his shoulders.

"I'm sorry to expose you to such talk, Emma. Lord knows Father would not like it."

"And yet Papa's the one with the tattooed arse."

"Hush, woman!"

Aloka's eyes belied his stern tone. His look of kindled affection stirred something inside her, something that fluttered in the area of her womb. Emma stepped closer to him, though she did not touch him.

"Perhaps you'd like to come to the coach tonight, and show me all the places your tattoos might go?"

"Oh, Emma! My dearest—"

"Just say yes."

Any other answer would be unbearable, after she'd worked her courage up so to ask him.

His answer had been yes, yes with all his heart. Aloka stood the second dog-watch, feeling a bit ashamed of how he fluttered inwardly with anticipation. One would think he was the maiden and not she. When the watch ended he went below to his cabin to have a little refreshment and wash. He was to meet Emma at a quarter past nine, and he would not be on duty again until midnight.

Aloka's heart would not stop racing, and he felt oddly weary and uncomfortably hot in his cabin as he stripped before the bucket where he would wash. He removed his shirt and gave a low moan. The rash was much worse, it covered his torso, arms, and with his shaving mirror Aloka was able to see it was all over his back. Light headed, he climbed into his cot to think. Much as he had hoped and dreamed of intimacy with Emma, he could not go to her blotched over with this...whatever it was. He had a vague notion of sending for Mr. McNeath.

His thoughts were disordered, and he sat in his cot with his head drooping, his chin on his breast. Aloka was aware of a great feeling of anguish in his breast, but after a time he couldn't recall the exact reason why it was there. His head hurt intensely, much as it had when he'd woken in the cell in Botofogo. He felt so entirely wretched, especially at recollection of those dark hours, that he lay down. Aloka told himself he would rise directly for he had a strong sense he must be somewhere, there was something he had to attend to.

Promptly at nine Emma was washed and perfumed. She'd decided it wasn't proper to meet him in a dressing gown with her hair loose, even though she'd invited him for that purpose. She was fully dressed with her hair pinned up, and doing her best to control her anxiety. Emma remembered what her mother once told her, 'All men want is what is different to themselves, and to be loved and respected', and the more earthy advise of the Hawaiian ladies, who could be quite graphic. When the ship's bell struck four times—her heart pounding in time, for it was now ten o'clock—her anxiety was reaching a fever pitch.

A tap came at the coach door and Emma sprang up from her cot. She stopped herself before opening it, and called out "Who's there?"

"A message from Lieutenant Blackwell."

Emma flung wide the door and Kuanoa pushed his way in. He literally bumped her with his chest, shoving her backward into the apartment, and pulling the door to behind his back. Emma's heart began to beat harder.

"What are you doing here, sir? What message have you from Aloka? Where is he, what's happened to him?"

"That I don't know. I do know he has missed his meeting with you, and I've come to take his place. I will initiate you into the ways of Venus. He will thank me for it."

"No, he won't!" Emma heard the squeal of panic in her voice. She took a deep breath. "You must leave at once. I do not want you here. I do not want you, and I shall scream for Captain Verson."

Kuanoa snorted and shook his head, reaching out strong, muscular arms for her.

"Captain Verson! Mr. Montelongo! Blondes! Blondes, to me!"

Kuanoa wore a shocked expression at her cry. Had he truly believed she would submit to him? His amazement increased when Captain Verson burst in. The captain was followed by Mr. Montelongo, with his dirk in his hand, and by the midshipman of the watch, Mr. Whittemore. A marine private brought up the rear. Emma's apartment was suddenly crowded with five men and herself.

"Miss Emma?" Captain Verson said, glaring at Kuanoa.

"He said he bore a message from Aloka, so I opened the door to him, sir. And then he would not leave."

"Sir, you will return to your quarters and never distress or disturb this young lady again." Captain Verson stood directly before Kuanoa, looking up at him. "I will brook no irregularity in this ship. You are an honored guest, but it is all one to me whether you pass your voyage in the great cabin or below in chains. Your behavior shall determine which. Do you understand me?"

Kuanoa regarded them all. Emma was standing before her berth with her trembling hands clasped in front of her, Captain Verson stoney faced, Mr. Montelongo beside him still gripping his weapon. He shrugged and nodded, pushing past Mr. Whittemore and the marine at the door.

"Mr. Whittemore, Mr. Price, accompany Mr. Kuanoa back to his quarters," Captain Verson said.

Kuanoa's quarters were no more than a few steps away, in the great cabin itself. Mr. Montelongo shut the coach door and, like a brother, held out his hand to Emma. Emma rushed over to him relieved. She'd always found Captain Verson a stern and forbidding man, somewhat like her own father.

"Captain Verson, forgive me. He frightened me so, I didn't know what else to do."

"You did right, Miss Emma. And there is nothing to forgive. Mr. Montelongo and I were taking a lunar on the quarterdeck when we heard your cry. The question is can you be comfortable, even with the latches upon the doors, with that man so close by? We can try signaling your father's ship tomorrow, and have you removed to *Albion* if you wish."

Emma felt she'd set a disaster in motion. The last thing she wanted was to explain this disgraceful sequence of events to Captain Blackwell and her mama. She was searching for words to decline, when a tap sounded on the door and a young voice called in, "Miss Emma! Miss Emma! Do come, Aloka has the sickness."

Captain Verson whirled round, crying out "What in God's name!", and threw open the door. Kimo stood there shaking with distress.

Emma could hear them talking in the wardroom, just the other side of the canvas door separating Aloka's cabin from the officer's dining space. Captain Verson, Mr. Montelongo, and Mr. McNeath. They said 'gaol fever' and 'ship fever', while Emma wiped Aloka's sweating face with a damp towel. She'd stayed in the cabin when the surgeon examined him, off in a corner next to Mr. Montelongo, and seen the ugly rash covering him, and how he could make no coherent responses to Mr. McNeath's questions. Aloka was in the throws of a fever, a hectic flush and sheen of sweat overlay his tanned skin.

She had not meant to listen to the officers' conversation, but it proved impossible not to attend to every word. Emma gathered there was a great fear of contagion. Mr. McNeath talked of miasmas and tainted air, and Captain Verson had already rousted out any sleeping officers and sent them away and posted Mr. Whittemore at the door to prevent anyone coming in. Emma hesitated much in rising to go speak to them; hadn't she been schooled in the fact a ship's business and men's affairs was none of her own; but the sight of Aloka decided her. She leant forward and put her cheek against his burning forehead and kissed him, then handed the towel to Kimo and went out of the cabin.

"Captain Verson, gentlemen, pray forgive the intrusion. I could not help but hear your discussion."

They'd fallen silent immediately when she stepped out of the second lieutenant's cabin.

Emma knew she must address herself to Captain Verson. "Sir, with respect. May I suggest Aloka be moved to the coach, where I can be in constant attendance on him? The officers may have their quarters back and he will be separated from the crew. The Hawaiians are near, but will know to keep off because of the sickness. In the morning you might signal *Albion* and have us both taken off if you judge it proper."

Captain Verson bowed to her. There was relief, she thought, possibly even admiration on his face. "You have great good sense, Miss Emma. But are you quite sure you will expose yourself to the risk of—"

"Quite, quite sure, sir. I thank you for your kind concern. I have the leisure to care for him. Under Mr. McNeath's direction, of course."

"Mr. Whittemore, go ahead and clear the way to the coach. All hands to stand aside, I do not want any more men involved. Then return and bear a hand with Mr. Blackwell."

The four officers; Captain Verson, Mr. Montelongo, Mr. McNeath, and Mr. Whittemore; bore Aloka bundled in his cot aboard a stretcher, to the coach. The most difficult part was the change of decks, negotiating the stretcher up the companion ladder. There was a great deal of sweating and maneuvering, and calling of directions to one another. The seamen having been warned to stay back, watched their officers' efforts with frowns and disapproving looks. At last they thumped Aloka down on the planks in the coach, removed him from the cot by means of a blanket placed under him, slung the cot anew and heaved him back into it.

"He shall be very well here, at least for the present." Mr. McNeath took Aloka's pulse one last time, and gave Emma instructions for Aloka's care. He turned to Captain Verson. "Let us discuss the fumigation of the wardroom, sir."

They were most assiduous in their precautions, the wardroom was fumigated with charcoal, and Captain Verson caused the berth deck to be washed with vinegar and water. The plan to remove the sick man to *Albion* was given up next morning, a fresh breeze having come up. *Albion*, lighter and faster, had already moved away and out of sight. The *Blonde* must proceed as she was, one lieutenant short, and Captain Verson set a course to round Cape Horn.

Emma's world shrank to the space enclosed by the bulkheads of the coach, and care of Aloka. In this she was assisted by Kimo, who helped clean up when Aloka vomited, and held him while he relieved himself into a pot. Emma was no stranger now to all those places his tattoos might go, for she washed him, and dressed him in a nightshirt that he would then sweat through. Her friends did not forget her. Besides attendance from Mr. McNeath and his mate, one or more of the officers stopped by daily. They took it in turns to see she had air and exercise on deck, and Li'liah offered to sit with Aloka while Emma slept in her berth.

On one of the last visits Captain Verson made to the coach before the working of the ship took up all his time and energy, he ordered another fixed berth built into it.

"I fear he may be too flung about in his cot," he told Emma. "It will be easier to lash him into a fixed berth." He gave her a conscious look. "We have been most fortunate, no one else has sickened."

"Amen, sir."

"May I say, Miss Emma, you are a very sensible woman. Just like your mother. I hope that doesn't displease you."

Emma assured him quite the opposite was the case, and sat down again on the three legged stool beside Aloka's cot after Captain Verson had gone. She propped up Aloka's shaved head and tilted water from a cup into his mouth.

"I licked moisture from the walls in my cell," Aloka said.

"Were you very thirsty, my love?"

"Parched."

"You shall have all you want now. Shall you take a little more?"

Aloka groaned and twisted away from her, rubbing his hands over his head, which appeared to pain him much.

"What has happened to my hair? Oh Emma, forgive me, I am no use to man or beast. No kind of fit man for you, no use to Captain Verson and the ship, and I have ruined your chances for a suitable match at home."

He had periods of lucidity when he would speak to her like this, full of anxiety, perfectly aware of his circumstances and surroundings.

"Only be well again, my dearest, dearest love."

He flushed and began to take panting breaths. Emma leaned forward and bathed Aloka's face and neck with a wet towel.

"I don't care for hairy women. Too great a chore to battle through all that hair to get to the tender parts."

Now it was Emma who flushed. She hoped he would not talk so when the carpenter and his mates came in to construct the second berth, she would have to leave the cabin if he did. Emma could not admit it even to herself, but she feared he would slip away while she wasn't with him. What then would she do, with a great hole in her life and her heart?

Aloka was her entire reason for being on that ship, for having left behind everything familiar in England, to journey to an unknown and savage land. Yet Captain Verson had called her sensible. If to be so meant fighting to keep Aloka with her, she would continue to nurse him round the clock. Had these been Mercedes' feelings too once—if they were so much alike—love, devotion, self-interest, and a certain amount of desperation?

Aloka's body was lifted unnaturally up, suspended, suspended, and then crashed back down into the berth. He was alternately sweating and hot, or freezing with his teeth fairly clacking in his head. He heard a female voice. "He casts off his blankets, and then he is nearly blue with cold when I can finally crawl down to cover him." It was Emma tending him! He wished she would come into his cot and cover him; cover him with her cool hands and her warm body. There was bitterness too, that she was seeing him in his present state. Bald, growing thinner, weak, and dependent. The violent motion of the ship continued unabated.

He slipped away, and imagined Emma was Mercedes, caring for him when he'd been dreadfully sick as a boy aboard his father's ship. Aloka was vaguely ashamed she should be trickling water into his mouth from a sponge, and massaging his feet. He tried to speak his gratitude, and apologies for causing her so much trouble. She always had a gentle caress for him, murmuring assurances he was to get better. Aloka felt this woman was holding him in the world, and would not let him set his feet on the rainbow.

Thoughts of his ancestors, who passed over a rainbow to the dwelling place of the dead, swam in his mind along with symbols of waves and the sea, and an old man performing an even older dance. Aloka heard the pounding of drums, the rhythmic stamping of feet, and saw images of lit torches, and lithely moving bodies. He glimpsed his father, furiously paddling a native canoe, weariness and strain upon his face. He himself was crouched, cold and wet, in the bows.

Ugly images began to flash before him like a phantasmagoria. Carvings of warriors holding severed heads, real warriors and actual heads with lolling distended tongues. Heavy war canoes rolling over live, shrieking bodies, a young boy swung by his ankles and bashed against the prow of a canoe. Suddenly a woman's face filled his whole field of vision. A very wide and bloated face, the eyes almost closed from the puffiness of the surrounding flesh. Aloka knew at once this was his mother. He was afraid, for this woman was intimately connected in his mind with that violent, dark side of his heritage.

Aloka woke with a start and a lingering feeling of dread and anxiety. He lay in his berth, listening to the sounds of the ship. The decks were being cleaned with holystones over his head, the *Blonde* was no longer in heavy seas. She moved with an easy surging motion, like a galloping horse. Pacific waters. Just as he was beginning to relax, drifting off to sleep, a woman's moan and whimper from above caused him another tremendous start.

He was lying in the lower of two fixed berths. A ladder of just a few rungs had been constructed at the foot, connecting the berths like a miniature companion way. Aloka sat up, planting bare feet on the wooden planks, and ran his hands over the white nightshirt he was wearing. The nightshirt was clean, but it was not a garment he should have chosen, much preferring to lie naked to sleep. Another little whimper recalled the reason he was dressed so, and, very carefully, Aloka stood up.

He had a bad moment when it occurred to him Emma might have sickened with the fever. But as soon as he peered at her in the upper berth, that fear was dispelled. Her lovely face had a normal rosy hue. She slept profoundly, bracing herself in the cot by custom of long usage, and whimpering from time to time. Aloka was weak and unsteady, but instinct was strong in him, and he leaned in to kiss her.

He caught sight of himself in a little square mirror over her berth as he did. Gone was the long hair any seaman, any warrior, might be proud of. Aloka's pate was covered by a half-inch thick fuzz of dark hair. His face was thin, more yellow than brown, there were bruise-like patches beneath his eyes, and his lips were cracked. He was no fit object, altogether unsuitable for this treasure of a woman.

In sleep she looked like an angel, or a very young child. Aloka backed away from her, bringing his hand up to rub his face.

Someone had been shaving him, he would otherwise have a beard like Methuselah. He sat down again on his berth to rest, and discovered his sea chest had been brought into the coach and was just at hand. As quietly as he could he rose, and took out his shaving things and clothes.

"Bear a hand there, Crosley, goddamn your eyes!" the bosun bawled out, quite near at hand.

Aloka was pulling the nightshirt over his head, and naked he jerked round to see if Emma had wakened. She slept on, the poor soul, exhausted by the trouble and care he'd caused her.

CHAPTER NINE

Blackwell came back into his sleeping cabin aboard *Albion* just as the holystoning started up. The hands disliked their captain to remain on his quarterdeck when the decks were being scrubbed. Blackwell commanded the yacht like a Royal Navy vessel, and he'd never been one to balk the custom of the service. He stripped off his clothes and climbed under the bedclothes with Mercedes.

Albion had come in to the port of Valparaiso the previous week, where she was anchored and awaiting the *Blonde*.

"Any sign of her?"

Mercedes was anxious for her children and the *Blonde's* people, the other ship had not been in sight since the doldrums.

"Not yet, no. Two frigates are coming in, the *Lautaro* and the *O'Higgins*. Part of Lord Cochrane's fleet, or I should say the Chilean Navy."

Word had reached *Albion* that Lord Cochrane had been hired by the fledgling nation to command a naval force in its fight for independence from Spain. At home Admiral Gambier had been acquitted at his court martial, while one of his most vocal critics, Lord Cochrane, was in disgrace over a stock market scandal. For the moment his lordship was struck from the Navy list, had even had his military honors stripped and his banner kicked down the steps of Westminster Abbey. It was rumored the South Americans were still paying him a princely sum. The flamboyant Cochrane had already reconnoitered the port of Callao and taken two of the Don's treasure ships.

"I expect we shall see *Blonde* within the fortnight, you are not to worry," Blackwell said. She would be concerned for her kin, not for Lord Cochrane and his exploits. "I trust she will not be too knocked about. What do you think of this tiny ship now?"

Blackwell was proud of the little vessel Mercedes had once maligned for her size. *Albion* had weathered the Horn just as well as could be expected. He had repairs to complete that would not take upwards of two weeks.

"She is a good, weatherly sea-boat," Mercedes said, in a gentle, mocking tone. "And fast. Very fast, if she is well handled."

"I'll handle you, Miss."

He was propped on an elbow, leaning over her, preparing to kiss her thoroughly. She returned his kisses, but he felt her discomfort. She kept that one arm hugged to her chest.

"Mercy, sweetheart, close your eyes. And put your arms over your head."

"Oh no! Then it would be you who needs to keep your eyes shut."

They stared at one another. Blackwell gently grasped her left wrist. "Are you going to obey me?"

She moved her arms over her head, a protest still on her lips, until Blackwell grasped both her wrists in a firm grip. She surrendered, turning her face into their outstretched arms, and shut her eyes. Blackwell kissed her lids, and her lips, and along her jaw. He put one large hand over the scarred flesh of her chest, and Mercedes fetched a deep sigh.

He kissed a line down her throat and collarbone, to the middle of her chest, and then took her nipple in his mouth. Blackwell was alternately gentle and aggressive, licking and sucking. She gasped, and that pleased him. At last he moved away, and lifting his hand he put a tender kiss on her scarred flesh, then looked up at her.

Mercedes' eyes were tightly shut, and from the corners tears leaked out. Blackwell was frightened, if he had distressed and offended her, made her cry, he didn't know what he would do. Go away and shoot himself, probably. He let go her wrists, hastening to push himself off her.

“Wait,” she said, opening her eyes. Her arms came about his shoulders, and she clutched him between her thighs. “Aren’t you going to finish what you started?”

It was probably the sweetest phrase he’d ever heard. He told her she was his dearest life, his greatest love, and he dove into her flesh. She arched up to meet him, allowing her wounded chest to rub against his. Mercedes clung to him, making him feel like he had at twenty.

“I won’t break, I promise you.”

At fifty-seven Blackwell was a long way past the vigor of youth, but he had a great deal of will and determination. Her words, the heavenly feel of her, her love and acceptance, brought forth his best efforts. He fancied he did please her, by the strength of her contractions against his body, and the way she nearly bit his shoulder when stifling her cries.

He held her a moment, and then started for the second time to shift his weight from her.

“Must you leave me so soon? I never have liked it, and now there is no need...”

He looked down at her a little dubious. “I shall collapse on you in a moment, you have worn me out so.” Yet he would do anything she wished. “Handsomely, now.”

She flattened one leg against the cot, he rolled in that direction, and clasping her against him, he brought her uppermost. Where would he be if she had reacted differently, cried and cursed him? He hugged Mercedes to his chest, pushing inside her again, as though they’d just become lovers.

“You are a very commanding woman of late. Have you noticed?”

This earned him a smile.

“Thank you, darling. For commanding me. And making me feel whole again, or at least that it does not matter to you that I am not.”

Blackwell was too stunned by her perception to speak and he only held her, for a brief and precious time.

Almost immediately after anchoring, the *Blonde* sent a boat across to *Albion* to request Doctor Sparrman come aboard at his earliest convenience to consult with Mr. McNeath. When Captain Blackwell asked Mr. Whittemore whether it would be inconvenient if he and Mrs. Blackwell were to attend, the midshipman answered, "Not in the least inconvenient, sir, I should think."

Captain Blackwell's gig was lowered into the water a short while later, with Doctor Sparrman and his medical accoutrement, and great bundles of fresh provisions Mercedes insisted on giving to the *Blonde's* gunroom. They were all anxious for who might require the doctor, but Captain Blackwell would never have questioned Mr. Whittemore. "I don't believe he should have answered so casual if it had to do with your children," he privately reassured Mercedes.

They were welcomed about the *Blonde* by mostly smiling, though worn, thin, and pale faces. Captain Blackwell stopped with Captain Verson on the weather side of the quarterdeck, while Mercedes, after greeting the officers, moved off to the taffrail where Aloka and Emma stood together.

"What is that red rash upon Mama's face?" Emma said very low, as she approached.

Aloka made a little ahem sound. "Father's beard."

"Oh!"

Emma said nothing more, though she looked disapproving. And then she could not contain herself, she gave a little skip and met Mercedes and fell into her arms.

After kissing Aloka on both cheeks, Mercedes said, "You have been unwell, my dear?"

Aloka was not in uniform, he had not been officially admitted back to duty, and his hair resembled that of a hedge-pig.

"A fever, dear Ma'am. The doctor believes it was a contagion I must have picked up in that filthy cell. You are not to be concerned, however, for your daughter saved me."

This was said in a cheerful tone but Mercedes, gazing from Aloka to Emma, was not deceived. Tears filled her eyes.

"I hope Doctor Sparrman's being sent for did not make you uneasy, Mama. It is poor, dear old Kapihe."

"He has a stomach complaint," Aloka said.

"Yes, and because of that, and for the sake of the King's people, and so Aloka might recuperate, we are thinking of taking lodgings ashore. What do you suppose Papa shall say to it?"

An honest answer would have been, he should say they were the pair of them both demanding and commanding women. Mercedes only remarked that she would speak to Captain Blackwell.

"A peculiar case, is it not colleague? A very peculiar, I should even say curious case."

The surgeon Mr. McNeath said this to Doctor Sparrman after a great many glasses of wine, while they sat apart from the rest of the company on the patio of the Blackwell's shore residence. There had been a grand supper, with many of *Blonde's* and *Albion's* officers in attendance, all four Blackwells, of course, and Lord Cochrane with his new wife, and several of his officers.

"Indeed, one hesitates to identify the complaint as typhus, with only the one sufferer." Doctor Sparrman tapped his cigar so the long train of ash clinging to it fell to the dirt floor. "For which we may give our thanks to the Almighty."

Doctor Sparrman had confirmed Mr. McNeath's diagnosis of Kapihe, much to the surgeon's relief. The chief suffered a bilious complaint and needed to be tapped, it was not typhus.

"Captain Blackwell told me Mr. Blackwell discarded his filthy clothing on the beach before the fortress of Santa Cruz," Doctor Sparrman said, "and later washed in the waters of the bay. Perhaps, colleague, we must reconsider how the disease is transmitted. Were it by tainted airs, that young woman should have long since perished." Doctor Sparrman made the faintest nod toward where Emma sat with Aloka, and Lord and Lady Cochrane.

"And the patient himself recovers well." In a very low voice Mr. McNeath added, "They have a reputation for brute resistance."

"Black savages." Doctor Sparrman nodded, a note of relish in his accented English. The old doctor harbored a respect for warriors, his ancestors having been of the Viking caste. "Let us hope Mr. Kapihe is similarly constituted, that he may withstand his operation. The Polynesians believe the soul, the center of life, resides in the stomach rather than the heart. Imagine the poor man's horror to have his soul tapped, as we mean to do."

"Thank you for your most generous offer," Aloka said to Lord Cochrane, in another corner of the patio. "I shall communicate it to Captain and Mrs. Blackwell."

"Please do," Lord Cochrane said.

Aloka and his lordship were behaving as if they had not been on the point of landing one another facers at their last meeting. Everyone was being decidedly civil, though Aloka could tell by Emma's stiff posture some of the company did not please her. He wondered how she'd taken Lord Cochrane's invitation to visit his country estate, a gift from the Chilean government. Aloka doubted less what her reaction to the offer of employment would be, that he'd received privately from the new admiral, for a command of his own in Chile's Navy.

"I much doubt my father, or any of us, shall move before Kapihe's operation though, sir."

"Oh, certainly." Lord Cochrane bowed.

There was nothing of shame or consciousness in his face, for his intrusion after that other surgery in the Blackwell's London residence. Aloka believed Lord Cochrane wouldn't have bothered with any of them, had it not been for the Chilean Navy's great need.

Emma and Aloka were alone on the deserted patio. In the mild Valparaiso evening, with the smell of lemon blossoms in the air from a grove of trees bordering the cottage, Emma sat, discontented, alongside Aloka. She had found the two houses in the port village, one occupied by the Hawaiians and the other by her family, and done the negotiation of terms with the land holder. Her father had judged it too taxing an effort for Mercedes to undertake, and had given Emma to understand if she wished for a shore residence, she'd best arrange it herself. She did know the Spanish, after all.

In spite of all this, and what she'd lived through on the *Blonde* with Aloka, Emma found she was still looked upon as just a girl. Katherine Cochrane, with her great bovine eyes, who was exactly Emma's own age was accorded more respect than she: apparently because of that particular bond between man and wife. Emma very much doubted Katherine had been more intimate with her ginger whiskered admiral than she had been with Aloka. She reached out and took Aloka's hand.

The flock of guests had long since departed, and her parents had retired. Emma pretended she hadn't seen Captain Blackwell lift Mercedes' hand to his lips, and the melting look he gave her as he steered her into their bedchamber. She would have thought, by their age, and with the operation Mercedes had endured, all that would be over. But it seemed her father was as importunate as ever. It never occurred to Emma to set any blame or criticism at Mercedes' door. There were certain things she could not see; any fault in her mother was one, nor the resemblance between father and son that struck everyone else so strongly.

Aloka squeezed her hand. "What do you make of this house party of Lord Cochrane's?"

"I would really rather drink bilge water than spend a week in the country with those two. But why do you ask me now, after you promoted the plan so to Mama and Papa?"

She let go Aloka's hand.

"You put me in mind of dear Ed just now." Aloka grinned at her. "I have a particular reason for wishing to travel out to this plantation. And it ain't for the company of his lordship and his lady—"

"You were very charming to her tonight."

"I know better than to bring the quarterdeck to the supper table. I am already cried out against enough as a goddamn savage."

Emma smiled, and gave Aloka an arch look.

"Admiral Cochrane says it is a two days journey by mule to the property," Aloka said. "If we contrive to travel separately, with one of the country people to guide us, we shall have two days and a night to ourselves."

Emma sat considering. Certainly Mercedes would not choose to go. She was delighted with the house, the only one sufficiently grateful for her efforts in Emma's opinion. There were flower, herb, and vegetable gardens for her to walk in, and her own and her neighbors' orchards. Local women had been hired to cook and clean for them, and Mercedes was content. Valparaiso was much like her native Monterey, she'd said. As for Captain Blackwell, he might put up with an English nag but he would never countenance a foreign mule.

"You are a clever savage," she said.

Aloka lunged at her. Somehow in the sequence that followed Emma ended up in his lap, kissing him.

Kapihe's operation was to take place in the Hawaiian's Valparaiso abode. Chilean houses of the middling sort had only one window, and that was in the main room. His surgery would be done on the *estrada*, a raised wooden platform that ran along one side of the long room, where the ladies were accustomed to sit and visit. The medical men were already there, methodically arranging their instruments; lancets, retractors, gags, graduated collecting bowls.

Captain Blackwell and Aloka and the ladies were present, though Captain Blackwell hoped to miss the operation itself. His little group had been particularly summoned by Kapihe, and could not absent themselves.

Kapihe came in and stretched obligingly out on the *estrada*, with his head in Li'liah's lap. He was clad only in a loincloth. Captain Blackwell believed this was for the sake of the sensitive Europeans, for Kapihe would otherwise have been naked for such an important event.

"Come closer *Ali'i* Blackwell, and Aloka, my son." Kapihe looked at them with an anxious gaze.

"How do you do, Kapihe? Are you ready to trust yourself to the white doctors?" Captain Blackwell asked in the native tongue. He very much hoped the doctors might give relief.

"My life is in your hands," Kapihe said with perfect trust, nodding and smiling at the medical men. "Should I go over the rainbow this day, I wish Aloka Blackwell to take my place as Hawaii's admiral. He may in the course of years, even if I do not. That is my wish."

The group of Hawaiians collected round to view the operation nodded approvingly, all saving Kuanoa, who wore a froward, grave expression. Kapihe made known more of his wishes, in the same fashion as their sovereign King Kamehameha II had done; except

Kapihe's last will and testament was not written down. The Hawaiians, every man and woman listening, could most probably have repeated the old chief's words exactly, using even the same tone and inflection.

The doctors moved forward when Kapihe had said his peace. Captain Blackwell and his ladies, Aloka, and some of the Hawaiian contingent retreated to the entry hallway. After some hushed general conversation, Captain Blackwell took Aloka's arm and urged him outside. When Emma began to follow them, Captain Blackwell gave her a stern look that made her blush and turn back to Mercedes.

A good road passed in front of the Hawaiians' cottage, bordered with brick made locally, and dropping in height on either side to the cultivated ground surrounding it. Captain Blackwell and Aloka walked along with pleasant views of fig, lemon, pomegranate, peach, pear, and apple trees; and the well tended *chacras*, or garden plots, of the landholders thereabouts. Valparaiso Bay could be seen from many vantage points.

"God preserve Kapihe, sir," Aloka said. "Can he have been serious about this admiral of Hawaii business? Could I be installed over other men's heads, having never been in their Service?"

Captain Blackwell considered. His son seemed to believe, as was perhaps common in the young, that he had all the answers. Matters of late had become more complicated than Captain Blackwell could have wished, with his children and in his professional life. Yet he had set himself up for a diplomat, and he supposed he must begin at once. He had a strong suspicion the Sandwich Islanders weren't the only ones with an eye on Aloka for military service.

"Very serious indeed, I should say." Captain Blackwell gave Aloka a long stare. "Though I know little enough of the size of their fleet, or its' organization, I do know that the *ali'i* are much like feudal kings in their powers. Each a state unto his own, prior to Kamehameha the First at least."

They halted on a rise for a moment before a sweeping view of the bay. Below bread was baking in many earthen ovens, and the homely smell drifted up to them. Aloka looked pale, not yet up to his former weight. Captain Verson did right to put him ashore for a fortnight to rest and recuperate.

"This is a most gracious land," Aloka said, studying the richly planted sloping ground reaching down to the sea.

"Do you remember Kauai at all?"

Aloka smiled. "Bits and pieces. I...I saw my mother's face when I was ill. It frightened me somehow."

"It was only the fever, son."

"I rather remember the house on O'ahu, with you and the dear ma'am, and Edward. And those odd old white people, and black Saunders."

Captain Blackwell bowed his head, trying to hide his grin. He felt obliged to correct him. "The old missionary couple Mr. and Mrs. Bing, and Saunders. A prime hand, for all she is a woman. I hope for Mercedes' sake she lives yet. They had a peculiar friendship." He paused. "So you are to visit Lord Cochrane at Quintero."

"Aye, sir, provided all goes well with Kapihe. Lord Cochrane is sending a man to act as guide. He has arranged for us to spend the one evening in route at the hacienda of a family by the name of Carrera. Emma shall not have to sleep out of doors."

Captain Blackwell grunted, he knew all this from Mercedes. He supposed Aloka had much on his mind, much to consider, but he gave him a lecture anyway on keeping a private log of the distances and directions they travelled. He advised him not to trust to the native guide. In case of accident or exigency, Aloka must be able to navigate back on his own.

Aloka listened and nodded respectfully.

Captain Blackwell took a deep breath. "It is Mercedes who gives leave for Emma to travel with you to Quintero. I have tried not to interfere with how she's brought up her children, for one thing she don't like it. For my part I can't fathom why either of you should cherish the company of Lord and Lady Cochrane." He took Aloka's arm momentarily, as they turned their steps back toward the Hawaiian's cottage. "However it might be, I would not interfere in your affairs, now you are a grown man, but that Mercedes has asked me to speak to you. This love, honor, and obey business runs both ways, do you see?"

Back at the cottage a tremendous quantity of fluid had been drained from Kapihe, and though he'd suffered much during the procedure, the relief he felt was great. The doctors finished and asked him how he did. "*Maika'i, ho'o maika'i*" he exclaimed, which was translated to them as "Fine, bless you." Li'liah, much affected, kissed the old chief's forehead with tears streaming down her cheeks. The last thing any of the Hawaiian contingent wanted was to lose one more of their own.

The native guide Lord Cochrane commissioned, Pedro Gregorio, was a man much like Mr. Martinez; short of stature, lean, with a lined, leathery, and tanned face. His humble attire belied the fact Don Pedro was a substantial land holder. He wore a linen shirt and cloth breeches, piped in colored listing at the seams and open at the knee over cloth gaiters and homemade shoes, the whole topped with a great pancho. He and his sons managed their own estates, and that of Quintero, gifted to Chile's new admiral.

He spoke in respectful and formal Spanish to Mercedes and Emma, while Captain Blackwell and Aloka stood by uncomprehending. He was invited to take *maté* tea and cake. Out of compassion Don Pedro made a short repast, the young people clearly anxious to begin the journey. The pleasantries concluded, he lead them to the stables belonging to the Blackwell's landlord, where he'd left his animals under the care of an adolescent boy.

It was not after all to be mules, and Aloka was glad of it. He was no horseman, and he feared he should be even more ridiculous mounted upon a mule. Emma on the other hand could command anything upon four legs. She immediately bonded with her rangy beast, the best of the three animals. What they lacked in beauty; being short, thin, and hairy; the little native horses made up for in wit.

"He says they are much like dogs," Emma told Aloka, turning in her saddle from chatting with Don Pedro.

Aloka listened to their Spanish conversation as they passed along the Almendral and then through the outlying regions of Valparaiso. This land was all under cultivation. Melons, pumpkins, cabbages, beans and potatoes and maize. Fruit trees of every variety: apples, pears, almonds, peaches, oranges, olives and quince. One of the words Aloka managed to distinguish in Emma and Don Pedro's discourse was *esposo*, husband, when Emma threw a significant glance in his direction. She was apparently telling Don Pedro a tale.

It was just as well, they were traveling together and meant to be bed-fellows. If Aloka had his way, husband would be no tale. He began to ponder on the possibility of convincing one of the local priests to marry them. From the reputation the English gave Catholic priests, it should only be a matter of price.

Aloka was shaken out of these ignoble thoughts when Emma called to him. They had entered upon the track that would take them to their resting place for the evening, at Viña a la Mar. He asked her to inquire of Don Pedro if they might make a halt, and he took out his pocket book and pencil. They stopped beside a high outcropping of rock, stretching out before and below them was a wide plain. Aloka made a quick sketch of the place and noted the time and their heading. He turned his book for Emma to see.

She narrowed her eyes regarding it. "How Edward would laugh."

"To be sure, I'm no great fist. None of us are compared to him. How I miss dear Ed, there is no one like him."

"Don't remind me, it will make me low, and I had much rather enjoy the ride. I should love a good gallop."

But for the first part of the journey there were none of those larks, for the way was through steep and rocky hills, and along precipices. The horses and a solitary mule carrying their dunnage and provisions and acting as *madrina*—a sort of godmother guide —showed their worth in sure-footedness rather than speed. They were always in sight of the sea, and with the towering Andes on one hand and the ocean on the other, the track seemed easy enough to keep. Aloka was a dutiful being, however. As he'd agreed to his father's council he periodically made notations of their course.

The countryside around Viña a la Mar was a pleasant contrast to the rocky rugged shore. A vast plain opened up to them, extensively planted in grapes. Beyond the vineyards the hills were covered in fine grass, upon which sheep and cattle grazed.

"Much like Devonshire," Emma said.

"Except for those great mountains."

At ninety miles distance from the sea-shore the Andean cordillera loomed up, piercing the ever present cloud layer near the summits.

"Oh no, nothing like that in England."

Shortly before dusk they arrived at the country estate of the Carrera family, a modest house, slightly larger but much in the style of their Valparaiso shore residence. They were cordially received, and at once Emma was offered milk flavored with cinnamon to brace her up after the fatigue of the journey.

Aloka thought at first they were a household made up solely of women. A venerable mother and three daughters, the loveliest among them was recently made a widow by Chile's war for independence. Aloka and Emma were given an excellent supper after the local fashion, and afterwards a brother of the family came in. Seventeen year old Jose Antonio had not yet become involved in politics, as had the rest of the men of his family. He had come in for the dancing, and to practice his English upon Aloka.

Aloka was only too happy to oblige, Emma being wholly taken up with the ladies. It gave him an odd feeling to sit so long mum and dumb. He had an interesting talk with Jose Antonio, who spoke to him of the surrounding countryside, and the distance yet to be travelled to Lord Cochrane's estate. It was from Jose Antonio that Aloka learned, much to his relief, that he and Emma were to pass the night in a little stone cottage high up in the vineyard.

Before they proceeded to this earthly paradise, like any well mannered guests, Emma and Aloka had to participate in the evening's entertainment planned by their hosts. This consisted in a dance called the *cuando*, which was first performed by Jose Antonio and one of his sisters, while another sister played the guitar and sang.

"It represents a sort of loving quarrel between those who are meant to be together," Jose Antonio explained.

Aloka and Emma were made to partner in an attempt at the dance. Aloka, holding himself very upright and stamping his feet in imitation of the *zapatear*, sang the words of the song Jose Antonio had translated for him.

When, when,
when, my love, when,
when will the day come, that
joyful morn,
when they bring the two of
us hot chocolate in bed.

Aloka thought Emma so graceful, so full of spirit, beauty, and strength, but it was his powers of imitation of the favorite song and dance that earned the most vocal praise. Aloka glanced quickly at Emma, afraid she might resent the caressing ways of the Chilean ladies. Still it was Emma to whom Aloka gave his arm when they were at last allowed to take their leave.

They went out into the soft night carrying two lanterns, and escorted by Jose Antonio, Don Pedro having gone to pass the night at the rancho of nearby relatives. On the way to the stone cottage in the vineyard, fifteen minutes' walking brought them to it, Jose Antonio explained to Aloka the track to take to a charming waterfall and pool. Aloka wished to visit the spot next morning, before proceeding on their journey.

Jose Antonio watched with a look of envy as the couple entered the little dwelling and closed the door behind them. His was not the only gaze in the vineyard following Aloka and Emma into the stone cottage.

The cottage was of one room only, which served as a combined dining, sleeping, and sitting area. Their canvas bags with their clothing and other possessions had been brought in earlier. Aloka was hanging a blanket from the rafters to screen off an area for washing and to place the chamber pot. With shaking hands Emma pulled linens and another blanket from her satchel to make up the bed. Four stakes were driven into the earthen floor, with leather thongs tied across them, and a thinly stuffed mattress rested atop.

"The water is ready for you," Aloka said.

Emma straightened from making the bed. She gave him an awkward smile, pulled a dressing gown from among her clothing, and slipped into the washing space. Until now, as she washed the dirt of the journey from her skin, she had not felt tired. But she'd been under various strains throughout the day, not the least of which had been the rather tortuous evening they'd just spent with their hosts. Emma's emotions before the Carrera sisters' envy, and their admiration of Aloka, were complicated. He was a fine figure of a man, with a character and personal attributes to match. They believed him all hers, but at that moment she doubted she was woman enough to make and keep him so. For courage, Emma repeated to herself what Mercedes had told her: "All men really want is what is different to themselves."

Aloka met her with a brilliant smile, rising from where he'd been sitting on the edge of the bed, wearing only trousers. He led her to the bed, squeezed her hands, and disappeared round the partition where he made a quick wash. He told her that long ago, when he was a little boy and had bathed in the Pacific ocean and rivers of the Hawaiian Islands, he'd resented extremely this business of washing from a bucket.

"You have the advantage of me," Aloka said, emerging round the blanket. "You've seen me without clothes, I never have you."

"You may look now, if you wish." She'd taken off her dressing gown, and lain down under the bedclothes nude. She might be green, but she wasn't stupid.

With a seaman's care Aloka placed the lantern on an overturned barrel that served as a bedside table and lowered the flame of the oil lamp. He raised the bedclothes, and eased in beside her.

"Lord, my love, you are the most..."

Aloka pushed the bedclothes from her then, raised himself over her, gazing down at her body as he moved his hands underneath her and brought her up against him. In the next moments he covered her with kisses. Emma sighed and gave herself over to him, she felt his hands, his mouth, touching and caressing and kissing and suckling. She opened her legs to him when he put one hand between her thighs, and stroked her in the most tender, intimate way.

Emma opened her eyes and looked at him, feeling moist and melted at her core, and longing for him to do...she did not know quite what.

Aloka's face was serious, and his voice low and husky. "If it hurts too much, tell me and I shall stop."

He heaved himself over her, Emma opened her legs around him. Aloka began kissing her again, and at the same time she felt his hard flesh nuzzling her. She'd seen him naked before, but certain parts of him had never looked then as they did now. Emma was a little horrified; she could not imagine how it would fit.

When he pushed inside her, she was sure it would not work. The pain was such that she whimpered in spite of a resolution not to. Aloka immediately stopped his movements atop her.

"Should I..."

"No, darling."

She could barely choke out her answer, but she raised her knees and clasped him with her legs. Aloka groaned and sank deeper into her flesh. Somehow when he was all the way inside her, as Emma felt he must be now, it was less painful. The beginning part had been excruciating, but she now felt she could endure it until it was over. She stroked a hand down his chest, feeling his muscles winding and unwinding as he moved over her, and the beginnings of something other than discomfort stirred in her womb.

His face was once again very grave as she gazed up at him. His expression, the grunting sounds, it was almost as though he were in pain. Aloka opened his eyes, and gently caressed her cheek.

"It is not happening for you, is it my dearest love?"

Emma returned him a blank stare, not knowing what 'it' could mean. She pulled him against her, he thrust powerfully into her twice more, and then suddenly jerked himself away with a muted bellow. That was not pleasant either, to be so much one with him, and then suddenly bereft. Emma gasped, there was something wet on her belly.

Aloka rose with another groan.

"Do not stir, my love, I will be right with you."

He went around the partition. Emma stared at his feet and calves beyond the edge of the hanging blanket. She thought in a rather disordered way that even his feet were manly.

She'd been quite obedient. She was still lying there uncovered, startled and wet, when he returned with two towels.

"Do not use the same one..." Aloka wiped his seed from her flat belly. He handed her the second towel.

He wrung out and hung both soiled flannels in the washing space, went to the makeshift table beside the bed and doused the light, before climbing back in with her. Aloka immediately took her in his arms.

"So you are thinking, that is what all the fuss is about?"

She didn't know what to say, wondering how he could have guessed her thoughts so exactly. Emma hugged him tighter.

"It will get better, I promise you. Much, much better."

Now she was worried. Had it not brought him pleasure, had it not been what he'd wanted and experienced with other women?

"Weren't you pleased? Was I not...good with you," she said in a small voice.

"Emma, my dearest, dearest love. You made me feel like a prince, an absolute king! No. I meant, in future, I hope and trust, my love, you shall feel exactly what I do."

"Oh, how I hope so too!"

He made a noise of approval, and they were content and silent after that. She turned in his arms and lay with her back to him. This was the best part so far.

"Aloka?"

"Uh!"

"Forgive me, darling, you were asleep."

"Well I'm not now. What is it?"

Neither his tone, nor the gentle touch of his hand was harsh.

"I was just wondering when we can be intimate again?"

Aloka chuckled, and kissed her shoulder.

"Tomorrow, earliest, I should think, my little minx. I don't want you to be hurt, here."

He spread his fingers over her womb.

"But...but, those bumboat women. They lie with one man after another, do they not? Why—"

"Those poor women are used, my love. You are to be loved and cherished."

"Must you coddle me so?"

"Most certainly. When you are more used to me, than we shall see. Go to sleep now, I shall wake you early. I want to see this Lagunilla Jose Antonio told us of. I want a bath, and a frisk. With you. Naked. In a pool."

Two hills away Kuanoa made his camp. He'd been tempted to take Emma when they'd walked out of the main house through the vineyard. But then he would have had to kill both Aloka and the young man belonging to the place. That would set the local people on his trail, a thing he did not at all desire. He'd followed them closely enough to hear their plan to visit a secluded pool next day, and Kuanoa decided to wait. It would be easy enough to kill the Blackwell whelp. He'd brought with him a killing club of his own making. The boy was still sickly, green, a puppy. By the time word reached Valparaiso, if it ever did, he should be long gone into the mountains with her. Kuanoa whiled away the remainder of the evening imagining all the things he would do to Emma once he captured her, and had broken her leg so she couldn't run away.

Aloka was up early next morning saddling the two stringy horses to the sound of birdsong, but he hadn't preceded the Carrera's servants, who were already about their morning tasks. With the lead ropes of the horses' bridles in his hand, Aloka stuck his head into the cooking house.

"*Buenos dias, Señor*," one of the good women said.

"*Bueños dias, Doña. Uh, chocolate? Mi mujer, chocolate.*"

This was greeted with a flow of Spanish and indulgent smiles from the women in the kitchen. They produced a pewter mug, quite large and with a hinged lid, and briskly filled it with chocolate enough for two.

He plodded up the hill to the stone cottage, the horses behind him, with the chocolate clutched in his fist. Despite his dark skin, the people here in Chile considered him a thoroughbred Englishmen. At home in England, in spite of his perfect British accent, he was nothing more than a Black Savage. Aloka thought of this as a mere curiosity, such things could weigh little with him this morning. As long as that dearest of women continued to love and accept him, the rest of the world could think what it would.

Aloka imagined making a life in this gracious country with Emma, and a command of his own in the Chilean Navy. He tied the horses leads to a ring driven into a wood block in the lee of the house, and turned to the cottage door with a beating heart. This little outing would give him a chance to tell her of Lord Cochrane's offer. Life was bursting with possibility. He longed to share everything with her, to make her feel that pleasure in intimacy he experienced most of all.

Emma was alone in the cottage when she woke, and she perfectly remembered Aloka's plan for an early outing. She felt slightly bruised and sore, and she should have preferred to lie abed. Then she thought of that simpering Lady Cochrane, she was surely as tough as her, and that was sufficient motivation to rise and wash. She gathered up her riding clothes and came back to the bed to dress, frowning down at a blood stain on Mercedes' bed linen. Emma stepped over and threw the latch on the door, so she should not be surprised, even by Aloka, as she put herself and a few other things in the room in order.

She had even packed their canvas bags, when the cottage door was tried.

"Is it you, Aloka?"

"Yes, my love."

Emma opened the door. She was so used to life aboard the *Blonde*, she forgot she need not be concerned out here in the middle of the Chilean countryside. Aloka came in with a wide grin, beautiful white teeth flashing against his dark skin. He praised her for her continued caution, and her industry in gathering up their dunnage. Emma caressed his cheek, he was new shaved. She was delighted with the chocolate he brought her.

Emma and Aloka sat side by side on the *estrada*, trading sips of the delicious chocolate tempered with milk and cinnamon. They kissed, and said rather stupid, endearing things to one another. When they'd finished the shared breakfast, they took care of a few domestic chores. Aloka carried out the buckets of night soil and unused water, and Emma rinsed the pewter mug at a rain cask outside. Together they loaded the two horses with their baggage—the better to be quickly away with Don Pedro later—and with some regret left the little cottage that had witnessed their first union.

The beautiful lagoon proved compensation for their early departure from the cottage. Lagunilla was formed by a tributary of the river Aconcagua, where crystalline water pooled in a natural stone basin, fed by a cascade tumbling over boulders above, and running away into the forest below. A thirty minute ride at a sedate pace, always climbing steadily uphill, brought them to the spot. Aloka hobbled the beasts in the manner he'd seen Pedro Gregorio do the day previous, in a grassy clearing below the lagoon.

"Come along, now."

Aloka held out a hand to her. He'd unsaddled the horses, and piled their packs and the horse gear together. He tucked one of the sheepskin saddle rugs under his arm, looking excessively pleased with himself. There was a low rumbling sound and the ground beneath them vibrated strangely. Emma jumped toward Aloka.

"Earthquake," he said. "There, its over."

They'd experienced many minor tremors since arriving in Chile, and when they were sure it was over they went hand in hand to the bathing pool. Aloka dropped the blanket at the base of an evergreen tree, in a grove fringing one side of the pool. He had his clothes off in a trice, ran toward the pool, and with a great leap and war whoop somersaulted in.

"Cold, is it?" Emma asked when he surfaced. Still fully dressed, she minced up to the water's edge. "It looks cold."

"'Course it's cold, my love, its melted snow from those grand mountains," Aloka called to her. "But it ain't worse than the Wandle, and it's considerably cleaner."

Emma pursed her lips. She'd been taught to swim in the river outside their door at Merton Place. Mercedes had never allowed her to swim alone with Aloka, but he had always been there in the water. An expert swimmer, ready to assist her, at the same time jeering and laughing at her, and calling instructions.

"Faint hearted, is it?" Aloka cried out.

She gave him a sharp look, ran back to where his clothes were and doffed her own. Emma raced forward and dove into the pool, almost upon his head. They were like river otters then, swimming, diving, jumping in while holding hands. They did indeed have a frisk. Aloka kicked down to the bottom of the pool, and judged it to be three or four fathoms deep. He climbed high upon the granite boulders on the cascade side of the lagoon, beat his chest and yelled, and jumped off into a neat swan dive. Emma tried jumping from the lower rocks, but she didn't care for the sensation of water forced up her nose.

Aloka surfaced in back of her from his last dive. He reached out a hand and touched the goose flesh on her shoulder.

"You are cold, and I am winded. Care to get out, my love?"

They scrambled out of the pool, and Aloka brought the sheepskin rug into the sun near the water's edge, and close against the protection of the tumbled boulders.

"Come, Emma, I'll warm you."

She was standing there with her arms clutched over her breasts shivering, and thinking of running to put on her clothes. Instead she took his outstretched hand, and let him lay her down upon the rug. He stretched out over her, the long muscles of his legs and torso pressed against her. Emma felt warm and shielded. Then he started kissing her, and she forgot the cold.

"Emma, I want to try...will you turn over, my love."

Emma opened her eyes, looked up at him. She'd been waiting for him to pierce her, for the pain, and then the pleasure she trusted him to make follow. Emma's eyes refocused away from his face and widened. With all the strength of her arms and legs she shoved Aloka from her, rolling towards him as she did.

The force with which Kuanoa brought the killing club down on the spot where they'd lain jarred the weapon from his hand. Aloka and Emma jumped to their feet. Aloka gave a swiping kick to the club with the side of his foot, sending it spinning into the pool. Made of hard wood, it immediately sank. He pushed Emma behind him with one arm.

"Run, Emma. Don't stop, don't look back. Go!"

Emma bolted, scrambling up over the rocks in the direction of the cascade. She could not run the faster way round the lagoon without passing Kuanoa. She crawled out as far as she could along the edge of the rocks, and then she jumped into the lagoon, came up and stroked for all she was worth to the opposite side of the pool. Hauling herself out, panting, Emma glanced back at the men.

They were circling one another, Aloka crouched with one arm extended toward Kuanoa, as though to keep him off. Kuanoa was jumping about, splay legged, slapping his thighs and displaying a distended tongue. Emma sprinted for the horses, her heart beating painfully. Once there she reached into her pack with shaking hands for clothing, and stopped.

Her only thought up to then had been run, dress, ride. But where was she to go for help? To the Carrera women and young Jose Antonio? A half hour ride to the hacienda, another half hour back. By then all would be over. And if Kuanoa were the victor? The thought made her blood cold. He would come after her, he'd come this far. Aloka must survive, not he.

There was Aloka's sword belt with the light cavalry sword and purser's dirk in it's sheath. She took up the sword belt and moved back through the trees in the direction of the men, a vague notion of throwing the sword to Aloka forming in her mind. As she neared Emma heard the sounds of close combat, grunts, and the smack of flesh on flesh. She halted and watched Aloka land a series of blows. He was no stranger to a close fight, but Emma remembered her father saying the Pacific islanders practiced wrestling from boyhood.

And then Aloka did not retreat fast enough after closing to engage, and Kuanoa caught him in a cross-buttock move. He threw Aloka to the ground and landed atop his chest. Aloka was no light weight but Kuanoa was heavier, and he got both hands round Aloka's neck.

Emma was close enough to make out his words, "...weak *Haole*," she understood the Hawaiian perfectly well. "You couldn't survive a week in those mountains. I can. I will take her into those mountains, where no one will follow. No one will find us. I'll fuck her until the fierce spirit goes out of her eyes, and beat her until the only will she knows is my own."

She didn't want to hear any more, she didn't want to see any more. Aloka's face was turning purple, his tongue lolling from his mouth. With her heart in her throat, Emma realized the sword would not do: she might injure Aloka. She slipped the knife from its sheath, dropping the sword and sword belt. Emma fixed the blade, spiked end out, clenched her teeth and ran forward.

She launched herself onto Kuanoa's back. He reared back in astonishment, driving the knife she aimed at the base of his skull even farther in. Blood sprayed into her face, bathed her hand. Hot, horrible smell. It covered Aloka's face and chest too. Kuanoa sagged. Emma let go her terrible grip and slid off Kuanoa's slick back. She crawled to the edge of the pool and tumbled in. Underwater Emma let her breath out in a prolonged scream.

Aloka spat out blood, choking and gasping for breath. He pushed the heavy weight off him and rolled onto all fours. He remained there head down like a dog, sucking air and gagging up a mixture of chocolate, blood, and bile. His breath returned at last and he looked up, blood dripping from his hair and upper body. Emma's head popped up out in the lagoon, their eyes met. He caught a flash of her horror and pain and she instantly sank down again.

He turned his head to look at Kuanoa. Dead. Thank God. Thank Emma. She'd saved him, again. Aloka struggled to his feet, stumbled to the pool, and tipped in. He kicked down deep under water, and scrubbed the blood from his skin and hair. When he surfaced Aloka spotted Emma at the far end of the lagoon, bobbing up out of the water and then sinking down.

He swam the length of the pool underwater, to further cleanse himself, and came up just in back of her.

"Get out now, Emma. Come."

She was trembling. Aloka put his body between her and Kuanoa.

"Don't look," he said. Though she'd not obeyed him in anything yet, and saved them both.

He put his arm around her waist and pulled her along to their packs. Aloka had to dress her, putting a shift over her head and doing up the laces of her corset, she was shaking too much to do it. Her teeth clacked together. When Emma was clothed right down to her boots, he shouldered the packs, picked up the saddles and rugs and led her to the horses.

The dear animals greeted them with big eyed, innocent gazes. Still naked, Aloka quickly saddled both the horses. He took the hobble from his own animal's legs, and untied the leather thongs securing a length of native line, the *laza*, to the saddle.

"Where are you going? You're not leaving me?" Emma spoke for the first time.

He took her in his arms. She did not cry, but she trembled as though she would shake to pieces.

"Listen now, listen. You did what you had to do. I am going to move the body. People come to this place, and we cannot leave it out in the open. Then I shall be with you at once."

Aloka looked into Emma's face. She was a practical, intelligent, even fierce woman. She'd just proved it. He willed her to summon up her reserves of strength. Emma nodded and moved away to her horse, leaning against it, her face turned from him. The poor dear soul. Once they were away from this place, that had seemed such a paradise but a half hour ago, he would stop and hold her for a long, long time.

He found his sword belt and sword on the ground near Kuanoa's body. The horse was restive, its ears twitching back and forth, snorting and blowing. The smell of blood was probably the reason why, there was certainly enough of it. The horse blanket Aloka brought to the pool edge was ruined with blood. He would have to compensate Don Pedro, or whoever owned it, the Chileans were particular about their equipage. He averted his face as he yanked out his knife, remembering the popping sound it had made going in. And then he rolled Kuanoa over onto the blanket, and looked into the face of obsession.

Sexual obsession had an ugly aspect. Kuanoa's tongue hung from his mouth, a terrible grimace on his face. Aloka had a flash of recognition; images carved on the prows of canoes. He bundled Kuanoa in the rug as they did bodies in their hammocks at sea, securing it round with twelve neat turns of the *laza*. The other end of the long braided hide line he knotted round the horse's neck, with his shirt and trousers beneath like mats. He led the animal forward.

They dragged the body to an enormous spill of boulders. He found an opening between rocks, and halted the horse. With much huffing and heaving, Aloka wedged the body into a crevice between earth and stone.

Straightening from the nasty work, sweating and blood smeared once more, the words of a Spanish toast came into his mind.

May no cross mark his remains,
May his burial ground remain unblessed,
And may he lack a loyal son to close his eyes in Christian rest.

Aloka sagged against the nearest boulder. He was not religious, but he'd been raised and grown to manhood in a Christian country. He knew with certainty where his loyalties lay, and he turned away from the burial place of an evil man: A traitor to the human race. He would proceed to Hawaii with that good man, his father. He would not separate Emma from the comfort of her family. Not now.

He tethered the horse to a low branch, and picking up his knife Aloka jumped into the pool to wash one last time. A moment later he hauled himself out, glaring at the blood pooled in hollows of the stone, wondering what he must do about it. Then a great cracking boom like the report of a ship of the line's broadside stunned him.

His horse screamed, a sound he'd never heard before, and tearing the lead rope free it galloped away. Aloka crouched for a moment, the earth unstable beneath his feet. A low loud rumbling sound persisted, and despite the still day the trees whipped violently back and forth as though in a strong gale. He took up his sword and sword belt with the knife he'd washed clean, and sprinted for the clearing where he'd left Emma.

She and her horse were huddled like children, their heads together, and they looked up at him with equally wild eyes.

"Earthquake. Big one."

It was still going on. The trees continued their tossing motion. Emma and Aloka found it hard to keep their feet, the ground undulating beneath them more than the deck of a ship at sea. They clustered together, Emma pressed against Aloka's chest, and both with a hand upon the horse. In the next moment they heard the whinnying call of Aloka's horse, the beast charged over to them, and they were four frightened creatures together.

When it was over, no more movement nor cracking, rumbling sound like the vengeance of the gods, Aloka detached himself to put on clothes.

Both spoke at once. "I will take you—" Aloka began, and Emma broke in with, "I want Mama."

Aloka and Emma mounted the poor shaken beasts and turned their heads to the Carrera's hacienda. There would be no going on to Lord Cochrane, they would return to Valparaiso. Emma needed her mama, and if Aloka were honest, he did too.

They rode past the stone cottage. The place that had sheltered them was a pile of stones and sticks thrown upon the ground, as though a giant hand had slapped the little structure down.

The main house, the cook house, and outbuildings at the Carrera's were in much the same tumbled down condition, though a barn was yet intact. Chimneys had fallen in and walls collapsed, and the toll should have been high in human life had the household still been abed. But they were all up about their business and Emma and Aloka found the Carrera women, Jose Antonio, and their servants clustered outside the ruin of their house.

Aloka immediately dismounted and, with the other men, began clearing the brick, tiles, wood and debris from the cook house entry. Three walls of the structure survived, though the roof had collapsed, but they removed the rubble and made it serviceable again. Then they all set about salvaging items from the main house; mattresses, cups, odd bits of furniture. Aftershocks shook the earth, and sent them scrambling away over the wreckage into the yard.

After one of these tremors Aloka took Jose Antonio and his mother aside.

"Don Pedro must be fully taken up with his own people. Emma and I shall return to Valparaiso on our own. She is most concerned for her Mama, and for our people there."

No one noticed the change in Emma, the earthquake was enough to explain her shaken withdrawn behavior. She came forward and shook hands, and exchanged kisses and well wishes, but it was clear she was as restless as the horses.

"I thought you would never come away," she said in an angry tone, once they'd departed.

Emma encouraged her animal into a gallop when they were out on the great plain, on a tract of level ground. Aloka had no choice but to spur up his horse and follow. The day previous there'd been peaceful herds of grazing sheep and cattle, today as they raced past they heard the constant lowing and bleating of the poor beasts.

"'Vast there, Emma!"

When he caught up to her, Aloka made her get down from her horse.

"Come, Emma. We cannot use the horses so, it is a day's riding in front of us, and we do not know what is ahead. How the land might have altered."

Emma looked at him after this scolding and burst into tears. He tied the horses with long leads so they could graze and recover their wind. Then Aloka took her hand, plopped down, and brought her onto his lap.

He held her for a long space while she sobbed. He even rocked her a little, and it reminded him of when she was an infant and they had all held baby Emma on their laps. Their first kiss had been a long, long time ago. Aloka murmured to her in an effort to reassure, calling her tender names, and stroking her hair.

The first thing Emma said when she could speak was, "How can I be anyone's little love after...after what I've done."

She gave him an almost defiant look and Aloka immediately felt his danger. How was he to help her understand the complex emotions of battle, of taking another life, when he did not comprehend them himself.

"All men feel what you feel, Emma. All men with a heart and a conscious. I've seen officers suffer it, the hands, our father, in fact. We all think, can I call myself a gentleman, would they love me at home if they knew?"

"But you were under orders. Murder. I've done murder."

"No. You killed a man who was murdering me, and he would have—"

"Please don't...don't say it. I shall never be able to un-hear his words, I shall never be able to un-see—"

"Men get up to great evil, that women should never be party to. But there is no use in pretending, and you must try to put the events of this morning away where they cannot hurt you."

"Is that what you, and Papa, and other fighting men do?"

"We try, my love, we do not always succeed. You must not speak of it, of course, but this does not mean you've done wrong. You defended yourself, and me, and what you did is between you and your god."

She was calmer then, and Aloka fancied he'd given her some comfort. Emma said she was ready to move on, and he made her swear she would not charge off again. Aloka was far from easy in his mind, Emma continued silent and haunted. He was ashamed to admit he was fearful lest she be afraid to be intimate with him again, that being what they'd been about when they were attacked. Those wretched things Kuanoa had said were enough to frighten a much more experienced woman. He thought of this on a level far below the surface, however. Outwardly he was taken up with the journey, and the changed countryside round them.

On a hill where the track hugged a sheer cliff face, they came round a blind switchback and found the way ahead blocked by a rock slide. The ledge was so narrow they could not turn the horses round, and were obliged to step them backwards until the path widened. It was a procedure the beasts did not care for, yet Aloka and Emma had reason to bless their sure-footedness, and their intelligent and tractable natures.

Once again at the base of the hill, they stopped to consider. Behind the precipitate path they'd backed down the land rose steeply, a great hill of boulders, loose rock and earth. They would find no good footing for horses by climbing higher, even for the nimble *madrina* mule it would have been an impossibility. On the other hand where the sea had broken violently at the base of the cliff the day before, there was now exposed beach.

"The sea has receded a prodigious way," Aloka said.

At the foot of the cliffs was a wide, wet stretch of sand and shell. The sea was breaking farther off shore, exposing rocks whose existence was unknown yesterday. Aloka and Emma exchanged a glance.

"There is really nothing else for it," he said, urging his horse downhill to shore, "though I don't like it above half."

They rode across that new beach, with its exposed sea life. Anemones, crustaceans, mollusks; the atmosphere was pungent for many of these creatures, and numerous small fish, were expiring.

Aloka gazed out to sea, it was most unnatural. "We need to step along lively, Emma. I want to get to higher ground."

Emma urged her horse forward and closer to the cliffs, and allowed the animal to seek its own path upward. Gaining a high plateau, they halted to rest the horses. Aloka checked his pocket book notations.

He picked up the trail again, and they rode on. At the ford of the river Margamarga, Emma rode down the crumpled banks to the spot where they'd crossed with Don Pedro. Aloka urged his mount forward, in case she meant to plunge her horse into the swirling current. The water level had risen, and there was a great deal of debris carried along in it. Tree limbs and branches, turf and soil, raced by.

"Not here, Emma, it can't be done."

Aloka pushed his horse between her mount and the river's edge. Emma's face was puckering in an effort to keep back tears. So close to Valparaiso, and her mother, to be turned back. On the other side of the Margamarga were the outskirts of the town itself. The pony she rode helped him, it willingly turned away up river. Aloka reached out his hand to her, but Emma kicked up her horse and trotted ahead of him. She kept her face turned to the river, constantly scanning for a place to cross.

They found an area where the river forked around a spit of land, and crossed in two stages. The water was very chill. They halted on the opposite bank, while Aloka pulled out his compass and checked the direction they must bear for Valparaiso. He hoped he could bring her there before full dark.

At dusk they began to encounter the camps of refugees from Valparaiso, in the hills surrounding the town. Aloka supposed they were too frightened to return to their houses. But as they rode through the Almendral they found there was hardly a house left standing. He gazed out to the Bay of Valparaiso, no British ships of war, no merchantmen lay at anchor, but far out the topmasts of what might be Chilean Navy ships.

"Emma, slow down," he called.

She'd forced her horse into a trot and was charging for their cottage. His heart misgave him, thinking what they might find. Emma threw herself from her horse, running toward the rubble where the house had been, calling "Mama! Mama!" Only one wall was left standing; the chimney had collapsed inward; the two little bedchambers were completely destroyed.

Aloka jumped down and ran to her. "Emma, we—"

She shook him off. Emma looked at him with an almost hostile gaze, while his was imploring. He felt at that moment he would give anything for Mercedes' safety, that she should be there in Valparaiso. Emma needed her so.

In the relative quiet, for the birds were not making their usual evening stir, Emma and Aloka heard a harsh voice. "Goddamn, hell, and death! It won't be moved!"

They could have never guessed it would be such a relief to hear McMurtry's complaining voice, and they ran toward it.

"Bless me, Black Savage the younger!" McMurtry was startled into crying out.

He was perched atop a pile of bricks and broken wood beams and clay mortar, along with a pint sized dog with a curling tail. Li'liah and the other Hawaiians stood crying and wringing their hands at the base of the pile.

"Which it's the old native admiral stuck beneath here, sir, and I can't shift this last cross beam."

Emma looked as though she would burst with anxiety, nearly as distraught as the Hawaiians.

"Come down at once, McMurtry," Aloka called, restraining Emma from scrabbling up the pile.

"Is he still alive?" Aloka asked in a discreet tone of McMurtry, with the little dog beside him.

"Copped it, sir, I believe."

Aloka shook his head, looking grieved, and threw a sidelong glance at the Hawaiians.

"The Missus?"

"The Missus is at the church, or in the church yard, because the church fell down with everything else, helping the padre with the wounded. She's brave, Miss," he said this to Emma. "Nor would she consent to stay put, until I promised to come out and help our native friends and her neighbors."

Emma came and leaned on Aloka's arm, her body sagging with relief.

"The *Blonde* and *Albion*?"

"Sailed in company yesterday, sir. Report of an English vessel, the *Rose*, in distress near Valdivia. Our Missus wanted to stay ashore, you and the young Miss being away like, so Captain left her here under care of the foreign medico."

Aloka turned and gave Emma a quick embrace. "You see, she's well." He went to the Hawaiians, and greeted and condoled with them. "We have these two horses. Let us see what can be done."

"Yes, do," Emma called. "I'm going to Mama."

Aloka opened his mouth to object, but Emma was already speeding away in the direction of the Iglesia Matriz. He exchanged a glance with McMurtry. He did not want Emma running about unescorted, particularly now, but if he followed her he was sure to receive a cold, angry rebuke. Then there was the matter of dear old Kapihe wedged beneath brick and rubble. He shook his head and motioned McMurtry to follow him to the horses.

"Orders aren't for them, sir," McMurtry said, repeating the great Vice-Admiral Lord Nelson's home truth.

Emma was aware she was considered burdensome baggage in certain quarters, though Aloka had never made her feel that way. Were he to cease to think her special after all that'd happened, or even worse tiresome and needy, she was not sure what she would do. There was little reason left in her, it was emotion that drove Emma toward the arms of security, comfort, reassurance, and love.

Outside the crowded churchyard she stopped, scanning the anxious faces, many blood stained and dirt soiled. Emma searched out her mother's more refined English dress, her dear, dear face. She moved around the periphery of the yard, and at last there she was, standing in conversation with a man holding a mule harnessed to a large wagon. Doctor Sparrman was on the ground nearby, sitting up, with a bandaged foot stretched before him.

Emma's knees trembled, she caught her breath and clasped her hands together over her breast.

Her mother looked smaller somehow, older. Mercedes' hair was not done in the usual way, she wore a single hasty braid at the back of her head. Her face was careworn, tired, worried. Then she looked up and met Emma's eyes. That dearest most beloved of faces was suddenly shining with joy.

Mercedes was deeply relieved Emma was back, but she wondered why Emma clung to her so. She appeared well and whole in her person, and she did not cry. Instead she buried her face against Mercedes' neck and shoulder the way she'd done when she was frightened as a child, though now she had to stoop to do it. Mercedes' heart began to thud with fear, and she held Emma away from her.

"Where is Aloka?"

"He's fine, Mama. He's with McMurtry." She gulped back a sob. "Poor old Kapihe is buried under their house. They are going to use our horses to try to shift the beams and retrieve his body."

Emma sucked in a shuddering breath. "I am so happy you are safe, Mama. So happy." She seemed to recollect herself, and went over and gave Doctor Sparrman her hand. "How do you do, Doctor?"

"As you see, Miss Emma, most pitifully. It is an ignoble injury, I twisted my ankle running from the house, crying 'Earthquake! Earthquake!"

"You were not more frightened than any of us, I'm sure, sir. It was most dreadful."

"Indeed, but your mother assists me in attending these poor people. They must come to the doctor rather than the doctor going to them. She has hired this peon and his mule to carry wounded Spanish prisoners. They must be borne by their countrymen all the way to Santiago."

Emma turned to her with a questioning look.

"The Spanish prisoners from Lord Cochrane's last action are here in a dreadful state, and Admiral Ávala is the senior naval officer among them. I could not live with myself if I did not try to do something for my mother's old friend."

Captain Blackwell had been baffled, angered, and frustrated at every turn. At sea aboard *Albion*, the earthquake had felt as though the ship was suddenly and violently got under way, and then been dragged across a series of submerged rocks. When *Albion* answered her helm once more, Captain Blackwell had immediately gone alongside the *Blonde* and spoke her. He'd shouted across to Captain Verson he would make all sail and run into Valparaiso. He feared what he might find on land, the violence of the event being what it had at sea.

The *Blonde* sailed with the English vessel *Rose* in tow, and must make her way to port at a slower pace. Yet when *Albion* neared Valparaiso Bay Captain Blackwell found he couldn't take her into port. The sea had so far receded that he feared there was not sufficient depth for his ship's draught, and furthermore there were many exposed rocks. He had one of the cutters manned and provisioned, and advised Captain Bowles to keep *Albion* well out in the offing. Captain Blackwell was rowed into Valparaiso.

As he made his way through the Almendral, the nearly deserted Almendral, with the houses all thrown down, one of Lord Cochrane's officers, an Englishman in the Chilean service, ran up to him.

"Captain Blackwell, sir, *Albion* was seen standing in. Lord Cochrane sends to ask if you will take some of the refugees aboard? They are crowded onto our ships, sir, with many more outside the city in tents. Even the supreme director, Mr. Bernardo O'Higgins sleeps out of doors."

"I am grieved to hear it, Mr. Miller," Captain Blackwell said. "I have only just come ashore, and unless and until I know the disposition of my own wife and family, I cannot speak to the accommodation of refugees."

Captain Blackwell bowed and moved off. Narhilla gave young Mr. Miller a hard stare as he passed him.

In the twilight Captain Blackwell gazed on the tumbled down ruin of the cottage Mercedes so liked she'd wished to stay there alone, without him. He turned searchingly round, and heard the dulcet sounds of seamen cursing close by.

The difficulty for Aloka and McMurtry in helping unearth people trapped beneath the ruins of their dwellings, was not to crush them in the process. The little dog was a great hand in this matter, for he leapt down into the crevices and barked like a fiend if there was danger to the one trapped. McMurtry and Aloka were already calling him Hero.

Captain Blackwell found them trying to free a young couple who, lying late, had been trapped in their bedchamber. He gave Aloka his hand.

"How do you do, Father?"

"I should be better if I knew where Mercedes and Emma are, and how they do?"

"They are at the church with the padre, tending the wounded, sir."

It was very quiet, no end of day bustle in the deserted neighborhood, no sounds of birds settling in for the night. A tremor suddenly struck, and for a moment even the seamen had difficulty keeping their legs. There were screams from beneath the heap of rubble next to them. In the silence that followed Aloka gave Captain Blackwell the news of Kapihe's death.

"Mr. Blackwell, Narhilla, Barnes, come with me," Captain Blackwell said, after the biggest after shock yet had subsided. "McMurtry, you will continue here until these people are safely out, then proceed to *Albion*. Desire Captain Bowles to send a boat ashore tomorrow noon."

"Aye, aye, sir," they said all round.

Aloka was a tired, bedraggled, much begrimed sight. He was limping, and in Captain Blackwell's opinion not much improved by his shore excursions. He was almost foundered like the two little rangy ponies belonging to Don Pedro. Reaching the Iglesia Matriz in the dark, Captain Blackwell learned Mercedes and Emma were caring for a detachment of wounded Spanish prisoners a short distance out of town.

"Listen, now, sweetheart," Captain Blackwell told Mercedes, when at last he found her among the wounded. "We brought a tent and blankets. You do what you have to do, and then come lie down. You had best send Emma straight away. I don't know what she and Aloka got up to, but he is fairly dropping with fatigue."

Captain Blackwell had been angry that she should place herself in the middle of two armies. Yet he knew he could not dissuade

Mercedes when she took certain notions in her head, so he'd decided he must just be grateful she and Emma had escaped harm in the terrible earthquake.

In the early hours of the morning Mercedes left Don Ignacio de Ávala and the other wounded men. Gazing up at the glory of stars overhead, she wondered if Edward was studying the firmament at that moment in England, peering through one of Doctor Herschel's massive telescopes.

Outside Captain Blackwell's tent, Barnes was on watch duty. He knuckled his forehead to her, and whispered, "Watch and watch, Missus. Captain took the first one." He raised the tent flap for her.

Mercedes moved over to where Blackwell lay, snoring gently. He no longer emitted those raucous noises he'd done when they'd first met. A stint as a prisoner in the Sandwich Islands had cured him. The old surgeon of his then command had remarked that Captain Blackwell was the only man to have his health improved, rather than ruined, by a prolonged captivity.

She took off her blouse, corset, and boots with relief, and prepared to lie down beside Blackwell in skirt, stockings and shift. At the other end of the small shelter, Emma and Aloka were curled together like cats. The sight pleased Mercedes somehow, and made her smile. She lay down thinking of Edward, longing for her family to be whole and all together again.

Mercedes was on the verge of sleep when Emma suddenly shrieked and sat up. Aloka was immediately there beside her, she turned into his arms. Both of them looked in their direction. Mercedes feigned to be asleep. Blackwell helped her at that moment by heaving a deep sigh and throwing his arm over her.

Jolted out of the sleepiness that had been upon her moments before, Mercedes watched them covertly. Aloka coaxed Emma to lie down beside him. She heard Emma begin to weep, and Aloka making soothing noises. Mercedes' own heart hammered for a time, wondering what could have put that note of grief into Emma's sobs. Her daughter rarely shed a tear.

She could not make out what was said between them, which was all the better. Mercedes feared it might be an intimate matter that she'd no business to discover. At least she did not have to worry Blackwell would wake, he would sleep on until the changing of the watch, or some emergency arose. Mercedes went to sleep to Aloka's low pitched voice, like a lullaby, in spite of her apprehensions and the heaviness of her heart.

Near the end of the morning watch, past six o'clock in the morning, Mercedes awoke. She was tired still and the sadness of the last few days weighed on her. The reason she'd come to attend the Spanish prisoners had more to do with belief than any sound logic. Mercedes had lived among seamen the greater part of her adult life, and they were a superstitious race of men. She was aiding the prisoners so that one day someone would do the same by one of her military men. Hers was a doctrine of kindness and tolerance, and Mercedes hoped she would be helped in turn, in her dying time.

She could sleep no longer with these thoughts in her head, in spite of her fatigue. Mercedes dressed, while her companions slept on. Outside she told Narhilla she would check on the wounded, and then return directly. She'd only gone a short ways when she heard steps pursuing her.

"Ma'am! Dear ma'am, may I have a word?"

Aloka's hair was uncombed, sticking up in all directions. Against his dark skin, darker circles were visible under his eyes. Aloka's face was bruised too as though he'd been in a fight, and he looked so like Blackwell that Mercedes' heart went out to him, and she said something she had not meant to.

"Will you tell me what troubles Emma she should cry so?"

"I will. I knew you could not sleep through her crying. Mothers are not made so. You are not, at least."

Mercedes took the arm he offered, and squeezed it. They set off toward the river, away from the rest of the company.

"I...I thought at first you might have been unkind to her," Mercedes said. "That something had gone wrong between you. But I cannot continue to think it, not with the way she clung to you last night."

"Never, never in life would I hurt her, if I could help it. But I could not protect her in everything. She killed a man, and now her soul aches." Aloka paused a moment, as Mercedes gasped. "Kuanoa. He followed and attacked us. He would have strangled me but that Emma stabbed him. I am sorry, my dear ma'am, it was wretched, and ugly."

It cost Mercedes a great deal not to break down sobbing for her girl, which would do no one any good.

"I told her we could not speak of it, yet I'm afraid that will hurt her too. I could not tell Father. Imagine the trouble it would throw him into in his new capacity."

"My dear, with all my heart I am so sorry," she finally said. "I never imagined...if I ever had to do such a thing..." She paused and sighed. "I will comfort her if I can, but I am afraid I shall not be much use. You, or James, is better equipped than I."

Mercedes thought of Blackwell telling her once, she was ill suited for knocking other men on the head.

"I want very much to claim a right to give her all my protection," Aloka said. "To be with her when she wakes frightened. Do you think one of these Catholic priests would marry us, ma'am?"

Mercedes was a little shocked, in spite of the fact she had no religion outside of the Anglican church, and that because of Captain Blackwell. Her life had been far from conventional. She felt guilty besides. In the first place for having neglected the religious education of the young man standing before her. Secondly, because she too wished Aloka and Emma should be married before they reached the Sandwich Islands. No one knew the allure of those islands and their beautiful women better than she, and it would be best if Aloka were tied to Emma in a way that was meaningful to him.

"The good padres will not marry you without you are Catholic. You would have to convert. I could not recommend that, unless you were sincere." Aloka looked so downcast, she said, "Why do you not ask Captain Verson? A ship's captain is empowered to perform the marriage service."

Aloka now looked shocked, clearly it was an idea he had not considered, and he opened his mouth several times to speak and shut it again. What he brought out at last reminded Mercedes how young he was.

"Do you think he would do it when Father don't approve?"

"Even I don't know your father's feelings, my dear. I do know Jack Verson is an honest, honorable, generous man. You can but ask him, you and Emma together, I should think."

"Oh, dear ma'am."

He was stepping forward to embrace her when they heard a muffled scream that startled them both. Aloka and Mercedes ran back to the tent, where they found Narhilla standing before it, white faced.

"No one inside except His Honor and the young Miss, sir," Narhilla said, knuckling his forehead.

He held open the canvas door. Mercedes went before Aloka. Inside she found Blackwell with a sword clutched in one hand, and Emma held to his chest with the other. He turned a rather frightened, inquiring gaze on her. Mercedes turned about suddenly, and urged Aloka back through the entrance.

"Tell him, my love," Aloka said in Hawaiian, before he would be pushed all the way out.

Aloka guided the Chilean soldiers and their Spanish prisoners to the ford up river that he and Emma had used the day previous. The wagon carrying the wounded could here lumber safely across the two streams.

Back in Valparaiso McMurtry and the little curl tailed dog met them, and immediately took them along to the Hawaiians' camp outside their cottage. When all the rubble was cleared away, Kapihe had been found lying upon the *estrada*. Sluggish from his recent operation, he had not moved fast enough when the quake started. The chimney had fallen in and crushed the fine old admiral.

"Hero could not save him," McMurtry had confided to Narhilla. "He was already gone, the poor old savage."

"Which makes our Black Savage the Younger Admiral of Hawaii, I collect," Narhilla replied in the same hushed tone.

There was no talk of succession or promotion in the following days. When Kuanoa's body was not discovered, his already grieved companions assumed he'd died outside the environs of the town. There was also no further word of a command in the Chilean Navy for Aloka. Lord Cochrane did send to renew his request for *Albion* and the *Blonde* to take on refugees.

Captain Blackwell and Captain Verson did their part both afloat and on shore in humanitarian aid for the people of Valparaiso. But Captain Verson could not help but be of the opinion his first duty was to his mission, to see the Hawaiians safely back to their islands. The ship bore the bodies of their beloved sovereigns, and their own numbers were dwindling sadly. Neither captain took the least notice of Lord Cochrane's displeasure the morning they set their allotted numbers of refugees—British shop-keepers and their clerks for the most part—ashore in preparation of sailing.

Emma was made a sincere offer of a berth aboard *Albion*, Captain Blackwell fearing she might not care for the close proximity of the Hawaiians. He had something of an understanding with her now, the girl who'd always been such a cipher to him. Captain Blackwell had been able to comfort her for the first time in his life. She'd inquired how many days sail to the Galapagos Islands, where the captains meant to wood and water.

"A week, seven days, according to weather, I should think," Captain Blackwell said.

"Why then, Papa, I will stay where I am. It will be the least upset to everyone. I should not like the King's people, nor Captain Verson, to feel I am slighting them." She gave him a weak smile. "I am sensible of your goodness, and I thank you, but I can almost go without sleep for a week. In the Galapagos, if I cannot bear it I shall come aboard *Albion*."

"You always were a gentleman-like creature. Not unlike your Mama."

CHAPTER TEN

Early in the morning Charles Island was sighted, the southernmost of the Galapagos. On the decks of both ships, as they passed by under easy sail, the people gazed at Charles Island's rocky landscape, roughly three miles long and a thousand feet high, covered in prickly pear cactus. *Albion* and *Blonde* sailed on, past Gardiner Island and a singular rock formation through the middle of which a natural arch had formed. The two captains wished to come to anchor in Banks's Cove, the snug harbor of Albemarle Island, before nightfall. They might return to Charles or one of the other islands in the next days for wood.

Hood and Chatham islands were some distance away to leeward. Mangrove trees grew at the water's edge on parts of Albemarle Island. In others the shore was rocky, with fields of black volcanic rock. They observed black and brown sea-iguanas in abundance.

"Ugly devils," commented many of the seamen and officers aloud.

"I don't think so. They look like nothing so much as pint-sized dragons."

Emma said this in English and her companion, Li'liah, gave her a blank stare. To explain the mythical beast to the Polynesian lady was too much to consider at the moment. Emma thought how Edward would have delighted in the creatures.

"Those land lizards, I like them much, " she said in Hawaiian.

Li'liah gave her an indulgent smile. Aloka could not be with them, he was the officer of the watch at the moment, and very active about the deck. She and Li'liah were walking on the forecastle, where Aloka came to speak to the old experienced quartermaster at the conn from time to time. Emma felt an affectionate pride in his professionalism and competence. Mercedes had once told her the sight of Captain Blackwell upon his quarterdeck always made her heart glow.

Emma was thinking about the calmer hours ahead when they would be anchored at Albemarle Island, the ship's business of provisioning going forward, and of requesting a private meeting of Captain Verson. They had waited until now in order to put distance between themselves and Chile, and so they should not appear importunate—that was what Emma and Aloka hoped—in their request to Captain Verson to marry them. She did not see how anyone could refuse Aloka, who was such a man of parts and good qualities.

The multitude of sea lions swimming about those waters looked into their faces with great, shining, and slightly astonished eyes. They would not flee when a firearm was leveled at them. The birds were so unafraid of man and his machines, they landed all over the rigging and spars. Li'liah was delighted when two tiny creatures alighted on her feet.

She laughed heartily, and leaning over to look more closely at the small finches, the upper part of her gown fell away. The thermometer stood at a warm eighty-five degrees, so Li'liah didn't bother to pull the gown up when she straightened. She was content to have her lower half only shielded in the way of her home islands. The seamen working close by immediately jerked their gazes away. Even Aloka flushed and looked conscious when he happened to glance in the ladies' direction.

Emma didn't mind the sight of Li'liah's naked bosom, having seen that and more living in such close proximity. She even felt some fraction of the men's admiration for Li'liah's well-formed and firm breasts, arms and shoulders. But having been brought up in England, Emma was also conscious of the tension of the men round her. They were unused to such provocations in their ordered wooden world. Though she hated to quit the deck and all the fine sights, as soon as she decently could Emma challenged

Li'liah to a game of *kōnane* in the great cabin. Emma knew Li'liah could not resist trouncing her once more in the Hawaiian's favorite pastime.

The men on deck, Aloka among them, blessed Emma for her merciful spirit and great good sense.

The ships had not been able to get into Bank's Cove before nightfall. The wind died and they were becalmed between Albemarle and Narborough Islands. Toward the end of the middle watch a light breeze came up when third lieutenant Mr. Verson had the deck. His vigilance lapsed in starting the lead, he might even have dozed at his station. When he did order the lead started, the *Blonde* was in eight fathom water, the next cast found her in six fathoms. Before the lead could be cast again they struck.

Captain Verson ran up to the quarterdeck in his nightshirt, with a sword buckled round his hips. The *Blonde* had struck a shoal and stuck fast. Captain Verson roared orders that caused sail to be taken in, and the boats hoisted out to take soundings round the ship.

"By the gods, Miss," Boki said, bracing himself in the doorway separating the great cabin from the coach. "What is all the hallooing about?"

Boki was a good looking sturdy man of a little less than thirty years, with the Hawaiians' generous lips and wide spaced dark eyes. He and Li'liah, and the others in the King's suite looked to Emma as an authority on seagoing affairs.

"I believe we struck something, by the way we were brought up. Do not be distressed, we will be sent for if there is the least—"

"Could you not ask?" Li'liah cried. "Send to Aloka!"

Emma flushed. "I cannot, dear ma'am, indeed I cannot." Her resolve weakened before further entreaties, until at last she cried out, "They have their hands full, trying to save the lot of us!"

This did not make the Hawaiians more comfortable, and Emma was relieved a short while later when Aloka knocked at her door and walked in. Boki and Li'liah and a half dozen of their companions were crowded into the coach at Emma's invitation.

"Ah, I am happy to find you all together. Captain Verson sends his compliments, and we are just getting out the boats to try to heave her off." Aloka was standing with his hat under one arm, his free hand clutching a timber overhead. "Once the stream anchor is carried out, we shall strike topmasts and yards, and carry out the two bower anchors. It may be necessary to lighten ship, if we cannot get her off."

There'd been many English words in his explanation, and he met with blank stares.

"We might have to start our water, pour it into the sea, cast off ballast and heavy stores. Even shift the guns, though I hope it don't come to that."

Aloka tried a smile, meeting more confounded looks.

"In any case, we have *Albion* to support us. And between her boats and ours we can bring everyone safely on shore." Aloka exchanged a look with Boki. "Everyone, the living and the dead, sir."

The Hawaiians nodded in approval. Among themselves the *ali'i* shared the belief old Kapihe had chosen well in the next Admiral of Hawaii. When the men of the King's suite saw the furious activity going forward; the carrying out of the two bower and stream anchors, the rigging of blocks and tackles upon the cables; they volunteered to take places at the capstan and windlass to help heave the ship off. Nor were they above manning the pumps, these men of the Hawaiian nobility.

"The ledge of rocks or shoal we have been upon, lies in 0° 16' S and 91° 25' W. Once we had her heaved off, the ship began to make water as much as three pumps could free." Captain Verson wrote in his journal, sitting at his desk in the *Blonde's* great cabin. "I therefore determined to prepare a fothering sail, to stop a leak on her starboard quarter against the time when we could heave her on shore to properly address the damage. As he had seen a ship fothered with great success while on the North American station, I confided the operation to Lieutenant Verson's supervision. This was performed very much to my satisfaction, and the ship made no more water than one pump could free."

Captain Verson leaned back in his chair. While they repaired the ship he was temporarily restored to his cabin, the Hawaiians choosing to stay ashore in two huts left by some previous visitors. In order to bathe and fish according to their own customs. Captain Verson was grateful for the privacy, the few sentences in his journal did not do justice to what he'd lived through in the days since the ship struck. At one moment he thought his son might be lost to him, broken more in spirit and resolve than he'd been by the depredations of prison.

Though it had not been strictly necessary, Captain Verson considered the fothering of the ship a happy stroke. Young Jack's spirits recovered somewhat after he'd led the effort that stopped the leak, and the incessant heavy labor of pumping ship. Repairs were well in hand and going forward. Using both *Blonde's* and *Albion's* boats, they'd lightened ship double quick in order to careen *Blonde*. The provisions had been got ashore, along with the sick, who were sheltering in tents. He had dispatched parties for wood and water to other islands. The water could be kept ashore in casks until their departure. There were men fishing in Bank's bounteous cove, and soon he would detail hunting parties and have the men putting up seal meat.

Captain Verson heaved a sigh, and bent to his journal once more. "In justice to the Ship's Company, I must say that no men ever behaved better than the Blondes have done on this occasion. Animated by the behavior of every Gentleman on board, every man seemed to have a just sense of the danger we were in, and exerted himself to the very utmost."

A knock sounded on the door. Captain Verson glanced up at the chronometer. Mr. Blackwell was punctual to his time.

"Mr. and Miss Blackwell, sir," the Marine sentry said.

"Come in." He rose to greet his visitors.

Captain Verson exchanged salutes with Aloka and extended his hand to Emma.

"Miss Emma, how do you do? Come, take a seat, if you please."

Captain Verson led Emma to a seat on the stern lockers. He sat down beside her, hoping to impart that he understood this to be an informal visit. Aloka chose to remain standing, one hand behind his back. Captain Verson expected to see his officers worn and reduced, after the exertions of the last days, but he could not understand why Emma should appear quite so fatigued and unhappy.

They waited in awkward silence, while Captain Verson's steward brought in wine and a plate of aged biscuits.

"Thank you for having the goodness to speak to us, sir," Aloka began. Captain Verson bowed, looking from one troubled young face to the other. "The case is this, sir. Miss Emma and I wish to be wed, in the Anglican service, and before we reach the Sandwich Islands. The *Blonde* having no chaplain, sir, I...that is, we, wish to make so bold as to beg the favor of you, of uniting us in matrimony here aboard ship."

Aloka's words came out in a rush at the end, he was obviously sensible of the boldness of his request. Bold, indeed. Captain Verson never carried a chaplain if he could possibly avoid it. His life and habits were too irregular to bear the scrutiny and scruple of the church and its representatives. For irregularity though it was hard to beat these two, half-brother and sister, wishing to be joined in holy matrimony.

"Is this what you desire, Miss Emma? You will forgive my saying, you will both pardon me, I trust, on the basis of long friendship. You are not at all in your best looks."

Emma flushed, but then looked him directly in the eye. "I do wish to marry Aloka, Captain Verson, as soon as ever may be. If I am not in my best looks, it must be because I have been too long kept from the comfort and solace of love."

Captain Verson jumped up from his seat, and began to pace. He needed to turn his back for a moment, so they wouldn't see how deeply Emma's words affected him. He wished Juan Luis might walk in, to have his own comfort and solace near at hand.

"We ... we know what will be said, sir," she said. "Incest."

Captain Verson stopped in his circuit, deliberating between his regard and gratitude to Captain Blackwell and what his feelings directed him to do in this case. He took a few moments to compose himself, and, still standing, turned to face Emma and Aloka.

"An ugly word. Nearly as bad as sodomite."

For a moment the three of them gazed at one another and rank and class and gender fell away, leaving them just humans.

Captain Verson cleared his throat. It was his cabin, his ship, his decision.

"Those are just words, and words do not define us. Actions do." He exchanged a nod with Aloka. "I have only ever known you both act in the most clear-headed and creditable manner. Do you have the consent of your parents, Miss Emma?"

By their faces, Captain Verson understood this was a question they'd both been dreading.

But Emma answered in a strong voice. "I do not, nor have I asked it. For you see, sir, I am of age."

"It is your choice to make." He bowed. "Quite proper. Your Mama, Miss Emma, once told Juan Luis only a hypocrite would ever hold what a man loves against him. I would be ashamed not to take her part. I will perform the marriage service, here aboard *Blonde*, at whatever hour you care to name."

Captain Verson watched their expressions change. Happiness and relief. Relief, he thought, was uppermost.

"I would wish, however, that it should be at such a time after you have sent across to *Albion*, to acquaint Captain and Mrs. Blackwell of the fact."

Mercedes had persuaded Captain Blackwell they must attend the ceremony, it would look odd before the Hawaiians were he to absent himself. It might to some of the crew as well; people married their cousins all the time. Nothing could induce him, however, to stay to the supper afterward in the newly wedded couple's honor. For all Mercedes' complacency respecting their children, he could not shake the notion he'd done her daughter an ill turn bringing his bastard son back from Polynesia with him. He felt sure this could not be the match Mercedes would have wished for her most darling child.

Captain Verson invited Captain Blackwell into the great cabin immediately he came aboard *Blonde*. Mercedes was stopping in the coach to assist Emma with her wedding dress.

After they'd lifted their glasses of Madeira to one another, Captain Blackwell said, "*Albion* will sail on this evening's tide, immediately after the...ah, ceremony. Boki speaks for them now, and he has decided we should go ahead with the news of King Liholiho's death, and prepare them for the return of his people and the sovereign remains. There is not a moment to lose."

Captain Verson bowed his head.

"I offered them passage aboard *Albion*, but they have all declined." Captain Blackwell smiled for the first time. "They seem to feel a great reluctance to leave the *Blonde* and her people."

Captain Verson looked at him kindly. "Allow me to say, your son and daughter are first among those who have inspired respect and esteem among the Hawaiians, and everyone aboard."

Captain Blackwell started a bit.

Though they were alone, Captain Verson leaned closer and lowered his voice. "I know what it is to be disappointed in a child, James. To feel that child's disappointment in return. But love survives it. Emma and Aloka, and your absent son Edward, must ever claim such a feeling from a father's breast."

Captain Blackwell was more startled still, but he put his hand out and grasped Captain Verson's hand in a firm grip. "Thank you, Jack, you are a wise man. I suppose if my children are any better than they should be, it is only due to that best of women I was blessed with."

"To Miss Mercedes, then!" Captain Verson raised his glass.

"To Mercedes, with all my heart."

Mercedes led Emma out of the coach and into the great cabin. The Hawaiians were there, and the three officers. Jack, Juan Luis, and Aloka stood chatting together, while the two captains conversed a ways apart. Mercedes was relieved to see a relaxed, almost pleasant expression on Captain Blackwell's face. It did not last, however, as Emma's entrance meant the official business of the gathering could commence. Captain Blackwell's smile faded as soon as Mercedes put Emma's hand on his arm.

The captain's desk had been placed like a lectern with the Bible and a Book of Common Prayer open atop it, and thither they all moved. Juan Luis and young Jack were happy to stand as witnesses. Neither had great prospects in the Service, or cared more for the irregularity of the proceeding than the people involved.

"Her mother and I do," Captain Blackwell responded, when asked who gave the woman away in marriage.

Mercedes noted the grave, noncommittal countenance Captain Blackwell often wore in his professional capacity. It was the mask behind which he hid his feelings. She took his arm, squeezed it, and he covered her hand with his.

Mercedes felt a mother's deep desire that life should be easy and kind to her children. Since leaving England, Emma had unfortunately to do with illness and death. Death of a most disturbing kind, if there were any other. She wished Aloka might bring her happiness, comfort, love. She wanted Emma to have all that. She was a good person and deserved it, Emma was unselfish and kind hearted. Many couldn't see past Emma's beauty and her sharp tongue to her better qualities. As for Aloka, she'd always loved him, since the day Captain Blackwell came back from Kauai with a naked little boy trailing in his wake.

The ceremony was concluding. Those whom God hath joined together let no man put asunder. Aloka was given permission to kiss the bride. He made it a very chaste kiss, rubbing noses with her at the end. The uproar of approval at the *hongi* from the Hawaiians covered somewhat the awkwardness of Captain Blackwell's handshake with his son afterward, and the peck on the cheek with which he saluted Emma.

Aloka was in the gunroom explaining, over a cup of grog with Jack Verson, the Hawaiian belief that the center of life resided in the stomach, rather than the heart.

"But to say a fellow is a man of belly just don't sound so well as to say he is a man of heart."

Jack gave Aloka a quizzical look, and stood up. "Good night to you, Al. As before, my very best wishes to you and Miss Emma."

Aloka knew Jack could not understand his lingering over grog and not hastening in to his new bride, waiting for him in the second lieutenant's cabin. Emma had declined to remain in the coach, because she'd spent so many restless nights there. It was not because she wished to share the quarters and the duty of a serving officer, as some supposed. Emma hoped those demons of thought that visit during the night would not pursue her to his berth. The truth was both Aloka's heart and belly were unsettled, the responsibility of marriage weighed upon him, and he sat there cup in hand, hesitating.

If he'd needed any confirmation of what his father's good opinion meant to him, Aloka found it in the heartache Captain Blackwell's grim and disapproving manner had caused him during the marriage service. The cold handshake afterward, his father barely embracing him and muttering, 'Do your duty, son.' Mercedes had been her natural and loving self, and had seemed happy for them. But she and Captain Blackwell had hurried off as soon as the ceremony concluded. Perhaps it was his father's duty to object to a match such as theirs.

Aloka pondered the concept of duty, to both English and Polynesian, and tossed off the last of his grog. It was his duty now to look after Emma, and past time he should be about it.

Aloka walked in to his cabin, to find Emma lying under the bedclothes of the higher slung of two cots.

Only her face and hair were visible, she had the blanket pulled up to her chin, and she stared at him out of those lovely eyes.

"I thought you would never leave off pratting and come in."

"This is how it is to be then, married life, recrimination and insult right from the start?"

But he bent over and gave her a resounding kiss. A kiss, in fact, that made her arch her body toward him.

"Well, take off your clothes, won't you?"

He immediately did, and put out the dark lantern. Aloka fitted himself into the cot beside her. Emma lay half over him, one of his legs between both hers.

"I know I should not say this, with you and the other officers working like fiends from hell, but I am so tired I could cry."

"Emma." He gave her a squeeze. "If you want to sleep while I hold you, I shall not complain or cry foul."

"Won't you?" She gave his cock a gentle tug.

Aloka gasped, and moved her hand away.

"Let me tell you something about that, Miss. A man can become this way just thinking of a woman, much less seeing her lovely body. And I should have to be made of wood if I could resist a lovely, naked woman lying beside me."

"There must have been a great deal of wood on deck the day Li'liah's top fell off."

Aloka snorted. "They were grateful when you led her away. But you are not to talk in that, how shall I say it, loose way."

"Except to you, my love?"

"Just so."

Aloka decided to quit pratting, and turn to his duty. He became serious and intense in his kisses and caresses, concentrating gentle strokes on the most tender parts of her. Emma's bosom began to heave; how the sight delighted him; and he pushed the bedclothes completely from her in order to take in the full view of her incomparable body.

She squirmed beneath him. "You wanted me like this, did you not?"

Emma turned over and presented him with a view that nearly caused him to lose all thought, but of possession. Aloka grit his teeth, moved up close behind her. He continued to stroke her while he joined his body to hers. How well they fit together, how perfectly suited. Aloka watched her intensely, pain and strain on his own face. He was determined this time she should have pleasure, and it was with equal joy and relief he saw her turn her face into the bolster and cry out. The strong contractions of her body confirmed it, and Aloka barely pulled away in time.

"Aloka?"

"Uh?" He was now standing beside the wash hand stand.

"Does being intimate help one sleep?"

"I've always found it work wonderfully well for me."

Moments later he was arranging himself next to her in the berth, regretting the remark. She would not care to be reminded he'd lain with other women, many of them in fact. But Emma, lying with her back to him, merely snugged her body against his.

"I feel so deliciously relaxed, I think I shall sleep for an age. I may oblige you to do this every night. For the sake of my rest and health, you understand."

"Why, I believe I can manage it, if I must."

"You are generous...in that way."

He detected a change in her tone. Had she been on the point of saying 'with your favors'? Aloka embraced her warmly, and kissed her neck.

"Only you, Emma, my dearest love, shall I have and hold from this day forward. Shall I love, honor, and comfort."

He heard a sweet little sigh, and shortly after her even breathing as she slept. Some duties were far pleasanter than others.

CHAPTER ELEVEN

Blackwell was back in the two room house in Oahu that the crew of his former command *L'Unite* had built for Mercedes and Edward. It was night time, the middle watch, and he was lying in the great wood bedstead with Mercedes. In the next room his two young sons, Edward and Aloka, were curled asleep like puppies on fine, soft mats.

The outside door into the bedroom burst in. Blackwell could not untangle himself from the sheets in time to reach his sword or war club, before the warriors were upon them. He heard the great crack of the killing club on his skull and Mercedes scream at the same instant. Then he was present in spirit only, hovering over the scene, his corporeal person a bloody corpse lying upon the bed.

He watched the warriors drag Mercedes naked from the bed, shrieking and straining against their gripping hands as she tried to reach his body. Edward and Aloka rushed in. At that point Blackwell wanted to shut his eyes against the scene, but he hadn't any to close and must gaze on. Aloka darted over to his weapons and was immediately taken up in a strong clasp. The warrior tossed the boy into the air, and caught him on the downstroke by the ankle, holding him upside down.

The room went silent as Mercedes ceased to scream and rushed over. She caught the boy against her body. "No, no!" Now the warriors saw a different woman, a fierce, proud creature, prepared to fight. She clutched Edward and Aloka, one little boy against each hip. This they respected, and the invading party immediately moved out, taking their captives with them.

The last glimpse he had was of the three of them bound together with sennet twine round their wrists. Blackwell's heart ached, he knew the fate of captives of these raids. The women would become slaves to men who would come to them in the night, wearing masks to preserve their dignity. And the little boys, his dear sons, would be kept for sacrifices when the war canoes were launched.

He watched, helpless to aid them, taken out by a single stroke of an ancient weapon. Mercedes was her younger self, her body whole; with not a stitch to cover her lovely nakedness. Blackwell knew she would be suffering in her good Christian heart. A sudden vision flashed before him of Edward being thrown beneath a war canoe, his pale face and inscrutable blue eyes turned accusingly on Blackwell, while Aloka was swung by his ankles toward the canoe's prow.

Blackwell woke with a start and a pain in his chest, his arms felt paralyzed at his sides. For several moments he lay this way, immobile and afraid. The compass over his head, the creaking of the rigging and the ship's hull under pressure of sail comforted him, and Blackwell's heart returned to its duty and a regular beat.

He swung his legs out of the berth and sat up, rubbed his hands over his face, and left the cabin.

Mercedes looked so peaceful in repose, so unlike the poor shrieking creature of his dream, that Blackwell only meant to gaze on her and not disturb her rest. The ship gave an awkward gripe, however, and he was obliged to plant his feet rather firmly and clap hold of a timber overhead. She was a light sleeper and woke on the instant.

"Jim?" She sat up. "Are you ill?"

"No, its ..."

"The children? The ship?"

Her tone had a slightly frantic edge and he saw how it must be for her, woken in the middle of the night, hardly sure where she was. Blackwell came forward and edged one great ham onto the side of her berth.

"No, sweetheart, nothing like that, no emergency. Forgive me if I frightened you. It's me, I...I need you. Will you come lie with me?"

"Oh!" She threw her arms round his shoulders, relief in her voice. "Of course I will."

He moved to pick her up out of the berth, but she said, "I need to use the quarter gallery first, darling."

If she was surprised he should be waiting for her in the dark just outside the privy, rather than in his double berth, Mercedes did not show it. She grasped his arm with both her hands, and even kissed his shoulder as he led her to his sleeping cabin. Not for the first time, Blackwell wondered what he'd done to deserve such a woman.

He wondered again when they were lying together in his cot, and Mercedes immediately reached for his cock.

"But, you are not—"

"No. Did you think I woke you just for that?" It was obvious what she thought, for she still held him in a warm clasp. "Is there no end to your tender love, sweetheart? Most wives would cry out at such behavior."

His wife merely shifted against him, and moved her hand to rest over his heart.

"Are you going to tell me what troubles you?"

"I suppose I must, since I roused you out."

Blackwell would not have told her, if he could have decently avoided it. He'd rather not speak of battles, real or imagined; least of all to a lovely woman. He felt this way in spite of what he knew of Emma's experiences, and how women were not such very different creatures to men.

She kissed him when he finished speaking. "Here I am with you, dearest James. Your sons are grown men. Edward in London, how I miss him! And Aloka somewhere at sea by now, would not you think?"

"That is just the thing. I know it was only a nightmare, but for some time past I've been feeling that I've done ill to bring you, and all of us, back here to the Islands. If we'd remained in England, Emma would not—"

"Life cannot be managed. You and I both know that. If it could, we probably would not be together now."

"God between us and evil." He picked up her hand and kissed it.

Because of that evil dream the cry of land ho! next morning, a hazy, misty morning, did not strike the same pleasure into Captain Blackwell as he found in the faces of his officers and men. *Albion* ghosted along, everyone straining for glimpses between the parting mists, of verdant slopes and a welcoming people. Close to the shore were green lawns dotted about with coconut and breadfruit trees and, much to the delight of the seamen, the native huts. No sight could be more grateful to a seaman, after a long cruise, then the places sheltering welcoming, dusky flesh. Beyond this pastoral scene rose a dense forest where waterfalls could be glimpsed in cascading glory.

"It don't look inviting, sir," Captain Bowles was explaining, "there is a wicked reef that appears to close the mouth of the harbor, and the sea breaks most violently against it. But in fact there is a channel, with upwards of half a mile between the east end of the reef and the shore. We surveyed it in the year four when I was with, why with you, sir, that is to say...with Captain Verson."

It was still uncomfortable, speaking of that time. Captain Blackwell had not been along on the survey of Hilo Bay because he'd been a captive on Kauai, and his first lieutenant Mr. Verson had command of his ship.

"Now we shall have the benefit of your diligence, Nathan. You say there is good holding ground?"

"The channel leads to a wide and safe basin, sir, with good bottom, gradually shoaling from ten feet to five fathoms a mile or so from shore."

Albion was on the point of opening the mouth of that channel, when the morning mists lifted and Captain Blackwell and his crew beheld a sight that made him call for all hands to put the ship about. Two hundred war canoes lay in Hilo Bay. Each capable of holding between forty and eighty men. Fierce skilled warriors in their prime.

Captain Blackwell called for his best telescope and studied the shore and the bay. By this time the presence of a foreign vessel had been noticed, and several fishermen in the roads were approaching *Albion*.

"Let them come aboard, Captain Bowles," Captain Blackwell said.

He wanted to find out what was afoot.

Two fishermen came up the side, tanned, lean, middle aged men, Captain Blackwell's own age or older. They gazed forward and aft once on deck, with exclamations of wonder at the ship's size and armament. Captain Blackwell thought these declarations rang false, and were more along the lines of what they felt was expected and due out of pure civility.

"*Aku* hunters," Captain Blackwell addressed them directly in their own language, "who is to be fallen on by those war canoes?"

Their surprise was such that he thought it best to make himself known. "I am the *ali'i* Blackwell, sent by His Britannic Majesty's government as consul-general to the Hawaiian Islands."

Now the two fisherman were agape, overawed, and they exchanged knowing nods. One said, "*Ali'i* Blackwell, I did hear of a white man—" but left off when he caught a glimpse of the pursed lips of his companion.

"It is a party to be led by Kapihe's brother Karaimoku," the second man said. "Against the upstart on Kauai. Ata Gege's son."

"Grandson, do you mean?"

"The very bugger. Soon as word reached Kauai of the death of our dear sovereign, what does the savage do but seize the moment to rebel and set himself up as King."

For the first time Captain Blackwell noticed the intent stares of the ship's officers and crew. He could hear them thinking, 'Black Savages ain't in it.'

"Who rules on Hawaii, at this *ahupua'a*?" he asked in English and then in Hawaiian.

The men answered quite readily that Karaimoku and Ka'ahumanu were joint regents in the King's absence, and Ka'ahumanu was at present in residence at Hilo. Captain Blackwell was on the point of questioning the fishermen further, as to the news reaching the Islands of the sovereign deaths, but he caught sight of an approaching canoe.

This was no ordinary canoe but a double hulled one, two canoes lashed together with a raised platform between them. For battle or for visits of state; the canoe was intricately carved at both ends. Captain Blackwell recognized the craft moving rapidly through the water toward them. It was paddled by ten muscular men working in perfect union, first stroking on one side of the canoe and then on the other, shifting their paddles at exactly the same instant. Here was precision, it was rather like what was required to put a ship about smartly, never missing stays.

The two native fishermen backed away when the regal visitor came up the side and strode confidently onto the quarterdeck. Ka'ahumanu was an impressive woman, tall like most of her countrymen, and weighing above two hundred seventy pounds, with a fierce eye and a proud bearing. She wore a *tapa* cloth skirt, dyed red in respect of her station, and was quite bare above the waist; with great dignity, Ka'ahumanu strode straight up to Captain Blackwell. Taking a caplet of flowers from her own head, she placed it on his, and proceeded to salute him in the native fashion.

It was an intimate greeting, witnessed by all on deck, but one about which Captain Blackwell felt no discomfort. Nothing of the dread that other side of the Islander's nature inspired. Captain Blackwell and Ka'ahumanu turned to Captain Bowles. They had last met some twenty years before, when Captain Blackwell and Mr. Bowles had witnessed King Kamehameha beat his favorite wife, the nineteen year old Ka'ahumanu. Captain Bowles bowed slightly to receive the flower wreath Ka'ahumanu moved to place on his head, and straightening, looked directly into her capacious bosom. A furious blush suffused his already ruddy face.

This seemed rather to please Ka'ahumanu, for she went round the deck with Captain Blackwell as he showed her the ship with a gay, almost girlish air. The queen's attendants were astonished. Captain Blackwell remembered how she'd once called Mr. Bowles handsome, and received a beating for her impudence.

"Should you like to go below, Ma'am?" Captain Blackwell asked, on bringing Ka'ahumanu back to the quarterdeck. "Captain Bowles, would you care to join us?"

"Captain, is it?" Ka'ahumanu said in Hawaiian, glancing over her shoulder as they passed into the captain's cabin. "No longer just Mister."

A person of Ka'ahumanu's bulk could not fit comfortably in a sloop's between decks, and there was not much to choose between the two captains in terms of height and girth. They were fairly cheek by jowl once seated in *Albion's* cabin. Mercedes was the only one that seemed to fit in the setting, small and delicate as she was, and Ka'ahumanu eyed her askance.

The queen spoke to Captain Blackwell in a way that might have been called mannish by Europeans. She was the regent, or joint-regent, of her nation, and the Islands had had women rulers or *ali'i* time out of mind. Her speech was bold, straightforward, and the timbre of her voice pitched low, rumbling forth from her great barrel chest. Captain Blackwell was put in mind of another such woman: Aloka's mother. In his diplomatic capacity, Captain Blackwell's first concern was to know whether the sad tidings of Liholiho had reached Hawaii.

"In O'ahu the British whalers brought this tale," Ka'ahumanu said, "of the death of our King, who is my son by kinship. They hourly expect the ship with his remains. Here in Hawai'i we did not believe this news, until the eclipse." Ka'ahumanu paused with a significant look, and desired Captain Blackwell to translate for their companions.

"An eclipse of the moon, you see, foretells the death of a great chief," Captain Blackwell explained to Mercedes and Captain Bowles.

Captain Blackwell had to inform Ka'ahumanu it was not just her adopted son and his queen who'd perished, but Kapihe and Kuanoa also had been lost in Chile. The British ship carrying the sovereigns' remains and her surviving countrymen would arrive in several weeks.

Mercedes refilled teacups, and they all stared down into them or gazed out the stern windows, while Ka'ahumanu absorbed this news. Whenever an *ali'i* died there was a re-distribution of his lands to kinsmen, and Ka'ahumanu was related to everyone.

"I am sorry for Karaimoku," she said at last. "He has an affectionate nature, and Kapihe's death will grieve his tender heart. To say nothing of his hopes that Kapihe would appear over the horizon, in time to launch his ships in war with Kaumuarii—he calls himself George. Karaimoku hoped Kapihe might be aboard your ship, this ship. He did not come himself because he is ashore with the *ali'i* of Maui, those backward sods."

A little surprised at this last, for Ka'ahumanu was a noblewoman of Maui, Captain Blackwell instead told her how much he'd esteemed Kapihe. He did not mention Kapihe's choice of successor, and with a feeling of trepidation Captain Blackwell asked about this so called George.

George was in fact Aloka's half brother. They were both the sons of princess Kalani of Kauai. Captain Blackwell had known Kaumuarii as a boy, when they called him the *Ali'i Kāne*. The one who would inherit from Ata Gege. Upon his leaving the landholdings of Ata Gege, Kalani had thrust Aloka after Captain Blackwell, insisting he should be taken away, fearful less the child be killed by his brother when they came to manhood. 'There can be only one king'. Her words rang in memory. As a father and as England's representative in the Islands, Captain Blackwell gave full attention to Ka'ahumanu's account of George.

Kaumuarii, a young chief of Kauai, had spent some years in North America, where he had taken the name of George. Liholiho's absence seemed a favorable opportunity to George, of gaining possession of his native island and its resources. He was descended from an ancient line of kings, and had easily raised sufficient warriors to support him. When word of this rebellion reached Oahu, where Karaimoku resided, he instantly sent to the several islands to rally the chiefs. Karaimoku himself had come to Hawaii some days previous, with his followers, to gather his forces.

"No one wants a return to the warfare of the bad old days. That is why Karaimoku is acting so swift, old though he is. This young puppy must be put down. Maui has sent a few unseasoned young *ali'i* and a handful of warriors. You cannot imagine our hunger for men." Ka'ahumanu licked her lips, and the two Englishmen loosened their stocks almost in unison. "Come to Karaimoku's council of war this evening, *Ali'i* Blackwell. I shall give you a pilot and whatever else you require for your ship."

Captain Blackwell glanced at Mercedes. It was plain from the intelligent, apprehensive look on her face that Mercedes understood the better part of their conversation in Hawaiian.

Noticing the exchange of glances, Ka'ahumanu said, "You can bring as many of your men as you wish, and *wahine* Blackwell." She nodded at Mercedes. "Women are not unwelcome at councils of war. We are not like white men."

Captain Blackwell sat back in his chair at those words, and told Ka'ahumanu he would consider of it. Then he led the way in the exchange of presents, and the visit concluded pleasantly.

Ka'ahumanu stepped onto her double canoe, and arranged herself on its platform, wearing an English bonnet. She was pleased with her prizes, and she looked back complaisantly at the two tall figures standing in discussion on the ship's quarterdeck. Ka'ahumanu wondered what a fine stout man like the *ali'i* Blackwell could want with that skinny, delicate looking woman of his. *Wahine* Blackwell was sick too, if she was not much mistaken. Ka'ahumanu had little sympathy for women, and indeed men, who were in her opinion poor goers.

Mercedes had mixed feelings sitting alone in *Albion's* cabin, amid the soft mats, fine woven bowls, wooden paddles, and *pa'ūs* and *malos* of *tapa* cloth that had been the gifts of Ka'ahumanu. The voices of the two captains drifted down to her. Mercedes had felt Ka'ahumanu's contempt for her as a person of no family or connections, and this invitation to a council of war stung too, as though that should sway Captain Blackwell in his decision to attend. Of course she must be guided by him, they all must—he was England's representative in the islands—and she could not imagine that he would want her there.

Her sleep had been fitful these last several nights, the tropical climate seemed to be sucking the spirit out of her. Mercedes hoped she would adjust, Captain Blackwell had brought her there for her health. His welfare was uppermost in her mind at the moment, and Mercedes wished he were able to go ashore with a file of Marines and a full boat's crew of officers and good English tars at his back.

That was not to be, they were not a man-of-war. Her own good English tar came in to her directly.

“Mercy, sweetheart.” He was huffing and blowing a little himself, making his way to a seat. “Tell me what you think, eh? Not all white men disregard their lady’s opinion, you know.”

She had to smile at that. “I was just thinking I should be much easier if you had a dozen lobsters, and your barge’s crew to accompany you.”

“Bless you, sweetheart, there’s no need of that.” Captain Blackwell smiled, then looked down. “You do not put much store in my abilities, I fear, now I’m grown old.”

He reached out and squeezed her hand. “Karaimoku himself is a man of sixty, I am told. You are not to worry, there is no danger in this meeting. There will be none heeded but cool old heads at war. Besides, I believe I shall be welcomed, something of the prodigal returned.”

“Oh, James.” She went over and put her arms round his shoulders. “They’d best treat my prodigal well. Remind them there is a 46-gun ship just over the horizon.”

Captain Blackwell gave a bark of laughter and patted her arm over his chest. “Perhaps I shall.”

“Who do you take with you then?” Mercedes asked, settling on the small sofa beside his armchair.

“Captain Bowles must come, he is a great favorite of Kaʻahumanu—”

“In case I had not noticed.”

“Just so. And I shall take young Parsons with me, he shows an interest in their language and culture.” Captain Blackwell had no young gentlemen aboard, no marines, and Parsons was a junior lieutenant, or second mate in merchant-ship parlance, which of course the captain would never use. “And my boat’s crew, in course, as you so kindly suggest.”

He would attend this meeting, perhaps amidst hundreds of warriors, and take with him only a half dozen men. Yet Mercedes would not have him hanging fire and anxious. She thought back to his waking her the previous night; she knew in his professional life decision and action were all. Captain Blackwell came to what he really did want to consult her upon.

"Ka'ahumanu has given us a residence ashore for the duration of our stay. It would be churlish to refuse, and aside from that I think you could do with a change of scene and fresh vittles. You won't mind my saying so, sweetheart? You look a little peaky."

"Why, that's ungentlemanly in you."

They tried to laugh it away, not to betray to themselves that her health could once again become a serious issue.

"Would you like to go in to shore with me this evening, and begin settling in?" Captain Blackwell said. "Or do you prefer to wait a day or two? I can ask Captain Bowles to take possession in my stead, that should satisfy Ka'ahumanu." He was not above a little simper. "And you can come ashore at your leisure."

Mercedes wanted to keep up the lighthearted vein. "I daresay Ka'ahumanu shall be best pleased if we send in Captain Bowles as the advance guard. I should prefer to wait a day or so, if you please. I know its childish, but I don't like to arrive in a new place by night. But...will you return to the ship or sleep ashore tonight?"

Shore: with all its allures, the soft tropical night, willing, warm, and whole women. There would be no difficulties for a man like Captain Blackwell. A fine, manly figure still, in spite of his age, and of high social status. He could command any number of lovely coffee skinned wenches.

He jerked himself out of his chair, and went down on one knee before her. "Where ever you are, my dearest soul, that's where I shall be. Of course I will return to the ship, since you choose to stay. You are my country, Mercedes, you must know that."

At first she couldn't speak. "I love you too, Jim." Then, in order not to break down into full blubber, she put her chin up. "And you would never leave your gig ashore overnight in any case."

Mercedes was right about that last; he would never leave one of his boats ashore unattended. Blackwell had lived among the natives long enough to know their ways, at least to some degree. They considered all property in common, saving that of their chiefs, and would see nothing amiss in taking the gig for a sail round to the leeward side of the island should the spirit move them. She was quite out though, in her notion that a file of marines, sea-officers, and men might protect him. The Hawaiians were uncommon efficient warriors in close combat; they could take down the marines before the lobsters had time to raise their muskets. One blow from a killing club and, as in his dream, its on to the next life.

None of this would he breathe to a soul, except perhaps to his son. Aloka and Emma had seen it for themselves. His gig came ashore at a most convenient landing place, alongside the outlet of a freshwater river, ideal for watering a ship. Blackwell gave orders to his boat's crew. On the walk to the *maneaba*, the meeting place, Blackwell enlightened Captain Bowles and Mr. Parsons on the political economy of the islands.

The islands were divided into *ahupua'a* or districts, ruled over by a high chief, his lesser chiefs and kinsmen, and his men of business. A priest or two was also usually involved. Many of these high chiefs were noblemen, members of the island's *ali'i*; in past times each island had also had its own king and queen. Ka'ahumanu was the daughter of the king of Maui. At present the islands were united under one king, the descendants of King Kamehameha the Great. Given the structure of their society, it was natural that each *ahupua'a* would have its cadre of warriors. To unite them in a single cause was the purpose of the meeting they were to attend.

Blackwell was heartily glad, on walking into the *maneaba*, he would not be the one to mold these men into an army. As with any gathering the men stood about in groups. The younger men were clustered together, talking and laughing loudly, some leaping about in demonstration of their skill in the steps of various *hula*. The local men of Hilo were huddled up, glancing with disdain at the first group. And then there was a gathering of men of a certain age, grave looks upon their faces, standing apart and distinguished by the staffs they held, each ornamented with feathers.

It was this group of *ali'i* Blackwell approached, recognizing Kanakoa of Oahu, and feeling an unexpected relief that the man was still alive. The Hawaiians are not ones to forget a face, they speak and dance their history from generation to generation, and Kanakoa instantly knew him.

"Blackwell," he said, with a flash of white teeth, "I heard you had returned. I shall be happy to make you welcome on O'ahu. Why do you not carry your staff of office?"

"Kanakoa, I trust I find you well?" Blackwell bowed. "I will be sailing to O'ahu presently, thank you. My staff is with my son, it is by rights his own."

Kanakoa considered the staff in his own hand. "My father passed me his, and then he went over the rainbow."

The venerable old man had also been known to Blackwell, and he reached out and grasped Kanakoa in the native handshake. They bowed their heads together for a moment. No comment was required. One did not say 'I am sorry for your loss', because the Hawaiians believed death did not entirely remove their loved ones from this sphere.

After a decent interval, Blackwell said, "May I present my officers?"

Captain Bowles and Mr. Parsons were presented, and then Kanakoa did the honors for them among the *ali'i*. When Ka'ahumanu and Karaimoku walked in, Blackwell and his party had already found their places.

A hush fell in the *maneaba*, the Hawaiians had great respect for their chiefs and here were the joint regents of the entire archipelago. Ka'ahumanu took a seat upon a raised wooden platform covered over in fine mats, and made a motion of her arm like a benediction. All of the men sat down. Had Mercedes attended, she would have noted there were no other women present.

"At Maui the *ali'i* and *haku'āina* agreed it would be proper to send two hundred men in canoes." Ka'ahumanu glared about, immediately launching her attack. "Where are those men? Karaimoku has seen none arrive in O'ahu, and he has been forced to come here seeking them. Will you in Maui make me ashamed to call you brothers?"

A confused discourse broke out as the Maui chiefs tried to defend themselves.

"I wish you had waited until the black *tapa* covered me," Ka'ahumanu thundered, "before taking away my father's honor."

Ka'ahumanu's strong words caused another outcry, the Maui chiefs declaring they were quite willing to send the two hundred strong armies they'd committed to. The sticking point appeared to be they did not desire to go themselves to war. Blackwell had judged the Hawaiians a fierce and warlike people, so that here was his first diplomatic surprise. He could not make out if the Maui contingent dreaded a renewal of the bloodshed of Kamehameha's time, or had grown accustomed like sensible beings to a peaceful, stable way of life. Then again, some particular fear of Kauai and her kings might be at work.

An older man stepped forward from the group of *ali'i* Blackwell was attached to, and held up his hands. He was small, with a brown and leathery skin that contrasted with his pure white hair.

"Hear me, ye chiefs; ye who have warred under the great Tamehameha. Karaimoku and I were born upon the same mountain in this Island, and together we breasted yonder foaming waves. In manhood we fought side by side. When Karaimoku was wounded, I slew the chief whose spear had pierced him; and though I am now a dried and withered leaf, never be it said that Kaikeoeva deserted his friend and brother in arms in time of need. Who is on Karaimoku's side? Let him launch his war canoe and follow me!"

Such a shock went through the gathering that Captain Bowles and Mr. Parsons stepped back as though evading the recoil of a great gun. Everyone was on their feet, the young warriors snatching up spears and killing clubs, war whoops rising up to the dark skies. A glance at his companions showed Blackwell pale faces, surprised, and perhaps a little frightened. The idea that Mercedes might have been there made Blackwell shake his head. He reassured them all was well.

Karaimoku would not launch the canoes that night, but he took advantage of the fervor to organize the men, giving commands for parties to be formed under particular chiefs, and setting the next rendezvous on Maui. The two hundred war canoes in Hilo Bay belonged to Ka'ahumanu's followers, and they, together with Karaimoku and the gathered chiefs would proceed next to Maui, then Oahu. And at last together, to fall upon the rebel George in Kauai.

Blackwell was trying to recall every word of old Kaikeoeva's speech, he'd never heard a finer, and he wanted to share it with the Englishmen, and perhaps write it down. He glanced over at Ka'ahumanu and surprised a self-satisfied look on her face. Gone were the wounded pride and chagrin at the backwardness of her

Maui connections. It made Blackwell wonder if there had been something of performance in what had played out at this meeting.

CHAPTER TWELVE

The chiefs had pressured Captain Blackwell to take part in the war against the upstart George, to use *Albion* as a transport to carry men across the treacherous channel between Oahu and Kauai. His refusal had been steadfast and unmoving. Karaimoku's war party departed three weeks before the *Blonde* arrived in Hilo. Captain Blackwell's duty was to rendezvous with *Blonde*, and not to interfere in the internal upheavals of a sovereign nation.

Captain Blackwell was too old to be incited with the prospect of glory in battle; he knew what it was to kill other men. He had an *amor patriae* and though he would have continued in his own country's wars, the battle in the Aix Roads had shown him how little his heart was in it. His first diplomatic decision could not but please his lady. In that quarter at least, Captain Blackwell could feel some satisfaction. Color had returned to Mercedes' cheeks, and she had nearly as much spirit and cheerful energy as in previous times.

They'd taken up their shore residence, trading sleeping quarters with Captain Bowles. He'd come back aboard *Albion* with a look of relief that seemed to indicate a certain affright with his conquests ashore. The *Blonde* meanwhile continued a happy ship, in spite of her commander's taciturnity. Captain Verson was a deeply introverted man, but he was a good seamen, and a better leader of men. *Blonde's* people were intent on profiting from their refreshment and run ashore.

Aloka and Emma joined a party from *Blonde* sent to map the great volcanic crater Kilauea. They peered from its black edge into a chasm the cartographer's calculations later put at over 900 feet deep. From parts of the crater smoke and flames constantly rose. Closer to Hilo, Aloka hiked up the Honolii river and rode its many waterfalls down with other daring young *kanakas*.

The bloom on those two young faces, Emma's and Aloka's, accounted for a great part of Mercedes' improvement. She had but to look at Emma to feel happy. She was indeed the beauty of the world, as good Doctor Russ had once said. Mercedes was thinking of her and Aloka at church earlier, very correct and polished—he in his lieutenant's uniform, and she in a neat morning gown—never touching one another, as she walked home from the service arm in arm with the local missionary's wife.

Hawaii, Oahu, and Maui all had missionary establishments. White missionaries and their families, living on land and in houses granted by the *ali'i* and built and maintained by the people. Kauai had a Tahitian missionary, Mercedes had been told. She strolled along, enjoying the soft air, the sounds of the dry coconut fronds clacking in the mild breeze, and the peeping of the small yellow birds that were always about the green grasses. Old Mr. and Mrs. Bing were on her mind, once the only missionaries in the Sandwich Islands.

"Does not it gladden your heart," Mrs. Lyon said to Mercedes, "to see the natives in their Sunday clothes? Quite apart from the enlightenment of their benighted souls, were our presence here to produce nothing more than the desire of clothing, the benefit to the people would be great indeed. Besides all the decencies, and the virtues that spring from the decencies of life, the additional incitement to industry which the desire of clothing affords is of incalculable value to a people in a state of incipient civilization."

Mercedes had the distinct impression, from Mrs. Lyon's mooing tone, she was reciting something she'd heard her husband say, or seen written down in a letter.

"Every want that stimulates the breast, becomes a source of pleasure when redressed." She quoted Goldsmith, feeling piqued at the religious and commercial zeal of the Americans.

Mrs. Lyon was looking perplexed, as if trying to work out whether she'd been insulted. From round the back of the house Ka'ahumanu had given for their use, the great queen herself appeared. She wore nothing but a *pa'ū*. Ka'ahumanu was otherwise bare, her astonishing large breasts and trunk like thighs exposed below the short *tapa* cloth skirt. Mercedes stepped out of her path and made the queen a curtsey as she passed. Without looking at them Ka'ahumanu arranged herself upon her carriage, and nodded to her bearers. Mrs. Lyon's mouth was agape.

Emma appeared from the back of the house, clad much like Ka'ahumanu below her slim waist. On top her breasts were covered by an abbreviated chemise of the type she'd fashioned for Mercedes, to cover her wounded chest. In one arm Emma clutched a float board, feathered round the edges. She was followed by Aloka, carrying his own float board and sporting the native breeches round his loins.

"Mama!" Emma called to her. "Her Majesty is taking us out. She was a cracking great float boarder in her day."

"You should see the size of the one she uses now," Aloka said *sotto voce*, as he passed them, winking.

Mercedes and Mrs. Lyon watched the two hurry off after Ka'ahumanu's litter. The lively step and eagerness of the young people bespoke health, beauty, and vigor. Mrs. Lyon's mouth was still open, while her eyes followed Aloka's manly form with great attention.

"Well," said Mrs. Lyon, seeming to feel some comment called for, "she is after all merely your daughter-in-law."

"How badly did you blow her up after that?" asked Captain Blackwell, when Mercedes told him of the incident.

"I fancy we shall not be troubled by any further visits from the Lyons." Mercedes sighed. "I should like to be well with the Christian community but—"

"But your children and your husband are half heathen, so it will not do."

"She made me angry. And when my blood is up I become defiant. I'm too proud I know, too proud of Emma, too proud in general. Just like a Spaniard."

"I saw them at it," he said, then abruptly closed his mouth.

From the deck of *Albion*, where he'd been discussing the ship's trim with the Master and Captain Bowles, Captain Blackwell had seen the interested stares of men on both British vessels. Aloka, Emma, Ka'ahumanu, and her people, passed the two ships at anchor on the way out to meet the waves on their float boards.

Little of duty went forward after that, with all eyes turned on this novel spectacle. It was interesting to watch, Captain Blackwell would freely admit, as the natives launched their boards into the surf and rode the waves. The most adept at it could stand upon their boards. But the fascination had as much to do, he thought, with the costume Emma was wearing. Somehow with her breasts shielded by that little bit of cloth, Emma was more alluring even than the bare-breasted native women.

Captain Blackwell blushed.

"Sure it is immodest," Mercedes said, "but the longer I live the less I think of what Mrs. Lyon calls the decencies. They are young and beautiful, why should they not show their bodies and paddle about like sea creatures. I wish I could." She looked at him and laughed. "You should have seen the way Mrs. Lyon looked at Aloka in his *malo*. Devoured might be a better word. Ogres ain't in it."

Captain Blackwell laughed heartily. He treasured Mercedes and he told her so, ill-natured Spaniard though she was.

Emma and Aloka would have got up to further capers; they had heard a shipment of horses was to be landed at Kona on the other side of Hawaii, and were talking of sailing over to watch; but that a messenger from Oahu arrived with a letter for the two British captains.

'O'ahu, May 6th, 18XX

My Lords,

With very respectful congratulations on your arrival, I am requested to present you the cordial salutations of the people of O'ahu, Hawai'i, Maui, and Kaua'i, where latterly the rebellion of the upstart Kaumuarii George has been put down. The king and princess of these Islands are highly satisfied at the event, and send their united and respectful request, that if it may be agreeable to yourselves, you will be pleased to favor them with your company on shore in O'ahu, bringing with you your ship's officers, the Admiral of Hawai'i, and our beloved countrymen and our late sovereign's remains. The present is a time of great sympathy among the chiefs and people. I myself will come on board at your arrival in O'ahu to bring you to the presence of their Royal Highnesses. Allow me, my lords, the honour to be,

Very respectfully and truly yours,

Karaimoku

regent of Hawai'i'

A short letter, most handsome as Captain Blackwell put it, and one that caused consternation on many sides. Boki, Li'liah, and their companions could not help but feel a depression of spirit, given the hopes with which they'd left these islands for England, and the sad circumstances under which they returned. For Aloka, the reference to the Admiral of Hawaii inspired something like dread.

Blonde and *Albion* sailed in company for Oahu before Aloka had a chance to talk matters over with his father. He longed to open his mind to the one person who'd always advised him before on a professional level. Now Aloka was not at all certain he would meet with a willing and sympathetic ear. He might have forfeited his claim to his father's patience and indulgence. The most important of his choices though, Aloka could not regret.

He put his arm protectively over Emma's dear form in his cot. Alone with her in the second lieutenant's berth of the *Blonde*, Aloka felt himself the most happy and fortunate of men. His only wish was this feeling might last.

"Emma?"

"Ummm?" She was rosy and languid from his attentions.

"It might not be so nice for us in Oahu, as it was on Hawaii."

"Could we not go back?"

"I don't know." The truth was he didn't know much of anything when it came to these islands, that were supposed to be his native land. "Would you be terribly unhappy were I to remain as I am, a lieutenant in the Royal Navy."

Aloka felt her body, relaxed against his, stiffen just slightly.

"Return to England? There would be a great deal of pretense. People will remember we were raised together."

She turned under his encircling arm to face him. Aloka was aware of her penetrating stare in the gloom of his cabin.

"I should be very, very sorry to part from Mama. I fear...there may come a time when she shall really need me, as much as ever I needed her, when I was a pup."

"Oh," Aloka said. That could not be argued with.

She lifted a hand to stroke his face. "But my whole happiness is tied to yours, my dearest love. I am prepared to be one of your followers, and go with you from ship to ship, or island to island. However it might be—"

His kisses and embraces silenced her for a moment.

She whispered into his ear. "I'm prepared to do this, at least until I'm not."

He chuckled, his heart feeling lighter. If she had faith in him, Aloka believed he could face the future with tolerable fortitude.

Aloka was not alone in the two English ships in feeling it might not be so pleasant for them in Oahu. Mercedes lay awake in her narrow berth aboard *Albion* brooding on the life she'd led on Oahu, during the long time James had been captive on Kauai, and the people she'd known there. Kanakoa was alive. Hale and hearty, and still at the head of a few thousand men, was how James put it. She wanted to seek out her usual comfort, in his arms. But it felt unseemly, ungentlemanly, since it was he she'd transgressed against. Mercedes would also have to pass through the great cabin to reach the captain's quarters. The great cabin was Ka'ahumanu's bed place for the passage, and Mercedes didn't feel equal to it. Cowardice was what it amounted to.

Next morning the two ships were in the approaches to Honolulu Bay. The *Blonde* fired a fifteen gun salute, which was immediately returned by the forts on shore. Two forts; one near the beach, and a second placed up the face of an extinct volcano. The forts had not been there at the time of Captain Blackwell's previous sojourn in the islands. Aboard the *Blonde*, after she'd been moored, Captain Blackwell contemplated the much changed Waikiki. He stood with two other oldsters, Captain Verson and Kairamoku, staring at the shore from *Blonde's* quarterdeck.

"The near battery mounts 42 guns of different calibers," Karaimoku said. The guns were probably of various nations as well, Kamehameha never having been nice about where his armament should come from. "The other fort in the crater mounts eight guns."

"How it has changed," Captain Verson said. "So many more dwellings. The church and the mission house, with Miss Mercedes' little cottage, were the only wooden structures before. Now there must be a dozen very fine houses of two stories, and that handsome one of stone and wood."

"That is my house," said Karaimoku in English. "I beg you and your officers will honor me with a visit, after your presentation to the King and princess tomorrow."

Bows were exchanged. Everyone on the frigate's deck was impressed with the intelligence and circumspection of Karaimoku. He turned to Captain Blackwell. "Is all ready *Ali'i* Blackwell?"

"Indeed, sir." Captain Blackwell bowed in his turn, and motioned toward the main chains where man ropes had been rigged. The coffins of Liholiho and his queen had already been carried across to *Albion*, which would take them and the king's suite into the inner harbor. Li'liah, Boki, and all the other chiefs had already gone aboard, where they met Ka'ahumanu, who'd come over in *Albion* from Hawaii.

Karaimoku stopped in leaving the quarterdeck in front of Aloka, who was lined up with the other officers. Trained to obedience Aloka stood still and upright, his hand having moved slowly from his sword hilt as soon as the older man faced him. He stood between Mr. Montelongo and young Mr. Verson.

"Allow me to name my son," Captain Blackwell said. "Second lieutenant of this ship, Mr. Aloka Blackwell."

A long silent considering look, and then Karaimoku extended his hand. Aloka immediately came forward and shook in the native, by the forearm, and then in European fashion. Aloka declared himself honored in Hawaiian.

"I will look forward to a private meeting tomorrow, lieutenant," Karaimoku said. "I have your brother George prisoner ashore. He must be dealt with."

Karaimoku turned to Captain Blackwell. "He is nothing like George." He made a haughty gesture, walking away, as though tweaking a high shirt collar. The Hawaiians were known to describe people by both word and gesture.

Captain Blackwell and Aloka exchanged a brief glance. There was astonishment, even pleading, in the younger man's face.

State canoes were sent out to meet *Albion* once she was in the inner harbor, to bear away the bodies of the sovereigns. Boki, Li'liah, Ka'ahumanu, and the king's remaining suite, even young Kimo, Aloka's servant, were put into two of the ship's boats and rowed ashore. A numerous gathering awaited them. The *ali'i*, the nobles, were naturally in the front and closest to the breaking surf. Among these were Ka'ahumanu's sisters, one of whom was the mother of Liholiho, and the other mother of the present king, his successor. The English were taken aback by the great wailing *mele* that went up from the people, the chant of grief started by Ka'ahumanu and the other queens when they were within sight of one another. The fort near the beach fired a minute gun until the caskets were brought on shore.

McMurtry was one of the boat's crew helping to hand the brown people out on shore, and as he did so he scanned the gathering at the water's edge. His ugly mug screwed up in a look of satisfaction when his eye found what it was searching for. A knot of Europeans, white faces on the fringe of the crowd, the deserters and malcontents from all nations that made up the Hawaiian king's dockyard force.

On the pull back to *Albion*, McMurtry said, low voiced to Narhilla, "I smoked 'em, didn't I? And one blackamoor too."

The European faction was no where in attendance next day, there was only a great concourse of native people on the beach. Karaimoku and Boki came out to *Albion* in the morning. They returned on shore in her gig carrying Captain and Mrs. Blackwell, and accompanied by the *Blonde's* barge with nearly all her officers, the surgeons of the two ships, and Emma.

Captain Blackwell picked Mercedes up out of his gig, in order to set her dry-foot ashore. Emma thought Mercedes looked pained and anxious. Aloka did not offer her such gallantry, merely extending his hand to help her out of the *Blonde's* boat, which was just as well. What was a little water up to her ankles, when she'd already gone float-boarding in the deep water and breaking waves.

On the beach the parties were arranging themselves. Captain Blackwell and Captain Verson went first with Karaimoku, and Kanakoa, the hereditary king of Oahu. Emma had observed her mama and Captain Blackwell greet the king first upon coming ashore. Captain Bowles, *Blonde's* first lieutenant, and Mr. Montelongo came next, escorted by Boki. Aloka, who gave an arm each to Mercedes and Emma, walked in this group. Each of the Europeans, down to the *Blonde's* reefers, had a native chief for escort on the way to the *maneaba*. On either side of their path, though kept at some distance from them, Emma looked out upon a sea of native faces.

She whispered a question to Aloka, who passed it on to Boki. They'd been shipmates a long time, and become friends.

"The way to the *maneaba* is tabooed, so they must keep back," Boki said. "We have not given up all the old ways."

Many of the native men, the native faces and voices, brought Kuanoa to her mind, and she felt singularly grateful to the old ways. The chiefs who were their escort, on this day, were all dressed in European black suits. Some even wore stockings and shoes.

The lady chiefs they found, upon entering the *maneaba*, dressed also in black silk or crepe. Their only ornaments were feather caplets or necklaces, which stood out strikingly against the severe black clothing. The *maneaba* was a half mile from the beach, located inside a tall enclosing wickerwork fence. It was a native structure with doors opening to the four cardinal points of the compass, and quite large. In length fifty feet and in width twenty-five, with wood pillars thirty feet high holding up the ridge pole of the meeting place. At the opposite end from where Emma and the whole procession entered, sat the king and princess of the Sandwich Islands.

A boy of ten and a girl of eight sat upon a cane sofa on a raised platform at the far end of the room, flanked on either side by

Ka'ahumanu and the other queens, her sisters. Draped over the sofa the sovereigns were seated upon was a magnificent garment covered in feathers of brilliant yellow, red, and black. Their escort, saving Karaimoku, dropped away and took up places in two lines of *ali'i*, men and women, that stretched from the raised platform to the southern entrance of the *maneaba*.

There was a great ceremony of presentation, where every one of the Europeans was named to the king and princess, and then all of the *ali'i*, starting with the most important—the queens—and ending at the bottom of the meeting house. Once this long introduction was got through, the Europeans were led to seats of honor next to Karaimoku's chair, and across from the queens. Emma's head spun with the names of the people she'd met, the great majority beginning with 'K' and containing a multitude of vowel sounds. She much doubted she could remember a one correctly.

Captain Blackwell could have named them all; it was a particular genius he possessed, that might have saved his life on more than one occasion. The introductions and handshakes concluded, Captain Blackwell stepped forward to deliver the message of his sovereign to the Sandwich Island nation. He spoke in Hawaiian to say he would address them first in English, and then translate for them in Hawaiian. As he said this, Captain Blackwell gave the American missionary on Oahu, who would normally have translated his English, a quelling look.

"His Britannic Majesty commands me to salute the regents of the Sandwich Islands in his name, and to make known to the reigning king, and the principal chiefs, the sorrow he felt at the death of their late king and queen, whilst on a visit in his dominions. His Majesty King George of England could not further testify his regret at the death of the sovereigns than by giving an early audience to the surviving suite. The manner of their reception, and the treatment they met with in England, could be best detailed by Boki and those to whom God has granted a safe return to their native land."

There was a stir and murmurs of approbation from the chiefs who'd been in England, when Captain Blackwell reached this point.

"The King of England has moreover caused the expenses of the Sandwich Island chiefs, while in England, to be paid by the Government; and has appointed Captain James Blackwell of the Royal Navy to wait upon them, and to attend to their wishes in the capacity of Britain's official consul to the Sandwich Islands. His Britannic Majesty has sent one of his royal frigates to convey the remains of the late king and queen, with their surviving suite, to their native land; and to assure the actual government of the Islands of his sincere wishes for their welfare and happiness, and his hopes that, with the blessing of Providence, they might continue to prosper, under a peaceful and well-ordered administration."

Karaimoku stood and made his acknowledgements, adding that the regents and chiefs were well pleased with the message and the messenger sent by the King of England. The old chief looked gratified too. Captain Blackwell was remembered in those islands and spoke their language like one of them. He and Karaimoku turned to Captain Verson, for the distribution of the presents.

The Hawaiian chiefs received their tokens of King George's esteem with pleasure and a good grace, but there was absolute joy on the part of the young King Kiaukiauli with his present. Two midshipmen came forward at Captain Verson's signal and presented the young king a Windsor dress uniform, complete with a scaled down but very beautiful sword, and a hat with a long plume. The joy on the youngster's face made everyone saving the austere Protestant missionary smile. He leapt up and instantly threw off his black mourning clothes, donned the British uniform, and proceeded to prance about. This put a period to the solemn and formal proceeding. Refreshments were brought in; and the gathering broke up into informal groups.

Not everyone was pleased. Ka'ahumanu nearly knocked the wind out of one of her attendants when she clapped him in the stomach with the silver teapot she'd received. The queen's gaze was fixed upon the little capering king, and his sister. The princess sat demurely upon the sofa still, her eyes turned to the missionary to discover if her modest behavior should be noticed and approved.

"She would not wear the *pa'ū* that cost more than a year to make," Ka'ahumanu said, to no one in particular, though Emma and Captain Blackwell were just at hand. "She deigns to sit upon it, but must wear a gown of black silk."

The queen looked at Emma, up and down, scrutinizing her high waisted figured muslin gown. Emma refused to be put out of countenance. She studied the beautiful feather garment the little princess sat upon.

"I should wear it," she said, "I don't think I have ever seen a finer, or more beautiful garment."

"Emma!" her father said in a low voice, as though she'd uttered some gaucherie.

Ka'ahumanu smiled, a sudden brilliant flash in an otherwise forbidding face. "And deservedly so." Nodding to them both, she told Captain Blackwell she should see him at the serious conference at Karaimoku's house.

"I know it is a royal *pa'ū*, sir, so you need not cry out about it," Emma said to forestall him.

Captain Blackwell looked as though he were restraining an oath. It saddened Emma that the sympathy that had grown between them in Chile had apparently not been of a lasting nature.

"Be so good as to accompany your Mama back to *Albion*. The *Blonde's* reefers and boats' crews will attend you. This meeting at Karaimoku's is for senior officers only."

Emma considered answering, "Aye, aye, sir." But she had never yet dared take certain liberties with her father, and had no notion of beginning in a room full of people. Emma nodded, and turning round she found Mercedes standing there. Her mama wore that unhappy look that was always there when Emma and Captain Blackwell disagreed.

On the half mile walk to the landing place Emma was silent, considering. It had been a discouraging shore visit thus far. She was used to a certain degree of admiration and regard; she made no doubt that the eyes of the midshipmen walking in back of her were fixed upon her figure; yet she should have to get over being the Queen of the May. Emma must have been much stupider than she was not to have noticed it was not she receiving the keen attention of the Hawaiians.

Aloka was the object of an almost panting interest among the lady chiefs, if Emma did not mistake, in his lieutenant's uniform. The Hawaiians loved finery and show in dress, and he'd received a great deal of scrutiny from the men as well. In the short time she'd spent at the reception in the *maneaba*, she'd heard low voiced comparisons between Aloka and his half-brother, George, who was apparently given to appear in European clothes. She understood the attraction and interest Aloka excited; a native son returned with his perfect English manners and address, his mariner's profession. This was to say nothing of the fact he was a fine figure of a man. They could eat him up.

Emma felt down-hearted, even a little sorry for herself. She knew Aloka looked just as well out of his uniform as in it. They were nearing the landing place and the boats. Emma decided to tell Mercedes of her unease, but her mother pulled her arm loose from her grasp. Mercedes skipped forward and fell into the arms of a black person standing beside *Albion's* boat.

Saunders had not changed overmuch, the coiled braids that sprang up all over her head were shot through with grey, but she was dressed, as accustomed, in seaman's duck trousers and loose fitting tunic. She and Mercedes grinned into one another's faces, holding hands still. Mercedes remarked more lines on Saunders' face when she smiled, and knew the same was true of her own.

"Will you come aboard *Albion* for a visit, Saunders? She is a yacht, not a man-of-war."

"She is a fine ship, Missus, for so she must be called with a post-captain commanding her. How keeps the Captain? I saw him from a distance yesterday."

"He's prime, Saunders, I thank you."

Here they paused. It was not right to play question and answer in front of the *Blonde's* officers and the boats' crews. Mercedes smiled and inclined her head in the direction of *Albion* with a questioning look at Saunders.

"I shall be honored, Missus, with a visit to *Albion*."

"Right you are, there, mate," McMurtry said to Saunders, as she settled in the bow of *Albion's* boat. She knew her place so far as not to sit in the stern with the Captain's wife and daughter.

Once aboard *Albion* Mercedes desired Mr. Parsons to show Saunders over the ship.

"We were shipmates in *L'Unite*," she told Mr. Parsons, "the Captain's command last time we were in these islands. Please bring Saunders to the great cabin at the conclusion of the inspection."

Mercedes was gratified to see, when Mr. Parsons escorted Saunders in to the cabin, that they had struck up an easy rapport. She'd hoped it would be so. Saunders was a thorough going seaman, and Mr. Parsons man enough to respect that in whoever he should meet. The same could not be said for McMurtry, who brought in the refreshments and banged them down on the table.

"Christ, McMurtry, you've knocked the tea things all ahoo," Emma said.

Mr. Parsons bowed and took his leave, followed by McMurtry, with an uglier expression than usual fixed on his ill-conditioned mug. He was a jealous creature and since Saunders had once been Mercedes' servant, he felt she should be treated like one. Rather than being fed on cake and tea like a lady.

"Sit down, please, Saunders. Allow me to present my daughter Emma Blackwell. Emma, this is Saunders...I'm sorry, I don't know your first name."

"Which it's Priscilla, and now you know the reason why. Saunders will do, ma'am." She nodded at Emma, who was setting the tea cups back on their saucers. "I'm honored to meet the wife of the new Admiral of Hawaii. Master Al and I shall have much to do with one another in future."

Saunders had known Aloka when he was a bare bottomed toddler, so she felt at liberty to use the old name given him by the L'Unites.

Mercedes exchanged a glance with Emma. "Is it so much known then, Saunders, this Admiral of Hawaii affair?"

"Oh, aye. I don't know how it is but the water round these islands speeds their news rather than slows it down, and if it has to do with their own, the people seem to gather it from the very wind and waves. But there are two factions, do you see? Those that have accepted the Jesus book, as they call it, and those that don't."

They all stared at one another for a space. Mercedes had been brought up outside any traditional religious faith, with her mother a courtesan, and she'd communicated what she thought of as her heathenism to Emma. As for Saunders, who'd once been loaned out by her plantation masters to ships anchoring in Antigua as a comfort woman, it was doubtful she believed in much of anything saving her own survival.

"That will be useful knowledge for Captain Blackwell, I thank you Saunders."

"They are infinitely happy King George has seen fit to send the skipper, of all people. Especially the cool old heads among them." Saunders gave Mercedes and Emma a considering glance. "They are not so good at news outside their families and tribe. May I beg to know how Master Edward does?"

"Oh!" Mercedes exclaimed, realizing Saunders most probably thought him dead. "Edward is well indeed! A fine grown gentleman living in England, studying at a great university."

She saw the relief in Saunders' face, and Mercedes and Emma were both touched by it. Mercedes was suddenly unable to speak for the great lump in her throat. She should have given Edward's regards to Saunders immediately in his place.

"He is still odd as odd can be," Emma said, "but the academics and philosophical gentlemen have discovered a genius in it. And he is very dear to us, we love and value him much."

"Do you know, Missus," Saunders said, looking almost affectionately on Emma, "she looks very much like you."

"Anyone who knew my mother, Mr. Martinez for one, declares she is the image of my Mama. If Emma looks like me it is because she is my daughter, and daughter-in-law. We fouled the hawse of the missionaries in Hilo with that one, you may be sure."

"Goddamn!"

Saunders had been unable to restrain herself, and looked a little sheepish. Mercedes and Emma both laughed self consciously. Here was honesty in its purest form.

"Now you have discovered all my secrets in the first five minutes, Saunders, tell me how you do. How is Colonel Frasier, and your life here?"

Saunders frowned and looked down for a moment. "Ann Frasier died close on three years ago. Colonel Frasier, as she was called, wanted it known, her true persuasion, after death. She thought it would be easier for me to follow her, into the position of master shipwright for the king."

"Goddamn!" Mercedes and Emma exclaimed together.

Then there were smiles and laughter, all of them feeling on a more equal footing.

One or two of the *ali'i* recollected Edward, and they asked Captain Blackwell and Aloka, at the meeting at Karaimoku's, after the *akua*. Edward was affectionately called 'little god' by some of the Hawaiians for the prodigious skill in drawing, and rendering to the life birds and landscapes, that he'd first exhibited in those islands. Aloka gave a comfortable account of his brother to those interested older men, while feeling inside a distinctly uncomfortable anxiety and apprehension. Aloka felt today somehow damned, rather than blessed, by the gods.

The general meeting was attended by the *ali'i* and the officers of *Blonde* and *Albion*, with a sort of joint chairmanship between Karaimoku and Captain Blackwell. Karaimoku appeared in black trousers and a loose fitting black tunic, while the majority of the *ali'i* had traded their black mourning suits for the native breeches and mantel. Karaimoku asked if King George had sent them laws by which they might govern themselves, this being one of the missions of the Hawaiian delegation that had visited England.

"Laws I do not bring you, but this paper with a few remarks from our leading ministers concerning the governance of your affairs." Captain Blackwell advanced a packet to Karaimoku. "I beg you will look over them at your leisure, and if you approve the measures, adopt them as your own. These are in no way dictates from the British government, which has no wish to interfere with the business of the chiefs of Hawaii, who must be the best judges of what suits the people."

Karaimoku accepted the package with a pleased countenance, nodding with satisfaction at Boki, who must have given advanced warning of King George's response. The regent named a day in the coming week when the *ali'i* would gather, and invited Captain Blackwell, to translate and discuss the content of the British message. At this point Karaimoku turned the discussion to one of military affairs, the strength of Kamehameha's armament, and Hawaii's desire to work in concert with the British for the protection of the nation. More particularly he began to address the succession of leadership in Hawaii's maritime force.

Aloka had mixed feelings about being spoken of as the next Admiral of Hawaii, as though it were already decided, a foregone conclusion. To him an admiral was a great man indeed, a much older and wiser man. Aloka focused his attention instead on the important description of the king's arsenal. Six hundred muskets, eight four-pounders, one six-pounder, five three-pounders, forty swivels, and six small mortars.

"And there are twenty-one schooners carrying swivels, some of which are commanded by foreigners." Karaimoku stared pointedly at Aloka, and the two British captains.

There was further discussion, and then the topic of when mister lieutenant Blackwell could be stepped down from his present duties aboard the *Blonde* came up, and Captain Verson immediately agreed to a proposed date. Aloka felt his heart hammering in his chest. Should he not speak up now? But Karaimoku was suddenly dismissing the officers of the *Blonde* and *Albion*; all saving his father and himself; with assurances of good will on the part of the British, and cooperation on that of the Hawaiians.

Refreshments were brought in, and after they had partaken of Karaimoku's good things, the three of the them sat down together again.

"Much as I should like to honor my brother's wishes," Karaimoku said, "and I have no doubt you are an excellent mariner, Aloka, I cannot sanction your elevation to such a high station without proof of your loyalty to our king and nation."

Aloka had been frightened at the prospect of becoming an admiral, but he found he feared even more the loss of the position. The consequences attending on his not finding a berth, so to speak, in those islands began racing through his mind.

"I am not sure how that is to be done, sir." Aloka's voice sounded strained, even to his own ears. "In England, we receive a commission and swear an oath of allegiance."

"How it is done in England is of no consequence here." Karaimoku's gaze was an odd mixture of ferocity and sympathy. "You may show your allegiance to King Kiaukiauli, this Regency, and the people, by executing George. He is your half-brother, these things are best done by family."

Aloka's head jerked back in surprise. He stole a glance at Captain Blackwell, whose look was grave.

Karaimoku heaved a great sigh, and his face relaxed, as though he'd been relieved of the greater part of a burden. "Traitors to the nation must die, Aloka. I believe that is the same in England as it is here. You must go to George and ask him what manner of death he prefers. He is housed here, in my old dwelling, with two of his women unfortunate enough to be taken with him."

Aloka sat reflecting a moment, silent in his chair, while two weathered faces studied him.

"I'll speak to George, sir," Aloka said. "To discover his wishes. The fate of a traitor is the same in all nations, as you say, sir. Must I also carry out the sentence?" Aloka wanted to be clear about such an order.

"You will find out what death George prefers, and kill him in whatever manner he chooses."

Orders could not be plainer. It sounded barbarous, savage. But was it any worse than burn, sink, or destroy, flogging round the fleet, run up to the yardarm with a noose around the neck?

"In that case, sir, I will undertake to speak to George. Were you to require an oath, sir, I could not swear to you that I will carry out the sentence. Such a thing I may choose to leave in other hands, with deep regret and an understanding of the consequences."

Aloka looked over at his father as he concluded, and caught the flash of an approving look. That put some heart into him.

Karaimoku slapped his large hands down on his knees. "You cannot say fairer than that."

The prison that housed George was no stinking pestilential pit like the one Aloka had known in Brazil, far from it. He was accommodated in the thatched house Karaimoku had recently quitted, together with his wives, and a few servants courtesy of the two regents. The house was in the native style, large, airy, and fit for an *ali'i*. The floor was laid with small black stones covered over with large mats, and the roof lined with pandanus leaves. The only sign it was now a gaol were the warriors with muskets and clubs stationed at each entrance and the several window openings cut in the thatch.

Aloka was escorted to the house by Karaimoku, Ka'ahumanu, and several courtiers. Captain Blackwell had chosen to return to *Albion*. Everyone understood this was a duty he was to perform alone, and the natives all stopped at the door. They had a conference with the sentry, while Aloka went in. It was a high-ceilinged dwelling so that the interior was quite dim, and as Aloka moved toward the light of a brace of candles, he did remark the house was stripped of furnishings.

He found George seated at a solitary desk, on which the candelabra rested, studying some papers before him. Beyond the candlelight, in a corner of the apartment, Aloka heard feminine voices and caught shadow like movements. George was clad in European breeches and shirt, and as he looked up at Aloka, he tugged at his collar to straighten it.

"So they've sent you, have they?" George spoke as though they'd parted the day before. "Aloka, son of Princess Kalani and her fourth, fifth...dozenth husband?"

Aloka made a leg. "At your service. Son of the princess's fourth husband, Captain James Blackwell. How do you do, George?"

"As you see, mewed up in this goddamn place, when I should be king on Kaua'i."

"There can be only one king, and that is Kiaukiauli."

"You would bow to a boy, a mere puppy? When you and I were his age, we had made our first voyages. Gone over the seas and seen other lands, places of promise, where a man can make his fortune and his name."

Their eyes met and Aloka was moved by what he most dreaded, a fellow feeling for his half brother.

"I have been to the Pacific Northwest, many times, anchored in her fine deep bays, and traded in the wood of enormous forests. We could sail between the American mainland and the orient, masters of our own vessels, answerable to no man."

George was a good looking man, and what Aloka supposed must be called attractive. He was not so tall or broad as many Hawaiian nobles but, standing, they looked one another in the eye. He made again that gesture of plucking up his shirt collar, and turned toward the rustling in one corner of the room. In an imperious tone he called, "Come here."

There was hesitation in that corner, the whisper of voices, a sudden resounding slap. A young woman, more a girl, moved into the ring of candlelight.

"This one is from there, an American native." George declared, roughly squeezing her lovely brown cheeks between strong fingers. "I won her of one of the great Northern chiefs. Take her, she's yours. You see I want to be true brothers, and share everything, be *punalua* with you."

Aloka felt his heart recoil. Co-husband. George used the Hawaiian expression for a group of lovers, multiple husbands and wives.

Mistaking his reaction, George said, "Don't like this one. Nahina!"

Another woman moved into the candlelight. A plump lady with a froward ill-tempered expression, clearly Hawaiian and clearly defiant.

"No, I—"

"Don't know what to do? Come, brother, let me enlighten you."

From the desk George took up the parchments he'd been studying when Aloka walked in, and handed them to him. Aloka had seen these sorts of illustrations before; certain men in both services, army and navy, were veritable collectors; of men and women depicted in the sexual act. What Aloka could not like were the expressions on the women's faces, as though they were in pain.

In a confidential tone, George said in his ear, "Ever had dry sex? You make them put crushed coral and herbs, well, you know where. There is nothing like it, I do assure you."

Aloka looked George in the eye, and set the drawings face down on the desk. He now knew what the English expression 'made my skin crawl' felt like.

"You seem to mistake the intention of my call upon you. I did not come here to make alliances of any kind."

"I saw you with your women this morning, on your way to the *maneaba*. What you can want with that old, sick one, I cannot tell. But the other! By all the gods she is the most—"

"Do not speak of them, either one!"

George was taken aback, he pursed his lips, fingering his collar. Aloka began to see that George imagined himself a man of the world.

"Don't get into a taking, brother. Bring her to me, let her decide for herself if she likes me."

"Never!" Aloka could have picked George up by his frilled shirt and throttled him with it. "I've come to ask what manner of death you will have, George Kaumuarii, son of Kalani, grandson of Ata Gege. There can be only one king and that is Kiaukiauli, and since he is but a boy, the regents in his stead."

"Would you fight me? To the victor the honors, the women, the admiralty?"

"I would. But you should die in any case, it's your sentence for rebellion."

George sniffed. "Drowning at sea then. That will do. I hope you are prepared to do cold murder, little brother."

"Don't call me brother." Aloka glared at George. "I have only one brother, Edward James Blackwell of Cambridge and London." He tried to compose himself. "Drowning it is then, George Kaumuarii. I shall call on you again." Aloka turned pointedly to the two women. "The guards at these doors are to keep George in. You will be allowed to pass if you wish it, no one will detain you."

He bowed to all three, turned about and strode away.

"You do not even ask after our mother," George called. "Do not you care whether she lives?"

Aloka's back stiffened, but he did not break his stride toward the door. He had such a sick churning in his stomach that the urge to get away was stronger than the duty he felt to a mother he could not remember. The patter of feet pursuing him did not make him turn either. When she was abreast of him, Aloka saw it was the younger woman. He let her pass in front of him and walked outside.

They both breathed in the sweet warm air as though it were a tonic. Only the sentry remained at the door, the regents and their courtiers having gone away. After studying the night sky for a moment, Aloka set off in the direction of Karaimoku's new house, saying gently to the woman, "This way if you please."

He walked along trying to conquer the revolted feeling in his vitals, and work out the few words he would say to Karaimoku and Ka'ahumanu. A remote part of his mind pondered what he was to do with the girl at his side, when a figure moved at him from out of the dark.

"Master Al!"

He went into a crouch, his hand on the hilt of his sword. Though Aloka could not see the speaker, there was something in the voice that made him relax his fighting stance almost as soon as he'd taken it up.

"It's Saunders, Master Al. Remember me?"

Aloka came up close to her. In his relief he grasped her forearm in the native fashion, her sinuous muscled arm, and smiled into her face.

"Saunders! Bless me, I can hardly believe it."

"The Captain asked me to round up some *kanakas* and take you off in a native craft. After you speak to the chiefs, in course."

She and a half dozen men escorted him the rest of the way to the regent's house. Aloka relaxed somewhat in the presence of Saunders, and went in to Karaimoku and Ka'ahumanu more composed. The two chiefs had many years and much experience between them, and they did not detain Aloka, nor question him too closely. The regents released him after a mercifully short meeting, to seek the comfort of his ship.

Aloka took Saunders aside as they neared the landing place.

"That woman, I do not know so much as her name, has been badly used. Will you find her a place to lie tonight?" He peered imploringly at Saunders. "I dare not take her aboard *Blonde*. Captain Verson may cut up rough, to say nothing of Emma. Tomorrow I may be able to arrange something for her. I shall consult Mercedes."

"Abused her, did he?" Saunders glanced over at the young native woman, who had a wary eye upon Aloka. "Goddamn scrub. She can sling a hammock with me, I live alone since the Colonel passed."

"Oh, Saunders! I am deeply sorry for your loss."

"Thank 'ee, Master Al. Let's let the girl know then, shall we?"

There was some relief on the part of the young woman when the plan was revealed to her. She'd apparently feared going aboard ship, since it was on a ship that all her troubles began. She watched with disinterest while Aloka stripped off his clothes and threw them into the canoe meant to carry him to the British ships.

"What are you called?" Saunders asked the young woman. "Not what that brute's been calling you. Your real name that your Momma used."

"Anushka. Little Anushka, she used to say."

Aloka dove into the surf. He wanted to stop the sound of the pain in that woman's voice, drown the recollection of the words exchanged with his brother, and wash the sick and despairing feelings away in the clean sea.

In the cabin of *Albion* they heard the officer of the watch hailing a boat, and then the thump of the craft against the ship's side. Blackwell emerged on deck a few moments later, having left the women in the cabin wringing their hands. Peering down into the native craft Blackwell saw neither Aloka or Saunders.

One of the *kanakas* looked kindly up into Blackwell's face and said, "He comes this way, *kupuna kāne*," and pointed his paddle. It was a respectful address, but Blackwell didn't care for being named grandfather by any old sod. He gazed out over the water. His eyesight was not what it once was, for he did not see Aloka in the water until he was quite close to the ship.

Blackwell retreated to the quarterdeck, to preserve his dignity. Aloka swam alongside, pulled himself out of the water and came up the entry steps. Once on deck he did not throw his head back and shake himself like a dog in his accustomed manner. In fact there was something in Aloka's bearing that made Blackwell throw aside reserve and hasten over to him.

Aloka's clothes and shoes were handed up from the canoe. Once dressed Aloka said, "Good evening, sir. May I have a word?"

Blackwell nodded and motioned to the quarterdeck. As Aloka passed him, he stopped suddenly, reached out and pulled Blackwell into an embrace.

Aloka clung to him, and when they disengaged it required some moments of pacing together, on the weather side of the quarterdeck, before either one was composed enough to speak.

"I told the old chiefs I would do it, " he said quietly. "I met George."

For several steps Aloka paced with bowed head.

"I feel I have to. There is something wrong with George, like Kuanoa, using his women most brutally. He has an astonishing sense of entitlement, never asked after the fate of the men who followed him into battle. He is—" Aloka made that gesture of pulling up his collar, but with a revolted look upon his face "—wicked."

They stopped in their pacing and faced one another. Blackwell knew a thing or two about evil, from past experience.

"Mad dogs must be put down, son."

Aloka nodded once and glanced away, clenching his jaw.

"Will you...will you come with me, the day it is to be done?"

Aloka asked nothing improper. It would not be amiss for Britain's consul general to attend aboard the Hawaiian king's ship. The execution would be an affair of state.

He put his hand on Aloka's shoulder. "If you want me there, I shall be."

Aloka let out a breath and sagged a moment under his hand. Then he said something that startled Blackwell.

"Thank you, Father. I'm so afraid."

His son turned and they resumed their pacing. Aloka had been in any number of sea battles, boarding parties, and cutting out expeditions. He had the courage of a young lion and had killed in the service of his country. This was different, of course, it was his half-brother. And it was not battle, but a cold killing with the other man disarmed and helpless. Blackwell was still puzzled by Aloka's words, and the emotion in his voice.

"What if," Aloka said, very low. "What if George was made that way because of his parentage?"

Blackwell was astonished, not least because he immediately found himself prepared to urge that Aloka and Emma's offspring should not be monsters of iniquity.

"You cannot give way to those kinds of thoughts," Blackwell said. "You must simply live life, accept what comes. The way you have accepted this hard duty about George."

Aloka looked down at the deck, and then straight at Blackwell.

"He had the temerity to speak of our women. At that moment I wanted to stop his breath forever." Aloka shuddered, and then with an effort squared his shoulders. "We must not keep the ladies waiting longer."

The sight of Mercedes and her gentle manner toward him brought a great choking lump into Aloka's throat. He remembered how he used to hide his head in her skirts and weep, when he'd been wounded as a boy. He would like to have done so now, to feel the reassuring stroke of her hand on his hair. Aloka hurried Emma into the native craft and away to *Blonde*, barely able to exchange more than a greeting with Mercedes, and certainly not speaking to her of that poor wretched young woman left ashore.

His sole object was to regain the familiarity of the British man-of-war, and more especially his little private den. Once undressed and swinging gently in his cot, with Emma beside him, Aloka unburdened his heart. But though he did tell her of Anushka's desertion, George's more lubricious proposals he could not bring himself to relate. Aloka hoped that Emma, and Mercedes, should never so much as look on his half-brother George.

"It is a terrible duty has fallen on you," Emma said, "and I shall certainly do something for this woman. It might have been me, depending on the favor of strangers, had they succeeded in Brazil."

"Don't..." Aloka unclenched his teeth. "Don't speak of it, my love. I cannot bear to think of you ... I grieve for my part in almost allowing you to be taken."

Emma pressed closer against his side. She began to caress his chest, and as her questing hand moved lower Aloka caught it up in a firm grasp. He was so oppressed he could not even seek solace in her flesh. There needed to be some joy in his heart for that, and at the moment there was none.

"Just let me hold you."

She asked him, not in a pushing manner, whether Captain Blackwell would accompany him when it came time to carry out the sentence, and whether she must not.

"Father has consented to be a witness on behalf of government, and you must certainly go on shore with your Mama."

He took a great shuddering breath, and wiped tears from his face. She kissed him tenderly, saying nothing, and lay back down against his chest.

When he'd recovered somewhat, Aloka said, "I desire you would not even see the ship off. Oh Emma! I wish I could just lie here with you, and never turn out again."

CHAPTER THIRTEEN

A strong breeze out of the North came up on the day the sentence was to be carried out against George Kaumuarii. The barometer had fallen steadily for the last twelve hours, but Aloka was obliged to turn out in command of the sloop *Kamehameha I*. His usually cheerful face had taken on a grave and stern expression not unlike Captain Blackwell's. Aloka had filled the intervening days working with the crew of *Kamehameha I*, getting used to their ways and they to him.

He had to learn a new vocabulary of commands as expressed in Hawaiian, and Aloka wished he'd started sooner. *Kokua na kelamoku apau*, all hands on deck; *ho'alu aku i ka lau*, slacken the sheets. *Kamehameha I's* crew could nearly all pass for able seamen, but naturally the native men were no where near Royal Navy style where discipline and organization were considered. Secretly, Aloka had been glad to get away from the island on sail handling exercises. He was guilty as well, for having thrown Emma so much upon her own devices. In these last days Aloka's strongest desire had been to put distance between himself and his half-brother, and the wretched duty ahead.

Aloka had not left Emma alone overnight, of course, always returning in the evenings to the little wood house alongside the London Missionary society church. The previous occupants Ka'ahumanu had unceremoniously ejected in their favor. It had at first been assumed by the local *ali'i* that they should all be living together, Captain Blackwell and Aloka and their wives. But

Captain Blackwell made it clear the idea did not suit, and he'd taken Mercedes to a half finished stone and wood dwelling that was building far up the slope of Diamond Head. The only small glimmer of gratification Aloka had in those unsettled, uncomfortable days was in having found a berth for George's brutalized wife Anushka.

"Saunders knows a thing or two about abuse," Mercedes had said. "She was so badly used in Antigua, she told me she never could have children. If anyone can help Anushka recover it would be Saunders, and Saunders is willing she should stay as long as she needs to."

God bless Saunders, Aloka thought. The one flicker of goodness in an appalling sequence of events that was by no means over.

Albion's boat touched gently against the side of *Kamehameha I*. Captain Blackwell came up the side onto the deck and Aloka saluted before he could stop himself. Captain Blackwell returned the salute and then turned with a conscious look to his coxswain Narhilla, following him up the side. Narhilla was bearing a set of iron manacles for wrists and ankles.

"Your second in command?" Captain Blackwell asked.

"Maaro." Aloka motioned at a man standing behind him near the wheel.

At a nod from Captain Blackwell, Narhilla delivered the set of irons from *Albion* to *Kamehameha I's* lieutenant. Aloka moved to the gangway as the state canoe was seen to put off from shore, carrying the two regents and the prisoner.

"Good luck, Master Al," Narhilla whispered. He passed Aloka before going down the ship's side into *Albion's* boat. "God be with you."

Aloka felt that lump of emotion rise in his throat, the same he'd been fighting for days to keep down.

The strong strokes of the paddlers, chanting as they came, brought the state canoe rapidly alongside the sloop. Ka'ahumanu, Karaimoku and their suite came aboard, and then George was handed up the side. His hands were bound with sennit cord, so he was unable to climb the ship's side unassisted. George jerked his arms loose of the seamen's grasp once on deck. There was a haughty set to his face. He would not deign to look at any of them saving Aloka. George stared at him intently, with a look of cold hatred and contempt.

"Take that man below and clap him in irons."

George was led away between two sturdy warriors at Aloka's command. Maaro followed behind them with the irons. Aloka had rehearsed some of the proceedings of this day with his crew. He went to supervise the bringing aboard a worn native canoe, part of which might have been used as a float board but that it was to be George's sepulcher: by ancient custom of the people.

"In some lands they set the condemned man adrift in the canoe to starve to death," Ka'ahumanu said to Aloka. The canoe was on board, and he stood with the regents on the quarterdeck. "We are not so barbaric."

George would be put, manacled, into the canoe and sunk.

"The ship is ready to get underway, with your leave." Aloka bowed to the regents, received their nods, and walked forward and called out the orders to unmoor ship.

The men chanted at the capstan, and Aloka looked apprehensively at his father. There was no singing and chanting on the deck of a Royal Navy ship.

Captain Blackwell merely shook his head. "I do not like the look of it."

Aloka knew he spoke of the weather, the glass falling, the strengthening wind.

"Karaimoku says these conditions only ever foretell heavy rains, but I shall not be unhappy for sea room."

From the activity on board the *Blonde*, as *Kamehahameha I* sailed past her, it seemed Captain Verson was in agreement. The frigate was unmooring. Aloka and Captain Blackwell lifted their hats to the quarterdeck of the man-of-war as they passed. Black Savages they must seem today to the English officers and seamen, who knew on what business they were about.

Both Aloka and Captain Blackwell were aware it would not take long to sail to a point the regents would deem propitious for George's end. They would not sink the land. It would take place in deep water, the realm of the sharks and whales and great tuna, but within sight of the land they were defending by George's death.

Aloka had an odd sensation as though time were running out for him too.

"Tell me something of my mother and my grandfather, Ata Gege," he said to Captain Blackwell. "Something good, if you please, that will not make me shudder to be a part of them. Of all this."

Captain Blackwell wore a serious considering expression. They each had a hand grasping a stanchion, the sloop was breasting high swells as she beat to windward. "Kalani gave you up to protect you from Kaumuarii. She was afraid he would murder you to assure his succession to Ata Gege's place. She wanted me to make you a chief among the white men."

"She worried for me, and now look what I am come to. I do not even know if she lives, because I could not bear speaking to him. How is that as compensation for her sacrifice?"

"Kalani did what most mothers would do. She must have seen what Kaumuarii was becoming, even then. Your grandfather Ata Gege was a violent man, but also a man of war and of honor." They caught Ka'ahumanu signaling to them, and exchanged a pained look. "He once told me, before a battle...be calm, be voiceless, be valiant, drink the bitter waters, my son, turn not back, onward unto death."

George was hoisted up the after hatchway companion ladder by *Kamehahameha I's* lieutenant and bosun. They attended him, shackled hand and foot, as George shuffled across the deck. The rotten canoe was in the water, with lines fastening her head and stern to the sloop's larboard main chains. The prisoner was turned to face the regents, who each made him a speech. Not as long a one as the elders otherwise might have done, because the wind had risen and the motion of the sloop, though lying to, was lively. A squall of rain hit them, as George was lowered into the already leaking canoe.

George shook his head to clear his soaked hair from his face and lifted his manacled hands toward his shirt collar. Aloka stood in the chains, one arm wrapped around a shroud. He leaned down toward the canoe, an axe gripped in his hand.

"You will do this then?" George shouted at him over the roar of the wind. "And be damned forever, you and the whelps you may have with your luscious wife!"

Aloka glared at him, raising the axe, and suddenly the expression of George's face changed. His look of hatred and malice melted into a wide eyed innocent and pleading stare.

"Don't do it, little brother, we were nourished at the same breast, our boyish sports were in common. Remember how we played and laughed?"

Aloka held George's gaze as he swung the axe, hacking a hole in the canoe's bottom. George screamed and spat at him, the sea flooding into the little craft.

"Let go the falls," Aloka called.

The seamen on deck cast off the lines holding the canoe alongside. A wave swamped the canoe and reached far up the sloop's side, drenching Aloka as he clung to the shrouds outside the ship. He forced himself to look at George, who was cursing him in a language neither Hawaiian or English. A language that sent a chill to his heart. The awful and frightening rant was cut off as water closed over George's head. Aloka leaned far out to watch as the pale face receded into the deep. George Kaumuarii's long hair stretched upward as though reaching for the surface. Another great sea dashed against the ship's side, nearly tearing Aloka from his perch.

He felt strong arms grasping him, and his father and Maaro pulled him inboard. Aloka stood swaying before the regents and his crew, all eyes were turned expectantly on him. The tears on his face could not be distinguished in his sodden condition. Aloka wanted nothing so much as to retreat to his cabin, to hide, and give further vent to his misery.

The words he'd thought of and almost spoken after another traitor's death came to him. They seemed to desire a speech, so Aloka stepped forward and raised his voice.

To Hawai'i: and may he who wishes to defend her
die an honorable death,
And may he who is a traitor to her be dishonored
to his last breath,
May no cross mark his remains,
May his burial ground remain unblessed,
And may he lack a loyal son to close his eyes in peaceful rest.

In response the men broke out in a favorite chant.

A shark going inland is my chief,
A very strong shark able to devour all on land,
A shark of very red gills is the chief.

Aloka felt a little sickened, both unworthy and unwilling to be compared to the great king Kamehameha. He was no conqueror, no great leader of men. All he'd done was murder his half-brother.

"Take us back to Honolulu, Admiral!" Karaimoku thundered above the roar of the wind and driving rain.

Aloka looked about him, he saw the grave concern in Captain Blackwell's eyes, and forced himself to come alive to the world round him. The world of the living. He ordered his men to their stations in a strong voice, and then he took Ka'ahumanu and Karaimoku to the break of the quarterdeck to shelter from the rain.

"Sir, Ma'am, with respect," Aloka said. "It would be a danger to the ship to return to Honolulu. We are much better where we are, I should even like to take her farther out to sea. The gail is blowing right on shore."

His father, who'd accompanied them for the conference, wore a look of relief and nodded his head.

"It may be a danger to the ship," Ka'ahumanu said, "but it will be a greater one to the nation should we not return. The people will think that George Kaumuarii has won, and conjured this great storm to deprive the land of her regents and protectors."

Aloka stared at Kamehameha's queen, and he could see by the gravity of Karaimoku's face that he was in agreement with Ka'ahumanu. He could not take council with his father, much as he would have liked to. There was only one captain—admiral, his guts twisted at the idea—in command of *Kamehameha I* and it was his decision alone. He had to weigh the beautiful sloop, the welfare of his men, against the stability of the nation he'd just killed for.

Aloka stepped out into the full force of the elements and shouted out, “All hands to make sail.”

Captain Blackwell came up from below, having convinced the regents to take refuge in the sloop’s cabin. He might be as old as they, he was in fact older than Ka‘ahumanu, but he’d spent his life on the deck of a ship in all weathers.

“An oil skin would not be unwelcome, however,” he said, as though he’d spoken his thoughts aloud.

Aloka looked at him, surprised that he was clinging to a stanchion on the quarterdeck beside him. Captain Blackwell’s heart went out to him. How he should like to see the youthful cheer again, rather than the pain and grief that had settled on his face of late.

“Kimo!” Aloka called to the young man now serving as steward. “Fetch an oiled cloak for Captain Blackwell. We do have them, you know, primitive though we are.”

Captain Blackwell was glad to see the ghost of a smile cross Aloka’s face. He nodded at the crew on deck, all wearing ponchos of *tapa* cloth rubbed with animal fat.

“They don’t smell nice, to be sure,” Aloka continued, as Kimo arrived with a cloak, “but you shall not mind it.”

When Kimo left them alone on the starboard side of the quarterdeck, Aloka turned to Captain Blackwell and his face crumpled. “Oh, father!”

Captain Blackwell reached out a hand and patted Aloka’s shoulder, grasped his arm. After a time, he said, “Easy there, son. I should wonder about you did you not feel as you do, though Kaumuarii was an evil sod.”

Aloka rubbed a hand over his face. A useless gesture, for the rain immediately wet it again. “Thank you, father. I wish you was safely ashore or on your ship with the dear Ma’am. Yet I don’t know what I would have done without you.”

“You’d have lived through it, son, all the same.”

Aloka shook his head, sniffling. “Not the same. No. But I can be grateful you are aboard for I am short a quartermaster. Getting back into Honolulu, if we can do it at all, shall be a near run thing.”

Across the grey heaving sea, through a break in the squalls of rain, they caught a flash of white topsails. "The *Blonde*," they both said at once.

Aloka's mentioning the dear Ma'am, as he always called Mercedes, turned Captain Blackwell's thoughts in that direction. He hoped she was snug and safe in the house upcountry.

As though reading his thoughts, Aloka said, "I hope Emma don't stay in the cottage, so damned close to shore, and goes upcountry to your place."

"Amen to that, son."

Emma had reached the house upcountry before things went sideways. She and Mercedes were huddled together in the main room of the new house. Much as she'd wanted to stay near the quay to meet Aloka on his return, Emma had not liked the look of the harbor in Honolulu. There were many ships in port, and an odd swelling of the sea had already caused several merchant ships to drag their anchors. As she left the cottage, Emma saw her father's ship *Albion* struggling to unmoor and set sail. Captain Bowles, she knew, would have hesitated to the last minute, in order that the ship should not quit the port without her captain. That helped decide her, and Emma ran to her parents' house with the wind pushing her along. She and Mercedes could hear tremendous crashes outside, the roar of the wind, and saw the trunks and fronds of coconut trees flying past the window openings.

"Dear god, I wish there had been time to ship deadlights," Emma said.

The wind was howling through the house, part of which had no roof.

"I wish we had deadlights to ship. Oh, how I hope your father and Aloka..."

"So do I, Mama."

And then they both screamed and clutched one another. The new roof was torn off and carried away out of sight. A deluge of rain poured in on them. Emma took Mercedes under her elbows and guided her to a corner of the room. She was careful to stay away from the chimney, remembering the earthquake and the death of Kapihe. They crouched with their arms round each other, already wet down to their small clothes. Emma felt Mercedes shivering.

“Mama, we can’t stay here like great helpless ninnies in the rain. Oh! I am so vexed with him I could spit.”

“Why?” Mercedes stammered out between chattering teeth. “And...with who?

“Aloka, in course, and I shall tell you why. He—”

“Mercedes! Mercedes Blackwell!”

Someone was shouting outside, a strong native voice, and then the figure of a large man loomed in the doorway. Emma was surprised when Mercedes began pushing herself to her feet. She put a restraining hand on her mother’s arm.

The native man strode into the room. “Come away. We go upcountry.” He actually stepped between the two of them, and took her mother’s arm.

“Sir, I beg your pardon, we shall do no such thing. Unhand my mother, if you please.”

“Emma, no it’s—”

Mercedes staggered and would have fallen but for the native man supporting her.

“Come, daughter, we go upcountry. There is shelter, with the other women and children.”

Emma clamped her lips shut and took Mercedes’ other arm. It was of the first importance to get her mother out of the weather. She hoped it would not be far. They were slipping in the muddy earth, practically carrying Mercedes between them, in danger every minute from flying debris. They struggled uphill, always uphill, on a path Emma could not discern but which the native man seemed to know perfectly well. He moved swiftly, Mercedes could not keep his pace long. When they were in a dense forest, the wind abating somewhat the farther they went from shore, the native man turned and took Mercedes up in his arms.

Emma was astonished, even more than when the man entered her parents’ house. What would Papa make of this? Just as quickly she became angry again with the pair of them, father and son.

“Take my arm,” the native man commanded.

They wound their way faster along a terraced track in the forest, with the native man carrying Mercedes and Emma clinging to his arm. At last the big man ducked into a cave, one Emma had not distinguished in the black hillside. The ceiling of the cave rose ten feet over their heads, and was deep enough to hold a collection of women, children, and men. They had lit small fires, quite protected from the wind and rain outside, the flames reflected on the black lava rock walls of the cave.

The native man set Mercedes down on mats amid a group of women. Emma thought she remembered some of them from the *maneaba*. He spoke in a low voice to the women closest to Mercedes, then moved away toward the entrance of the cave.

"Who is he, Mama?" Emma whispered.

"King Kanakoa, you met him before. These are his wives." Mercedes nodded at the ladies seated round her, and introduced each one. Mercedes knew them all by name, seemed already intimate with them.

How they managed it Emma could not tell, but the king's wives kindly produced dry cloaks and short *pa'ū*, *tapa* cloth skirts, for them to wear. Then they were offered a refreshment of poi and coconut milk. Emma was relieved when Mercedes' shivering and teeth chattering stopped. After they had warmed and dried themselves, and eaten, Mercedes appeared refreshed. Together they moved a little ways apart on the mats. Emma was fashioning a top of one of the *pa'ū*, winding it about her breasts like a bandage, when her mother reached out to her. Mercedes put her arms round her and leaned her head on Emma's shoulder.

"Tell me what's wrong," Mercedes said, in that way she had of going straight at a problem.

"I've hardly seen him these last days. We were together all the time on Hawaii, and then we come here and—"

"He cannot have foreseen the hard duty that awaited him here."

"I know. I understand his reasons for being so much away in his ship, and why he has cared so little to be on shore. But it is more than that. He has not wanted to..." Emma glanced at the king's ladies sitting so near, "...well, you know. He tells me there is no joy in his heart. What if there never is again?"

"Oh, Emma, that won't happen. He's so young, he'll recover from this. You will help him. The same way he helped you after...the earthquake."

"It's not the same. He thinks...he is afraid if we have children they may be monsters like George. Or deformed physically, and he shall have to kill them with his own hands. That is what Li'liah told me men must do. Can you think of a more soul destroying thing, how much more grief can he endure? It would be no wonder if he never wanted to touch me again. And he shall not want for the consolation of other women. Not here."

It had all come out in a rush. Her tears fell fast with the confession, and Emma had not finished.

"And even that is not the worst of it. I am already with child."

Her mother's reaction shocked her: Mercedes smiled.

"A baby! Oh Emma!" Mercedes kissed her. "I did not think I should live long enough to see your children."

"Mama! Have you not been attending? Is there something wrong with you?"

Emma was instantly ashamed; ashamed, guilty, and aggrieved.

"I'm afraid there is, my love, and I'm far past the point of wishing to pretend otherwise. Except that it hurts your father so. And you, my love!"

They clung together for a moment, both crying now and at first unable to speak.

"I could not even walk here on my own, and should probably have expired but for you and the king. I am happy I shall meet at least one of my grandchildren. You and Aloka have as fair a chance as any of having a healthy child."

"I wish it were so. Oh! How I wish I could convince him, and myself, it were so."

Mercedes stroked Emma's hair the way she'd done when she was small. Except now Emma could have held Mercedes on her lap.

"I am beyond any desire for pretense, Emma, but I find I'm not beyond cowardice."

Emma looked at her searchingly. Her mother was the strongest, bravest woman she knew.

"When you are a mother you have to face things you don't want to," Mercedes said, as though to herself, and then she looked directly at Emma. "You have to grow up, my love. You have to believe, with all your heart and soul your child will be healthy, and make it so. You can believe it, Emma. You and Aloka are not related."

Mercedes drew a shaky breath. "I was unfaithful when...when...before your father, before James, returned from living with Ata Gege. Aloka's people."

Captain Blackwell's sojourn in Kauai, Aloka's birthplace, had always been to her more a thing of family legend than reality. She stared at Mercedes, who compressed her lips with an odd, guilty look.

"Seven months after James came back to Honolulu, you were born."

"Not my father—"

"He is your father. In the same way Severino Martinez is more my father than Admiral Gambier ever was. Captain Blackwell was there when you were born. It was his service—you know his dreadful wounds—fed and clothed you, so you could grow up secure and privileged at Merton. The only thing he didn't do was conceive you with me. And your real father, if we must call him that, is a far better man than mine ever thought to be!"

Mercedes' breast was heaving after her long impassioned speech. Emma felt the weight of her mother's words. Still she yearned to know more, questions tumbled over one another in her mind. Hadn't she a right to know?

Emma waited until Mercedes was calmer, and then she whispered, "Papa knows then?"

It occurred to Emma this would explain much in her relationship to her father, which had always had a singularly strained quality.

"We didn't speak of it. We don't speak of it. Infidelity, it's...different for men."

"You mean his bastard was no disgrace to you, but I should have been for him?"

Mercedes gave her a sudden angry and reproachful look. "Lord, Emma, you vex me so I could spit."

They both laughed then and leaned in to touch each other, and felt easier together.

"My...my real father, as you venture to name him? The one who did conceive me with you, so we make no mistake."

Mercedes took her hand, gave it a squeeze. "Kanakoa, my love. The *ali'i ai moku* of Oahu. I'm not going to beat about the bush, you are a grown woman, you have a right to know."

Emma leaned back against the lava rock forming the sides of the cave, smooth where they sat, pitted and rough elsewhere. There was a time, not long ago, when she would have been pleased to learn she was a princess, the daughter of an exotic king. Hadn't she once thought Mercedes too fine a woman for Captain Blackwell? Now she was flooded with unexpected emotion.

A feeling of loss and uncertainty about her place in the world stole over her, the view she held of herself and her kin. There was a growing sense of her father's, that is, of Captain Blackwell's goodness to her, and the ungrateful return she'd made him. But far below the surface lived something like relief. She could tell Aloka he need not fear for any child of theirs. A child who would bind them to one another. Emma instantly began to worry whether she could share this with Aloka, for then wouldn't Captain Blackwell come to know of it. She would be the cause of more pain to her parents.

"I was weak," Mercedes said. "Then and now, and I beg you will forgive me. Speak to me, Emma. I could not bear an estrangement, not now, not ever."

Mercedes was gasping for breath, and the foremost feeling in Emma's confused and troubled heart was concern. It was more than that, she felt near panic before her mother's strong emotion and immediately put her arms round Mercedes.

"Nothing to forgive, Mama. I would never...I could never...I shall always love you."

She patted and soothed, and Mercedes, leaning against her, began breathing easier. Emma wondered what the king's ladies must make of the pair of them, blubbering away. She suddenly envied them their stout healthy bodies wrapped in copious folds of *tapa* cloth, their children and grandchildren gathered round them. Emma thought about the mother she'd known growing up, the one also of family legend, who had fought with swords and sailed on ships. Mercedes had fallen asleep in her arms. Emma looked on her now. Small, ill, and fragile, a cave was no fit place for her.

Near the cave's mouth Kanakoa's men came and went, conferring with the king. He turned suddenly toward the group of wives and children and caught Emma's eye upon him. Kanakoa strode over to them.

"*Kamahameha I* has come in. We go to bring our regents ashore."

"I'm coming with you!"

Her declaration woke Mercedes. There was no one to tell Emma her duty, that she mustn't or couldn't. Kanakoa only regarded her mildly as though to say, why don't you then.

"Mama, will you be—"

"She will be with us," one of the king's wives said. Aside, to Emma, she added, "She nursed my daughter once, and did everything she could to save her. Go daughter, go to your man with an easy mind."

Mercedes kissed her. "Bring Captain Blackwell and Aloka back with you to fetch me, my love," she said bravely.

Emma hugged Mercedes, and Keao the king's kind wife. She swallowed down her fear and doubt and ran after Kanakoa, already departing with his entourage of men.

The seas were higher in the approaches to the Bay of Honolulu than Karaimoku, or any of the old hands, had ever seen. Captain Blackwell was forward on the forecastle, gazing through the rain to conn the ship, Aloka remained aft standing beside the helmsman. It was impossible to see the reef for the heavy weather, but Captain Blackwell and most of the native seamen knew the long narrow approach to the harbor intimately. The issue might not be so much avoiding the coral reefs, with that unnatural spring tide beneath them, but collisions with other ships or being run on shore. There was much shipping trapped in Honolulu, and Captain Blackwell looked out anxiously for *Albion*.

"Two points a larboard," Captain Blackwell called aft in a strong voice.

Looming up in the near distance at the mouth of the bay Captain Blackwell made out through the haze the outline of a ship.

At one moment she was hull up, and in the next she was swallowed in a trough of sea so great only her topmasts were visible. *Kamehameha I* was under storm trysail and closely reefed top sails, yet she tore along, great seas coming aboard as her bow dipped. Suddenly the two ships were passing on opposite tacks and Captain Blackwell recognized *Albion*, with a jury bowsprit, clawing her way out to sea.

She was plunging and staggering beating to windward, but she was making way. The two ships came near so that for several moments they were almost looking into one another's faces, and the decks of both vessels erupted in cheers. Captain Bowles and the Albions raised a great huzzah, clearly heard even over the roar of the elements, and answered by the crew of *Kamehameha I* in a manner that lifted Captain Blackwell's heart. He willed her on to open sea, relieved that his ship, at least, was being saved by the skill and daring of Captain Bowles and *Albion's* crew.

Expertise and boldness were not enough to save the shipping in Honolulu Bay, where nature and the elements were in control. *Kamehameha I* came in at such a clip with the wind behind her, she was immediately in danger of grounding on coral in the troughs or collision with other ships. A Russian merchantman, the *Mina*, disengaged herself from having run on board a German ship, and careered straight for *Kamehameha I.*

"Stand clear of the cable!" Aloka roared out.

Captain Blackwell braced himself, ready to sing out when to let go the anchor, he wanted good holding ground away from the other ships if he could get it. A tremendous crash and impact from aft, and Captain Blackwell was thrown face down on deck. He struggled to his feet.

"Let go the best bower!" he called.

He looked aft at the two helmsmen at the wheel as they responded to the order to down helm, their deeply bronzed faces frightened. Captain Blackwell was unsure who gave the order; Aloka was no where in sight. The ship began slewing sideways to the seas. Captain Blackwell wanted to order a sheet anchor readied and a reef let out of the main topsail to keep her head to the wind, but it was not his command.

He ran aft, and with relief met the lieutenant Maaro giving those very orders. *Kamehameha I's* bow was already coming round.

"She's seems to be holding," he shouted at the lieutenant, longing to ask after Aloka.

"I will ready a sheet anchor, and the Admiral is aft. The great Russian has dished us, Father."

Quite nearly a navy like response, was Captain Blackwell's odd thought as he made his way aft. The deck beneath his feet was canting down toward the sea, and he slid to a halt near a group of seamen at the taffrail. He peered over the rail in time to see Aloka's head pop out above the boiling surface of the sea. He shook his hair out of his face, clinging to a line over the stern, and began to pull himself up hand over hand.

Aloka tumbled over the rail, completely sodden and panting for breath.

He gulped in air. "She has taken off the rudder and the rudder post, carried away the starboard quarter gallery, and stove in the stern lights. The sea is coming in fast."

His eyes met Captain Blackwell's.

"All hands forward of the mainmast," Aloka called.

As the men struggled up the deck, slipping on the wet surface and holding to the hances, Aloka took Captain Blackwell's arm and held him back.

"We may be grateful the regents were not in the cabin when the Russian ran us down. They came on deck as soon as we were level with the fort. How we are ever to bring them ashore I do not know. I regret to say it, the barky, she's done."

Seamen never speak of sinking, not even when they are father and son. Captain Blackwell and Aloka staggered forward up the quarterdeck together, Aloka behind with his hand on his father's shoulder.

There were a hundred and more natives on the shore. A shore that now began near the Mission church and house, and its companion cottage built by the English. The winds had dropped and they were no longer in danger of solid flying debris, the heavy rain seemed to have dampened it, but the sea continued high.

Emma felt lost in the crowd of natives, very much a foreigner in unknown territory. On the trek down the mountain from the lava caves there had been many young women like herself in the party, concerned for their men. Emma was unique only in that she had her breasts covered. Kanakoa and his followers took no notice of her, none offered their arm, or was the least concerned for how she did.

Emma tried to remain near the king nonetheless, one of his followers. They reached a vantage point with a view of the bay. Two merchant ships and one Russian navy brig were on shore, farther out other ships were dragging their anchors, some dismasted and none unwounded from collision or the seas. Among the wounded ships was *Kamehameha I*, on which the interest of all the people round her was focused.

How Emma wished for one of her father's perspective glasses. She looked round behind her over the heads of the natives, wondering if she should run to her parents' house, and then spotted a most welcome sight.

"Saunders, thank god!" Emma cried, making her way through the crowd.

Saunders gave Emma a nod, asked very low after Mercedes, then proceeded to push her way through to Kanakoa. Behind her trailed a file of dockyard men, the woman Anushka, and now Emma.

The sloop *Kamehameha I* lay less than half a mile away, a distance most of the natives were capable of swimming, much less reaching in their canoes or on float boards.

"She has her boats too, your majesty," Saunders was saying of the sloop, "but no boat can swim in this here sea, sir. We can try bringing a gun down from the fort, and firing or launching a line out to her. A great Russian slack-arsed tub has stove in her stern quarter, your honor, do you see? She fouled five other ships besides, saw it happen myself."

Saunders in fact had a telescope slung over her shoulder, and she offered it to the king. Kanakoa studied the ship thrashing about in the seas of the bay in front of them. Emma's hands itched to take the glass.

"Make it so, then, master shipwright," Kanakoa said, gravely handing her back the glass.

The men around him were galvanized into action, and a large contingent began moving off with Saunders for the fort.

Emma ran after them. "Saunders! May I borrow your glass?"

Saunders unslung the telescope and gave it her. "We shall place the cannon as near as we can manage to the old quay, Missus, you can meet us there."

"Thank you, and bless you Saunders. Do you think it will answer?"

"We can but try. I owe your mamma and the Captain that much, and more."

Anushka, though she appeared loath to lose sight of Saunders, stopped and said anxiously to Emma, "Can he still be alive, out there on that ship?"

"I have no doubt he is gone from this earth, else the ship would not have returned."

"The people are saying Kaumuarii George caused this great storm."

"Vengeance from beyond the grave?" Emma frowned, angry at the suggestion for a number of reasons. But there was incomprehension on the poor suffering woman's face. "Dead is dead, Ana," she said not unkindly, "and no man has power over nature. You are living in this world, he is not."

Aboard *Kamehameha I* they were watching the movements on shore with intense interest, after having discussed the possibility of launching a boat. Aloka and Captain Blackwell were unaccustomed to collective decision making, they gave the regents one of their telescopes and took themselves a ways apart on the forecastle.

"Maaro, a deep sea line bent to the capstan," Aloka said. "The larboard watch into the tops."

The watch on deck was busy tending the scraps of sail keeping the ship's head to the wind. There was water in the waist with the level rising, and although the ship carried only nineteen hands, with all of them forward of the mainmast it was rather crowded. They should all have to retreat to the tops soon enough.

"By God, she's a clever one! How glad I am I did not boot her off the ship in Brazil all that time ago."

Aloka jerked round at his father's exclamation, and Captain Blackwell handed him the glass. Through it he saw the natives had hauled a six pounder cannon to the shore, and were setting it up on a great platform, complete with its gun carriage. They had also a modified capstan, a multitude of small barrels, the accoutrement of the gun, and in the midst of all was Saunders directing the work.

"That's what I thought she was about!" Aloka declared, taking the glass away from his eye. "She is going to try to cast us a line. Maybe we can meet her with our own." He looked over his shoulder at the deep sea line the men were bending to the capstan. "Bless her! Dear god, Emma's with them!"

"It's an infernal device, Missus, a rocket," Saunders said, in answer to Emma's asking what she was assembling. "Picked them up from a Canton trader. I meant to use the gunpowder to fill canister, but they may serve as they are. Trick will be lighting the bugger in this wet."

Emma turned and moved through the crowd asking the women she'd come down with, if they knew how to build a shelter. The master shipwright needed one over the gun platform. Someone put a small axe in her hand and Emma ran upcountry with the people, in search of saplings for poles and broad forest leaves for a matted roof.

Aloka lost track of Emma in the crowd. He lowered the telescope feeling he would give anything to be on shore with her in his arms. "Saunders is readying a mortar, or something like Cochrane's incendiary rockets."

"Let's hope it saves us rather than blowing us up, this time. And can carry with it enough line to reach us."

"Amen, amen," Aloka said, and clapped his father on the shoulder. "Emma is scampering about on shore, where she would never be if Mercedes were in need of her."

Saunders had the rig ready on shore, the line bent to the capstan with the inboard end secured to the rocket. The deep sea line between was neatly coiled on the platform, and the whole arrangement weighted in place by the cannon.

"We shan't fire it unless this other don't serve," Saunders told the crowd of native men round her.

Emma stood off to one side with a knot of women, warriors and chiefs, Kanakoa among them, when the first rocket went off. The explosion was accompanied by much cheering, and the sound of the line whipping out off the platform. There was a sense of elation, they jumped in the air and hooted. Working together they'd built a stout shelter double quick and been able to fire the rocket in the worst conditions. Trailing a tail of sparks the rocket skipped across the surface of the sea, and sank far short of the sloop.

"No!" Aloka shouted.

A body whipped past him at a run, and Kimo jumped from the larboard bow and launched himself into the sea. Round him was tied the deep sea line. Aloka watched the rocket, aimed too low, sink quite close to shore.

"Ahead of orders! Do you see?" he shouted angrily at no one in particular.

Kimo's head bobbed up some way from the ship, and there was a collective exhalation as the young man struck for shore. They lost sight of him for some moments in the trough of a swell, the line continued to pay out. Scanning the surface with their telescopes, they glimpsed his head and an arm. Kimo seemed to be waving in distress.

"Oh Lord," Captain Blackwell said. "The boy's in a whirlpool."

"Stopper the cable!" Aloka called.

Should he pay in the line, bring it back aboard with the capstan? Aloka thought of the weight of the deep sea line once wet. Kimo would be pulled under by the weight of it, and the turbulence of the sea.

On shore someone called out there was a swimmer in the bay. Saunders snatched up her glass. She gave it over almost at once to Emma though, in order to return to the task of readying the second rocket and bringing in and coiling down the line that had paid out.

After much scanning of the surface of the harbor between the sloop and their position, Emma saw a dark head and a brown arm thrust briefly above the surface. She shrieked and called out to the people round her. She ran down shore toward the Nuuanu stream, where she'd glimpsed the figure in the water.

"They are forming a chain," Captain Blackwell declared, looking through his telescope at the activity taking place where the Nuuanu stream emptied into the harbor. "A human chain, it is the completest thing!"

Aloka alternated between the rescue trying to take place, and Saunders and her group.

"I wish Emma may not be among them," he murmured to his father, about the group after Kimo.

"She will be if she thinks you are out there."

"They've got him out!" Aloka said. "I think they have. Maaro, look here, is that Kimo?"

He handed over the glass.

"The very candlenut!" Maaro declared. "And the bugger slipped the line."

"Shorten in cable!" Aloka ordered. "And the next man to act except under orders shall answer to this *ali'i* of the candlenut shade!"

Captain Blackwell turned his back to hide the grin that arose at those words, *ali'i no ka malu kukui*. A chief of the candlenut shade, meaning of questionable genealogy. Of a sudden his heart was filled with pride for his mixed race son, and an odd desire that he should live to see the sons and daughters he would raise.

Saunders had elevated the rocket's mounting carriage, and she lit the fuse of the second rocket from a slow match burning in a tub underneath the shelter the people had built. The fuse stayed alight and the rocket exploded in a singing arc, the line whipping out behind, this time trailing an even more spectacular tail of colored sparks. Another cheer went up from the natives clustered on the shore, and a group of them rushed into the waves.

At first Emma didn't know what they were about, and then she saw them positioning themselves along the length of line as it fell to steady it in its path toward the sloop. A modified version of what they'd done at the stream with the human chain. Emma ran forward and dove into the oncoming waves.

She surfaced some ways ahead, looking round to orient herself with the line, and dove again. The next time she came up, and the next, the native men waved her on as though aware of her royal status. Emma dove deep and swam hard in the turbulent sea, and reaching the surface gasping she had to kick over to the nearest native man.

The man clutching the fallen line said, "Hand on my shoulder, sister."

They bobbed there together, smacked in the face by waves, all active and kicking below the surface. The native man made a loop in the end of the line and passed it over Emma's head and one shoulder, so that it lay between her breasts.

"The Admiral comes this way." The native man moved his head in the direction of the ship.

"Don't see him."

Emma stared, following the line leaving *Kamehameha I's* hawse hole, and then she gasped. She sucked in a great breath, arched her body into the oncoming wave and swam hard.

When she surfaced a third time after that dive, Emma spotted him and raised her arm above the surface. Waving, waving frantically, her strength on the ebb.

Aloka popped up next to her and they patted one another, gasping. He mimed pulling the cable over his head and pointed down. Emma nodded, took another great breath and dove with Aloka.

He kicked down hard, she followed. When they were at a depth removed from the worst tossing of the surface, Aloka took the coil from over Emma's body, passing her end through the loop still over his chest. He pointed at Emma and then the surface, reached over, grasped her foot and shoved upward.

Emma's head cleared the surface and she sucked in air, followed by sea water as a wave broke over her head. She choked and spat, took in several gulps of air and sank back below the waves, trying to discover Aloka.

He surfaced a ways from her, clutching the knot he'd made in the two deep sea lines. She swam over to him, and he put her hand on the lifeline.

"Go back." He pointed toward the shore.

She shook her head no, water flying in all directions. "Together. Or I won't."

Aloka gave her an exasperated look, and passing his hands around her body, exchanged places with her to put her before him.

"Move then, woman, to the ship is shortest," he said. When Emma began pulling herself along the line in front of him, he added, "My dearest love."

Captain Blackwell reached a hand down to her as Emma came up the steps in the sloop's side. He and Maaro lifted her aboard once they could reach her, and Captain Blackwell clasped her to his chest in a close embrace.

"You are the bravest, strongest, most admirable woman."

Before he could ask, she said, "Mama's upcountry, at the place of refuge. I promised her we would all come to fetch her away."

"Bless you, sweetheart."

They turned to Aloka with tears standing in both their eyes.

Aloka wiped the water from his face with both hands. "No one listens to my orders," he said privately to them.

"Shorten in cable!" Aloka called. "Handsomely does it, handsomely now!"

He turned back to Captain Blackwell, and put his arm round Emma, who was shivering. "Father, you will help me with the regents, if you please."

They stepped over to where Ka'ahumanu and Karaimoku and their people were huddled together in the bow. Aloka's heart was aglow. Gratitude, love and happiness, even triumph lived there, where he never could have imagined they would be, on this day of all days.

CHAPTER FOURTEEN

The tropical storm was a milestone in their lives, one of those events after which life was forever different and unalterably changed. It was the end of Emma's and Aloka's first youth, the time before their two children were born. Captain Blackwell experienced an immediate and lasting backlash from the great storm, in the form of recriminations started by the British merchants in port. He was accused of insufficient zeal in coming to their aid, and of preferring native interests over those of the Crown.

"Father cut up rather old fashioned," Aloka had said, "when they suggested he could command King Kanakoa's men."

The ill will of his countrymen was not nearly the change of the most moment to Captain Blackwell, however, it was that Mercedes had never really been well since the blow. He'd written his letter to government requesting to be relieved of his diplomatic duties more than a year since; not as a consequence of the old clash of his two worlds, but because his role as consul general necessarily took him away to the different islands. He did not wish to leave Mercedes alone for any length of time, though she now had ladies constantly in attendance upon her. To help her with what Mercedes called her squalid needs.

Captain Blackwell made his way through the Chinese section of Honolulu. At an earlier hour than he usually looked in on her, he'd gone to Mercedes' room that morning and stood in her doorway. They'd run out of the laudanum Dr. Russ had sent with them on the trip out. Captain Blackwell had found her, when she thought no one was by, writhing on the bed and moaning. He was not aware there were tears streaming down his face, as he walked along thinking of her, the shops opening and the town coming to life round him.

The cancer was not in her breast this time, she said the pain lived somewhere deep in her innards. He'd offered to take her back to England, there was a chance Dr. Russ still lived, and where there were other physicians and hospitals.

"No, James, much as I long to see Edward again," she said. "I thank you, but I cannot. I would not have you to myself for the entire voyage, and I am not sure how long...and besides I should miss Tomi and Ana."

Her grandchildren, and her children, were the greatest joys of her life. Captain Blackwell couldn't imagine what it cost her to suppress her pain in the short times she now allowed each of them into her bed chamber to visit. He turned into an herbalists and apothecary's shop, with the intention of buying opium.

He was concluding what was to him a foreign and distressing business with the elder of the two Chinese shopmen, to come round to his house later with the purchased item and demonstrate how it was to be taken. Captain Blackwell had never been a man for strong spirits, and he did not indulge in *awa* the local *kava* drink, disliking the physical and mental numbness that ensued. But he'd be damned if he would give the oriental draught to Mercedes or the pipe, or however it was done, without he should also brave it himself.

Aloka burst into the apothecary's shop."Father! There you are at last. *E hoa!*"

Captain Blackwell turned with a blush and an indignant look at Aloka. Shaking his head dismally, he extended his hand to the old shopman and made his acknowledgements. He bowed and then allowed Aloka to lead him out of the shop.

"What is it, son? Pelting about like a mere squeaker."

"I don't feel like one," Aloka said, a hand to his chest. "I ran up to your house, back down, all over town, looking for you. Fortunately, you are hard to miss, lumbering about Nu'uanu avenue. Step out lively, Father, show a leg! A packet from England has come in."

Captain Blackwell was not moved by the news, unless she had carboys full of laudanum aboard, nor could he understand Aloka's high spirits. He did not protest on the run to the quay, because he could not spare breath to do so.

On the wharf the usual bustle of unloading and disembarkation was taking place, and Captain Blackwell reconciled himself to meeting the packet's master. In his official capacity he would listen to the man's requests and desires while in the port of Honolulu, and make sure port duties were paid.

Aloka took his arm in a strong grip and motioned in front of him.

A tall golden haired young man straightened from looking into one of a collection of chests grouped on the quay, and turned toward them.

"Oh my God!" Captain Blackwell cried. He started forward and embraced Edward.

Edward returned his embrace and his slaps upon his back, one for one, then stepped back and gazed directly at him for just a moment.

"How do you do, Father?"

Edward had the same Apollo good looks, his features aged of course. Somehow he was still more handsome.

"Edward! So much better now you are come. She will be beside herself, your Mama, so very pleased."

He turned, still clasping Edward by one hand, and grinned upon Aloka too.

"Look what he brought with him," Aloka said.

Edward bent down again and lifted the lid of the chest he'd been peering into. Inside was bottle after bottle of laudanum, carefully packed in lamb's wool.

"Dr. Russ sent them."

Captain Blackwell wiped the tears from his face, and murmured, "God bless the Doctor, and you too, Edward." He cleared his throat, gazing with affection on his sons. "Aloka, be so good as to ask one of your men to run up a bottle to the house straight away. Momo is with her this morning. I shall follow immediately, but I ain't so spry as I once was and you have already run me off my legs. If you have not alerted Emma, you had better take Edward to her at once, or I would not answer for the consequences. Then bring him to see his Mama."

That would give time for Mercedes to have a comfortable dose of laudanum, so she might meet the great surprise of Edward's coming in some level of comfort.

"Aye, aye, sir," Aloka said. "But we have not done yet with surprises."

He nodded to two gentlemen behind Captain Blackwell.

"Father, allow me to name my particular friend, John Wesley Park," Edward said. "Doctor Park, m'father, Captain James Blackwell."

They shook hands, the doctor's grip firm and assured. The gentleman standing beside Edward's friend needed no introduction. Captain Blackwell and his brother Francis were already embracing, and clapping one another heartily on the back.

Mercedes was in better spirits and looks than she'd been for many and many a day. She was even dressed, her hair washed and put up, and sitting in the main room of the house Blackwell had built of stone, Northwest coast timber, and native thatch. The pain was there, but it was underneath the drug, far below the surface. Not the all consuming nightmare it had been in these last days when she'd been unable to move from her bed. She caught the amazed glances of the people that were with her daily. Dear James, Saunders, Ana—they sometimes called her granddaughter Anita to distinguish the two—and Momo. Edward sat beside her holding her hand.

Edward had been with Mercedes some little time. She'd learned that, after the examiner had tipped his hat to Edward, he'd found the notoriety of being Senior Wrangler at Cambridge insupportable and packed his instruments for the Islands. She gazed on him fondly. He was unchanged aside from the more manly cast to his features. He'd always spoken freely with her and Emma, but he was more conversant now, easier somehow in his skin. Mercedes attributed it to love.

"May I present my particular friend, Mama, Doctor John Wesley Park." After the introduction, he'd given the other man a look that spoke volumes. At least to Mercedes.

"How do you do, sir. Did you meet at Cambridge?"

"I'm a physician, Ma'am, not a doctor of philosophy or a scholar like Edward."

"He attended Dr. Russ in his last illness. That is how I made Wesley's acquaintance."

"How sorry I am to hear of Dr. Russ's death. Such a brilliant man."

"Tio Severino, too, Mama," Edward said, with something of his old bluntness.

She cried then, thinking of the man who'd been a father to her. Severino Martinez had been an unfailing constant in her life. The best of parents; kind, consistent, and direct. Edward turned his head away from her tears, though he held her hand tightly. Doctor Park told her about Mr. Martinez's last days, attended by both he and Edward, and that was a consolation to her.

Mercedes sniffled. "He would say, 'Don't be a fool, girl. Stop crying, be grateful.'"

"I don't see how dying of a wasting disease is anything to be grateful for," Edward said, very low, so only she and Doctor Park heard him.

"No, so it isn't either. But everyone dies." She spoke softly too; James and Francis were conversing a short distance apart. "At least I am at home, with my family and people I love near me. I am only sorry for..."

She couldn't speak that particular thought, looking across at James.

Emma came in the front door just then, followed by Aloka with a child on each arm. Ana and Tomi shrieked to be put down, and they ran to Mercedes and leaned into her lap, one on each side.

"How pretty you look, Mama," Emma said, stooping to kiss her cheek.

"Grandma, you got out of bed!"

"It's a special day, you know, because your Uncle Edward and Francis have come. And our new friend Doctor Park. Honolulu is in great need of medical men, sir, should you choose to practice. Though you must accustom yourself to being paid in pigs and poi."

"Pigs and poi!" the little ones hooted.

Aloka came last and kissed Mercedes' cheek. "How do you do, Mama? Shall I take these little brutes away?"

"Never in life, my love, don't you dare."

Mercedes gave Tomi and Ana a squeeze. They shot off together as though fired from a gun, careened into James's legs, and ricocheted out the door into the back garden.

Aloka and Emma went to pay their duty to Captain Blackwell, and then sauntered hand in hand out of doors after the children.

"He calls you Mama, now," Edward said. "Never would before."

"Maybe because Kalani died. He and your father went to Kauai, to the village of Ata Gege, after the hurricane and...Aloka had another half-brother, you know, who was executed for treason."

Edward gave her a skeptical look.

"Afterwords, he could not rest until he found out what happened to her. To bring her the news of George Kaumuarii's death himself, like the honorable man he is. They found the village deserted, fallen into decay and three parts reclaimed by jungle and the sea. But Momo is from that village." Mercedes nodded at a substantial woman passing by. "One of my many helpers. The surviving people moved up country, where your father and Aloka eventually found them. A few came here to Honolulu, like Momo."

"What happened to them, if I may be so bold?" Doctor Park asked.

"The missionaries and the *haole*, what they call foreigners, happened to them, sir. The missionaries would insist they leave off head-hunting. Not that that is a bad thing, but it destroyed their society. Their system of obligation and kinship bound them together, and with nothing to take its place the young men, the warriors, left to pursue warfare on a larger scale. Many of them led by George Kaumuarii, Kalani's other son."

"The one that was hanged?" Edward said.

Mercedes nodded. "In a manner of speaking. And then there was the *ōku'u* sickness, probably cholera. Momo says Kalani died during the time of sickness, but hush, here are the children."

When they'd dashed off again, she said, "Aren't they the most darling little things?"

Edward looked after the darlings unmoved."I should think we must be grateful they don't have horns in the middle of their heads."

"Edward!" she and Doctor Park cried out.

To his credit, Edward ducked his head with a conscious look.

"And Emma is a wonderful mother," Mercedes declared.

"Of course she is, Mama. Look at the example she had."

Later in the evening, when Mercedes had begun to think longingly of the amber colored liquid in the bottle beside her bed, Francis came and sat beside her.

"We have not yet had a chance to talk." She smiled kindly on him. "Tell me all about how you came to be sent to the far side of the world."

"Government was only too happy to have anyone by the name of Blackwell posted here, it pleases the chiefs inordinately, so they looked me up. As it happened, I was at loose ends. A man without a home or employment."

"Oh, Francis! I am—"

"Never worry yourself, my dear. It is over, history, and I would not have you alarmed for my sake. I was not so fortunate or so wise in my choices as my brother, and must forego the rewards of constancy and devotion. I always thought, Mercedes, you would have made a wonderful diplomat's wife."

Mercedes grimaced. "Forgive me, Francis. I can't tell you how happy I am you are here. It will be a great comfort and relief to James. I believe I must retire."

After saying this Mercedes looked up. Many concerned faces were staring back at her. She extended her hand to Captain Blackwell, and he immediately came and helped her up, and escorted her on a round of good byes and goodnights.

Mercedes and Captain Blackwell were making their creeping way to the bed, after he'd helped her to the close stool.

"Call one of the ladies, James."

He'd shaken his head no; and now they both spotted the man bowing to them just outside the double doors opened to the back garden.

"It's Yeung, the China-man. I had forgot. I shall send him away."

"No James, if you please." Mercedes gave his arm a feeble squeeze. "I need it."

He went quite pale. "Are you sure, sweetheart?"

"I am longing to consume that whole bottle over there."

He took her to bed and helped her in.

"You will not join me. Only watch, so that you can help me do it another time."

His heart was wrung, to see this immaculate woman so reduced, and of course he would refuse her nothing. He tried to smile at her, a weak attempt, and went to fetch in Mr. Yeung.

The older man set promptly about his business. He asked for an oil lamp, and bringing the accoutrement out of a neat leather case, and the opium from an inside pocket, he began to prepare the drug. As the sweet noxious scent filled the chamber, Blackwell's courage failed.

"Mercedes, forgive me, I...I can't do this. Shall I ask the young doctor to step in?"

"Bring Saunders, if you please." She spoke through gritted teeth.

Saunders came back in with him, took in the situation, and went immediately and knelt beside Mercedes and Mr. Yeung. She passed her eye over the pipe, the flame, the thread of heated opium poised over the bowl and she nodded at the older man. Mr. Yeung filled the bowl and held the pipe to Mercedes' lips.

Mercedes exhaled a luxurious cloud of smoke. They watched her sigh and relax in the bed, her eyelids fluttering.

"Now then, sir," Saunders said, turning to Mr. Yeung, "show me the part I missed, if you please."

Blackwell sat down in a chair near the bedside and put his head in his hands.

Mercedes felt a flood of cold relief that seemed to start in the hottest most painful part, deep in her insides, and radiate outward until she tingled all over. She imagined or dreamed she'd seen a man's head taken off by a canon ball, and she was running, slipping on something slick underfoot, with terror in her heart. She ran on, frantically climbing one ladder and another, always upward, and emerged at last into dazzling light. On the deck of a ship a man in uniform gave her a quizzical, pained look. In the next moment she was inside a comfortable ship's cabin being kissed by the same gentleman, and enclosed in protective and loving arms.

She opened her eyes in a dark room and lay there listening. All was quiet in the house, and beside her slumped in a chair was the man she'd been kissing. No longer in uniform, grey haired now, but he was still the same dashing officer in her eyes. With an effort she extended her hand and grasped his knee.

James woke, sat up straight, and rubbed his hands over his face. "What is it, sweetheart?"

"Drink."

He brought her a tumbler of water, eased her upright, her head lolled against his shoulder like a doll's, and held the glass while she drank.

With her mouth thus unglued, she said, "Thank you, darling, you've always been so kind to me."

He eased her back amid her pillows, and she kissed his neck twice as he did. Tears came into his eyes, and he sank heavily into his chair.

"You will have given your chamber to Edward and Doctor Park, and Francis has mine?"

James nodded. Mercedes lived on the ground floor of the house, in what used to be a pleasant sitting room, to make it easier to bring in water for her baths and because she could no longer manage the stairs.

"You must take off your clothes and come to bed with me."

He gave her a doubtful look. She had not invited him to her bed for a very long while. On top of everything else, Mercedes fancied she did not smell nice. She who had once perfumed her skin with creams and washed her hair with scented water. Mercedes thought she would cry if he refused her.

James never let her down. He stripped off his clothes and settled carefully beside her, seeking her hand under the bedclothes. Mercedes leaned her head against his shoulder.

"It's all the small things," she said. "Going to the bathing pools, walking to the shore and Emma's house, cruising on your ship, those things I miss. It's been so long since I've made you a meal, or been a real wife to you."

"I wish you did not think I love you for what you can do for me, sweetheart. I know it is my fault for the way I behaved when we first met—"

"I was just dreaming of the way *I* behaved when we first met. What has happened to Francis?"

The pain was at a distance, she felt almost normal, and Francis's odd speech came to mind.

"She threw him over, your friend Zahraa, for a much younger man. A man barely older than Farrokh, and to cover her transgressions Zahraa accused Francis of having to do with Miriam."

Mercedes gasped. Farrokh and Miriam were Zahraa's children by the Dey of Oran. They'd all lived together once in a seraglio, before Francis and Zahraa had become entangled.

"*Pobre hombre.* He spoke of constancy and devotion, and how much more fortunate you'd been than he in that regard. It made me feel such a hypocrite."

He turned his head and looked at her, astonished.

She held his eye. "You never pretended anything with Aloka, I should not have done with Emma. I was inconstant. You know she isn't yours?"

To her unutterable relief he squeezed her hand. "Sure I'm not the sharpest weapon in the arms chest, sweetheart, but I can count. Either she was a seven month's wonder, or...I once told you any child you bore would be yours and mine and most heartily welcome. Do you remember?"

She shook her head, eyes filled with tears.

"I meant it, I mean all the things I say to you. You are the light of my life, and I cannot even remember a time when I was not in love with you. Life must not have been worth living back then."

"Oh James! I love you too. And how I wish I could make love to you."

"Listen now, sweetheart." He moved closer against her, put his arms round her and whispered, "If you hurt at all, tell me, and I shall fetch you a draught or call the doctor. You give me too much credit, and I hardly think—"

"I think it. You are still a healthy man. Why should that part of your life be over because—"

"Hush, Mercy, please."

She lay there thinking how odd it was, with his being a professional man of war and ten years older, that she should die first. He must have thought so too, Mercedes heard him sniffling.

"At my advanced age, you know," he said, clearing his throat, "desire has more to do with phantasy and imagination. Shall we pretend?"

"With all my heart."

"Then let's pretend I just gave you a tumble, a right good rogering." She actually giggled at that. "We're happy and content, lying here together, and everything's right with the world. You would say something like, 'Jim, that was the best I ever had. In bed you're like a...like a—"

"Like a hero, darling, my own one."

EPILOGUE

"Tomi, get off your sister this moment or I shall fetch you such a swipe!"

The little boy stopped in mid-throttle and looked over at her. Emma and Edward were seated together on the veranda of a house that had arrived in pieces, brought by a ship from the Pacific Northwest.

Emma rose from her chair, taking off her slipper to menace her son, and to show she was in earnest. Tomi immediately sheered off and ran out of the yard and away in the direction of shore. Ana sprang up, her hair all ahoo, and pelted after him.

"Are not you rather hard on the little brute beast?"

"Aloka never treated me so."

"But don't he just now," Edward muttered, turning his head aside.

"What did you say?"

Edward turned further away from her, hung his head, and said nothing.

"McMurtry!" Emma called to a ten year old boy scuffling his feet in the yard. "Keep company with Tomi and Ana if you please."

Emma sighed and flopped back into her seat next to Edward. She sometimes felt like fetching her brother a swipe with her shoe, and might have done but for the thought Mercedes would not like it. Then too, poor Edward had come back just in time to watch their mother die. Mercedes had lived but two weeks after his and

Francis, and Doctor Park's arrival. She looked over at Edward, his hands clasped between his knees.

"Dear Edward, I think of her all the time. Would she bring me up for topping it the brute with my children, do you suppose? With all of them." Emma waved her hand around, meaning to encompass her house, her yard, her life, her husband.

There were a number of children round about them, of various ages, nearly all half-castes. Children of Europeans and natives whom neither community wanted. Aloka and Emma had taken them in.

Edward unbent himself and stared at her for a moment with his intense blue gaze. "No, Mama was never one for nonsense, she would be proud of you. You know she would be, your heart is in the right place Emma."

Tears came into her eyes, as they always would these days. You couldn't be raised by a woman like Mercedes without you learned a thing or two about kindness. She took Edward's hand and squeezed it, grateful to him.

Some bitterness remained in her heart though, for the way their mother had died. A world where the best and dearest of women could meet such a cruel end; drugged and in pain, with no pleasures in life left to her, speaking to them in one word sentences; was one without sense or justice. When Mercedes asked her not to bring the children with her to visit, Emma had known her mother was near the end.

Her grandmother had died of a similar malady, and Emma wondered if all the feelings she had now were what Mercedes was experiencing in that long ago time when she'd embarked on her own ocean voyaging. Unlike Edward, Emma didn't know much about the universe and its workings. Yet now she thought when people spoke of someone dying peacefully in their sleep, that was just a fiction. Death was a struggle, even for a small, feeble, much loved woman lying in her own bed.

Emma wiped her face and they watched Ka'ahumanu pass by on Beretania, in a pony trap pulled by several of her *kanakas*. Ka'ahumanu was dressed in an enormous tent-like peach colored silk dress trimmed in black lace, with a great leghorn hat sporting artificial flowers from Canton perched on her head. Emma and Edward inclined their heads to the queen, they were still

Ka'ahumanu *ma*, Ka'ahumanu's people, though somewhat in disfavor. After the great storm Ka'ahumanu had embraced the Jesus book, and become Ka'ahumanu the Pious. She found Aloka and Emma and all the Black Savages not quite the thing. She'd booted them from the cottage next to the Mission house and church, and it was just as well. They needed far more room—for their coconuts, as Emma privately thought of the mixed race children.

She could have provided Ka'ahumanu a pony to go with her trap. Kanakoa had been given four horses in trade, and not knowing how to value them and furthermore appalled at the way they ate their heads off, he'd given them to Emma upon her asking. She knew horse flesh, and she was keeping the fine creatures to herself for the now. Emma was training the horses to the harness, and she might have given one to Ka'ahumanu had she esteemed her better. But she would not have dared involve herself and Aloka by such a gift in the unhappy rivalries developing between the *ali'i*.

It seemed to her the last time the community had been united was during the memorial for Mercedes outside Honolulu Bay. Her mother had decided that, much as she did not wish to deprive them of a grave to visit, she did not like the idea of moldering in the ground. She had asked Captain Blackwell to have her body prepared in the way of the Hawaiians and her ashes scattered on the sea, the natural element of her beloved. *Albion* had not sailed far that day, with a great procession of native canoes and float boards, and a royal sailing canoe in company, to send Mercedes' spirit over the rainbow.

Immediately after her ashes were committed to the deep, another sailing canoe was lowered over the side of *Albion*, and Captain Blackwell left them. He looked shattered, his face tear streaked. The last thing he said to Emma was, "I don't know how I can be expected to go on without her." He went over the side, and paddled away in the direction of Kauai.

"How could you let him go?" she'd demanded of Aloka as soon as they were alone together. "He's old. Do you want to lose them both?"

"What would you have me do? He needs to be alone with his grief."

For Emma that was the start of the strife, though she was beginning to acknowledge it had been there all along. She had not heeded it while her mother was alive, and they'd all been consumed with making her suffering less. Aloka was unhappy.

He did not care for being a "jobbing, merchant captain" as he called it, for Ka'ahumanu and the other chiefs. Sailing shiploads of sandalwood to Canton, and returning with the hold crammed with luxe goods for the *ali'i*, whose chosen form of warfare had become trying to outshine one another in the way of dress and accoutrement. It reminded Emma of the little she'd seen of the behavior of 'coming out' in London. Factions were developing and Aloka did not like to be in the middle. On the one side was their old shipmate, now Governor Boki and the merchant community, and on the other Ka'ahumanu and her followers and the American missionaries. Emma could not blame Aloka for his discontent.

Yet she'd been unprepared for him to say, on the very evening of her mother's memorial, that he thought of going to Brazil, joining Lord Cochrane's fleet in the fight for that country's independence. After she'd blown him up Aloka had apologized, for burdening her on that day of all days. But there it was. He missed the Royal Navy, he wanted his profession and to be a frigate commander. Aloka wasn't as happy as she was in the islands. It was powerfully hard to face, another separation, but Mercedes had warned her. Women were the ones that held families together.

"I'm trying," she said out loud to Edward.

Edward merely nodded. She shared the kind of intimacy with him that allowed them to be silent for long spaces, and then pick up a conversation at random. Tomi came charging round the corner of the house, jumped on to the porch, and leaned, panting, into Edward's lap.

Edward eyed him askance.

"I know something you don't," the boy said.

"My man, I make no doubt of it."

Ana and McMurtry arrived and joined them on the porch. Emma didn't know how anyone could look on the poor little sod's face, McMurtry's that was, and not feel for the boy who looked so like Captain Blackwell's old steward, buried now these several years. Tomi was put out by Edward's disinterest in his news, and was scowling mightily.

"I want to know what it is, my love," Emma said, drawing the boy to her side.

Tomi shook her off for the sake of his dignity before the other children, and stood up straight and important.

"Which it's Grandpa has come home!"

Emma stared at him, and then she was up and flying toward shore. Thank god, thank all the gods! she thought. She ran to meet the man she'd once thought, and openly avowed to her shame, not good enough for her mother. How that had changed in the last years, in those last terrible days when he'd held Mercedes' hand and been unerringly kind, helping to care for her. He'd done everything for her the women had. Emma heard a great whoop in a voice she knew well, and then there in the surf bringing the canoe ashore with the *kanakas* was her father. James Blackwell wore a long sleeved linen shirt to cover his burned scarred skin and a *malo*. Aloka was clapping him upon his good shoulder.

"There now, don't take on so. Did you think I wasn't coming back?" Blackwell said. He'd never expected a reception like this from Emma, tears and falling upon his breast. Her half resentful glance told Blackwell he'd said the wrong thing, that she might have thought she'd lost both parents. He hugged her close and whispered, "Forgive me. I love you, I would not hurt you for the world."

Emma kissed him, and stepped aside so others could welcome him ashore.

"How do you do, son?"

Edward was standing just out of reach of the waves. Blackwell walked up to shake hands with his grandchildren either side of him, bounding about like young hounds.

"Better, Father, now you are here."

They shook in the European way and then Blackwell pulled Edward into a close embrace, and gave him the *hongi* salute, smiling into his face. "You're fine the way you are, son, and I love you."

Blackwell stayed with Emma and Aloka and their ménage that night, not wanting to return to the house he shared with Mercedes just yet. In any case they were rearranging themselves over there, to give him back his old bedchamber on his return. There'd been one rough spot, he'd nearly broken down again, when Tomi and Ana were saying good night to him.

"Is Grandma coming back soon too?" Ana asked in a shrill and hopeful voice.

A great lump of emotion had leapt into his throat and he looked, dismayed, at the two expectant young faces.

"Remember Grandma died, and when you are dead, you do not come back." Through her tears Emma went on, gently, "We're sad because we don't get to see her anymore, but we could not have wished her to live longer and suffer. She stayed as long as she could, and now Mercedes will live forever in our hearts."

"Bless you, sweetheart," he murmured.

"Kiss your Grandpa now. *Aloha ahiahi, Kupuna kāne*."

Aloka swept the twins up in his arms.

Alone with his children later that evening, Blackwell said, "I saw her in a dream." He nodded round at them, by way of explaining his return, looking at Edward, Aloka, and Emma in turn. "I was going in by the wicket to the cemetery at Deane, when there she was just up the road. I went to her at once, in course. Mercedes put her dear little hand on my arm—I can still feel it—and she said 'take me home, Jim.'"

About the Author —

V.E.Ulett

A long time resident of California, V.E. Ulett is an avid reader as well as a writer of historical fiction.

Proud to be an Old Salt Press author, V.E is also a member of the National Books Critics Circle and an active member and reviewer for the Historical Novel Society.

Coming soon from V.E. Ulett, a new historical adventure series with a fantastic edge.

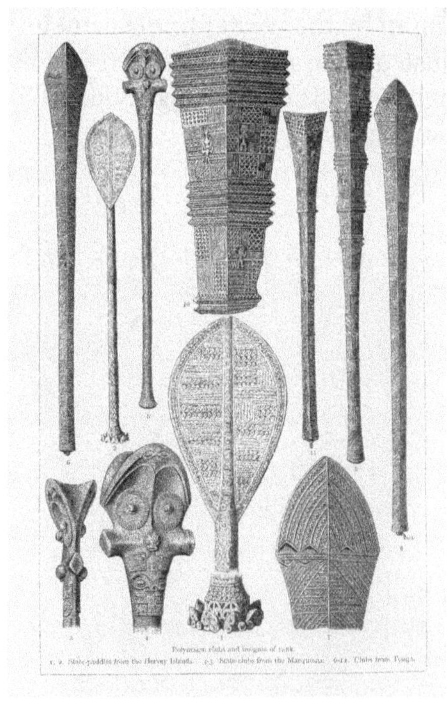

About Old Salt Press

Old Salt Press is an independent press catering to those who love books about ships and the sea. We are an association of writers working together to produce the very best of nautical and maritime fiction and non-fiction. We invite you to join us as we go down to the sea in books.

www.oldsaltpress.com

More Great Reading from Old Salt Press
A romantic adventure from the days of wooden ships and iron men

A small, audacious British frigate does battle against a large but ungainly Spanish ship. British Captain James Blackwell intercepts the Spanish *La Trinidad*, outmaneuvers and outguns the treasure ship and boards her. Fighting alongside the Spanish captain, sword in hand, is a beautiful woman. The battle is quickly over. The Spanish captain is killed in the fray and his ship damaged beyond repair. Its survivors and treasure are taken aboard the British ship, *Inconstant*.
ISBN 978-0-9882360-6-6

"Not for the faint hearted – Captain Blackwell pulls no punches!" - Alaric Bond

The repercussions of a court martial and the ill-will of powerful men at the Admiralty pursue Royal Navy captain James Blackwell into the Pacific, where danger lurks around every coral reef. Even if Captain Blackwell and Mercedes survive the venture into the world of early nineteenth century exploration, can they emerge unchanged with their love intact. The mission to the Great South Sea will test their loyalties and strength, and define the characters of Captain Blackwell and his lady in *Blackwell's Paradise*.

ISBN 978-0-9882360-5-9

Eleanor's Odyssey

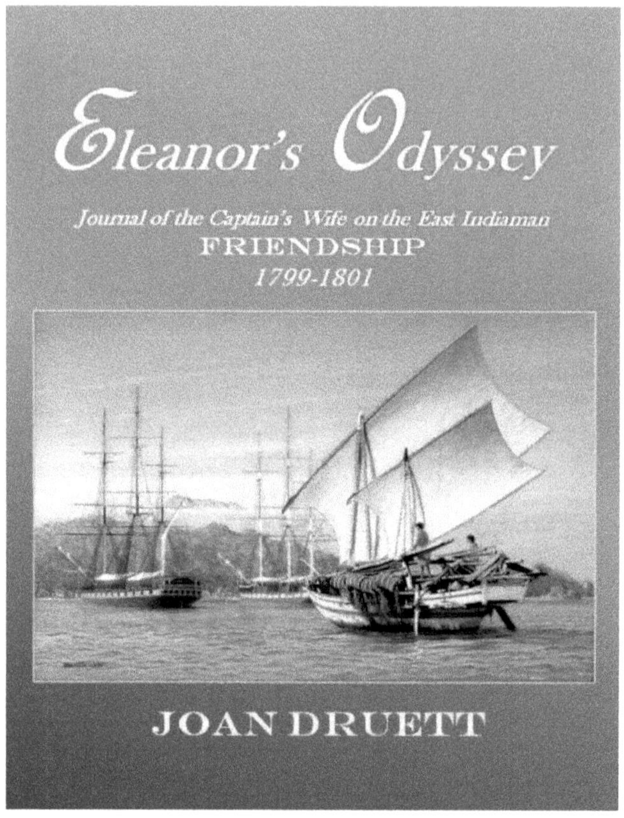

It was 1799, and French privateers lurked in the Atlantic and the Bay of Bengal. Yet Eleanor Reid, newly married and just twenty-one years old, made up her mind to sail with her husband, Captain Hugh Reid, to the penal colony of New South Wales, the Spice Islands and India. Danger threatened not just from the barely charted seas they would be sailing, yet, confident in her love and her husband's seamanship, Eleanor insisted on going along.
Joan Druett, writer of many books about the sea, including the bestseller *Island of the Lost* and the groundbreaking story of women under sail, *Hen Frigates,* embellishes Eleanor's journal with a commentary that illuminates the strange story of a remarkable young woman. 978-0-9941152-1-8

Another gripping installment in the Fighting Sail series

A tired ship with a worn out crew, but HMS *Scylla* has one more trip to make before her much postponed re-fit. Bound for St Helena, she is to deliver the island's next governor; a simple enough mission and, as peace looks likely to be declared, no one is expecting difficulties. Except, perhaps, the commander of a powerful French battle squadron, who has other ideas.
With conflict and intrigue at sea and ashore, *The Torrid Zone* is filled to the gunnels with action, excitement and fascinating historical detail; a truly engaging read. 978-0988236097

Dawlish Chronicles
Duty and Daring in the Heyday of Empire

"Britannia's Shark" is the third of the Dawlish Chronicles novels. It's 1881 and a daring act of piracy draws the ambitious British naval officer, Nicholas Dawlish, into a deadly maelstrom of intrigue and revolution. Drawn in too is his wife Florence, for whom the glimpse of a half-forgotten face evokes memories of earlier tragedy. For both a nightmare lies ahead, amid the wealth and squalor of America's Gilded Age and on a fever-ridden island ruled by savage tyranny. Manipulated ruthlessly from London by the shadowy Admiral Topcliffe, Nicholas and Florence Dawlish must make some very strange alliances if they are to survive – and prevail. 978-0992263690

The Shantyman – He can save the ship and the crew, but can he save himself?

In 1870, on the medium clipper ship *Alahambra* in Sydney, the new crew comes aboard more or less sober, except for the last man, who is hoisted aboard in a cargo sling, paralytic drunk. The drunken sailor, Jack Barlow, will prove to be an able shantyman. On a ship with a dying captain and a murderous mate, Barlow will literally keep the crew pulling together. As he struggles with a tragic past, a troubled present and an uncertain future, Barlow will guide the *Alahambra* through Southern Ocean ice and the horror of an Atlantic hurricane. His one goal is bringing the ship and crew safely back to New York, where he hopes to start anew.

Based on a true story, The Shantyman is a gripping tale of survival against all odds at sea and ashore, and the challenge of facing a past that can never be wholly left behind. 978-0-9941152-2-5